THE ETERNITY ARTIFACT

Tor Books by L. E. Modesitt, Jr.

THE COREAN CHRONICLES
Legacies
Darknesses
Scepters
Alector's Choice
Cadmian's Choice*

THE SPELLSONG CYCLE
The Soprano Sorceress
The Spellsong War
Darksong Rising
The Shadow Sorceress
Shadowsinger

THE SAGA OF RECLUCE
The Magic of Recluce
The Towers of the Sunset
The Magic Engineer
The Order War
The Death of Chaos
Fall of Angels
The Chaos Balance
The White Order
Colors of Chaos
Magi'i of Cyador
Scion of Cyador
Wellspring of Chaos
Ordermaster

THE GHOST BOOKS
Of Tangible Ghosts
The Ghost of the Revelator
Ghost of the White Nights

THE ECOLITAN MATTER
Empire & Ecolitan
(comprising *The Ecolitan Operation*
and *The Ecologic Secession*)
Ecolitan Prime
(comprising *The Ecolitan Envoy* and
The Ecolitan Enigma)

The Forever Hero
(comprising *Dawn for a Distant Earth*,
The Silent Warrior, and
In Endless Twilight)

Timegods' World
(comprising *The Timegod* and
Timediver's Dawn)

The Green Progression
The Parafaith War
The Hammer of Darkness
Adiamante
Gravity Dreams
The Octagonal Raven
Archform: Beauty
The Ethos Effect
Flash
The Eternity Artifact

*Forthcoming

E THE ETERNITY A RTIFACT

L. E. Modesitt, Jr.

A TOM DOHERTY ASSOCIATES BOOK
NEW YORK

THE ETERNITY ARTIFACT

Copyright © 2005 by L. E. Modesitt, Jr.

This book is printed on acid-free paper.

Edited by David G. Hartwell

Book design by Mary A. Wirth

A Tor Book
Published by Tom Doherty Associates, LLC
175 Fifth Avenue
New York, NY 10010

www.tor.com

Tor® is a registered trademark of Tom Doherty Associates, LLC.

ISBN 0-765-31464-9
EAN 978-0-765-31464-2

First Edition: October 2005

Printed in the United States of America

0 9 8 7 6 5 4 3 2 1

For Robert and Nesby, in memoriam,
in proof that dreams are carried unto the generations.

"Love of knowledge is the basis of all scholarship and lies eternally at the root of the tree of civilization."

"The eternal love of God surpasses all other loves, and is to be valued above all worldly and other transient affections."

"Love is a delusion, an eternal romanticization of lust perpetuated by oversexed males."

"A true artist's love of life, of the endless and eternal, and all that it encompasses, is expressed in every brushstroke."

"What separates artifices and artifacts from mere assemblages of components, what defines them and their use, is the love with which they are constructed and applied."

PREFACE

The last—and most unusual—discovery of the ill-fated and underfunded Deep Space Exploration program of the League of Worlds was Chronos [see "B², " "DSE, Section 4-1," "Galactic Anomalies"] . . .

Chronos is a perfect sphere of compressed matter in a state that appears as neither regular matter, nor that which would be classified as neutronium. Its diameter is 15,020 kilometers [1.178 T-norm], with an approximate mass of 1.9714×10^{15} kilograms [density is roughly 280 T-norm]. Remote tests and probes indicate no atmosphere, and a surface that is perfectly polished [variation less than .0001 mm.] under a thin layer of galactic dust and detritus. Chronos rotates on its own axis with a period of eleven standard hours . . .

Based on the accumulation and composition of surface matter, the trajectory of the body, the images and sensor readings, the DSE team estimated that Chronos had been formed between 4 and 10 billion years ago. This preliminary finding ignited controversies in all major systems, and two other brief expeditions [see "Covenant Rim Expedition" and "CW Chronos Probe"] were mounted. Their instrumentation was less elaborate, but essentially confirmed the findings of the DSE expedition . . .

Equally remarkable is the body's location and velocity. Chronos was detected beyond the outer edge of the trailing arm of the Galaxy moving at a thirty-degree in-clination to the galactic ecliptic and tangent to the arm at a constant velocity of 66 km/sec. Because of its speed and gravitational characteristics, confirmation of its prop-erties was both difficult and costly, and those expenses were a major factor in the ter-mination of the DSE program . . .

After the initial furor over the findings of all three expeditions, all the systems of the Galaxy abandoned the enigma that was Chronos to its lonely journey, citing the difficulties and costs involved in further explorations . . .

—UNIVERSE OF WONDER
J. Joshua Moorty, D.Sci.
Pan-Media
Delhi, O.E., 4323

THE ETERNITY ARTIFACT

PROLOGUE

GOODMAN

Tyang Ku Wong stepped onto the dais and crossed to the podium. Podiums haven't been necessary in millennia, except for symbolic reasons, but symbols are critical to humanity, whatever the culture. From where I stood on the west side of the dais with the half squad of White Guards, Ku Wong would be less than ten meters away.

The Hall of Deliberation was hushed as the recently elected people's advocates of the Middle Kingdom waited to hear him. I already knew the basis of his address and the policies he intended to follow as First Advocate. That was why I was there.

My hands felt like they were sweating under the pseudohand full-gloves that ran from fingernails to elbow. So did my face, under the real-flesh that wasn't my own. The sweating was an illusion, not from nervousness, but from a systemic reaction to the nanothin layer between my flesh and the foreign DNA of the arm-gloves and head-flesh.

With the other White Guards, I remained perfectly motionless.

Ku Wong stepped behind the podium. The front was carved in the likeness of a spray of bamboo stalks behind the seal of the Middle Kingdom. He let the

silence draw out before he spoke. The instantlinguistic made what he said intelligible, but that was only because I'd had practice. Years of it. Speaking was still
easier than comprehending.

"... the people of the Middle Kingdom have made their wishes known, and
you are here on Tiananmen to enact the laws and policies necessary. The elec-
tion has made it clear that the Middle Kingdom must be run on principles of enlightened humanism and secularism, and not by the dead hands of ancient
prophets and barbaric gods. In an age of enlightenment—and we of the Middle
Kingdom are indeed blessed to live in such an age—there is no place for religious and cultural paternalism. There is no place for unbridled feministic anar-
chy. There is no place for unfettered capitalism, nor for dictatorial government
command-and-control. Most important, there is no place for the worship of
power for the sake of power. We will continue to oppose all the ancient evils,
whether based on superstition and blind belief or upon unchecked power and
greed. We will oppose such policies and beliefs both within our worlds—and
without—and we will stand firm against those who would force such upon us,
or who would endeavor to seduce us with poetic polemics of the past . . ."

A roar of applause filled the Hall.

I had no doubt that Ku Wong's words sounded better in their original Man-
darin, but the instalinguistics were accurate enough. I waited for the next round
of applause.

"... in the course of human events, each people has the choice of whether
the day ahead will be a bright tomorrow or a faded yesterday chained by memories of a despotic past. The worlds of the Middle Kingdom have chosen tomorrow, unlike those of Covenanters, who have proved that they will drag all
around them, such as the ill-fated Libracracy, into a despotic religious tyranny,
or those of the Alliance. Tomorrow *will* be ours . . ."

Just before the applause rose to the highest point, I twisted my hand slightly.
The miniature nanodarts flashed unseen across the space that separated me from
the First Advocate.

He paused, looking surprised. "... will be ours . . . for we have . . . prepared . . ."

A few in the front row—the new ministers—leaned forward. Ku Wong
never stuttered.

Abruptly, a pillar of flame flared where he had stood. It was so hot the
podium turned black even before the pyrotic darts finished their reactive con-
sumption. The darts had been so small and so comparatively slow that the kinetic energy screens had not been triggered. The multiple microlaunchers in my
uniform had disintegrated, and the residue would show nothing.

For less than a second, the Hall of Deliberation was still. Then, chaos
erupted.

"Covenanters! Murder!"

With the other guards, I dashed forward. We formed a barrier around the ashes that had been the First Advocate of the Middle Kingdom. Nanetic barriers dropped into place, separating the dais from the Hall proper.

"White Guards! Re-form on the wings!" The commands came from nowhere, but the voice was that of General Tse-Sung, the Advocate of Security.

We re-formed. Energy fields flashed over and around us. I waited as hard-faced men and women in brilliant white appeared, with the shoulder braids of Security on their singlesuits.

One team appeared to my right.

"Lao Xun, forward!"

Xun stepped forward. The Security specialists aimed scanners and analyzers at him.

The head analyst nodded. "To the right. Wait there."

"ChoWang, forward!"

I stepped forward. The analyzers took minute samples from the backs of my wrists and cheeks and neck. The only weak points for my visible body parts were my eyes themselves, but the politics of scanning eyes had limited DNA sampling there and retinal scans.

"Clear. Step to the right."

I formed up next to Lao Xun. Neither of us spoke.

For the next two hours, the Security specialists scanned everything and everyone. The scans were not only for DNA, but for internal weapons. The scans showed that I was ChoWang and that I had no internal weapons or anomalies. That was as it should have been.

All I had to do was to remain calm and carry out the duties of the Guard I had removed and replaced. To do otherwise would have called attention to who I was, and would have been as fatal to me as my nanodarts had been to the First Advocate.

Another two standard hours—and two more screenings—passed before we were dismissed and confined to quarters. This mission had been completed satisfactorily. Getting back to New Zion would be tedious, but not a real problem.

While the universe might suspect that the Council of Twelve had decreed the First Advocate's death, no proof of my actions or identity could be traced to the Council. Even if I were caught, the automatics would ensure no evidence would remain, and that was another reason why I planned most carefully. If that fail-safe had not existed, the results would have been catastrophically embarrassing to the Council.

In some senses, an operative's easiest tasks were the missions. In working for the Council, the members and their personal crusaders were more dangerous to you than the operatives of other governments.

As I waited for the opportunity to leave the barracks, I couldn't help but wonder what the next assignment would be.

SEEKING

1 FITZHUGH

At times, every professor believes that his classroom represents the abnegation of intelligence, if not absolute abiosis. This feeling has been universewide since long before the Tellurian Diaspora. Lughday was no exception, especially not for my fourth-period class, Historical Trends 1001, the introductory course, one of the core requirements for undergraduates.

I walked through the door into the small amphitheatre classroom and toward the dais. Forty bodies sat waiting in four tiers, arrayed in a semicircle—all avoiding my scrutiny. At times such as the one before me, I could only wish that the university did not require all full professors to teach one introductory course every year, at a bare minimum. I'd drawn fourth period—right after lunch, and that made it even more of a challenge.

I stationed myself behind the podium, the representation of a practice significantly untransformed in almost ten thousand recorded years of human history—and for the last five, savants and pedants had prognosticated the decline of personal and physical-presence classroom instruction. Yet in all instances where such ill-considered experimentation in technologically based pedagogical methodology had been attempted in an effort to replace what had worked, if imperfectly, the outcomes and the ramifications had ranged from social catastrophe to unmitigated disaster, even as my predecessors in pedagogy had predicted such eventualities.

Technology and implementation had never constituted the difficulty, but rather the genetic and physiological strengths and limitations of human cognitive and learning patterns. From a historical perspective, successful technological applications are those that enhance human capacities, not those that force humans into prestructured technological niches or functions.

As I cleared my throat and stepped to the podium, the murmurs died away. I glanced down at the shielded screen before picking a name, smiling politely, and speaking. "Scholar Finzel, please identify the single most critical aspect of the events leading to the Sunnite-Covenanter Conflagration of 3237."

"Ser?" Finzel offered a blank look.

For the second class of the first semester, blank looks were not exactly infrequent, not for beginning students, especially for those from nonshielded continents or from the occasional off-planet scholar. "I realize neolatry precludes your interest in matters of past history, but since the Conflagration resulted in the devastation of Meath, extensive damage to the Celtic worlds of the Comity, and significant taxation increases for the entire Comity, and since both the Covenanters and the Alliance have continued to rearm and rebuild their fleets, with a continued hostility exemplified most recently by the so-called pacification of the Mazarene systems and the forcible annexation of the Walden Libracracy . . ."

That not-so-gentle reminder did not remove the expression of incomprehension, but only added one of veiled hostility. I used the screen to check his background. As I'd vaguely recalled, he was from Ulster, where he could have netlinked and been provided the answer.

"Scholar Finzel," I said politely, "Gregory is a shielded continent, and the university is a shielded institution. You are expected to read the texts before class. For some reason, you seem unable to comprehend this basic requirement. I suggest you remedy the situation before the next class." I turned to a student with a modicum of interest in her eyes. "Scholar MacAfee?"

"According to Robertson Janes, ser, there were two linked causes of the Conflagration. The first was the malfunction of the communications linkages of the Covenanter fleet command, and the second was the widespread perception among the population of the Alliance worlds that the Covenanters intended to spread a nanogenevirus that would transform all herbivores into hogs." A hint of a smile crossed Scholar MacAfee's lips.

"You're in the general area," I replied, "but I don't believe that Janes said the Covenanter fleet's command communications malfunctioned. Do you recall exactly what he wrote?"

MacAfee frowned.

"Anyone else?"

"Ser?" The tentative voice was that of Ariel Leanore, a dark-haired young woman who looked more like a girl barely into seminary, rather than at university.

"Yes?"

"I think . . . didn't he write something . . . it was more like . . . the expectations of instantaneous response resulted in the ill-considered reprisal on Hajj Majora . . . and that reprisal made the Sunnis so angry that they passed the legislation funding the High Caliph's declaration of Jihad. There were rumors about the Spear of Iblis, but those were noncausal . . ." Leanore paused, her voice trailing away.

"Very good, Scholar Leanore." I stopped and surveyed the faces, seeing that most of them still hadn't grasped the impact of Janes's words. "The expectations of instantaneous response . . . what does that mean?"

All forty faces were blank with the impermeability of incomprehension. When I had been in the service, I had believed that such an expression was limited to those of less-than-advanced intelligence. The years in academia had convinced me that it appeared upon the visages of all too many individuals in the adolescent and postadolescent years, regardless of innate intelligence or the lack thereof.

"What it means . . ." I drew out the words. ". . . is that instantaneous communications and control preclude the opportunity for considered thought and reflection. The Covenanter command had the ability to order and carry out an immediate reprisal. They did so. They did not think about the fact that the Covenanter trading combines on Hajj Majora had, within the terms of their culture, acted responsibly against those Covenanters who had manipulated the terms of exchange in a manner that could be most charitably described as fraud." I cleared my throat. There are definite disadvantages to auditory lectures, especially without even sonic boosting, but my discomfort was irrelevant to those who had enacted the shielding compact. "Now that you know that, why did I initially suggest that there was only one critical aspect to these events?"

"You suggest that both events listed by Janes share a commonality, ser?" That was Scholar Amyla Sucharil, one of three exchange students from the worlds of the Middle Kingdom.

"Not only the events cited by Janes, but those cited by Yamato and Alharif."

"Isn't it communications? They all deal with communications, ser," suggested Leanore.

Young Ariel might have been tentative, but at least she was thinking, unlike most of the others. "Exactly! Both the events cited by Janes were the result of misunderstanding and misapplications of the use and function of communications, if in different societal aspects. If you apply the same tests to the examples of Yamato and Alharif, you'll find a similar pattern." I smiled, not that I wanted to, because it was likely to be a long afternoon. "History illustrates a pattern in communications. In low-tech civilizations, only immediate personal communications can be conveyed with any speed, and those are often without detail. As more detail is required, communications slow. As technology improves, there is

always a trade-off between speed and detail, because improving technology results in greater societal and infrastructural complexity, which requires greater
detail. Until the development of fullband comm and nanoprocessing, this trade-
off existed to a greater or lesser degree. For the past millennium or so, however,
the limitation on communications has not been the technology. What has it
been?" I surveyed the faces, some beginning to show apprehension as they realized that they did not know the answer, and that I might indeed call upon them.

"Would it be understanding, ser?" ventured Sucharil.

"Precisely! Just because you have the information, and even a hundred near-
instantaneous analyses, doesn't mean that you truly know what to do with it,
particularly when the analyses may be conflicting, depending on the background assumptions and the weight of the evidence. This was particularly true
in the case of the Conflagration, because of the cultural imperatives of both the
Covenanters and the Alliance. Even today, any analyses dealing with the interaction of those cultures are problematical."

"Ser? Why does it matter that much?" That was from Emory David. "The
Comity has a thousand world members, and the Covenanters have less than two
hundred. There can't be more than seventy Alliance worlds."

"What is the first rule of interstellar warfare?" I replied.

"No planet can be effectively defended against a determined attack . . .
ser . . ." replied Scholar David.

"And what are the beliefs behind a jihad?"

Finally, comprehension began to illuminate a few faces.

"You mean, ser, that they don't care because they'll go to paradise?"

"Or Heaven, if they're Covenanters doing the Will of the Divine, and seeking to ensure that we do not recover the Morning Star," I replied dryly.

"But . . . that's a myth without foundation . . ."

I could not ascertain the source of that incredulous murmur.

"Not to true believers, it is not. Not even in this so-called enlightened and rational times, and certainly not upon the Worlds of the Covenant. The Morning
Star, or the Spear of Iblis, the Hammer of Lucifer, whatever the specific term, is a
symbol of forbidden knowledge, knowledge that is considered only the province
of Iblis, Satan, or their demon children. If there is one aspect of all true-believer
religions that remains constant across time and history, it is that certain aspects of
technology or science are forbidden by the deity because use of that knowledge
usurps the powers and privileges of the deity. Such theocracies will therefore
commit great violence over issues or scientific practices that would appear common to many of you." I inhaled slowly, for a pause. "With regard to this, even if
the Comity is more secular in outlook, once the theocracies have used force
against our interests, such actions require force in response, or the perception of
weakness will cost even more in the long run. We lost the populations of ten
worlds. The Covenanters lost thirty and the Alliance nearly forty. It has taken
close to ten centuries for them to recover, half that for us, except that a dead
world remains that for longer than we or any other humans will be around to

recolonize. A hundred worlds scoured . . . would you like it to happen again, on Ulster, or Lyr? Or perhaps Culain or Liaden?" I paused. "Or perhaps the Covenanters are somewhat sensitive to the power of position, in which case, what happens to be the other leading secular polity? The one with whom they share the closest stellar congruencies?"

"The . . . Middle Kingdom?"

"Correct. Now . . . my skepticism is almost without limbi, but most recently the First Advocate of the Middle Kingdom died in circumstances resembling assassination—right after he had delivered a series of addresses severely critical of the theocratic expansionism of the worlds of the Covenant. What might happen if the Middle Kingdom were reputed to obtain some forbidden knowledge, something resembling the Spear of Iblis? To borrow an ancient metaphor, how long before the sabres began to rattle? Again . . . just over, if you will, information?"

There was silence in the room, although I could hear someone murmur, "It couldn't happen again . . ." I refrained from suggesting all too many people, particularly politicians, had said those words, or some variation, over hundreds of centuries, generally to everyone's regret.

"Now . . . I'd like each of you to take a moment to reflect. I would like each of you to come up with an example from history where information and how it was handled was critical in determining the fate of something—an army, a fleet, a nation, a world." I held up a hand to forestall the objections. "I know. Once you're away from Gregory, you can netlink and get a reply, ordered by whatever parameters you suggest. The point of this exercise is to develop your judgment so that when you do that in the future, you will have a greater understanding of what that information actually means."

This time the majority of expressions were those of resignation. I supposed that was an improvement. If they thought what I was requiring was difficult, they hadn't even considered what was going to be required in the later stages of applied manual mathematics. I'd learned, years earlier, that if I leaned on the students hard in the opening classes, the classes got easier and more rewarding toward the end. Unfortunately, doing so, and maintaining a cheerful demeanor in the process, was arduous in the first weeks of the semester.

I didn't quite breathe a sigh of relief when fourth period was over and I left the classroom, walking down the ramp to the main level. There were times I could feel my hands tightening, wanting to throttle certain students. The best ones cared for knowledge as a tool, and the worst only sought a degree with marks that would guarantee entry into some multi or another or into the Comity bureaucracy, which was worse, from what I'd seen, than that of academia. I could not help but wish, at times, that I were back teaching in the days prior to the Disapora on Old Earth, where everything had been broadband and without the direct face-to-face student contact that reminded me all too often of how little most of them cared for knowledge itself.

But . . . that time on Old Earth had been before the discovery of the subtle but far-reaching effects of broadcast energies, even at extraordinarily low power, on neonatal and prematuration mental development. The Comity had banned wide-scale public and private broadcast of information and power, and relied on monoptic distribution systems, unlike the more conservative governments, such as the Covenanters and Sunnite Alliance, for whom cost-benefit analyses included individuals with environmentally damaged attention spans. I couldn't help but snort to myself. My students had short enough attention spans without additional technological assistance in shortening them further. The continent of Gregory, as many other continents on Comity worlds, had even more stringent requirements than the baseline regulations in force throughout the entire Comity of Worlds.

Once back in my office, little more than an overlarge closet three meters on a side, I settled myself behind my console and keyed in the codes to call up my in-comms—there were no personal direct-links at the university, or for that matter, anywhere on the continent.

The first message was from the provost—just a message, and no text.

Congratulations on being nominated for a senior fellowship with the Comity Diplomatic Corps. Your continued diligence in seeking outside validation and recognition of your talents, accomplishments, and credentials has not gone unnoticed . . .

I just looked at the message. The last thing I wanted was a senior fellowship with the CDC. Years back, my service tours had convinced me of the futility of government service. I certainly had not applied for such a fellowship. Had the provost nominated me? Why? Had I been that much of a thorn in his bureaucratic side? It didn't matter. In the unlikely event I happened to be selected, I'd politely refuse. There were more than enough brilliant junior professors who wanted such empty honors and would be happy to accept.

I moved to the next message.

2 *GOODMAN*

The five-story building in New Jerusalem was identified as the Zion Mercantile Exchange. It wasn't, although there were legitimate trade and commerce offices on the main level. At the end of the east corridor, I stepped through the gate to the lifts, cleared by a minute sample of my true DNA. My destination was on the second level. At the third doorway on the second level, I offered my wrist once more to the DNA-coder.

"Request clearance codes."

"Kappa seven-eight-nine-six, Josiah three, Walls of Jericho, Hatusa version."

"John Paul Goodman, cleared." The endurasteel portal irised open, long enough for me to enter one of the sanctums of the Covenant Intelligence Service.

One of Colonel Truesdale's bright young men looked up from his console at me. "The colonel will be with you in a few minutes, Operative Goodman."

I was a senior CIS operative, not just an operative. I didn't correct him. Instead, I settled into one of the straight-backed chairs to wait.

Fourteen and a half minutes passed before the aide said pleasantly, "You can go in now, Operative Goodman."

"Thank you." I offered a warm smile and walked through the door that opened as I neared and closed behind me.

The inner office looked to have a panoramic view of New Jerusalem through a wide expanse of glass. That was an illusion. Two men awaited me. Colonel Truesdale sat behind a table desk, and a dark-skinned man with gray hair sat in a chair to his left, facing me.

Colonel Truesdale's eyes were hard and glittering blue. They didn't match the genial laugh and the warmth of his voice. "Operative Goodman, you've heard of Major Ibaio."

I nodded politely. "Yes, sir." Who hadn't, after his exploits in pacifying the Nubian Cluster? Or rooting out the followers of the antiprophet among the Mazarenes? He hadn't had much to do in the ongoing annexation of the Walden Libracracy. He wouldn't have been needed. The Waldonians didn't believe enough in anything to fight that hard.

"Take a seat."

I sat in the remaining chair.

Major Ibaio's dark eyes scrutinized me from an even darker face. After a moment, he spoke. "The Comity is undertaking an unusual expedition. They have refitted a former colony supply ship. The *Magellan* is the largest possible vessel that can fit through a Gate. The AG drives are the most powerful ever installed and have been under construction for the past three years. The shuttles are larger than couriers. The vessel is heavily shielded, and armed with the weaponry of a standard Comity battle cruiser, and it will be part of a scientific expedition."

A colony vessel with beefed-up drives armed like a battle cruiser for a science expedition? That made no sense. Why were they giving me that kind of mission? What I knew about any science besides weapons and the general basics wouldn't enabled me to pass for a lab tech, much less a scientist. Or was it a way to get rid of me?

"The Comity government has seldom invested heavily in any research exploration, but it seems more than probable that their scientists have located a planet with alien forerunner technical artifacts—or a renegade Technocrat colony that escaped the Dirty War, then failed." Ibaio smiled coldly. "You understand the possible value."

"In thousands of years, no one has found any alien artifacts—not anywhere in the Galaxy. It's unlikely that any of the renegade Technocrat scientists escaped."

"Exactly." Ibaio's voice was colder than before. "The Comity would not expend such funding if they were not absolutely certain. They may even be seeking the Morning Star."

The legendary Hammer of Lucifer, the Spear of Iblis? Had they ever even existed? I wasn't about to ask that question. "I'll do whatever is required, sir, but I'm not a scientist—"

"Your job is both simple . . . and very difficult," interrupted the colonel. He smiled warmly once more. "We don't expect you to bring back scientific discoveries or artifacts. That would be asking far too much of any operative."

That didn't reassure me much.

"What you are to do is to leave an AG signaler that will allow our ships to locate the planet or station or locale independently."

AG signalers didn't exactly float in orbit off strange planets. That I knew, but I wouldn't have recognized one if it had been set before me.

"Needless to say, you cannot carry such aboard the *Magellan*. That means you'll have to build it from scratch."

I was getting a very bad feeling about what the colonel had in mind.

"We don't intend to confront the Comity directly. That would be . . . unwise, but it is difficult to monitor an entire planet, even for the D.S.S." The colonel smiled once more. "You'll be given an in-depth indoctrination for both your cover and for your mission. Your cover will provide you access to the equipment you need. You will spend the next month in a regime of forced nanite education and indoctrination. By then, you'll look and act like your cover."

More surgery and forced nanite education? What stories I'd heard about them hadn't been good. "How many operatives are you putting through this?"

Truesdale ignored the question. "You will be William Gerald Bond, Comity armorer second class. He has been assigned to the *Magellan*, but will be late in reporting for cadre training because he is currently finishing a patrol cruise on the *Drake*. That will allow us time to prepare you. Along with other techs of lower rank, armorer Bond has been under surveillance for some time, and we have his DNA. Because this is a long mission, we will have to alter the medical records at Hamilton base and those carried on board the *Magellan*. We cannot risk changes to the main databases, but the subroutines should hold unless there is a deep audit. Even so, that will require your escape relatively soon after the ship returns. Any other information you can supply will be most useful as well."

"Might I ask why an armorer?"

"There are several reasons," Ibaio replied. "First, scrutiny of mid-and lower-level techs is somewhat less. Second, armorers have access to AG-driven message torps and regular armed torps. The torp drives have the components that can be converted to the necessary signaler."

"Do we know anything about where this place is?"

"Distant enough to require several Gates to reach it. The details will be covered in your briefing and indoctrination, Senior Operative Goodman," Truesdale said smoothly as he stood. "I wish you well, Goodman. You're in Major Ibaio's most capable hands now."

Ibaio had risen as well. Unlike the colonel, he wasn't smiling.

The Morning Star—the Hammer of Lucifer, or what the Sunnis called the Spear of Iblis? Why was the colonel sending an operative? Why not a crusader who was deep-programmed? I could see why he didn't want to send a fleet directly against the Comity, especially when too many ships were tied up in finishing the pacification of the Libracracy, but a single operative?

3 FITZHUGH

After a long and frustrating battle with student preconceptions in the honors seminar about the reliability of standard historical methodologies, I stepped into my office in the History Annex and took a long deep breath. At times, I did indeed have difficulty in refraining from applying violence to those prone to incompetence.

Without thought I dropped into an alert stance as a slender man in a black singlesuit rose from the chair in front of my desk console. I *had* sealed my office when I'd left for class.

"Easy, Professor Fitzhugh. Jon Herrit. Comity Security. I've been waiting for you."

For me? I didn't even have to look puzzled. I hadn't seen a Security type in years, if not decades, certainly not since I'd finished the two Service tours that had paid for my undergraduate and graduate degrees. But then, those years and what they had entailed were best left in the past. "For me? I'm afraid that I can't be of much help to you—or Security." I couldn't help but wonder why so many security organizations wore black—or mostly black. Then, the black was doubtless only used when they wanted to be noticed.

"I'm certain you'll be of great help." Herrit smiled almost apologetically. "Before we go any further, though, I'd like to request that you check all your in-comms. That will make some matters clearer, Professor."

I didn't like his attitude, but I would have checked my in-comms anyway. So I settled behind the console.

The first message was from the dean, congratulating me on my success in obtaining a senior fellowship with the Comity Diplomatic Corps and granting me up to a three-year sabbatical, effective immediately at the end of the day—today. He also thanked me for obtaining the matching grant for my replacement, wished me well, and asked me to stop by for just a moment before I left. The next message was from the provost, both congratulating me and telling me how much the trustees would appreciate the outside validation of the expertise of the university faculty. The third message was from the Resources Office, noting that, during my sabbatical, my pay would continue to be posted to my designated financial institution and that all coverages would remain in full force, in addition to any coverages that I might obtain through the Comity fellowship.

I looked at Herrit. "Why don't you explain?"

"You've been requested as a consultant on a high-level, extraordinarily secret Comity project." He shook his head. "It's so high-level that I don't know what it is, or where it is."

"I'm supposed to accept without knowing anything?"

"Actually, Professor, you really don't have any choice. As you can see from those messages, the government has already made the arrangements with the university system. You will receive your university salary during this sabbatical. In addition, you'll be paid at the rate of a Comity assistant underminister for the duration of the project, or a full academic year, whichever is longer."

That was frightening. An assistant underminister made at least three times what I did, and anyone who wanted to pay me that much had either a difficult or dangerous task—or both. "You're Security, but this fellowship is with the Diplomatic Corps. Why are you here?"

"You're a very important man, Professor. Why, I don't know. My job is to make sure you get to the project safely."

"So . . . do you have any recommendations on what I should take?" My words came out sardonically.

"You'll be traveling, and that means packing light. I'd suggest as much material as you can load into a couple of cubes. A mixture of entertainment and professional reading."

"I'll have console and equipment access? Or do I need to bring a portable console?"

"I'm quite sure that you'll be provided with all the equipment you need, Professor. With your background, I'm certain you understand that."

I ignored the reference to the Service. That had been long ago, even if I did continue the workouts and exercises. They were useful to keep me in shape despite my more sedentary academic lifestyle. They also provided a most necessary outlet for a genetically supported tendency to violence—so that I didn't actually throttle dense students. "What now?"

"I'd suggest you say your good-byes to the dean, and then we go to your quarters and pack. We have a reservation on one of the late-evening elevator climbers to Orbit Station Beta."

While I'd had the feeling that the assignment was off-planet, since Leinster wasn't exactly the hub of the Comity, Herrit's words still sent a chill through me. "Where am I headed after that?"

"I don't know. There will be a Comity courier ship waiting for you. That's all they told me."

"What do I tell my family?"

"Your daughters are both grown, and you never recontracted. You tell your daughters that you're leaving on this splendid fellowship, and that it's a well-paid, once-in-a-lifetime opportunity. I have a comm address through which they can reach you."

"Carefully screened, no doubt."

"Very carefully screened, I'm certain, Professor." Herrit smiled. "You'd best cubeload whatever you want from your console here, and then I'll accompany you to see the dean."

As if I had much choice. I should have rejected the nomination that had appeared weeks before, except I had the feeling that no one would have listened. And I still had no idea why I was being drafted, or for what, only that the stakes had to be high. But why would anyone want an obscure professor of historical trends from the University of Gregory?

4 CHANG

Headed back from Alpha Station, I felt the ice forming on the back of the space armor collar. Brushed it away twice. Wouldn't want to have it jam the seal if I had to cram on the helmet. Cockpit heaters weren't working that well. Neither were the scrubbers. Frost was building on the bulkheads away from the boards. I triggered the comm links, tight-beam. "Flashpot, stacker two, on return. Cargo as manifested. No passengers."

"Stacker two, have you inbound this time."

"Affirmative." Idiot! "On return" had to be inbound.

"Stacker two, shut down and report to ops upon return."

"Flashpot, shift's not over."

"Operational requirements, stacker two."

"Stet. Will report as ordered." Operational requirements meant I got paid. Wasn't about to let Graysham short me on a technicality. Didn't get paid enough as it was. Never had.

Scanned the boards, the farscreens and repscreens that worked. Telltales showed a ship at lock one. Priority lock. Couldn't tell what. IFF wasn't working. Not much on Beta Station shuttles did except basic habitability, main controls,

drives, grapples, and dampers. Why I worked suited, except for the helmet. Mc-
Clendon was ass-end of the Comity, no orbit elevators. Would have been cheaper
and safer, but the tightwads wouldn't come up with the capital. Couldn't afford
more than basic maintenance. Sometimes, not even that.

Another ten standard passed before I confirmed Beta Station—dead ahead.
Would have been shocked if it hadn't been. Years since I missed on a straight-in.
"Flashpot, stacker two. Have lock five, visual and beacon."

"Two, cleared into lock. Straight to ops after shutdown."

"Stet." What the frig did ops want? Shouldn't say ops. Graysham was ops,
maintenance, and my boss.

Went to work. Manual approach. Light touches on the steering jets, quick
burst on the electrogravs. Shuttle settled against the dampers, cargo and personnel locks lined up perfectly. Magclamps sealed tight.

"Flashpot, two's locked. Shutting down this time."

"Stet, two. Report ops soonest."

Didn't bother with a reply. First, logged red status to ops. Then had to do
the shutdown checklist manually, and by memory. Heads-ups had died three
months back. No chance of repair. No one made McCann wafers anymore.
Could feel more chill building in the cockpit before I unharnessed. Carried my
helmet out of the shuttle.

Wesmin stood by the lock, waiting.

"Red status," I told him. "Report's in the station log."

"It's a wonder she's stayed up so long." Shook his head. "Graysham won't be
happy."

"He's never happy."

Wesmin laughed.

Made my way toward the lockers. Wasn't about to wear a suit longer than
necessary. Stripped off the suit, racked the helmet. Pulled a vest and shorts over
my skintights and headed inward. Took the crew tube. Didn't see anyone. Not
that likely at midnight Comity standard.

Ops was on the inner ring, where the grav fields were steady. Cube three
meters on a side. Gray walls. Graysham sat in a web chair. He swung away from
the comm board and console when I stepped through the hatch. Looked at me,
like he'd never seen me before.

Before he said a word, I hit him. "Two's down. Heaters are shot, and scrubbers won't take out the water. Whole board'll go on a long run, maybe even to
Alpha."

"We'll take care of that after you go, Chang. You've got one stan to pack your
gear." Graysham grinned—evil expression.

Wanted to smash his teeth in. Could have, too, except I'd need work. "Not
going anywhere. Contract says—"

"I could tell you that you've been relieved because you're a lousy shuttle pilot. That wouldn't be true. Or I could say that I hate the waste you make of your

looks, your arrogant fembitch attitude, and your tight ass. That'd be true, but it's not the reason. Besides, rundown as Beta Station is, I need good pilots, arrogant and tight-assed as they might be." He grinned again. "You've got a better job."

That was bullshit. Who was going to hire me?

"It's the kind even you can't refuse, Chang."

"Never been a job I couldn't walk from." I'd walk to prove I could, if I had to.

"The Comity Diplomatic Corps wants the best shuttle pilots. They were very specific. They tracked you down from that mess on Lyr." He grinned again. "I never knew you'd kneed a commissioner in the balls and broken all his fingers."

"Bastard embezzled operations funds and tried to blame a maintenance failure on another pilot." He'd groped me, too, but I wasn't about to tell Graysham.

Graysham waited.

So did I.

"The Corps wants you, one Jiendra Chang. They told me to tell you three things. It's the toughest piloting job you or anyone else will ever see. You'll never hold any certification anywhere in the Comity if you don't take it, and you won't ever get off-planet to go anyplace else."

"That's two." Maybe it was three, but he was holding something back. Friggin' Comity. Hated threats.

"The third thing was a name. That's all. Eliasha Eileen Chu-Wong."

Double frig! Tried not to react.

Graysham leaned forward, looking uninterested. He wasn't.

"Who loaded you with all this shit?"

"Oh . . . and I was told to tell you that, if you do this job right, you'll get back your star-class rating, and your deep-space master's cert. You'll also get paid at star-class rates whether you're successful or not for a minimum of one year."

Talk about reward-punishment. Whoever "they" were could break me, even in McClendon system, but offered stuff only Comity execs could provide. "Who said so?"

"The lady in black who's waiting out in the passageway. She arrived a little while ago on that Comity courier. It's an armed courier, Chang. Talk to her and go pack. Good luck. Even you'll need it." Graysham turned back to the comm board. Not a signal on it. Just a way of telling me he was done.

Stepped out into the passageway. She was three meters back. Wasn't smiling either.

"Who are you?" Already knew *what* she was. Muscles, alertness, and black vest and shorts, black skintights said Comity commando. Also meant they knew my background.

"I'm Alya Podorovski, Pilot Chang." Pleasant voice. Behind it, she was the fem-bitch Graysham thought I was.

"Where's this pilot job?"

"I don't know. My mission is to escort you onto the Comity courier waiting in the priority lock and get you to where we're headed. I suggest we go to your quarters and that you pack your gear. I doubt you have that many memorabilia." Her eyes went over me like I was raw meat.

Hate it when they do that, men or women.

5 BARNA

Peter Atreos walked into the front display foyer. He stopped before the rendition of the Grande Opera Theatre. After a moment, he shook his head. Without looking at me, he spoke. "When I look at this, I see all the faults, and none of the grandeur. Yet every detail is perfect."

That was because the opera house was an architectural melange, a performing space designed to please the patrons, not to showcase the performers or the production. I saw no reason to point out the obvious. Atreos was one of those patrons.

"Why do you leave that work in the display foyer, ser Barna?"

I shrugged. "It is good art. Someday, someone will buy it."

"You are a great artiste, but you are not a businessman." He planted himself before the replica of the holo-portrait of Rennis Zaphir. The original was in Zaphir's private galley. Atreos studied it closely. His eyes narrowed. I knew why. Zaphir had thick bushy eyebrows that dominated his face. They gave him an unkempt look, even in the formal singlesuit. I could have cleaned up the eyebrows a touch. Then the image would have reflected greater control of the power of Zaphir's iron will, but not the passion behind it, or the humor or the stubbornness. It still would have been Zaphir, but not as much Zaphir. The original showed that to an even greater extent. Originals always do, in a way that even a molecularly identical copy cannot, no matter what the scientific types say. That was why original works remained in demand. They always would.

"You have a reputation for talent and realism, ser Barna," offered Atreos.

"That is what I am known for." I could feel Aeryana's eyes on my back. She stood at the railing of the loft. When potential clients appeared, so did she. She looked down into the display foyer. I always felt her eyes. What artist would not?

"Great realism." Atreos's words were tinged with irony. He turned and looked directly at me. "Yet . . . realism . . . untempered by, shall we say, practical considerations, fails to serve the patron or the artist."

It would be best for me to say little. Aeryana was listening, and I knew what Atreos wanted. I nodded.

"You know that we are seeking a likeness of the new Directeur. The work would provide a handsome commission. You did not submit a proposal."

"I am here, ser Atreos. My work is known. If the Societe Generale sees fit to commission me, I would be most honored." I offered the slightest bow.

"The Societe General, ser Barna, cannot offer commissions to those who do not apply," Atreos replied. "The application deadline is tomorrow. You might wish to know."

I bowed again. "You are most kind and thoughtful."

"I am not, ser Barna. I would prefer not to deal with you. The others requested you be told." With a brusque nod, he turned and departed. He did not hurry, but he did not look back.

His parting sentiment was not unexpected. That he had come to the studio at all had been the surprise.

"Chendor!" Aeryana walked down the ramp from the loft. Her deep blue eyes flashed. Her jet-black hair was shoulder length, most unfashionable, but perfect for her wide forehead, oval face, and high cheekbones. She was angry, but I enjoyed watching her before she spoke.

"You turned him down! You are an idiot, Chendor! An idiot! You are a great artist, but you are an idiot. You are less than an idiot. You are an arrogant, artistic genius, and we will all starve because you never compromise." Aeryana's words burned. They always did. She was exaggerating. I had the studio, and it was on Rimbaud Boulevard, with an eight-room conapt behind it. We owned both, in fee simple without encumbrances. We could afford the Academie for Nicole. That was hardly starving in Noveau Rochelle, the city of the arts on Gallia.

"I do not see you subsisting on stale biscuits, my dear." After twenty years, she was more beautiful than ever, and some of the portraits of her in the conapt would take away the breath of the most jaded. They were not for others, but for me. I would destroy them, in time, but not for many years.

"You are impossible!"

"That is possible," I admitted.

"Will you never reach out to ask for a commission?"

"Atreos does not want me."

"The others do. They forced him to come here and ask you to offer a proposal."

"Anything I painted would not satisfy him. I would not have one of the most powerful financiers in New Rochelle dissatisfied with me."

"His satisfaction will never pay the bills."

"That is most true, my dear, but his dissatisfaction may keep others from paying them."

"You are impossible."

"I believe you said that before." I smiled broadly.

"Chendor . . . I don't know why I stay with you."

"Because I am an arrogant artistic genius. And because I love you. I have always loved you and looked at no one else."

"All that is true, Chendor, but don't you dare turn down another paying commission that good. Don't you dare!"

"I can't promise that, dearest."

Aeryana was shaking her head as she walked back up the ramp to the upper level, from where she managed the financial side of the studio. She was no longer angry. That I could tell.

Should I offer a proposal on the Societe Generale portrait? It would be simple enough, and the work would not be that hard. Then again, Atreos would tell everyone he knew in Noveau Rochelle all of the faults he saw in the portrait. He knew far more people than I did.

If I created a portrait that pleased Atreos, it would not be the kind of work for which I was known. I would then be accused of abandoning my standards. That could cost me more than I'd gain from the Societe Generale commission.

I looked up from my thoughts. Out beyond the front display window, a black sedan glided to a stop at the curb in front of the studio. It was a security vehicle. I recognized it because one had always followed Zaphir's limousine when he had come to sit for his portrait. I'd offered to go to his office. He'd said that he preferred the excuse of leaving it.

Two men got out of the sedan and stepped toward the studio door. It was going to be one of those days. Aeryana would be anything but pleased if I turned down a second commission, especially from someone wealthy enough for a security detail.

When they stepped into the front foyer, I bowed. "Greetings."

As I straightened up, I recognized the shorter man in the lighter gray. It was Georges Hillaire, the managing directeur of Banc du Nord. I'd done a portrait of his wife nine years back. It had been one of my better works, except for those of Aeryana, of course.

"Ser Barna?" That was the taller and younger man in the severe dark gray singlesuit. He had the figure of someone who had been an athlete and still kept in training. His eyes drifted to the representation of the Grande Opera Theatre. He nodded, and his eyes flicked back to me. They were dark gray. They were also far harder than I would have expected from a man who looked so young as he did.

"The same."

"I apologize," he went on. "Ser Hillaire had given me your name and had agreed to accompany me. I'm here to discuss a possible . . . commission."

The hesitation over the word "commission" suggested tentativeness, but Hillaire would never have accompanied someone who could not have afforded my work—and prices.

"We would appreciate a few minutes with you, perhaps in a less open space."

Some clients were like that. "The conference room is damped." I gestured for them to follow me.

Neither spoke until the door was closed. One of them added a secondary damping field. Hillaire wouldn't have done it. The younger man in the darker gray surveyed the octagonal chamber, with the cherry-paneled walls—and no artwork. He studied the piped-light chandelier, then the circular table, before seating himself in one of the four wooden armchairs.

I took the chair across from him. Hillaire sat at my left. He worried his lip with his lower teeth. I'd not seen that before.

"I am here on behalf of the both the Comity Cultural Service and the Diplomatic Corps," began the man I didn't know.

"You didn't say who you are," I offered.

"I could give you a name. It wouldn't be mine, but you could track it, and it would be real. As real as any name is, and it would even identify the company that pays my salary. It's not real, either, except as a financial entity."

"Why didn't you just give it, then?"

"Because ser Hillaire suggested I do not. He said that you would know it was not real. Our research indicates the same. That talent is part of the reason the Comity would like to offer you both a stipend and a series of works for a commission. The stipend would go to your wife, the commission to you."

"I'm certain Aeryana would agree to that." I laughed. "She might ask why both did not go to her."

The corners of Hillaire's lips lifted, then dropped.

"What is this commission?"

"A series of depictions of places and items of great and unique interest. I can only say that you have never seen their like."

"Can only say, or will only say?"

"I cannot say more because I don't know more."

He was telling the truth. That was interesting, and unnerving.

"The stipend would be five thousand Comity credits paid every Gallian month for up to three years."

That was even more unnerving. Over the past decade, my best year had been seventy thousand, my worst thirty. The Comity was offering a baseline stipend of fifty thousand. "And the commission?"

"An additional one hundred thousand baseline, up to three hundred thousand."

"I don't recall such generosity being a Comity policy. What conditions are you omitting?"

"You will be traveling on Comity vessels, not luxurious private transports. The work will be interesting, but demanding. It could take up to two years. You will have comm links, but they will be delayed and monitored. Most important, if you take the assignment, ser Barna, you'll have to leave within a standard day. We will need to know your decision by the end of the day."

"And if I don't accept?"

"We go to the second artist on the list. That's a Pieter Bounaiev. He's from Dneipra."

Bounaiev was good, but not so good as I was. The man in dark gray knew that. He also knew I wouldn't like to give such an opportunity to Bounaiev.

"You may have my decision now."

Hillaire frowned. I could tell he thought I would decline.

"I will accept on one condition."

"I don't have much latitude, ser Barna."

"At least twenty percent of the work must be mine to display as I see fit and to sell or resell freely."

He nodded. "If you will excuse me for a moment. I will need to check with my superior." He stood and walked out, clearly heading toward the security sedan and its shielded communications.

After the other left the conference room, Hillaire studied me. He had an air of gloom. "Must you always be difficult, Chendor?"

"Artists are. No matter how great what I am to portray may be, and no matter how well I depict it, it does me no good if it is sealed in the Comity archives. It will not do the Comity much good, either."

"Chendor . . . you always press too much. You could have the Societe Generale commission if you would but submit a proposal."

"Georges . . . that is begging, and I cannot beg."

"Cannot . . . or will not?"

"I cannot. You know that."

"All too well. That will be the death of you."

Or the making—and the line between the two was thin for an artist.

We waited.

Shortly, the gray man returned. His lips held a faint smile as he closed the conference room door behind him. He did not seat himself. "Twenty percent is acceptable, but . . . nothing that will reveal military or technological details. I have been assured that you will have a great deal of choice within those parameters, perhaps more than you would wish or imagine."

There it was. Take it or leave it. Risk portraying dull images for a high fee or . . . I almost laughed. The images in Noveau Rochelle were already getting dull. When else would I get a chance such as this? Even before I replied, the unnamed man knew that I could not risk not having a chance at whatever it was that the Comity wanted represented accurately and artistically.

"I accept."

"Good. I will see you an hour before noon tomorrow. You are limited to one large valise for clothing and no more than one hundred kilos for equipment."

For the range of what I might have to depict, a hundred kilos might be pushing it, but if I eased in another ten, I bet no one would complain. I intended to take everything from old-style oils, pastels, and charcoal to lightbrushes. The canvases and the light matrices would be the heaviest, but I could always roll some canvases into my valise and limit the frames.

"Ser Hillaire will be here an hour before I arrive to set up the financial details. The monthly stipend to your wife will be coming through Banc du Nord, and the first payment will be in the designated account before you leave—as will half of the minimum commission."

I walked them to the studio door. When I turned and headed back, I could see Aeryana coming down the ramp. "I've taken a commission—"

"I thought as much." Her words were tart.

"I have to travel off-planet for it."

"You turn down a perfectly good commission here in Noveau Rochelle, then take one that will send you off-planet? Chendor . . . I do not understand you."

"A stipend of five thousand a Gallian month for you for at least a year and a deposit of fifty thousand in advance. Both will be paid tomorrow before I leave."

"You're leaving *tomorrow*? For a year?" Her voice rose. "What about me? What about Nicole?"

"Aeryana . . . this is an urgent commission from the Comity Diplomatic Corps. It is so important that they have pressured Georges Hillaire to accompany them. You would have me turn down Hillaire? They must have discovered something of great import—an abandoned colony or perhaps the first alien artifacts. My work will be displayed across all the worlds of the Comity. Peter Atreos would look like a fool if he opposed my work. They will beg me."

"Chendor, those who have any taste already do."

"This is the chance of a lifetime."

"What will you be portraying?"

"Everything."

"Exactly what is everything?" Aeryana's words were measured.

"They said that they couldn't tell me."

"You believed them?"

"Georges Hillaire was with him. The funds are coming through Banc du Nord. Besides, who would pay fifty-five thousand credits if they did not want my art?" Even Aeryana knew that a contract disposal could be had for far less, should anyone wish to remove me.

Tears appeared in the corners of her eyes.

"You said I shouldn't turn down another good commission."

"Chendor . . . I didn't mean . . ." Her arms were around me. That was the best we could do.

6 GOODMAN/BOND

The face in the fresher mirror was still unfamiliar, long and horsy. The short hair was brown, wiry and curly enough to be unpleasantly unmanageable. I was glad for the short military cut. The skin was too dark for my taste, but not out-and-out black or even light mahogany.

After the survey, and another effort to become familiar with the new visage, I stepped from the small fresher into the single room of the pleasure girl's studio.

I was William Gerald Bond. Before long, I would be the only William Gerald Bond.

At the faint beep, I checked the locator. It showed that the girl was on the ramp headed up to the studio. I stepped behind the old-style hinged door. The bioplastic had been resmoothed and colored so many times that faint streaks of white discolored what had been solid brown.

Waiting for them to arrive, I thought about the last month.

When I had come out of the nanite cocoon, my head felt like it had been split, frozen, and pulverized. The result? I now knew more about being a Comity armorer than I'd ever wished. I also knew how to build an Atrousan-Graviton signaler. Major Ibaio hadn't left that to mere nanite indoc. I'd built three before he and his chief tech were satisfied—all except for a live power source. We'd used inactive ones. Wouldn't do to set off an AG signaler in New Jerusalem. I couldn't say I knew how it worked, only what components to use and how to put them together. I'd also had to practice repairs and diagnostics until my fingers and hands matched my mind.

"You're tougher than Colonel Truesdale thought." That was what Majer Ibaio had said at my last briefing.

"How many others didn't make it?" I'd asked.

"For this position, you were the only choice."

That meant Ibaio had planted others—or hoped to.

After all the in-depth conditioning and training, I'd still had to get to Hamilton. The first stage had been the most tedious, as a tourist going to the pleasure spa at Maewest. An identity switch, and I'd been Angus DeWeil, natural fabrics factor, on the way home to Hamilton. Now I was in Alexander, the city that had grown up around the Comity's military orbit elevators, and I stood behind a bioplastic door, waiting for an oversexed armorer and a lightly conditioned pleasure girl.

You know what the steps ahead are, but you don't think about them, and not about the big picture. You can go crazy doing that, especially if it involved the Comity getting its hands on the Morning Star. You think about what is next and how to react. The door was thick enough that I didn't hear anything until they were just outside, and she touched the ID bloc.

"Just a moment, big boy . . . not in the hall." A nervous laugh followed the words.

The door opened, and I lifted the stunner.

As the door closed, I hit Bond with a full nerve jolt, then dropped the intensity to stun before I triggered it a second time. Neither even had a chance to see me.

Two bodies lay on the floor—one dead and one unconscious.

I straightened the girl, then dragged Bond's form across the floor and into the fresher. There, I stripped off his uniform. Once I had the uniform off, I carried it out of the fresher and into the other room, laying it across one of the straight-backed chairs set on each side of the small table protruding from the wall.

Then I came back and stripped off his underwear before hauling the body into the shower/drainage basin. I didn't look at his face. I knew better. I had to wash the underdrawers. Distasteful, but necessary. I hung them on the clothing pegs on the back of door.

Before I went further, I pulled on the double-layered impermeable gloves, then turned the water on in the sink, as hot as possible. Only then did I take out the packet and slide it under the stream of water, just long enough for the outer film to turn red. I quickly placed the packet on the chest of the dead man and stepped back to the sink. There I let the water run over the gloves before I stripped off the outer layer, then the inner one.

I left the fresher and closed the door behind me. The pleasure girl was still out, but breathing normally. I glanced back at the closed fresher door. The packet had held special nanites—gray goo, so to speak. Special gray goo, designed only to dissolve certain kinds of cells—and to be active only for so long. Still, I wasn't about to step back into the fresher until that time was well past. Well past.

I crossed the room to where the pleasure girl lay. With a smile, I bent and lifted her, carrying her to the bed against the wall. I laid her out on it, so that she'd be comfortable.

She was pretty enough, and my new "I" had paid for her services. There was no reason not to enjoy them. It would certainly be in character—and I'd be gentler than Bond was known to have been. I'd just tell her the truth—that she'd fainted as she'd stepped into the studio. I didn't have to mention that I'd caused her to faint. The priors might not be happy when I was debriefed, and the adjudicators wouldn't be pleased, but I could always claim that I'd had to stay in character as part of my mission.

In another fifteen minutes, well before she woke, I'd have to go back into the fresher and rinse out the residue in the shower basin.

7 CHANG

Never got planetside after the courier left McClendon Alpha Station. Alya stuffed me into a clamshell in the courier's passenger closet. Boosted out-system at three gees. Couriers don't use full-grav protection. Too much mass.

Went through the out-system Gate like a hell-bat. Only dropped accel for pre-Gate and Gate. I'd held star-class, but wouldn't have tried that. Definite way of putting me in my place. Stupid, too. Hit the edge of a Gate, and you become instant singularity, maybe even a graviton wave. That's after the explosion, the hard radiation, and the general mess within light-hours.

No one asked me.

Courier docked somewhere. I pulsed the links. *Where are we?*

We're locked at a D.S.S. station in the outer fringes of the Hamilton system. The exact locale is classified. You can release the clamshell.

I used the inside controls to open the clamshell. Once clear, I looked around.

No one anywhere, but words projected from the overhead. "Your gear is short of the lock. Leave by yourself. You'll be met. Good luck, sweetie." The voice was Alya's. Hot pilot, but a definite fem.

Made my way to the lock. My one kit bag sat there. Took my time checking the pressure equalizations and temps before I opened the inner hatch and picked up my kit. Fog still formed when the lock hatch slid open.

Next hatch was to the station. Checked it more carefully. Indicators green. Opened the hatch and stepped across. More fog, and the faint acrid smell all asteroid stations had—oil and metal and ozone and people. Even nanite-based reformulators never get rid of everything. Faint grav shift. That told me one thing—the station was an asteroid type. Most likely nickel-iron, with tunnels. Easy to shield.

Gray-haired Comity D.S.S. commander met me outside the station lock. Wore the standard blue skintights and gray vest and shorts for stations and ships. "You're Jiendra Chang."

I nodded. Once.

"I'm Commander Daffyd Morgan. I'm the operations officer of the *Magellan*. You've been assigned to us, but the ship isn't quite ready for us to embark." He smiled, half-sympathetic, and half–hard as adamantine steel. "There's another aspect of your job no one told you. From this moment on, you're Lieutenant Chang, and you're under my command. Your pay is still civilian star-class, but the *Magellan* is the equivalent of a battle cruiser, and all the pilots are in the military chain of command."

Shit! I'd thought dealing with Graysham was tight-ass. Military was worse. "Yes, sir."

"Come with me. I'll try to answer your questions. Those that I can." He turned.

I followed. Gravity was at one Tee, or close enough. Passageway was melted through the asteroid. Deck was smooth and even. Bulkheads and overhead weren't. Station wasn't regular installation, then. "Commander, was the station created for this mission?"

"That's an interesting question." He didn't look back. "You tell me why you think so, and I'll tell you if you're right."

"The deck is smooth. Bulkheads and overheads aren't. Be hard to believe that of a regular D.S.S. installation."

He laughed. "You're right."

"What is the mission?"

"I can't tell you that until later." He stopped at an unmarked hatch and touched his hand to the scanner. Hatch opened silently. Old hatches weren't that quiet. Morgan's office was smaller than Graysham's cube on Alpha Station. Morgan dropped into a chair, gestured to the other one.

Didn't feel like sitting, but didn't feel like carrying the kit bag longer, either. So I sat and waited for him to tell me something I didn't know.

He grinned, almost friendly. "D.S.S. hijacked you, Lieutenant. Get used to the rank. You'll be using it for a long time—if you make it. If you don't, you'll still get star-class salary while you're here and your ratings back. That's if you don't knee anyone or smash their kneecaps."

Wondered how he'd found out about the kneecap incident. Had to have been fifteen years back. I waited.

"We need particular skills in shuttle pilots. Most D.S.S. pilots will handle vessels in deep space far better than any of you could ever hope. Most of you can handle small craft around stations, planets, and other moving bodies far better than your D.S.S. compatriots. Different skills, and we need the best of both." He paused. "You'll start specialized training tomorrow, along with Lieutenant Braun. She'll be here in a moment to show you around the station and help you get squared away. She was the first shuttle pilot here. You two will be sharing a stateroom here. You'll have your own on board ship."

Didn't want to share anything. Didn't know which was worse—sharing with men or women. Just different problems. "How long before we embark on the *Magellan*?"

"I can't say. That depends on too many variables. Between two and four standard weeks. You'll be busy enough not to worry."

"Can you tell me what I'll be piloting?"

"A very special shuttle that also is configured as a lander with unique capabilities. Don't ask me to describe those. You'll begin to learn all about them tomorrow."

A slight beep from the hatch indicated someone outside. The hatch slid open. Morgan stood. Figured I'd better, too.

Woman who stepped in was the kind whose looks I hated. Petite, creamy skin, dark mahogany hair—doll-like. Might have come to my shoulder.

"Lieutenant Braun, this is Lieutenant Chang." Morgan smiled, professionally polite.

"Gretta Braun." She turned to me. Black eyes like focused particle beams. I've seen cold. Hers were colder.

"Jiendra Chang."

The commander cleared his throat. "Lieutenants. It's fifteen hundred. I don't expect to see either of you until zero eight hundred tomorrow at the training bay. That's bay three."

"Yes, sir." Braun's voice was polite, pleasant.

"Yes, sir."

We walked out into the passageway. Except for us, it was empty.

Braun looked at me. "I have to ask." Her voice was level, warmer than her eyes. Anything would have been. "Did you really break all of Fingan's fingers?"

"No. Broke six. Maybe seven. They stunned me before I got the last three. How did you know him?"

"I didn't. I took the job after you left. I made head pilot a year back."

"What happened to Hengeist?"

"He had an accident and decided to leave."

Hengeist had been almost as bad as Fingan. Should have had an accident earlier. "How did you manage it?"

"I didn't. I just didn't try to save him very quickly."

I'd have bet Braun had done more than that. Also bet that it wasn't wise to say so. "Suppose you ought to give me the tour."

"I can do that." She paused. "I'd like to have one thing clear. No men—or women—in the stateroom."

That was fine by me. "You hadn't suggested it, I would have."

That got me a nod.

Braun turned and began to walk. "This passageway is upper operations, only for ops personnel—pilots and ops techs. That's why it's mostly quiet. Ops passageways are gray, the same as on D.S.S. ships. Crew passages are blue. Maintenance ways are brown, and the weapons spaces are red. Pilots can use any passageway, but it's best to avoid maintenance unless there's no other way . . ."

I followed, listening.

8 FITZHUGH

While Security agent Herrit had been absolutely accurate in all that he had said, he had not said more than that I was to be handled like a valuable and high-priority package—and that was exactly what occurred. We were sequestered in a luxury lounge on the elevator climber to orbit Station Beta. Orbit elevators represented the cost-effective and practical, but there is little doubt that they dealated the romance of flight, leaving it far less supernal, assuming it ever had been.

We sat in the private lounge, a space no more than three meters square, adjoining two even smaller bedchambers. Feather-light hangings of cream and blue framed the wall screen that showed Leinster slowly dwindling below us and the stars appearing as the elevator accelerated upward out of the lower atmosphere. There was a stripped-down console between our chairs, and I could have read, but I felt even less like reading than watching Leinster, especially with agent Herrit around. For me, reading has always been solitary.

I tried music, an ancient piece, the *1812 Overture*. I blocked the visuals. Battle scenes re-created with brilliant blue-trimmed red uniforms and prancing mounts disconcerted me too much, but entertainment multis weren't about to show filthy blue-and-white uniforms with barefoot soldiers leaving bloody footprints—almost no one listened to music without a visual component anyway. I was one of the remaining few to prefer the auditory over the visual.

Eventually, I went to bed, but didn't sleep that well.

Herrit was awake and dressed in his black singlesuit before me in the morning, and waiting in the small lounge after I'd freshened up—the mostly waterless way, since water has mass, and every tonne of water means a tonne less paying cargo or passengers.

The eggs Lyonais from the lounge formulator were patrician in style and presentation, but thoroughly formulated in taste, and I eased them down with the excessive caffeine of old-style bergamot tea, also formulated. After beginning my second mug of the ersatz stuff, I looked across the narrow pop-up table that separated us, for Herrit had said nothing.

"How many missions like this have you done? Conveying professors to unknown destinations?"

"Ensuring the safe arrival of people and items is one of our standard duties, Professor. You, of all academics, should know that."

"How long have you been with Comity Security?"

"A number of years."

"How many people have you injured or killed?"

He just looked at me. I knew what he was thinking—violence on the personal level was a sign of incompetence.

"Have you had to take special precautions in my case?"

Herrit laughed, genially. "My superiors have. They always do. Why do you think neither of us knows where you're going or for what?"

"If I'm that valuable . . . ?"

"Professor . . . you're an intelligent man, perhaps brilliant. There are a thousand worlds in the Comity. Most hold millions of individuals. How many other brilliant scholars are there in fields similar to yours? You can be replaced. So can I."

At that point, I stopped asking questions, not because I didn't have more, but because Herrit couldn't answer them any better than I could, and because I'd realized something else.

If . . . if what Herrit had implied was true, then I wouldn't know anything that would cause anyone to want me dead until I was wherever the Comity wanted me, and the Comity could doubtless find a way to keep me quite protected while I was working on whatever they had in mind. My safety before and during this fellowship was not the problem.

Afterward . . . *that* would be the problem.

And I still couldn't discern why the Comity Diplomatic Corps had any need for a professor of historical trends.

9 GOODMAN/BOND

At zero five hundred I walked into the transient quarters just inside the main gate of the D.S.S. base. I made sure I was grinning. Most of the techs were sleeping. As I stopped at the locker above the empty bunk, one looked up. I could feel the briefing info take. Gutersen, engineering tech, third.

"Bond . . . you ought to be grinnin'. I saw that girl."

"I'd be grinning more if I had another day. That's D.S.S. Good enough pay for pretty women, not enough time to enjoy 'em. Course . . . for someone like you, with a pretty wife . . ."

"Two hundred kays away." He snorted. "Don't you ever worry about where we're going?"

"A tech'd go crazy worrying about that. Never tell us much. What else is new?" I opened the locker and took out the kit bag. Everything was stuffed inside. My predecessor had not been a tidy man.

After cleaning up and changing, at zero six hundred I presented myself at the D.S.S. in-processing center, a long building another block toward the bluff overlooking the north shore and the circular harbor below. I'd presented the ID card and had it checked against my DNA twice before I got to the personnel section. There the personnel tech took the order card and my D.S.S. ID. I smiled easily as they went into the analyzer. D.S.S. cards were supposed to be unduplicatable. But then, D.S.S. didn't want anyone to know they weren't, and CIS wasn't about to broadbeam that the cards could be duplicated and altered.

There was only the slightest hesitation before the personnel tech nodded. "You'll be on the eleven hundred elevator. Be at the debarkation dock no later than zero eight hundred. Take the upper inclinator at the end of the avenue. That one goes straight to the ferry dock."

"You know where I'm headed?"

"Nope. Only says you're going to D.S.S. orbit station for further assignment."

The colonel might have learned that I was headed to the *Magellan,* but no one in D.S.S. seemed to know that. I still had to push away the questions that wouldn't help with the mission and the speculations about the Morning Star and what Major Ibaio had really meant by that.

The tech handed back the cards. "Make sure you empty your bladder before you enter the elevator. Otherwise, you'll be very unpopular before long. The elevator has only one speed, and that's high." She didn't look at me. "Next! Guillermo, Christan."

It was only six-forty-five, and I walked casually northward through the base. Fifteen minutes later I reached the end of the avenue. From there, the harbor spread out below. There wasn't much at the base of the basalt cliffs except two long piers. Each was accessed by an inclinator. From the bluff top, I saw the ferry to the terminal platform. It was an SES—the sort that had been around for thousands of years, even before the Tellurian Diaspora.

I stepped onto one of the platforms, to the right of a woman armorer, chief tech. Her eyes took in the second's badge on my sleeve, then my face. She looked away. I was too old to be a rising tech. That was what the colonel had wanted—the kind of tech no one really looked at.

At the end of the inclinator, I let the chief tech move farther ahead of me.

Another ID/DNA check waited at the ferry. It was amusing. No one had thought about the implications. The DNA check made sure that no one had stolen a D.S.S. ID card, but it didn't guard against forged cards where the DNA matched. Since all information had to be ship-carried from system to system, the key to D.S.S. security was the unbreakability of the ID card.

The ferry trip took less time than waiting for the ferry to depart.

There wasn't an ID check at the orbit elevator terminal. There were screens on which names and level assignments were posted. Mine was third level, fourth bay. I took my time, again, but a number of techs hadn't reported when I reached the bay.

D.S.S. elevators don't have frills—just flat couches in square bays. Military elevators are faster than civilian elevators. It takes a mere five hours to get to the Clarke point. The trade-off is that D.S.S. only operates eight climbers at a time because the higher velocities require more energy and greater spacing. I didn't recognize anyone in the bay, and took an end couch. The fabric was old and stained in places. My kit went into the locker under the couch.

Before long, there was the standard announcement.

"Strap in and do not move once your harness locks. The first half hour will seem relatively slow until the climber clears the thickest part of the atmosphere."

I settled into the couch.

You can't feel the speed or the acceleration with an AG-boosted climber, and they're much safer than the ancient elevators. If the guidance ribbon breaks, the AG unit automatically throws the climber into low orbit, and eventually a shuttle comes and tows it to orbit station. Only a handful have broken in hundreds of years. Most of those were sabotage. One I knew about all too well.

Mostly, I was bored and sore by the time we unstrapped and lined up to leave the climber. Everyone in the third level was headed to the same shuttle lock, marked by the blue arrows. I followed the arrows—and ended up in a queue before an open hatch. Gutersen was five techs ahead of me. Officers didn't queue, and they had a separate waiting area. The tech just behind Gutersen was dark-haired, curved even better than the girl from the night before. She turned. Her face was harder, much older.

Once inside the hatch, there was a circular full-body scanner—the kind you walk through that shows every bit of your interior. Just short of it was an open bin. On each side of the scanner were two D.S.S. Marine guards behind nanite-shielded screens. They both had riot-level stunners, and they were out. My turn came, and I stepped toward the single security tech, third class. He was younger than Gutersen.

"Drop the kit right there." The tech's voice was bored. He must have said that a hundred times a day. "Into the bin."

"Ah . . . ?" I thought some reaction was required.

"You're in the group for further assignment, aren't you?"

"Yes."

"Your orders stated that you were to bring only minimal kit, and nothing personal. You'll be issued a new kit when you report to your station. Drop it."

I dropped the kit bag. It vanished into bin, on its way to reformulation.

"Through the scanner."

I stepped through. Nothing happened.

On the other side was a personnel tech. She was second class, nice-looking but not special. "You're cleared, Bond. You'll leave at nineteen hundred. Pick up one of the temporary kits there." She nodded at a stack of plastic handkits. "Disposable skintights and toiletries. Enough for your transfer hop. You and your cadre will be in the aft section of the *Titania*. Take the second hatch, the green one. Follow it to the waiting area at the end. Facilities and food are there. Don't leave the area."

A transfer hop that required more than one skintight meant a long in-system journey. I was headed to the *Magellan* or to an isolated system station to rot. I picked up the temporary kit and walked toward the green hatch.

Equipment hummed faintly when I stepped through—another scan.

A two-hour wait before we loaded. That wouldn't be too bad. I stepped into the waiting area, a long narrow chamber that had one large lock at the end. The walls were greenish gray. Every military outfit I'd seen liked some shade of gray.

"Bond!" called Gutersen. He sat in one of the sling seats set in rows. "Come join us."

I grinned. "I see you made it."

"Told you we were going the same place," Gutersen burbled. "It's just got to be something big. Maybe it's one of those new super dreadnoughts. Always wanted to be in on something big. What do you think?"

Two hours with Gutersen might be longer than two weeks with anyone else.

10 CHANG

Threeday morning I was in the training bay—long chamber, overhead with barely forty centimeters clearance, equipment stacked everywhere, and corridors melted through the nickel-iron at all angles. Was barely on time. Wouldn't have been if Braun hadn't reminded me to reset my personal chrono the night before. D.S.S. used old-style seven-day, twenty-four-hour Old Earth clock and calendar. Braun was neat, quiet, and kept to herself. So did I. Better that way.

D.S.S. tech, second, met us. "Lieutenants, I'm Weibling, habitability systems tech. We need to get you fitted for armor. Commander Morgan said to get that out of the way."

Space armor? That meant deep-space ops—or ops in adverse habitability. Or both.

"You don't know where we're headed, do you?" I figured he wouldn't know, but sometimes the techs know more than officers.

"No, sir. We get the equipment parameters. That's all. I can tell you that you'll be handling everything from near absolute to perihelion hot, and mostly with no atmosphere. Grav range is from null to one-point-five Tee."

Braun frowned.

"Thank you." I managed a smile.

"This way, lieutenants, if you would."

We dropped back slightly.

"They've found an artifact planet. Forerunner or alien," Braun murmured. "Or an abandoned colony with something special about it."

"Has to be hard to land there, then. Wouldn't need us, otherwise."

She nodded.

We didn't say more. Followed Tech Weibling. Suit measurements took less than half stan. When we got back to the training bay, Morgan was motioning from the far end.

"Commander wants us," Braun said.

"Hope not." Wondered how she'd take the double entendre.

"He wouldn't. He's old-style D.S.S., and we're his subordinates. That's bad form and worse discipline."

"Were you ever D.S.S.?"

"Gagarin Academy—one very long tour after that. I swore I'd never come back."

Promise like that always bites back. Learned that a long time ago. Closet Covenanter once told me God has a sense of humor. Never believed in God. Universe as it is can be rough enough without a deity to mess it up worse.

We moved briskly but didn't rush.

The commander stood before a long cylinder with an open hatch. Inside was a shuttle cockpit. Even from ten meters away, I could see it had a board like I'd only seen once before, and that was when I was ferrying mining supplies down to Toomai.

"We only have one simulator here, but that should be more than enough."

"How many shuttle pilots will you be giving fams to, Commander?" asked Braun.

"D.S.S. is sending four former civilians, including you two. I'm a backup, and so is Major Tepper. We can handle the mission with two shuttle pilots, and two backups."

Four shuttle pilots for a ship? How big was the frigging thing? Dreadnought?

"The captain has also requested that, after you're up to speed on the shuttles, you two also receive basic familiarization and some simulation training on handling the *Magellan*."

"Begging your pardon, sir," asked Braun, "but why us?"

"The captain is a cautious woman. She also said that while you two valued yourselves above anything, that same pride would keep you from selling out to anyone and anything, including fear and disaster." Morgan offered a smile that looked easygoing. It wasn't.

More I heard, more it seemed like a bastard job.

"How big is the *Magellan*, sir?" Finally had to ask.

Morgan grinned. "Bigger than anything you've seen, Lieutenant. She's a former colony ship, reconfigured with double dreadnought drives. She's also armed like a battle cruiser."

Knew it was a bastard job.

Morgan cleared his throat. "Lieutenants, you'll both need full medicals. That's so we've got baselines in case of emergencies or injuries. Braun—you head to medical now. Your first turn in the simulator will be around eleven hundred. While you're in the simulator, Chang will have her medical."

"Yes, sir." Braun nodded, then stepped back.

Morgan waited until she was well away. Turned to me. "I've heard you're the hottest thing since Chatzel." He snorted—loud. "You may be one of the best shuttle pilots in the Comity, Chang, or even the very best, but you've never seen a shuttle like this. Learning how to pilot it is going to take everything you have." He didn't raise his voice. Didn't have to. Cut like a focused singularity.

Reminded myself I was getting paid star-class, even if I had to wear blue skintights, with the dark gray D.S.S. ship vest and shorts—and the shiny silver shoulder stripes that said I was an officer. Didn't feel like one. "Yes, sir. Must be a special shuttle."

"Very special, Lieutenant. You've got chem-jets, photon-thrusters, and AG drive. With the AG drive you'll be able to lift off and land on any planet up to one-point-six Tellurian with full gross."

"No magfield drives?" *That* surprised me.

"Where we're headed lost its magnetic field a long time ago, and we might be able to use the extra cargo capability."

That said old. Old enough that there couldn't be much living there. "Any armament?"

"You know how to handle it?"

"I've had torp training, and some background in close-in particle beams."

"Good." He frowned. "That wasn't on your record."

Lots not on my record. Didn't want it there. The more that's there, the more they can claim you screwed up, that you should have known better.

"What else isn't there?"

"Had a course in commando hand-to-hand, once. Bare and in armor." Wished I hadn't said that soon as I did. Bust some jerk's balls, and they see commando training in the file, and you're a mankiller. Rather claim accidental self-defense. "Just a short course. Never rated."

"I don't believe that. You like ratings too much."

"Wouldn't rate me." That much was true.

"I see. What else?"

"Little things you pick up everywhere. How to jury a bad board, that sort of thing."

"You shouldn't have to do that. Everything's new. You've got standard pilot links?"

"Yes, sir. Still star-class." He'd known that before he'd asked. Hadn't been able to use links on McClendon. Straight manual. Equipment there was too old. A mal-link'd be so painful the best pilot couldn't think straight. Even me.

"Good. Go ahead and strap in. You'd be wearing armor, but that'll come once Weibling gets them ready."

"Yes, sir." Couldn't wait for that. Working a shuttle in armor, even without gauntlets and helmet, is a frigging pain. Hot, too. Even hotter in a simulator.

Climbed in the simulator, and closed the hatch. Manual style. Inside center was standard, except for the armament panel to the left and the crimson-edged panel to the right of the joystick. Overhead panels had all the extras.

Controls were optimum manual. Millennia back, when nanotech and minimicrotronics first came in, the designers tried direct mind link—minimal physical controls. Then came the Dirty War, and all the mental-link pilots got hammered, blasted, dismembered, by the Gallian Unity pilots on manual controls. Took almost ten years to figure out why. Seemed simple enough to me. Humans are optimized to *do* things. You train a pilot with brains and reflexes. Reflexes let you do one thing physically while your mind does something else.

Every study ever done shows that humans don't mental multitask without losing efficiency. Women tend to do it better, but still get clobbered in combat by physical controls. Best deep-space combat pilots tend to be spatially oriented women on mixed controls—or artistic men. Macho males come off worst. Really pisses 'em off.

Triggered the links.

Online.

Stet. Morgan came through clear, just like his voice. *Your call sign will be Tigress.*

Wasn't amused by that. *For simulation training?*

No. From here on. If you've got the first shuttle, it's Porter. So when you're piloting shuttle one, the call sign is Porter Tigress. Second shuttle is Sherpa. Magellan's call sign is Navigator. Got that?

Got it.

Today you'll be piloting Porter. They handle differently, but we'll start with Porter. The board's live. You've got ten minutes before you start the prelaunch checklist. You take her through delock and stand off, and I'll give you orders from there.

Stet.

Forced myself to run through the system specs first. Got more than a few surprises. The shuttle had an empty gross mass of fifty metric tons. Most shuttles ran less than thirty. It was also stressed to fifteen standard gravs—more like an air combat flitter. Except its exterior was barely lifting body shape, if that. Next surprise was that the AG drives weren't shuttle drives. More like full-scale small ship AG drives. Could have piloted the shuttle from the surface of any Tellurian planet and halfway across any standard system with them. Third was the power of the photon-thrusters. Shuttle one was more like a small in-system cargo ship—an armed one stressed for atmospheric and planetary landings. Braun's idea about a lost colony made more sense. Doubted we'd find an ancient artifact. No one had in thousands of years.

Went on to touch and check every control on the board. The armaments I didn't know. Finally, I linked. *Don't know the armaments section.*

We didn't expect you would. We'll do a fam exercise on those this afternoon. You ready?

Ready.

Called up the checklist and started through it.

Locks . . . closed.

Ship-grav . . . off.

Fusactors . . . online.

Finally reached the end. Seemed to take forever. Always did.

Navigator Control, this is Porter Tigress, ready for delock and release this time.

Porter Tigress, dampers released. Cleared for delocking. Use minimal power.

Navigator Control. Porter Tigress, delocking this time. Had to rough-calc the power on the shuttle. Was used to something fifty percent the mass of the Porter shuttle. Could tell I'd overdone it and had to overbrake. Knew it was simmie, but the farscreen feeds jolted me. Simulation showed the *Magellan* as huge, bigger than most orbit stations, close to two kays in length, and close to half a kay in diameter—and smooth. No hull projections at all—sign of a high-speed real-space requirement.

Porter Tigress, vector two four zero, relative Magellan course line, inclination minus twenty-seven.

Navigator Control, understand vector two four zero, inclination minus twenty-seven. No objective in screens. Interrogative time to destination. Wasn't about to go charging off without knowing where, or how fast.

Wait one, Porter Tigress.

In the simmie, abruptly, an object appeared in the long-range farscreen—a rocky asteroid. Range was a good ten thousand kays. I blinked. Ninety-eight hundred. What the frig was Morgan doing? Asteroids didn't have that kind of relative motion. Frig! I was operating off a ship with high relative motion, not a geostationary satellite.

Porter Tigress, rendezvous with and take station on target.

Navigator Control, understand rendezvous and take station. Had scramble to get a relative motion plot and calculation. Sort of thing that can scramble your brain, because where it would be when I got the shuttle there was effectively "below" and "behind" the *Magellan.* Did a quick power calculation—and froze. Ran it again, quickly. *Navigator Control, Porter Tigress. Power reserves insufficient for return from target. Interrogative dust density.*

Dust density insufficient for photon scoops. Scrub target alpha this time.

Scrubbing alpha.

Target beta at zero five zero, inclination plus forty five. Interrogative rendezvous.

Beta was possible. With the relative motion, I wouldn't need as much power on return.

Navigator Control, rendezvous possible, with one-half stan on station.

Porter Tigress, commence rendezvous.

Commencing rendezvous this time.

Gave the thrusters a full jolt, calibrated fine as I could. Corrections take more power than doing it right first. Shuttle was slow to respond, slower than it should have been. Didn't match mass specs. Ran diagnostics, and found a twenty percent loss in conversion from the right fusactor. Shouldn't happen on a new shuttle, but Morgan wanted to play games. Cross-equalized power flows.

Made rendezvous in fifteen standard minutes, after one farscreen failure and loss of internal grav. I was dripping sweat.

Went through five different kinds of track-and-rendezvous problems.

Porter Tigress, return Navigator this time.

Stet. Returning Navigator this time.

Made a low-power controlled approach. Shuttle had too much mass to risk high-power quick mass-thrust decel and brake. Like I figured, converters acted up, but I managed to lock with only an extra tenth grav impact, within damper parameters. Went through the postlock shutdown. Made sure I did it step by step. Deliberate. You have to when you're tired, or you'll screw up something.

That's all for now. Morgan's voice came through the links. *Unstrap and come on out.*

Back of my vest was soaked. Pulled it away from the skintights before I opened the hatch and stepped out into the training bay.

Morgan looked up from the console. "Not bad." He nodded.

He was doing his duty. Still wanted to swat him. He couldn't have managed what he'd done to me. Almost laughed, then. He knew it. That was why he was backup. "Just hope that we don't have to do some of that for real."

"So do I, but those kinds of stresses get you a better feel faster."

Commander was right about that.

He motioned to Braun. She was talking to a tech. She nodded to the man and walked toward us. Her eyes raked me. "You look like shit."

Didn't want to talk about it. "How was the medical?"

"Star-class plus. Diagnostics want to know about every cell in your body, and how it got that way. They're way too personal."

"Always are."

She laughed, like a low growl.

"Lieutenant Chang, off to medical, then get something to eat. Sixteen hundred and you've got another session." Morgan looked up from the console again. Realized he was sweating. Glad to see that. He'd made me work hard enough.

"Yes, sir."

He looked away from me. "Lieutenant Braun. Into the simulator."

"Yes, sir."

Kept the smile off my face. Braun'd learn quick enough.

11 FITZHUGH

Security agent Herrit hurried me from the orbit elevator to the Comity Diplomatic Corps courier so swiftly that all I recalled was a blur of maroon-and-blue corridors and artificial light. When I stepped into the lock, Herrit stood back and guarded it. In my judgment, that was more to remind me that, despite my background, he was the one responsible for my safety. Once the courier lock had closed, and the vessel departed the station toward a destination still occluded from my comprehension, I was more than certain I would become another anonym in his long line of assignments.

"Please settle yourself one of the staterooms, Professor. Make yourself comfortable."

Those words, heterized into androgyny by remote projection, were the only welcome from the pilot.

"Can you tell me where we're going?"

"To your assignment, Professor. Once there, I'm sure you'll learn all you need to know. Please stow your gear and settle yourself in one of the staterooms. We're ready to delock."

I took the first stateroom, where I slipped my valise and gear into the single locker that barely held both. Then I dropped into the massive-looking armchair anchored to the floor, a more refined version of an acceleration confinement and security couch.

The door didn't lock, but that mattered little because the ship consisted, so far as I could tell, of two small staterooms, each with two bunks and—sealed off somewhere—whatever quarters and control spaces existed for the pilot or pilots.

During the trip, I did sleep more than I would have normally, probably because I'd slept poorly on the elevator lift to Leinster Orbit Station Beta. I ate less, because, while the stateroom had a formulator, it was basic. I didn't go hungry, but was not in the slightest tempted to overindulge.

Except for the time devoted to exercises, what I spent my time on was the small console, in order to make a dent in my professional reading, beginning with the *Review of Socio-Historical Trends*. Most of the articles were more abstruse than I preferred, but I did get immersed in a monograph by Fleming Sohcora postulating that the demise of a culture can be predicted by the degree to which the media and opinion leaders endorse and support the monistic doctrine of single supremacy—the triumph of "winner take all," if you will. He tied the rise of single supremacy monism to the fall of Western Hemispheric dominance on ancient Old Earth, the collapse of the Cephean Commercial League, and the relative decline of both the Worlds of the Covenant and the Sunnite Alliance. I had my doubts about applying the monistic model to theocracies, but he noted that, in such societies, "the deity is the supreme winner who takes all."

There was a provocative, but far less well documented and supported, article on secularism as religion, which suggested that secularism as such did not exist, and that secularists were merely believers in other deities—such as "wealth" or "power" or "egalitarianism"—and that such nontheistic beliefs were far more dangerous to a technological society than traditional religions and deities. In that respect, my forced isolation promised wonders for reducing the backlog of my continued delayed professional reading. On the other hand, after reading so much negativity, for the majority of scholarly articles in my field have always struck me as negative, when the ship locked in at the still-unnamed destination two days later, I was feeling more than a shade cynical.

Once the courier locked, I was ushered out into another unadorned bay, where the walls looked to be solid steel, coated with bluish plastrene.

Awaiting me was a D.S.S. lieutenant in blue skintights with the gray D.S.S. ship vest and shorts. His rank-strip gave his name as Ruano. "Professor Fitzhugh. Welcome to Project Deep Find. If you'd accompany me . . . Could I take one of your cases?"

I surrendered the valise, but kept my hands on the bag that held my datablocs and reference materials. "Where are we, if I might ask?"

"Deep Find Station, of course, sir."

"And where might that be?"

"We're in the Hamilton system, sir, but exactly where I can't tell you. Only one of the pilots could."

"I thought . . ."

"This is just a staging point, sir, until we board the *Magellan.* You'll have a stateroom here until that happens, and you'll have a chance to meet some of your colleagues."

No one had mentioned colleagues, and I had foolishly assumed that my "fellowship" was to be one of the bureaucratic advising types, buried studying secret files and providing analyses. What else could anyone wish from a professor of historical trends?

"This way, sir," prompted the lieutenant, after taking the valise.

I followed, trudging through the blue-walled and blue-lighted tunnel-like corridor. At the first intersection, we turned left, then traveled at least another hundred meters, to yet another corridor, where we turned right. Fifty meters later we stopped before a hatch with a DNA code device mounted on the wall.

"This is your section, sir. You'll find several of your colleagues in the lounge. Beyond the lounge are the staterooms. There is one with your name. There is a folder on the station in your quarters. It tells you where the mess is and where the briefing rooms are. Just remember to keep to the blue passageways."

The hatch opened, and I followed the lieutenant. He set down the valise, smiled, and stepped back. The hatch closed before I could say a word. Unless previously prepared, as in academic settings, quick repartee has never been one of my strengths.

Two women and a man sat around a table, in replica old-style captain's chairs. They had turned when I entered, but none of the three looked immediately familiar. The taller woman rose, peered in my direction, then smiled broadly and moved toward me. She had a round cheerful face. I could tell she was one of those people who love to hug everyone, and I braced myself.

"Professor Fitzhugh! I'm so glad that you decided to join our little expedition." She stopped short of a full-body crush, just flapping her arms around me before stepping back.

"So far as I could ascertain, the element of choice wasn't presented."

"An honored fellowship with grant funds and prestige to your institution—how could you possibly term that a draft?" countered the other and more angular woman.

"In my myopic and academic fashion, I must be misoriented, perhaps even believing in counterfactuals."

"You haven't changed a bit since New Dublin, Liam," noted the woman who had greeted me first.

Finally, the face and name came together—Alyendra Khorana. She'd been— she doubtless still was—an economic sociologist at St. Patrick's College. How a Hindji-Anglan had ended up in that bastion of propriety she had never made clear. "Are you still at St. Pat's?"

"Where else?"

I turned to the angular, if shorter, woman and to the long-faced man with eyes so light a brown that they were almost tan. "I've met Alyendra before, but I don't believe I've had the pleasure. If I have . . . please excuse me."

The gray-haired man laughed. "Tomas deSilva. Political science at San Juan University on Melloan."

"I'm Melani Kalahouri. Theoretical psychology, DeForrest Seminary." She appeared almost elfin in build and only stood to my shoulder.

"I'm told we're all colleagues," I said, "but no one bothered to tell me what exactly we are colleagues in." I had a growing suspicion after Melani had introduced herself, because theoretical psychology was the latest term for alien psychology, but it was now termed "theoretical" because no one had ever found any alien artifacts, let alone any aliens whose behavior and psychology might be studied.

"We're all in the social and behavioral science section of Project Deep Find," replied Alyendra.

"You've just told me more than I could get out of all the people who drafted me. What is Project Deep Find?"

"We don't know," replied Tomas. As he moved toward me, I could see that he was older than I'd thought, possibly even elderly, although that was hard to tell until a time within a few years of physical nonexistence. "That is, there have been intimations that there is possibly a renegade colony or even an abandoned alien planet. The locale is quite distant, and it is likely that only a single expedition can be mounted."

"That seems more than a little illogical," I pointed out. "To get to any interstellar locale takes a Gate. Once the Gate is in place, a return is possible."

Tomas raised his bushy gray eyebrows "I can suggest several assumptions behind your statement that are normally true, but are not necessarily so."

I wish I hadn't spoken so quickly. That habit has always created difficulties for me. "You may be right. What do you think?" That was a safe enough question.

"It seems unlikely that we would not be traveling by Gate. That would require a generation ship or a new technology."

"So there's something about the destination that means a Gate can't be used repeatedly?"

"That thought had occurred to me," deSilva replied.

"Maybe the star is prenova," suggested Alyendrya.

"Or approaching a singularity, or close to an event horizon," I said.

"All of that is possible." Melani smiled politely, yet warmly. "There may be other possibilities. Since we do not know, I think we should help Professor Fitzhugh get settled."

"Thank you." I bowed slightly. She was less imposing than Alyendrya, yet she'd spoken with a quiet authority.

For whatever reason we had been gathered, it had to be important to the D.S.S. and the Comity. Our small group suggested that we were far from the only scholars who would be on the expedition. I just wished I knew what Project Deep Find was all about, but, at the same time, I had a strong premonition that my satisfaction would be less than profound when the aims of the project were revealed.

12 BARNA

The unnamed Security agent stuffed himself and me into an orbit elevator. I had been right. He didn't say anything about the extra twenty kilos. They were mainly canvases and matrices. I could have done everything with light matrices, but light paintings aren't always the best way to depict some things.

Getting to orbit station took almost a full day. The orbit elevator was an older model. Nothing on Gallia was known for haste. From there, we took a shuttle to another orbit base. That was the local D.S.S. station. I found myself in a D.S.S. courier, headed to an unknown destination, if without the Security agent. The pilot's disembodied voice reassured me with generalities before subjecting me to confinement and crushing acceleration.

The only interesting aspect of the trip was the Gate translation. I'd never made one before. What artist could afford interstellar travel? I tried to hold on to the image of the translation and how all the colors reversed—yet didn't. After the initial acceleration that followed going through the Gate, I got out my equipment and tried to re-create the visual sense of what I'd experienced.

I wasn't sure I had, but the work was something very different. It just showed my small cabin, with the two bunks and the acceleration couch, except the pilot called it a clamshell. I tried to depict the cabin at the exact moment of translation when black was white, and the other way around, and when all the colors were *wrong,* yet right.

I'd barely gotten a first run at it when I had to stow everything for deceleration. I'd used the lightbrushes, knowing there wasn't time for oils. Charcoal wouldn't have done what I wanted, and I wouldn't have had time to fix it properly.

Several hours later, we ended up docked or locked, and the pilot's voice was ushering me out. Someone in a uniform—I thought it was a D.S.S. uniform with the blue skintights under the vest and shorts—was waiting outside the courier's lock. The foyer or bay was a hideous shade of blue. It also clashed with the D.S.S. uniform. It was the shade all the occupationalists had declared "stimulating" a generation before. If they had meant that it kept someone awake, that blue was stimulating. "Hideous" was a better term, and more accurate.

"Ser Barna?"

"That's me."

"I'm Lieutenant Ruano. I'm here to escort you to your quarters."

"Where is here? Where am I?"

"Deep Find Station in the Hamilton system, sir."

"When do I start work?"

"I couldn't say, sir. Commander Morgan would be better able to tell you."

"Could you take me to him, then?"

"I'm afraid not, sir. I'm here to take you to your quarters. Your temporary quarters, that is, until we move to the *Magellan* in a few days."

"The *Magellan* is a ship?"

"Yes, sir. Could I help you with one of those cases?"

I gave him the personal case. I wasn't about to trust anyone else with the two wheeled cases that held all my equipment, and everything except the extra canvases in my valise.

We walked close to half a kay, or so it seemed, along the blue corridor. I was breathing harder than usual, and I seemed to weigh a little more than I did on Gallia. That wasn't surprising, since Gallia was a bit less than Tellurian norm, and we were clearly inside some sort of D.S.S. space installation with the gravity set at Tellurian norm. I thought it was probably an asteroid station because the walls weren't jointed or fabricated, but seemed hollowed out of something and covered with the blue synth wall covering.

"Your section is just ahead, sir. That's where you'll be quartered, sir." The lieutenant stopped opposite a hatch. On it were the letters and number RA-1.

The hatch opened, and the lieutenant stepped back. He gestured for me to go first. I wheeled in the equipment cases. The walls of the room, a low-ceilinged combination of foyer and sitting room, were a pale green. The color was even more unpleasant than the blue of the corridor. There were no windows, and the artificial illumination wasn't even close to replicating natural light.

"Your quarters are labeled, sir, and there is a folder with directions to the mess. Please keep to the blue corridors."

With a nod, he was gone, the hatch closing behind him.

A large-boned, silver-haired woman watched me. Her hair was plaited into a braid then coiled on the back of her head. She was seated at one side of a square table with four chairs. They were synth-replicated wood, or what some bureaucrat thought might resemble wood.

I looked at the woman. With that silver hair, she was obviously nearing the end of her career, if not her life, and I wondered what she was doing here. "I'm Chendor Barna."

"Elysen Taube. Are you in the sciences?"

"I'm afraid not. I'm an artist. What is your field?"

"I am an old-style astronomer. I specialize in capturing and interpreting full-spectrum stellar images."

That was a kind of art in itself. I decided not to say so. Some scientific types resented any hint that their work was art and not science. "All kinds of stars?"

She smiled indulgently.

I ignored the condescension and waited.

"My work has dealt with the images of older galaxies, those formed right after the brane flex." A chuckle followed. "'Right after' is a relative term. The first hundred million years or so through the first few billion."

"How do you separate them out?"

"Finding them is the hard part. The universe . . ." She smiled. It was a warm smile, that of someone who could have been a grandmother, but probably wasn't. I wished I could have caught her image at that moment. "Why don't we get you settled? You'll have plenty of time to learn about astronomy, and I've always wanted to know more about art."

"You act as though we aren't going anywhere soon."

"Soon is also a relative term, Chendor. I've been here several days, and I haven't gotten a definitive answer yet. Astronomy may deal in millions of years, but I don't have that many years left. I'm certain that you, as an artist, have noted that. Like you, I'd prefer to get on with the project, but it's so large a project that organizing and assembling those involved takes time."

"How large a project?"

"A project that fills an asteroid station is a large project." She smiled that smile again, the one I wanted to catch in a portrait. "Why don't we get you settled? After that, if you would like tea, we can sit and talk. I do have an old-style teakettle. I brought a large amount of real tea. One cannot formulate tea."

I could use some tea. Maybe I could also persuade her to sit for an informal portrait, too.

13 *GOODMAN/BOND*

From the Hamilton D.S.S. orbit control station, we were crammed into an in-system transport, a photon-scoop slowboat that took five days to cart us out-system somewhere. Half the techs complained that there were no bunk screens, only single entertainment screens in the commons. They were spoiled. Individual entertainment screens?

At our destination, we were delocked and ordered along a long passageway, blue for crew. From the bulkheads alone, I could tell we were in an asteroid station. It smelled too good to be an old one. It had to have been built to support whatever mission I was being inserted into. The colonel had that part right.

We were herded into a long bay. Once the hatch closed, there were almost fifty techs in the bay. None of them were unrated. The lowest-ranking techs were thirds. No one showed up to order us around or brief us immediately. So I listened.

"... pulled me right off the *Charlemagne* ... had almost a full tour to go ..."

"I was headed for the *Guevara* ..."

"Never heard of her ..." That was Gutersen, loud as always.

"Special ops vessel . . . does sweeps along the Arm nearest the Alliance . . ."

"Better them than the Covenanters. Those guys are crazy. They believe that the whole universe was created by their God for them to control."

"Or fill with people. They say that every woman's supposed to have eight children. They don't believe in synthwombs or geneing either."

Eight was only the optimum. I'd known lots of people who'd only had four or five children, as well as some who had had ten or twelve. It was an individual choice, depending on what the man thought was best for the couple. The bishops and the crusaders don't get into personal choice, unless it's serious. I never knew a prior who intervened, although I supposed they could have, but that always meant the woman got deep-conditioned.

"They want it natural all the way."

"So do I," guffawed Gutersen. "Natural all the way."

The two both laughed.

One of the younger female techs snorted derisively. I had trouble with females on ships and stations. It didn't seem right, but I smiled along with the others.

"Attention on deck!" The words rolled through the bay.

Everyone snapped to. Two men walked to the front of the group. One was a commander, the other a chief tech ops tech.

The commander scanned the group. Mild-looking, except when his eyes hit on me. He'd have held his own with either Truesdale or Ibaio. He didn't speak until the bay got quiet. That didn't take long. "I'm Commander Morgan, and I'm the ops officer on the *Magellan*. This is Chief Tiernesco. You're the last contingent to be assigned to the *C.S.S. Magellan*. Some of you have been asking whether she's a dreadnought or a battle cruiser or what. I can't tell you, because there's no classification. She's a converted colony ship, but she's been rebuilt from the inside out. The mission is a deep-space science exploration run. That's the bad news. The good news is that you'll get better habitability here than on a regular D.S.S. vessel. You get staterooms, not bays. Tech thirds and below are four to a room. Techs two and above are two to stateroom . . ."

I wouldn't have to bunk with Gutersen. That was a relief.

"This could be a long mission, but it is a combat tour, even if we don't expect any combat, and you'll get double credit. The chief will fill you in." Morgan nodded to Tiernesco. "It's yours, chief."

Tiernesco didn't say anything until the hatch closed behind Morgan. "You all heard the commander. This is a combat tour. You all know what that means. The commander is strict, but fair. So is the captain. You'd have to go a long ways to find fairer officers, or better ones. But he doesn't like shirkers, and he doesn't like excuses. Neither do I.

"The ship's in the final stages of prep, and you'll be working with the fitters to finish things up. It's cheaper, and you'll also get to know things better. That's important, because gear won't always be where you'd think it should be. This layout is D.S.S., but it's different D.S.S."

The chief tech stopped. His eyes fixed on a tall thin tech. The tech shifted his weight.

Tiernesco offered a cool half smile before continuing. "Quarters assignments are posted on the screens at the end of the bay. You'll be heading to supply here on the station once you're dismissed. You'll pick up a full kit there. Then you'll take lock two and head up the tower to the ship. Once you're on board, you're on board, unless you're specifically ordered back to the station as part of your duties." The chief stopped to let his words sink in.

Whatever the D.S.S. was investigating, they certainly didn't want anyone letting anyone else know, even on the support station.

"Once you've gotten your kit, you all head to sick bay aboard the *Magellan*. You don't go anywhere else. Everyone . . . *everyone* gets a baseline med and DNA scan before starting duties. Once you've been scanned into the ship system, find your quarters and drop your kit. Then you report to your duty stations. Like every D.S.S. ship, it's blue passageways for crew."

I had to hope that the colonel's plant had managed to get my DNA into the med/security records. If not . . . I wouldn't have to worry about anything . . . ever. I pushed that thought away.

"Any questions?"

There weren't any. Senior techs knew that the answers wouldn't tell anything more.

"Dismissed to find your bunking assignments and to get your kits."

I slipped into the middle of the group walking toward the assignment screens at the end of the bay. I took my time, but not too much. Being either a jumper or a laggard marked you, and my job was to remain competently unnoticed. My quarters would be on the fifth deck, aft of frame 1340, with the other armorers and weapons techs. I was billeted with another second, Alveres. He was listed as a shield mech.

The supply tech took my ID, swiped it through the scanner. Within a minute, a kit duffel popped up on the conveyor beside him. "Here's your kit, Bond. Take it to the table there and check it. It should have all your uniforms and insignia. If everything's there, head up to the ship for your med-scans. Next!"

"Velasques . . ."

As the tech had said, everything was there, from shipboots to skintights, all to my measurements. I sealed the duffel, hoisted it onto my shoulder, and headed out of supply and along the passageway to the lock tower. Five of us lined up at the base of the lock tower, waiting as two shipfitters wheeled down a cart that almost filled the ramp that wound up the tower.

"Can you move any slower?" asked a third ahead of me.

". . . lucky you don't have to manage this," replied the lead shipfitter. "Flatten you thinner than passageway plastrene."

I followed the others. Sick bay was slightly forward of midships, and two decks below the main deck. Even after the delay at the lock tower, there were still ten techs lined up waiting for their scans. When my turn came, I passed over the ID and order cards.

The medtech didn't even look at me. "Into the scanner, Bond."

I stepped between the two panels and put my hands on the plates. There was a faint hum.

"You're clear and entered into the ship system."

How the colonel had managed it, I had no idea. I was just happy he had. If the scan had gone red, certain proteins in my brain would have gone to work, and . . . I wouldn't have known anything within moments. They don't tell you about that when they first recruit you for Covenant intelligence. It provides a certain incentive not to be caught.

"Thank you." I smiled and picked up my kit.

The tech nodded.

The main crew passage was two levels down. A spiral ramp just forward of sick bay led both up and down. I headed down, keeping to the right. I passed a shipfitter first. He didn't even look in my direction. Once I was down two levels, I headed aft. The crew passageways were narrower, only about a meter and a half wide, tight for two techs with gear, but I only had to pass a handful of others on the way back. A thousand frames was more than a kay. I had to shift the duffel from shoulder to shoulder four or five times.

D.S.S. didn't use ship slideways. They claimed the longer corridors gave the crew exercise. They also saved mass and construction expense. Our ships were more crew-friendly.

The stateroom was easy enough to find. Getting inside was harder. It was more like a long narrow closet with two built-in bunks. Each bunk had an entertainment screen at the end, flat video, and earplugs—decadent luxury for a fighting ship.

Alveres had taken the upper bunk. That didn't matter to me. I took my time unpacking the kit and stowing the uniforms and gear according to D.S.S. regs, but not precisely.

Then I was ready to head to the armory. It was "up" and slightly aft of where I was billeted. The hardest part was finding the crew ramp up. When I got there, the armory hatch was open. In the bay just inside were sliders and trolleys. They were configured for torps and probes, but they were empty.

A wiry chief appeared. The name strip on his vest read Stuval.

"William Bond, chief, reporting."

"Glad to see you, Bond. You're the last one in the division to report. How was the trip?"

"I could have done without the slowboat from Hamilton." I offered a head-shake. "And what they called food."

Stuval laughed. "That's the way it is. Food'll be a lot better here. You'll be working in the torp section. Mostly inspection and maintenance. We got some substandard torps with the refit kits. BuWeaps couldn't give us a complete load of new ones. Told the major that, with the stepped-up patrols along the systems bordering the Covenant worlds, there weren't enough brand-new torps for everyone, and we're not going into hostile systems. Captain complained, but it didn't change anything. You and Ciorio will have to make the bloc switches."

"Yes, chief."

"Major Sewiki is the head of weapons, and the assistant weapons officer is Lieutenant Swallow. Now, let's give you the quick tour, so that you know where everything is."

I followed the chief.

14 CHANG

By the end of fiveday, I'd been through six runs in the simulator, each one tougher than the last. Each exercise told me more about where we were headed. On the last two simmie hops, Morgan had me setting down on a planet, not like anyplace I'd been or even heard of. Gravs were close to one-point-four, but no atmosphere, and cold as Hel. No mag-field and a thirty-three-hour rotation.

Once I got off training, I went to the station system and plugged in the parameters. Nothing matched. Not anywhere in any cataloged system. Figured it wouldn't, but it was worth the effort.

Ten hundred was my sixday simulator session. I got to the training bay at zero nine forty-seven. Anson Lerrys was getting out of the simulator. Little guy, smaller than me by a couple of centimeters, but just as tough. Have to be at his size and with a name like Anson. Wiry and red-haired. Cute ass, and smiled a lot, though. Morgan had said we'd get two more shuttle pilots, but Lerrys was the only one who showed up. Gave him the same senior lieutenant's bars as Braun and I had. Had the feeling that the other one didn't make the cut.

Hung back until Morgan dismissed Lerrys, then moved toward the simulator.

Lerrys grinned. His forehead was coated in sweat. "Good luck, Jiendra."

Don't know how he'd found out my first name, but he had. Said it nicely, though. "Morgan in a bad mood, Anson?" Figured I'd give him back the first-name stuff.

"More like a 'show me your stuff' attitude."

"Appreciate it."

"Do the same for me if it comes to that."

"I will." I would, too. Couldn't help but like him, brotherlike. Wish I'd had one like him.

Morgan was wiping his forehead—like working the simulator was as hard on him as the pilot. Probably was. Looked at me. "You won't find our destination in the station's data system, Lieutenant Chang." He grinned. "Good try, though."

"You never know." I grinned back. Mouth felt stiff from all the forced smiles.

"You'll find out in time." Morgan cleared his throat and motioned to the open hatch of the simulator. "Today, you'll start on weapons fam and indoc. The shuttles are armed, but only with a pair of torps. There are no lasers, no particle beams, and no projectile weapons for space or atmospheric defense. Torps are technically the only weapons the shuttles have, but they also have photon nets and scoops for mass collection for the fusactors. In certain circumstances those can also prove useful."

"How much mass can the nets sling?" I asked. "How fast and how accurate?"

Morgan gave a wry frown. "Enough, if you're in-system. The accuracy depends on the pilot. Don't fiddle with those on this run. This is for the torps, just to get you familiar with the systems and the controls. The installation's not quite standard."

Didn't know how anything in the shuttle could be. Shuttles were each one of a kind.

He motioned me toward the simulator.

I went. Was . . . and wasn't . . . looking forward to the next two hours.

15 GOODMAN/BOND

By sixday, I was working with Ciorio on refitting the substandard deep-space torps. Because he was a tech first class, he was lead, and that was fine by me. We were in the torp bay, on the outer deck, right against the hull, with secondary shields. No one wanted a torp malfunction to break the ship in half or impact the drives, but the placement was psychological. If a torp went off inside the *Magellan,* the ship wouldn't be going anyplace.

You couldn't repair a torp, not without more work than made sense. The insides were miracles of microtronics—well, not miracles like those done by the Christ or the saints, but close to them. All an armorer could do was replace defective components and make sure that the systems checked out. I eased the second torp off the slider and onto the bench cradle.

Ciorio unsealed the power access. "Check power route."

I ran the links and the diagnostics. "Power off."

Ciorio took a deep breath. "Good. That's the nasty part. Model is a standard 503. Problem is that the control modules were too temperature sensitive. Not to space. They did fine in cold, but if the internals in the ship got above thirty degrees Celsius, the power cutouts didn't work. Makes working on them a real bitch, because you've got to cut the routing. If you miss by a millimeter, the torp's junk. That's why they sent us ten extras. Figured we'd screw up some."

"Have you?"

"First few times. Not anymore." Ciorio lowered his voice. "We don't tell 'em. If we fix all twenty right, we'll report that we had to junk five, fed 'em into the main fusactor. Otherwise, next time, they'll send us even more of the defective ones, load the repairs onto us."

"Major Sewiki . . . she's stet with that?"

"Stet? It was her idea. No good officer wants the techs working twice as hard to bail out BuWeaps and their screwups."

That made sense, in a way, but it went down hard for me. The whole idea of a senior tech and a field-grade officer disregarding command procedures—it undermined order and discipline. My first thought was that it didn't happen in the CSN, but I'd have wagered it did. It was probably even quieter, because no one wanted the crusaders or their priors to find out.

"Besides," Ciorio went on, "that gives us more torps." He turned back to the open section of the torp, using the nanoprobes to disengage the links. Sweat beaded up his forehead, but his hands were steady. I watched as closely as I could. I'd used Comity nanoprobes. I just hadn't been trained in anything like what he was doing.

"Is it only the 503s?" I asked, when he took another deep breath and blotted his forehead on the back of his wrist. "I'd thought . . ."

"Nah. 502s sometimes, but there aren't many of them left anymore, and they pulled the 504s before they started sending 'em out. Too many 503s in service. Corvettes are the ones that get screwed, cause they don't have but one armorer, and no equipment to do refits. Good thing we're not in a big war. You want to try it?"

That was the last thing I wanted. "I've only watched. I'd like to learn . . . if you're not worried about spoiling a torp."

"You came from corvettes, I'd wager."

"What can I say?"

Ciorio shook his head. "Got to learn sometime. Better take it real easy. One step at a time. I'll guide you, once I replace the module on this one."

He made it seem easy, and within fifteen minutes, we had the refitted torp back on the slider, ready to head back to storage.

"Now, we'll switch places," Ciorio said.

We switched. He eased the next torp onto the bench cradle.

As I'd seen Ciorio do, I unsealed the power access. "Check power route."

"Power off."

I looked down through the nanomags at the module in the open section of the torp. It wasn't much bigger than the tip of my fingernail without them.

"Look for the green supercon line. Don't want to touch that. Real delicate. The red links are where you want to cut, anyplace between silver beads."

That was simple enough, and I did know the nanoprobes. I've also always had good fine-muscle control. I made the cut.

"Good. Nice touch there. Sure you never did this?"

"Other stuff. Not this."

"All right. Now . . . you use the left probe to insert the disable code."

"That's the standard D-I-S-X?"

"Right"

I followed instructions, and the module went dull gray.

"There. Simple as that. Just ease it out. 'Ware of the supercon line."

In a few moments, I had the module out and into the disposal holder, sealed.

Ciorio eased the replacement module holder, nanite-protected against dust, up to the probes. I lifted the new module and eased it back into place. It fit perfectly. From Ciorio's exhaling, I had the feeling that didn't always happen.

"Now . . . you'll have to extrude a touch of the control line, on polarity two. Just fill the gaps where you cut."

I managed that as well.

"Next . . . reactivate."

"R-E-A-T?"

"For 503s. For 502s, it's R-E-A-3. Don't ask me why."

I got the code in, again without brushing the supercon, and retracted the probes. "Diagnostics?"

"Green. You can seal it up, Bond. We got ten more to do. We'll take turns. Don't get as tired or careless that way."

I'd managed to get through one thing I probably should have known and hadn't. How many more would there be?

16 CHANG

Had almost a week more simulator training. Not all of it was on the shuttles. Spent four sessions getting a basic fam on the *Magellan*. Then Morgan took Lerrys, Braun, and me to the control room, let us link and get the feel of the systems. Decided I'd never really want to drive anything that big on a regular basis. Another three sim sessions were on needleboats. Pretty much all drives and enough mass to carry three torps. Screwy configuration. Couldn't figure why only three torps with two tubes. Morgan insisted it was the stripped-down fusactor limits and that the original design had only allowed for two torps. *Magellan* had five needles, just like a battle-cruiser. We were backups. Regular pilots were junior lieutenants out of the two Comity space academies.

After another two days of simulator training, Morgan cleared me to take out shuttle one—the real shuttle, hot a simmie. It was locked on Deep Find Station's tower three, a good kay "west" of the training bay. Wore my new armor and carried my helmet. A shipsuit will get you through a decompression, but not a battle or a fusillade of space junk. Takes armor for that.

Morgan escorted me through the ops personnel tunnel. Armor was hot. I was sweating when we reached the base of the ramp up to the lock tower.

Morgan stopped. "Just take it easy. It's a fam run. I don't want you acting like a test pilot."

Commander was acting like he'd built the shuttles. "You put together the specs for them, sir?"

His head jerked toward me. Started to glare, then laughed, shaking his head. "Lieutenant, I don't understand why you ever had to break anyone's fingers."

"Because he didn't understand some words—like 'honesty' and 'no.'"

He nodded. "Too many people hear what they want and not what's said."

Was Morgan was a nice guy inside? So nice that he'd built an endurasteel shell? Or was the niceness was just politeness over practicality? Either way, not my type. Be either too solicitous or as immovable as a singularity.

He stopped short of the tower lock. Noted he was carrying a stunner. "Shuttle one's all yours, Lieutenant. No more than two hours out, and stay clear of the *Magellan* and the station until you're ready to return."

"Yes, sir." I stepped to the lock. Pulsed the codes and got a return scan. That was another thing about the shuttles. All had the security features of armed Comity scouts. Never seen shuttles that did, not until now.

Stepped into the crew lock, and went weightless. No habitability gravs until I powered up the shuttle. Set my shipboots on the deck and closed the outer lock door, then opened the inner door. Pulled myself into—or over—the quarterdeck. More like a closet with a hatch to the cockpit to the left, passageway to passenger section to the right. Behind the passenger section was one big cargo hold, with the drives and ship's systems aft.

I opened the hatch one-handed, holding the grip with the other. Like the simulator, only one seat in the cockpit. Inside console and boards were identical to the simulator. Strapped into the pilot's couch and adjusted the links.

Delta Control, this is Porter Tigress. Requesting clearance to power up this time.

Porter Tigress, cleared, Report when ready to delock.

Control, Porter Tigress, stet.

Ran though the checklist. Didn't seem to take quite so long, maybe because it was the real shuttle and not a simmie. Readjusted the restraints once the gravs came on. Another difference. Smaller shuttles didn't bother with internal gravs. Shuttle one was designed to carry passengers who weren't used to null gee.

Delta Control, this is Porter Tigress, ready for delock and release this time.

Porter Tigress, dampers released. Cleared for delocking.

Delta Control, Porter Tigress, delocking this time. Slid the shuttle clear of the tower with two measured bursts from the steering jets. Photon nets didn't work without forward velocity. Couldn't use the AG drives close to anything else with mass.

Cleared the station, took in the farscreen feeds. Even after the simmie, the real image of the *Magellan* gave me a jolt. Wondered how long before Morgan would brief us on our objective. Wouldn't be until after we left the station, maybe later. Still . . . had a good idea of what we were facing, just not where, or what was on it. Knew it had to be cold and higher grav.

Porter Tigress, advise incoming at your zero eight zero, plus twenty-eight.

Control, have incoming and will avoid. Incoming was a slowboat, heavy mass reading on the detectors. Probably the last supplies and equipment for the *Magellan.*

Stet, Porter Tigress.

Pulsed the thrusters, watching the separation until the shuttle was well clear of the station and the delimiting area. Brought up the fusactors to full power and eased in the AG drives. Acceleration was smooth, smoothest I'd felt in a long time. Great to have new equipment.

Could tell from the system repscreens that Deep Find Station was well out in the Hamilton system—Kuiper Belt distance. The station was an anomaly itself. Don't find many nickel-iron asteroids that far out—not solid and not ten kays in diameter. Also noted the varying dust densities created by the shields of the ships servicing the station. Wouldn't be that long before they'd show up on even commercial detectors—raylike corridors pointing to the station.

Spread the nets at twenty percent. No reason not to scoop up the extra mass.

For a good hour, just played with the shuttle, testing response, lag time. Made a couple of approaches to an irregular chunk of dirty ice. Harder than another ship or a station, but good practice. Hard enough that I was really sweating inside the armor. Felt good in a way simmies never do.

Checked the time again and swung shuttle one back toward Deep Find Station.

Delta Control, Porter Tigress, inbound this time.

Porter Tigress, understand inbound. Cleared to tower three. Advise slowboat is hot.

Understand slowboat is hot. Meant I had to make an indirect approach because the slowboat was linked to tower two and using thrusters to balance against the mass shifts created by the unloading.

Approach was low-power anyway. Wouldn't try high-power quick massthrust decel and brake with the shuttle's mass, except in an emergency.

Didn't want to leave the shuttle after approach and locking. Best equipment I'd had in years. More responsive than most men, and had more power. Didn't talk back, either. Or condescend behind my back.

Took my time with the shutdown checklist. Not too much. Screens said Morgan was waiting to debrief me—and to send Lerrys off. Wouldn't be fair to Lerrys to stall.

Delta Control, Porter Tigress, powering down this time.

Stet, Tigress.

Pulled myself out of the couch. Weightless without power. Hand over hand to the hatch, then to the lock. Hated to leave . . . but Morgan was waiting.

17 BARNA

Elysen had been more than willing to let me work on a portrait of her. It was more like a series of portraits, but I limited myself to light-matrix versions, because I could always store them. I needed to save the canvases until I knew what would be the best media for the images required by the project.

We had more than enough time for her portrait. I had little else to do until we got to wherever we were headed. I'd wandered the approved corridors, and even lounged in the officers' mess, where we ate, but the officers were all in a hurry, and, while Elysen would occasionally talk to the other groups of scientists, their words flowed over and around me.

The social scientists were worse. Their words conveyed certainty without artistry and without replicable fact. I tried to smile, but I'd never been that good at it. Aeryana had always insisted that I should never attend soirees without her at my side. That was because I could not manage more than three sentences of small talk.

For her portrait, Elysen had insisted on one condition. Anything that was permanent had to have her approval. That made it a greater challenge.

On sevenday afternoon, I was in the sitting room that we shared, trying to get her eyes right. They were green, but there was something about them that I hadn't gotten. She had gone off somewhere to check on her equipment.

The hatch opened, and I saw a lieutenant's uniform behind Elysen before she stepped into our quarters and the hatch closed behind her. The blue of the officer's uniform and skintights clashed with the blue of the corridor.

For all her size and large bones—and her age—Elysen moved gracefully, almost regally. Yet she had short active fingers on large palms. Those fingers seemed at odds with the rest of her build and her mannerisms. They were never still, even when the rest of her was motionless. She was more of a mystery than ever. There was more to her than met the eye. Years before, I'd decided that was true of all women. My own Aeryana was like that. She'd never liked me calling her my own, and I didn't. I still liked to think of her that way. A man's thoughts are his own. At least, I'd like to think that they were.

"How is your equipment?" I asked.

"It's fine. They were transferring it to my work spaces on the *Magellan*. I had to make sure they moved it right and that no one unpacked it. That sort of help could do more damage than they could imagine. Oh . . . you have the work space next to mine. I took a quick look. They've mounted all sorts of visual farscreens in there. They said it won't be long before we can go on board. That will be a relief. I won't need escorts to go everywhere." She turned on the old-fashioned kettle. "Would you join me in some tea?" That had become a ritual, of sorts.

"Please, if I'm not using too much of your supply." I set aside the lightbrush and stood, stretching. The stiffness told me I had been in one position too long.

She smiled, beatifically. I could have used that expression if I'd been doing a religious work for one of the Christian-related sects that had hung on over the millennia. The Covenanters wouldn't have liked it, though. Their art was far too rigid, with mechanical smiles on pregnant women, and a paternalistic deity stern with unbelievers and overflowing with grace for believers. I never understood what believing had to do with good or evil or why believing made someone more worthy in a deity's eyes.

"There's more packed in the equipment," she added. "It fits nicely into the padding and cases."

"How much did you bring?"

"Several years' worth." She smiled. This time the expression was mischievous. "That depends on how much I share." She turned to the easel, where my latest effort was projected. "I don't think my eyes look like that."

"They do, and they don't. They'd look like that in any holo or flat picture. Those don't capture what's in and behind them." I didn't want to talk about what I hadn't been able to depict through either direct capture or my own lightbrush strokes and pointillism. "Did anyone say when we'll be able to board the *Magellan* or when we'll be leaving? Or where we're headed? Do you have any more ideas about that?"

"No one mentioned any specific time. I did overhear one of the officers talking about his stateroom and how it was better than the station quarters." Elysen looked at the thin wisp of steam beginning to circle out of the pressure spout of the teakettle that rested on the small counter at one side of the sitting room. "I hadn't realized the pressure seal was leaking. Watched kettles do boil so much more slowly."

"Do you have any more ideas about where we're headed?"

"I had thought it might be an expedition back to Chronos, but the parameters aren't right, and they wouldn't need someone like me . . ."

I nodded politely. I didn't have the faintest idea what Chronos was.

". . . and they certainly wouldn't need you. They want records, and good ones, but they also want a sense of wherever it is. You couldn't ever get close enough to record anything artistically, not even with an AG drive. Chronos is a featureless sphere, and with a gravity two hundred eighty times that of Terran norm."

"Terran?"

"That's old-style terminology. It's unfashionable these days. Now it's either T or Tellurian, but it's all the same. It has been for millennia. Too many people have the illusion that changing the name changes the truth—or the lie—behind it."

How old *was* she? She drank tea, had silver hair, and eyes that were black and green at the same time, and that was a sign of great age.

"You're saying that they've found an alien civilization."

"I would judge that they have found ruins of some sort, and that they're quite a distance away. If the civilization were still present, this would be a military expedition—or a diplomatic one backed with great military force. They have certainly found something of great and unique value. I would also judge that it is of great antiquity—unimaginable antiquity."

Unimaginable antiquity? What would something like that look like? Was it still intact? Or did they want me to create an image of what it might have been from rubble and fragments?

Elysen poured the boiling water into the teapot. "It's not as hot as it should be. That's even with the pressure spout."

I'd never noticed the difference, except that I wasn't burning my tongue.

"Tea should be prepared with true boiling water, not water pressurized to less than boiling, but that is one of the small irritations of great expeditions."

The irritations would be forgotten as small only if the expedition were in fact a great one. That also was human nature. I took the cup and saucer from her. It was ancient porcelain of some sort, and I decided that a cup and saucer of that design should be on a side table in the next portrait. Somehow, I needed to combine the mischief, the hint of saintliness, the scientist, and the proper woman who loved tea, a woman out of her time, who was aware of it and yet comfortable with who she was.

18 FITZHUGH

After more than an old-style week on the station, with each day unending in its dolose monotony, broken by but conversations, either speculating upon the forthcoming project or upon the eternal haecceity of academia, I had managed to make a less-than-profound impression on the tortuous backlog of professional readings I had loaded into the blocs I'd brought. So much of what passed for analysis and insight was merely a compilation of events with explications designed to support a preconceived thesis. All too many equated a succession of trends or events with causality. Most of the theses, as well, were based on ideological wistfulness, rather than the rigor of speculative deconstruction. To stand outside one's history, culture, and language and see what has happened with acciptrine scholarly vision is among the hardest of accomplishments, and the least valued by those who deal with the certainty of a set universe.

As for entertainment, while both stateroom and work space had screens, what was available from the station's system was insufferably pedestrian and with little redeeming value—social, political, or otherwise. I did listen to my copy of Cavernisha's *Event Horizon Suite,* my eyes closed, enjoying the music. I also used the high-gee workout room.

While I pondered, as I did more often than I should, right after breakfast on twoday, Lieutenant Ruano stepped through the hatch into our sitting room. His official title was Mission Liaison Officer, although his diplomacy, tact, and delicacy hovered on the border of taciturn banality, and, when asked a question, his explanations could often have been classified along the range of between disingenuous and totally morological.

"Professors, please pack all your gear. We'll be moving you to the *Magellan,* beginning at ten hundred."

" 'The time has come,' the *Odobenus rosmarus* said," I added, almost under my breath.

"Liam, obscurity for the sake of obscurity serves no one," murmured Alyendra from across the table. "Least of all, you."

"I was talking about walruses."

"You are a walrus at times, and that's being charitable."

I had let slip from my memory the less than delightful acerbity of Alyendra's terseness. I resolved not to do so once we parted ways again.

"Will we be able to return here?" asked Tomas.

"That is highly unlikely," replied Ruano, smiling.

A simple negative would have sufficed, along with a polite apologetic commentary, but Ruano's social graces had more than obviously reached their limbus at the minimum requisites of military courtesy.

"Will you have a slider for baggage?" asked Melani.

"Ah . . . I will make sure there is one."

"Thank you," the petite theoretical psychologist replied. "It will be far easier for you than having to carry so much of our baggage and equipment."

Ruano paused. He looked at Melani, then looked away.

Alyendra concealed a smile.

After several moments, Ruano straightened. "I'll be back at ten hundred." He turned and departed.

After Ruano's abrupt withdrawal, we all retreated to our quarters and began the process of repacking. That encompassed some garments, in my case, in need of cleaning, a necessity about which I was more than infrequently guilty of procrastinating, particularly when I was the one required to undertake the ablutive actions.

True to his word, the good lieutenant returned at zero nine-fifty-nine, with a muscular tech and a slider for baggage.

We all had our gear stacked in the sitting room. I had carried out a case of Melani's that massed as though it held either lead or gold. I wasn't about to inquire what it contained. I also wasn't about to warn Ruano, but the tech who accompanied him was the one who lifted it onto the slider, almost as effortlessly as I had.

Once the tech loaded the slider, we followed the lieutenant out through the hatch and down the blue corridor, then a gray corridor, then another blue corridor, for quite a distance—it could have been close to a kay—before we reached a circular ramp.

"This ramp will lead to the lock and tube to the *Magellan*. At the top of the ramp, each of you will be scanned, and your ID/DNA entered into the ship's systems. That is necessary to allow you access to the equipment in your work areas and staterooms. Your bags and equipment will be scanned as well. I'll wait for you inside the *Magellan*'s lock, and from there, I'll direct you to your quarters."

The tech and slider preceded us up the ramp and had vanished before we reached the medical tech and the scanners awaiting us short of the lock. Out of custom and habit, I deferred, and was the last one to finish and rejoin the others in an open space beyond the lock chambers and inside the *Magellan*. The walls were gray, and the sole concession to decoration was the D.S.S. insignia on the wall to my right, under which was the name C.S.S. MAGELLAN, DSE-3.

Ruano glanced at us. "This is the midships quarterdeck, and we're on the main deck. All the other decks are numbered outward. The even numbered decks are those above us, and the odd numbered ones are below the main deck. Second deck is the one above us, and third deck is below. Fourth deck is above second deck, all the way out to forty-eighth and forty-ninth deck. Fiftieth deck and fifty-first decks are the outermost decks, and the largest in size, because they hold the locks for the shuttles, needleboats, and loading and unloading areas. Fiftieth deck covers the whole upper half of the ship, and fifty-first covers the whole lower half."

"Wouldn't it make more sense just to have circular decks?" asked Tomas.

"It would, except working out the grav system would be worse than the structure on a Gate. The compartmentalization would be harder, too." Ruano stopped. "We'll take the center lift up to thirty-eighth deck. That's where your quarters are. There's also a ramp beside it in case we go to low-power conditions."

There were three lifts, each capable of holding ten people.

Once we got to thirty-eighth deck, Ruano launched into another exposition. "As on Deep Find Station, the officers' mess will serve both the ship's officers and all of you who are detailed here as civilian experts. You may sit where you please, except at the captain's table. That is by invitation only . . ."

As Ruano went on, I wondered what it was about the lieutenant that annoyed me. I'd certainly made the acquaintance of more than a few self-important, petty personages in academia, and they hadn't annoyed me half so much as the young officer. That was something else I had let time obscure.

". . . All your staterooms are along this passageway. Your names are on the doors. You are to use only the blue passageways on the *Magellan*, just like in Deep Find Station. If the captain orders 'General Quarters,' you are to remain in your stateroom or in your workstation. You are responsible for the cleanliness of your staterooms and work spaces. You have a cleaning facility for your garments on the same passageway."

Ruano smiled with the satisfaction of an inept provost delivering an address to a hostile faculty. I'd observed more than a few of those encounters over the years, and Ruano was more adept than some of the provosts I'd encountered. That, unfortunately, wasn't saying very much for either the lieutenant or those long-departed provosts who had equated academic brilliance and blind adherence to formulae with leadership.

"Are there any questions?"

"Do you know when we'll be departing, and where we're headed?" asked Melani.

"I can't say, except that departure is not likely to be more than a few days away, if that."

"Do you know?" asked Tomas dryly.

"No, Professor. I do not. I doubt that any of the officers and crew do, except for the captain, the exec, and the ops officer."

Alyendra and I exchanged glances. Inquiring further would have served little purpose except to reveal greater ignorance on the lieutenant's part, and such forced revelation would doubtless redound to our disadvantage in the future.

"If not, I will leave you to settle into your staterooms. Your work spaces are two decks up on forty-second deck above, and you may find your way there at your convenience, either by the lift or the ramp. Please use the blue passageways. The mess hours are the same as on Deep Find Station . . ."

Once Ruano had taken his leave, I made my way to my quarters, grandiloquently termed a stateroom, holding as it did a single bunk, with a deep green blanket folded in place, a full-length locker, and an attached multifunction fresher room, barely a meter and a half square. The stateroom proper did have a wall console, so that I could read and compose in privacy, or access what was open to me on the ship's system, primarily what was termed popular entertainment. Unpacking my wardrobe, such as it was, took little time, and I was eager to see what my "work space" might be.

I went down the blue passageway and took the ramp up to the forty-second deck. There was an open hatchway, with the words SOCIAL AND BEHAVIORAL SCIENCE on the greenish wall beside the hatch, presumably the spaces allocated to me and those with whom I had been quartered on Deep Find Station, as well as others I had not met.

I passed one open door and saw Tomas inspecting a console beneath a wall screen. The next door held my name, and from what I could tell, my space was identical to that of the political scientist.

I had to admit that the equipment was first-class. There was a single screen on the wall, showing an asteroid, indubitably the Deep Find Station from which we had been transferred so summarily, and a console that would handle more than anything I could have asked for, including multiple simultaneous inputs from datablocs.

"What do you think, Liam?"

Alyendra stood in my doorway.

I didn't know what to think. The more I saw, the less I understood why

I had even been included on what looked to be a scientific search—or plundering—of a defunct colony. Although others had suggested an alien culture was the objective, that seemed a wistful reverie. We had not found a single trace of aliens or forerunners among the thousands of worlds we had explored over the past three millennia. Why would such appear now?

As for a dead colony, my own expertise lay in analyzing documented trends, and I doubted that such colonists would have left much hard evidence or documentation. Dying civilizations seldom do. Their arts replicate what has gone before. Their technology stagnates, with but minor adaptations of what was created earlier. Political systems atrophy, with most debates and conflicts over who holds power, rather than how it is wielded or for whose benefit.

"Liam?"

"Oh . . . I'm pondering why anyone would wish to spend so many credits on providing me with such equipment, when it's likely that my contribution to what they want will be so minuscule."

"Did I hear what you said?" Alyendra raised her eyebrows. "The great Liam Fitzhugh . . . a minuscule contribution?"

"To this? Yes. We'll be looking at a dead colony—or the remnants of one."

"Perhaps they left records in one of the languages you speak."

I hadn't considered that, but it was a possibility. I didn't consider it a possibility of high probability, but . . . it was possible. I nodded.

"And just possibly," she added, "someone wanted your insights. They think it's important enough that they've not let even the junior officers know. What do your remarkable insights say about that?"

"Military secrecy is so ingrained that I have doubts whether that signifies extraordinary significance. On the other hand, others might also reach the same conclusion, further obfuscating the magnitude of what awaits us."

Alyendra shook her head. "You could have said you don't know." She smiled. "Would you care to accompany me up to the officers' mess? We are approaching midday."

I bowed and offered my arm.

"I'm not that infirm. Not yet." She laughed.

So we walked to the lift.

19 *Barna*

In comparison to my stateroom, the work space was luxurious—but only in comparison. Still, it was an office-studio five meters by four, with an array of wall screens and enough power sources for all my equipment. Someone, somewhere, had understood that an artist needed to see, to take in images.

The center screen, a good two meters square, showed a color image of an asteroid, with a tower protruding from its irregular surface. After a moment, I realized that it was a real-time image, doubtless light-enhanced, of Deep Find Station. We hadn't moved that far, and I hadn't felt any motion at all when the captain had announced that we were separating from the station.

I settled into the chair facing the board. While I didn't understand everything before me, I had time to learn it. I would. As I leaned forward, the small master screen flashed, and the words SYSTEMS INSTRUCTIONS appeared. While I would have preferred to experiment, it couldn't hurt to watch and listen as the system explained itself.

The instructions were very simple. I had access to all outside screens under normal conditions, and any remote feeds or views gathered by the ship's shuttles or needleboats once those were entered into the system. If they were. Whether that content was put on the feeds I could access would be determined by the operations officer.

"Ser Barna?"

I bolted upright in the chair. My back twinged as I turned to the open hatch. Elysen stood there.

"Would you care to join me for supper, or whatever one calls the evening meal upon a military vessel?"

I returned the center screen to the view of Deep Find Station and rose. "I'd be honored, Doctor." I stood and bowed.

"Elysen will do."

"Only if you call me Chendor."

"Fair is fair . . . Chendor."

We took one of the lifts. We had it to ourselves. When we got off at the mess level, two ship's officers hurried before us—both women. They were pilots. They had winged insignia—in gold—above their name strips. One was blonde, full-figured but muscular, with short hair, and taller than I. The other was petite, with dark hair. Both were visually stunning, one like a goddess, the other almost doll-like. Beneath the vibrant beauty of the blonde was molten iron. The apparent serenity of the smaller pilot concealed cold steel.

I knew I'd have to try to recapture that image once I got back to the office-studio, the contrast between the apparent and the reality beneath.

"You're staring, Chendor."

"Yes. I'd like to capture that image."

"Just the image?" Elysen laughed.

"Just the image," I replied. "Beneath those exteriors are women I'd just as soon not get too close to."

Elysen frowned for a brief moment.

Women think they're the only ones who see beneath surfaces. Some artists do, too. I can paint what I see better than I can describe it in words.

The officer's mess was paneled in cherrywood. It was only a veneer, but it made the room warmer. The off-white ceiling and the dark green hangings helped, too. The tables and chairs were cherry synthwood as well, with pale green linens on the tables. A single rectangular table was set at one end of the mess. Every seat was taken except for the one at the head. All those who were seated there were more-senior officers. That was if I'd read the rank insignia right. The other tables were circular.

"It almost looks like a private club," I said.

"It is. There aren't thirty officers on the *Magellan,* and I'd be surprised if there were that many civilian experts," Elysen replied. "There might be three hundred or four hundred crew members."

"Where do you want to sit?"

She gestured. We stepped toward an empty table. None of the occupied tables had space for two, except for the one where the two pilots had seated themselves with a man—another pilot. He was red-haired. The three of them also would have made an interesting composition. At that moment, a senior officer stepped through a side door, and all those at the rectangular table stood.

"Carry on." The captain took her place at the head of the rectangular table.

We seated ourselves. Within moments, we were joined by two men. I remembered to stand. "Chendor Barna."

"Misha Nalakov, I'm an applied mathematical theorist." He didn't look like a theorist. He had the muscular build of an old-time smith, with black hair slicked back away from a hawk nose.

"Rikard Sorens." He was slender, with a narrow triangular face that dwindled to an elfin chin. "Materials engineering."

"This is Dr. Elysen Taube." I sat down after that.

"I'm an astronomer." Her smile was that of a regal grandmother or an ancient queen mother.

"What do you do?" Nalakov looked at me.

"I'm an artist."

"Oh . . . documentary, I suppose."

"Representational."

Both men looked at Elysen.

"Do you have a subspecialty, Doctor?" asked Nalakov.

"Old galaxies . . . postflex."

Sorens nodded.

A steward came to the table and set bowls in front of us. Another followed with a tureen and a ladle. The soup was orangish and steamed.

"Where do you think we're headed?" Nalakov looked at Elysen.

"Somewhere quite distant, I would think."

"The D.S.S. has to have found some sort of alien artifact. Astronomers, materials engineers, chemists, physicists . . ." The mathematician shook his head.

"With the military, you never can tell," Sorens replied. "They once had me consulting on the contents of an outer Oort object. It looked different to them, but it wasn't manufactured at all, just coated and polished by millennia in the outer reaches of the system. It was something that I couldn't add much on. The astronomers and chemists knew more than I did."

"They wouldn't put together all this for something small," Nalakov retorted. "They're too cheap."

"You're probably right. One way or another, we'll know more at the briefing tomorrow."

"You're an optimist," Nalakov mumbled. He was talking and eating.

Sorens smiled indulgently. I liked him.

At the table behind us, I overheard one of the social scientists. I'd been introduced, but couldn't recall his name. His voice carried.

". . . the human species is characterized, assuming the term 'character' is not exceedingly charitable, by its predilection to create divisions and barriers, even at times to assert that humans of differing skin shades were of other species, as a basis for establishing competing polities . . ."

Why didn't he just say that people used any excuse to assert that they and their group were special?

"Chendor?" Elysen asked politely.

I shook my head.

Elysen smiled, and her eyes flicked toward the adjoining table. Her voice barely carried to me. "Once you get past his tendency to use the largest word possible, Liam seems like a fairly pleasant individual."

"Do all academics do that?"

"Do you think I do?" Her voice remained a murmur.

"You always knew better."

"How would you know? We've known each other for less than two weeks."

"Artists always know." I could see what lay beneath the surfaces of people and what they created. I laughed inside at the contradiction I'd expressed. Elysen was right. I should look inside Liam Fitzhugh before judging. Then, would I see what lay beneath wherever the D.S.S. was taking me? Could I portray it?

20 CHANG

We'd finally moved onto the *Magellan,* late on oneday, after I'd taken shuttle two out on a quick fam, then eased her into the bay on the *Magellan.* Had to help block and secure the shuttle. Lerrys got stuck doing that on shuttle one. Second shuttle was more of a workhorse. No real passenger spaces, just cargo, and bigger and few holds. Made me wonder what they expected us to cart back. Still wondered from where.

Twoday and threeday, we did drills and fams on the equipment in the ops spaces on the *Magellan.*

Fourteen hundred on fourday, the captain announced that the *Magellan* was separating from Deep Find Station. Separating, not delocking. Probably because the *Magellan* was close to quarter the size of the station asteroid. Not mass, just size. Ship stood off the station running tests and diagnostics, but I knew we weren't going back.

Sixteen hundred, Morgan gathered all the pilots and what looked to be most of the ship's officers for a briefing in the ready room aft of ops on the *Magellan.* Forty-eighth deck, just below the bays that held the shuttles and the needle-boats. Had both ramps and ladders up to the bays. Lifts didn't go to the two outer decks. Ladders wouldn't be used much unless we had to operate in null gee. With all the officers it was crowded.

Lerrys, Braun, and me—we were the shuttle pilots in the briefing room. All of us civilians wearing senior lieutenant's bars. The other officers I knew by sight were the ship's pilots—Commander Morgan; another commander whose name patch read LILEKALANI—the exec; Major Tepper; Major Singh; and Lieutenants Beurck, Lindskold, Rynd, and Rigney. There were three other pilots I didn't know. Among all the pilots, Morgan, Lerrys, and Rigney were the only men.

After everyone was there, Captain Spier entered. With her was a civilian in an old-style blue shipsuit—not skintights. Iron gray hair, and he looked like he wanted to be anyplace else.

The captain stepped out in front. She took a long look around the ready room, then spoke. "All of you know that Project Deep Find is highly secret and of vital import to the D.S.S. and to the entire Comity. It is so vital that overall control has been delegated directly from the Comity Minister of External Affairs to Special Deputy Minister Allerde." She gave a quick nod to the gray-haired man in the shipsuit. "Minister Allerde."

Allerde cleared his throat. "Project Deep Find is the most ambitious undertaking attempted by any system in centuries . . ."

Wished that he'd get on with the superlatives and tell us what the frigging project was.

". . . so ambitious that not even the Comity Assembly knows the nature of the project. Every person involved in the project has been specially selected, and, with the exception of Captain Spier and Commander Morgan, none of you have been told even the most general details of this endeavor . . ."

Kept wishing he'd get to the point.

". . . Now that we are clear of Deep Find Station and will be departing shortly, I've been cleared to enlighten you on the overall nature of the project. Then Commander Morgan will follow with some of the specifics." Allerde cleared his throat. "Project Deep Find is a technological, historical, and archeological investigation of an abandoned city of an alien civilization. The ruins are incredibly ancient, but are remarkably well preserved. They indicate that the aliens most probably possessed at least some facets of a technology well in advance of our present accomplishments. I trust that you can all understand why such secrecy has been necessary and why this mission is considered so vital to the Comity—and indeed to all human civilizations." Allerde smiled professionally. "I wanted you all to know how important the Minister of External Affairs and the D.S.S. feel this is. Commander Morgan will fill in all the details that I've omitted."

Allerde and the captain stepped back.

Morgan moved forward. "All of you have experienced the mission training." He smiled, laughed softly. "Most of you thought it was a torture test to weed out all but the best. That's true. But the conditions in the simulators were as close to what you'll face as we could design."

Low whistle came from Lerrys. Felt that way myself, but couldn't whistle. Never could. Not so as I'd want to around anyone else.

"As Special Minister Allerde has indicated, our objective is what appears to be an outpost world of an ancient alien civilization. We will be traveling well beyond the galactic halo and deep into the void between galaxies. Our target is a renegade world that is crossing the void by itself. It has no sun, no satellites. It still rotates on its axis, if far more slowly than it once did. It's barely within reach using a three-Gate translation. We're calling it Danann. That may be wistful thinking, but it seems appropriate. The local gravity is approximately one-point-two Telluran standard. There's no atmosphere because it all either vanished billions of years ago or froze solid. We have incontrovertible indications that it once hosted a *very* high-technology alien civilization. I must stress, again, that level of technology certainly appears to surpass anything we have accomplished to date." Morgan paused.

Another confirmation that we were on a bastard mission—high risk, high payoff.

"Sir? Could I ask how we know that?" That was Major Tepper, the assistant ops boss.

"The D.S.S. has sent a number of ships out to investigate. Several did not return. Some of the local . . . conditions . . . were unexpected." He coughed to clear his throat. "How many of you know about Chronos?"

Braun nodded. So did Commander Lilekalani. I'd never heard of it.

"Chronos was—or is—a galactic anomaly. It is a perfect sphere roughly one-point-two T-standard, but with something like two hundred eighty times T-standard mass. Danann has almost exactly the same diameter, although it's not a perfect sphere, since it was once inhabited, and it's linked to Chronos. In fact, that linkage was how it was discovered. AG drives leave 'traces,' certain minute disruptions in the membrane of the universe. That's how graviton trackers operate. Because all concentrations of mass operate under gravitational conditions, they also leave such traces. One of the Comity scientists postulated that Chronos must have left an unusual AG track. His measurements and monitors discovered that the track of Chronos was twice as long as it should have been. That led to additional observations and a single unmanned Gate-probe. That probe discovered another anomaly and the discovery that the trace of Chronos was not just a trace of Chronos, but two traces, and that there was a good possibility that something lay at the far end of that distant track."

I'm no astrophysicist. Had to take Morgan's word for what he was telling us. Wondered how all the science led to the alien technology.

"That led to a gamble on the part of the Comity. They sent out Gates and ships. They found Danann. Estimates are that the world was abandoned more than six billion years ago. Rough topographical scans and one landing have revealed that one section of the planet was heavily urbanized—and abandoned in good order. We don't know how to preserve something for that long, but the Danannians did. That alone is a good indication of their technology.

"Danann is aimed at another galaxy. We don't know whether that is by chance or design. Long before it will reach that galaxy, it will encounter a region of silent singularities. The rough ETA is three years. Danann may well survive that transit, but we do not have the technology to explore that area and survive. That transit will take thousands of years at best. We don't know with enough certitude how much longer Danann will remain in an area of stable space . . ."

The old pot of gold at the end of the rainbow. The alien bonanza, except that it was going to slip beyond our grasp in a few years.

"This is a combat mission. While the D.S.S. has attempted to keep this mission dark, the refitting of the *Magellan* could not be totally concealed, and there is a good probability that we will encounter some difficulties. We will be accompanied by the *Alwyn*, the newest of the Comity battle cruisers, and she will be joining us shortly after we leave Deep Find Station. We will also have two fast couriers, the *Bannister* and the *Owens*."

Frigging right there'd be difficulties, as Morgan put it. Even a hint of that kind of technology, and every one of the major powers would be scrambling to get a piece, or stop the Comity from getting it.

"Can you tell us anything about what we might expect to find?" asked Major Singh.

"No. You all know the conditions on Danann. The simulator runs were programmed to duplicate those, as well as we could. I don't pretend to know enough to explain what the first ships found. They didn't, either. That's why we have a large contingent of civilian experts on board. While they're heavy on the science side, we've also included other disciplines as well."

"Are you saying that the first ships couldn't enter anything on Danann?"

"They didn't have the equipment to explore for any length of time or to penetrate the structures."

"What about defenses?"

"There are no obvious defenses." Morgan cleared his throat. "There is a briefing package on each of your personal systems. Before you ask any more questions, I suggest you study it carefully, and in depth." After another pause, he added, "The duty rosters are also posted. This is the ready room and primary duty station for the needleboat and shuttle pilots."

No one asked any questions. Not after Morgan had told us to read first and question later. Didn't like the way he'd answered the question about defenses, either.

I didn't have duty until twenty hundred. Went back to my stateroom on deck forty. Ship with fifty-one decks, hard to believe.

Called up the briefing package, then looked at the image of Danann. There was only one. Shot from low orbit, it looked like. Had to be light-enhanced. No internal heat to speak of, and no sun for reflected light. Showed just one hemisphere, and what had to be the biggest complex or city ever built anywhere, anytime. A perfect oval, visible from space, and under ice and frozen atmosphere.

Must have been three hundred kays across at the narrowest—and sat on a high plateau, looked to be on dark rock. Studied the description. Silvery structures, with gray-black ice some twenty meters thick over it.

Bastard mission, all the way.

21 FITZHUGH

At ten hundred—ten o'clock for those unused to D.S.S. terminology—I gathered with all the other nonmilitary civilian members of Project Deep Find in the mess. By my rapid enumeration, there were thirty-one of us seated at the mess tables, awaiting the arrival of whatever D.S.S. functionary had been deputed to brief us. I sat between Melani and Alyendra, a not-too-unpleasant situation. It might have been more pleasant had I not been slightly sore from an excessive session in the *Magellan*'s high-gee workout room.

". . . an alien artifact, perhaps even a ship," suggested Melani.

"It would have to have crashed in a location where they couldn't remove it," pointed out Tomas from across the table. "Otherwise, they wouldn't need an expedition . . ."

I still thought an alien artifact or civilization was improbable, but saw no point in spouting forth on that in the midst of so many who hoped for an alien encounter. If the aliens were or had been less advanced, that would only enhance the already-excessive human arrogance, and a superior culture—even the remnants of one—would spark jingoism and paranoia. I doubted that aspect of military culture had changed over the years since I had beheld it more intimately.

Three individuals entered the mess—the dark-haired Captain Spier, a gray-haired D.S.S. commander, and some sort of functionary in a blue shipsuit with angular silver braid on the shoulders. The three perambulated to the captain's table.

There, Captain Spier stepped forward. "You are all knowledgeable experts within your field, and among the most esteemed in your disciplines within the Comity. By that fact alone, you must have surmised that Project Deep Find is of vital import to the entire Comity. It is so vital that overall control has been delegated directly from the Comity Minister of External Affairs to Special Deputy Minister Allerde." She gestured to the gray-haired man in the blue shipsuit.

Allerde moved forward and in front of the captain's table. "Project Deep Find is the most ambitious undertaking attempted by any human government in millennia. It is of such importance that not even the Comity Assembly knows the nature of the project. Every person involved in the project has been specially selected, and, for that, you should all be pleased to know how highly regarded each of you is within your discipline. For all of that expertise, with the exception of Captain Spier and Commander Morgan, no one, either in the ship's company or among you, has been told even the most general details. Now that we are clear of Deep Find Station, I've been cleared to enlighten you on the overall nature of the expedition. Then Commander Morgan will follow with some specifics." Allerde coughed several times. "Project Deep Find is a technological, historical, and archeological investigation of an abandoned city of an alien civilization. The ruins are incredibly ancient, but remarkably well preserved. The aliens most probably possessed a technology well in advance of our own. So I trust this will explain why such secrecy has been necessary and why this mission is considered so vital to the Comity—and indeed to all human civilizations." Allerde smiled professionally. "Commander Morgan will fill in some details."

Allerde and the captain stepped back, then eased away toward the captain's entrance, where they stood.

The gray-haired commander stepped up before the vacant captain's table. "Good morning. I'm Commander Morgan, and I'm the operations officer of the *Magellan*. That makes me the officer in charge of the daily operations of Deep Find Project. Special Deputy Minister Allerde has overall control of the expedition, and Captain Spier, of course, remains totally in command of the *Magellan* and can override any of my decisions—or those of Deputy Minister Allerde—in the interests of the safety of the ship and its personnel."

That was understood. No military organization would risk vessels for "mere" science.

"The *Magellan* has delocked from Deep Find Station. Once the final cross-checks are completed, we will be leaving Hamilton system. We will be accompanied by the battle cruiser *Alwyn* and two couriers. Because each of you will receive a complete briefing package on your work-space systems shortly, I won't go into specific in-depth details. Our objective is what D.S.S. believes is an alien world crossing the void between galaxies. It has neither a sun nor satellites but is rotating slowly on its axis. We're calling it Danann. We have incontrovertible indications that it once hosted a *very* high-technology alien civilization, but that was more than several billion years ago. There is strong evidence that many of the structures remain intact, despite the passage of time, and undisturbed. That level of technology certainly appears to surpass anything we have accomplished to date." Morgan paused.

I could see heads nodding around the mess tables, and while I could not help but be intrigued and excited by the possibility of beholding the ruins of an alien civilization, I had to wonder why I'd been included among all the scientific experts. I had my doubts whether the lessons of human civilization and history applied to long-departed aliens. I also couldn't help but be annoyed by the choice of the name, because properly it was a possessive form of the name of an ancient goddess. If they were going to name the place after ancient deities, it should have been Danu, but no one had consulted me.

As Morgan spoke, the captain and the Special Deputy Minister made a quiet egress. I had no doubts that Special Deputy Minister Allerde was present only as a political prop so that, once the expedition was over, the Minister of External Affairs could assert that a high-ranking representative of the people had been overseeing the operation all the way.

"It is possible that this could also be a dangerous expedition," Morgan went on. "As mentioned earlier, we will have a D.S.S. battle cruiser as an escort, and we have attempted to keep those who know me objective and the stakes to an absolute minimum. Keeping such a secret, unfortunately, can reveal that the secret exists . . ."

That secrecy revealed as much as it concealed was irrefutable.

"We are also operating under a time constraint. Danann will remain in a position where the planet can be explored and evaluated only for a few more years, perhaps less than three. That is another reason for this commitment." He stopped and surveyed those in the mess before going on. "At the moment, anything more from me would be either superficial or superfluous. After you have a chance to study your briefing materials, either Major Tepper or I will be meeting with the various teams to discuss and develop operations in dealing with Danann." Morgan offered a pleasant smile, a nod, then turned and was gone.

His behavior fit what I would have categorized as a typical military approach—make a presentation so general that the only value was the basic announcement and follow it with a promise of more information, while avoiding all questions on the basis that they were premature before we read the briefing materials.

"I said it was an alien artifact." Melani was radiating both excitement and anxiety. "How can we even begin to understand how they thought?"

Alyendra said nothing.

"You must have noticed that we are among the few who are not specialists in the physical sciences," Tomas said. "I believe there are also an artist, a cryptographer, and a linguist."

If Tomas was correct in his assessments, we were indeed a minority.

Alyendra finally spoke. "Why all the secrecy? It's not as though the Covenanters, or the League, or even the Sunnite Alliance or the Middle Kingdom, could use the Comity Gates to get to us, or to wherever we may be headed."

An economic sociologist she might be, but Alyendra clearly didn't understand the trends of human history. I cleared my throat.

"If this is truly a scientific expedition, why such a fetish for secrecy?" she continued, her voice increasing in volume and stridency. "All of us could have prepared better if we had known where we were going and why—"

I cleared my throat again. This time I was louder. "Throughout human history, over time, no polity has long regarded the limbus of authority of another polity as sacrosanct, regardless of the difficulties in surmounting either political or geographical borders. No polity has ever resisted the temptation to attempt to possess and monopolize new knowledge and technology. If what the Special Deputy Minister and the commander have asserted is accurate, and the D.S.S. obviously believes it is, or they would not have committed such an inordinate accumulation of resources and expertise, then the potential for a brane-explosion of new knowledge exists for whoever can find it and exploit it."

"But a Gate is as close to invulnerable as . . . as a star itself . . ." That was Melani.

"That is indubitably so. Do you recall what occurred in the Dirty War or the Second Arm War?"

Melani frowned.

"Gates had been long established by that time. Each of the belligerents controlled its own system Gates. Not a single Gate of any belligerent polity was compromised or destroyed through direct military action, yet whole systems were decimated."

"They created Gate-ships," pointed out Tomas. "Those were ships that went through their own Gates and ended up outside the enemy's systems, and then they were converted into functioning Gates for the attackers."

"Exactly. Consider that those wars were over control of populations, territory, and human knowledge. Wouldn't the possibility of alien knowledge be worth the expenditure to create or use Gate-ships, either to gain control of such knowledge or even to preclude the Comity from monopolizing it?"

"How would they be able to build them so quickly?"

"They wouldn't. Those earlier Gates later formed the basis for enhanced interstellar contact—those that were not dismantled because of their excessive operating costs. Do you know how many Gates are positioned outside Hamilton system?"

"How would I know that?" asked Melani.

"That's the salient point. Unless a Gate is used, space is vast enough that no one would know it's there. If its first use is to translate a fleet . . ."

"You think they would come after us, after a D.S.S. ship like the *Magellan*?"

"The commander said we would have a full battle cruiser as an escort." To me that more than intimated that the D.S.S. anticipated a high probability of some form of hostilities.

"Then let us hope that no one sends a dreadnought after us," Tomas said quietly.

While I appreciated and shared his concerns, I would rather that he had not expressed them quite so directly.

22 CHANG

On fiveday, early, I was down in the ops workout rooms trying to get back in better shape. Never had the time on Alpha Station. McClendon contract had been a bitch. Not many there, and all D.S.S., except for one of the civilians. Dark-haired, working hard but smoothly in the high-gee area. Doubted I could match him. Wondered who he was.

All pilots to stations! All pilots to stations! I'd forgotten that the links worked *everywhere* in the *Magellan.* Shouldn't have forgotten that. She was a D.S.S. ship.

Ran through the shower and scrambled into my uniform and up the ramps—faster than the lifts for a few levels. Lerrys was in the ready room before me. Braun was right behind me.

Major Tepper was waiting, not Morgan.

"We've got a small problem."

Tepper looked across us and the five needleboat pilots. All were junior lieutenants. Lindskold, Rynd, and Rigney were the ones I knew. Rigney was the biggest pilot I'd ever seen, over 190 centimeters. Name strips on the other two said SHAIMEN and UNGERA.

"An out-system Gate has translated two battle cruisers and two frigates.

They've split. One of the cruisers and one frigate will reach us just before we reach our Gate."

"The others are positioned to keep us from returning to Hamilton system without a fight?" asked Braun.

"They're Sunni-configured, and once they've translated through a Gate, they don't back off."

"Why the Sunnis, sir?" asked Rynd.

"We don't know. It could be that they're the most desperate for any possible alien technology. Their systems are outflanked by the Covenanters and the Comity, and Old Earth blasted them the last time they encroached on League worlds." Tepper gave a tight smile, wry. "If we prevail, the Alliance will deny that those ships ever existed. There certainly won't be any records. Or if there are, they'll be raiders funded by some extremist splinter group. All that's beside the point." She looked hard at the junior lieutenants. "Sunnite ships carry lots of needleboats. Each needleboat can carry one antimatter torp."

Rynd winced.

Rigney nodded.

"We'll see what the spread is, but you'll probably have to launch in another three hours." Tepper turned in my direction. "You're the designated rescue pilot. Once we engage, you'll be suited and in shuttle one, but you'll stay cradled in the bay unless and until you're needed."

"Except for Lieutenant Chang, you can all go back to whatever you were doing until ten hundred. Then I expect you back here, ready to fly. If we need you sooner, you'll be alerted."

Major didn't say a word until we were alone.

"Commander Morgan picked you for this, Lieutenant."

The way she said it meant she didn't agree. Would have bet she'd done the pickups before. "Yes, sir. I didn't know."

"I wouldn't have expected you to. You know how all the equipment works, and you're the best overall shuttle pilot we've got. It's basically a close and grapple and return operation. No armor to armor, and you never leave the controls. Is that understood?"

"Yes, sir."

"Lieutenant, if you're launched, your only task is to pick up any disabled needleboats and bring them back, as quickly as possible. We can't afford delays. You will not recover any enemy artifacts or boats unless specifically ordered. Is that clear?"

"Yes, sir." Wasn't stupid. Bringing a needleboat that still carried an antimatter torp inside the *Magellan*'s shields was suicide. Hell, Sunnis had been known to strap antimatter bomblets in place of one of the recycler packs on their space armor. Never understood suicide tactics. Doubted I ever would. Just accepted that some idiots were like that.

"Good. Do you have any other questions?"

"Bringing back disabled boats . . . what bay do you use?"

"Fourth bay for salvage and repair. It will be the only bay open on your return. That makes it easy."

"The ship will be maintaining heading and acceleration?"

"That's the plan, Lieutenant. Delays might provide opportunities for others."

"How many others?"

Tepper looked like she wasn't going to answer. Then she nodded brusquely. "We don't know. We've learned of a major security breach. There are . . . religious implications . . . we believe."

Religious implications? What did aliens have to do with religion? If someone believed in an all-powerful god—or goddess—the damned deity had to have power over aliens and us. Who believed in a deity that wasn't all-powerful? Didn't say anything, though. Never did understand why people believed that crap. Life after death? Even the words were a contradiction.

"If you don't have any more questions, Lieutenant . . ."

"No, sir."

Tepper left. So did I.

Did a quick workout, then got a shower and a big breakfast No telling how long I'd be standing by.

At ten hundred, I was back in the ready room, and by ten-thirty, I was strapping into shuttle one. Wore full armor, except for the helmet, racked just back of the couch. Had to be able to reach it in instants, but links didn't work well through armor, unless you used a habitability connection like they did in the needles. Glad I wasn't running a needle. They piloted in full armor, helmets and all. Went through the prelaunch checklist and put everything on hold. Didn't carry a tech on a recovery. Nothing a tech could do.

Navigator Control, this is Porter Tigress. Standing by at prelaunch.

Porter Tigress, Control, stand by until further notice. Estimate bogeys in operating area in fifteen plus.

Control, Porter Tigress standing by.

While I waited, called up the *Magellan*'s farscreens through the links, and the lower command net. Could see the Sunni cruiser and frigate, closing. *Alwyn*— D.S.S. battle cruiser escorting us—could have outrun both. So could the two couriers, *Bannister* and *Owens*. They'd run for the Gate. No reason not to. They didn't carry but four torps and light shields. *Magellan* had too much mass to make that speed in a short time. Gate was too far. We wouldn't make it before the Sunnis reached us.

Alwyn moved to intercept. Sunnis split. Frigate accelerated plus fifteen on a course thirty relative. Would try to intercept from the port forequarter. *Magellan* should have screens to hold off a frigate. Had to wonder how many needleboats the two Sunnis would launch. They'd need plenty to offset the *Alwyn*'s firepower.

The Sunni cruiser turned on a tail chase directly toward the *Magellan*. *Alwyn* altered course, dropping back slightly, but maintaining position between the Sunni cruiser and the *Magellan*.

Frigate kept accelerating, trying to draw abreast of the *Magellan*.

I ran the parameters through the shuttle's comps. No frigate had enough fusactor mass to keep up that acceleration for long, not even with augmentation from photon nets. Good question as to whether the AG drives would melt down or the fusactors would shut down. Frigate had to be figuring on a one-way attack or a later pickup from another ship. Farscreens only showed the other two Sunnis—heading toward a stand-off near Deep Find Station. They'd be able to reach the frigate before any Comity ship could. There weren't any other ships anywhere close in our out-sector of Hamilton system.

Sunni cruiser began an accel-run toward the *Alwyn*. That didn't seem right. I checked again. Cruiser was aimed at the *Magellan*.

I could see the Sunni tactics unfolding. Cruiser would shift all power to acceleration and forward shields. *Alwyn* would have to shift power to screens and block or destroy the cruiser. That would slow the *Alwyn*. If the *Alwyn* didn't have to protect us, she could have just cut back at an angle, and the velocities would have been great enough that the Sunni wouldn't have been able to bring torps— or anything else—to bear for more than instants. With the Sunni cruiser on a collision course with the *Magellan*, the *Alwyn* had to stand and fight. Both couriers were well clear, closer to the Gate.

I kept listening on lower command band.

Bandit one, closing. Range is one-point-three kilo-kay ETC is eight minus. Bandit two, closing on Navigator, terminal vee. ETC is eleven plus.

Both Sunnis were working on a simultaneous attack, one on the *Magellan*, the other on the *Alwyn*.

Bandit one, all shields forward. ETC five plus. . . .

Couldn't figure why there was so little on the lower command, but realized that the *Alwyn* was a warship, and the captain of the *Alwyn* was probably senior to Captain Spier. Meant that he was commanding and using upper band—why it was blocked. They had to give me access on lower for recovery ops.

Farscreens showed a reddish blip that was the Sunni closing on the blue ovoid that was the *Alwyn*. *Magellan* was a larger oval, with the smaller red triangle that was the frigate coming in from the port side.

Magellan's internal shipnet came up with a warning. *All personnel! Secure for null grav, Secure for null grav.* Probably went out over all audio speakers, too, but I wasn't where I'd hear that.

On the farscreen, I saw that the *Alwyn* fired five torps, almost point-blank. Except point-blank in space combat was something like two hundred kays. Sunni cruiser didn't return fire.

Sunni cruiser's shields stopped the first torp salvo. Thought I saw a flicker of orange when the fourth and fifth impacted shields. Less than fifty kays separation when the second salvo went. This time the third salvo went on top of the second.

Sunni's shields went amber, vibrated green-amber, then dropped through the amber to red.

Attacking cruiser, your shields are gone. Surrender and decelerate, or be destroyed.

That message went out on all bands and was repeated in all of the major system languages. Recognized some, but not the others. Sunni piled on acceleration.

Alwyn fired another spread of torps.

I shifted screens to check the frigate, coming in faster, burning drives and systems. Clear suicide run. Looked like that, anyway. A good ten torps blew out from the frigate. Ten? Half were torps, and half were needleboats.

Torp spread flared out from the *Magellan*, five headed toward the frigate. Another five followed.

Ten torps? More than half the total load of a corvette.

Launching needles this time. Null grav in bays four and five. That was lower command band.

The frigate's shields went into the amber, but held, through the first salvo, and even the second. The Sunni torps didn't even cause the *Magellan*'s shields to flicker. Five Sunni needleboats spread—small targets for torps.

Lead needleboat from *Magellan* targeted the middle Sunni needle, one that looked larger on the screen.

Bandit one destroyed. Hold rear shields for debris. Another expanding energy globe appeared where the Sunni cruiser had been. Could make out chunks of matter going in all directions, but most of it was headed toward the area aft of the *Magellan*. Made sense, laws of motion and energy. Sunni cruiser had been accelerating toward us.

Turned concentration back to the port screens. White energy appeared on the screens where the two needleboats had been. When it cleared, both needleboats were gone. Sunni had triggered antimatter torp—or the D.S.S. needleboat had.

Four needleboats against four.

Both the *Magellan* and the *Alwyn* sent a salvo of torps toward the Sunni frigate, the *Alwyn*'s first. Salvos were synched so that all would impact the frigate's shields at the same time. They did.

This time, Sunni frigate's shields went amber and red, and then the frigate went from mass to scattered mass and energy all at once.

Left four Sunni needleboats still headed for the *Magellan*.

Torp from the *Magellan* took out one more Sunni needleboat, but the others missed, and kept traveling. Might hit something someday millions of years in the future. Probably wouldn't.

Alwyn was moving up on the trailing Sunni needleboat. Sunni didn't see soon enough. Alwyn's shields crushed the needleboat—another energy flare from antimatter. Thing was that when the mag containment went, no matter how, you got all that energy—enough that the *Alwyn*'s screens flickered amber, just for an instant.

One of our needleboats drilled one of theirs, then twisted behind the *Alwyn*'s shields. Wasn't sure how the pilot managed that. Good thing he did. More anti-matter combining with matter and lots of energy flaring everywhere.

I'd missed some of the action, because all the Sunnis were gone, but one of our needles was drifting. No propulsion. No debris around it, though.

Didn't wait for orders. *Navigator Control, this is Porter Tigress, request null grav, bay two, this time.*

Porter Tigress, Control, stand by for null gray bay two.

Control, standing by.

Going from full grav to null gee gave my guts a jolt, then passed. Checked all the boards, and pressures.

Porter Tigress, Control, bay doors opening, atmosphere barrier in place.

Control, Porter Tigress, understand bay doors opening. The nanite barrier that kept most of the atmosphere in place was transparent. Meant that everything out beyond the doors was visual black. Switched to enhanced farscreen through the links.

Porter Tigress, Navigator Control, bay doors open, cleared to uncradle and launch.

Control, Porter Tigress, uncradling this time.

Released the cradle blocks, then pulsed the steering jets, just enough, and we were clear.

Porter Tigress, you have one pickup. Needle Four. Navigator Control has no comm with Needle Four.

Control, understand one pickup and no comm. I have Needle Four at two eight one, plus nine.

That's affirmative.

Screens showed three needleboats returning. If the pilot of the disabled needle survived, we would only lose one needle and one pilot.

Once I was clear of the *Magellan's* shields, I cut in the AG drives and boosted toward the drifting needle. Pilot had been disabled while accelerating, and I'd have to overtake, capture, then make a powered return that amounted to an acceleration to catch the ship, and then a decel rendezvous with the *Magellan.* Needle's habitability and power wouldn't last long enough for a more gradual re-turn.

Tried comm two–three times on the out-run. No response. Still took almost half stan to catch the needle.

Finally shifted to closescreens as I eased the shuttle up aft and alongside the needle. It was tumbling end over end. Had grapples and nanite-sticktights ready.

Figured I'd try with my comm. Could be her directionals had been fried. Up close she might hear.

Needle Four, this is Porter Tigress. Approaching for recovery your port side. In-terrogative status.

. . . Tigress . . . no attitude control . . . suited . . . habitability negative . . .

After that, I got nothing.

Matched relative velocities with the needle, close enough for what I needed.

Planted the first sticktight on the fuselage aft of the cockpit, second went farther aft. Dropped the needle's end-over-end rotation to half what it had been before the lines parted. Good thing the shuttle massed so much more than the needles. Second set almost stopped the rotation. Biggest problem was that we were still bat-assing away from the *Magellan*. Couldn't do anything about that until I had the needle grappled and secure. Checked the return calcs. Had less than twenty before return went negative.

Timed the grapples—and clamped. Slight grinding, and amber flash off on the aft clamps, but I had the needle. Tightened up and ran the return numbers. Then began the turn and power accel. Tried to keep it at two gees. Needles didn't have internal grav systems, and there was no way to tell what shape the pilot was in. Two was as low as I could go if we wanted to make it back.

Navigator Control, this is Porter Tigress, recovery green. Returning Navigator this time.

Porter Tigress, understand green. Interrogative pilot status.

Navigator Control, limited comm, believe status is amber.

Stet, Tigress, will have med unit at bay.

Tried to get a comm link, even with direct contact. Nothing. Had to hope, but couldn't do anything but get back to the *Magellan*.

Took almost a standard hour before we were stabilized off bay four. The last part of the approach had been tricky. Screens were showing fuzz and junk aft of the *Magellan*, just beyond the shields. Remnants of the cruiser that had plowed into the shields and piled up there. Laws of motion again.

Navigator Control, this is Porter Tigress. Extensive debris aft of Navigator, range less than one kay.

Porter Tigress, understand debris. Scanning this time. Maintain separation.

Frig! Maintain separation? I'd had to navigate around all that crap, and they hadn't even warned me. *Control, maintained separation during approach. Just thought you'd like to know. Request clearance to bay four.*

Cleared to bay four.

Bay four was longer, not quite so high as bay two. Didn't enter all the way, about halfway. Weird when you're split with half the shuttle inside the atmosphere barrier and the other half in vacuum. Differential visuals.

Porter Tigress, Bay Control. Hold position. Cradle moving to recover.

Bay Control, holding.

Had to wait until they got the cradle under the grapples. Needle had mass, even in null grav.

Porter Tigress, cleared to release grapples. Hold position.

Opening grapples this time.

Seemed to take a good quarter stan, but the time showed three minutes before Bay Control came back.

Porter Tigress, clear to leave bay. Minimal power.

Departing. Understand minimal power.

After all that, cradling into bay two was a snap. Inside my armor, I was soaked.

Still had to go through all the shutdown checklists and final clearances from Navigator Control. Also had to report the overstress of the rear grapple and clamp. Finally, I did get out of the shuttle and made my way from the bay to the ready room.

Close to fifteen hundred. Battle with the Sunnis had taken less than a stan. Recovery had taken three.

Major Tepper was waiting. "Not a bad recovery, Lieutenant. Shaimen will make it. You cut it close on habitability."

I was glad to hear that Shaimen had made it. Worried about that all the way back. "Her needle was tumbling end over end. Had to slow it enough to use the grapples."

"You didn't mention that in the transmissions."

"It's in the system logs, sir. Didn't want to spend time explaining, not with the separation we were building."

The major nodded. "You hate to explain, don't you, Lieutenant?"

Should have been obvious. You can't explain to idiots, and usually don't need to for people who can figure it out. "Have trouble with it, sir."

"Chang. This is a military vessel and a military operation. Not everyone understands what you're doing out there. A few words of explanation would ease things for everyone. You might think of them as . . . system lubrication. People have moving parts, too. I can explain it this time, and I will. You're not used to this kind of operation, and you were handling a lot. But lots of people were handling a lot, and one of them didn't make it back."

"I'm sorry, Major. I'll try to keep that in mind in the future." Tried to look contrite.

Tepper snorted. "You don't do the contrition well, Lieutenant. Don't try it. Just explain."

"Yes, sir." Managed to smother a grin. Tough woman, but she was right.

"Any quick questions?"

Looked at her. Blotted the sweat off my forehead. "If this is so frigging important, why didn't we get a dreadnought as an escort?"

"Because there aren't any spare dreadnoughts, not with the latest mobilizations and maneuvers by the CWs and the Middle Kingdom, and the Covenanters with their latest pacification efforts. Even if there were, sending one might have been worse. It would have told the whole Galaxy how important this mission is. Every dreadnought's assignments are monitored by every other system. Instead of having two obsolete Sunni ships, probably turned over to the Children of Mahmed, we might have had a three brand-new cruisers chasing us."

"Obsolete . . . the shields?"

The major nodded. "Let's just say that there was more to this than meets the eye."

Didn't want to hear that. Not at all.

"Lieutenant Lerrys is standby now. You might want to get cleaned up before we translate. Gate ETA is in less than a stan."

"Yes, sir."

So I headed back to my closet stateroom and a shower. At least, I didn't have to share it with anyone. Major's words about there being more than met the eye nagged at me. So did a suicide attack by obsolete ships. Even obsolete ships cost billions of creds.

23 *Goodman/Bond*

I'd barely settled into the armory on fiveday after morning muster. I hadn't slept well. Alveres snored very loudly, and I'd have to adjust to that. Even the sonic earplugs hadn't helped. So much for the Comity's vaunted technology.

Then the captain had announced over the screens that the ship was on an exploratory mission to an unusual planet that might have some artifacts, possibly even alien ruins, but that we wouldn't know much more until we got there. Crew scuttlebutt was that there were real aliens. That didn't make sense. There were lots of scientists aboard, but no Comity Marines. There weren't any diplomats, either. If there were real live breathing aliens, we'd be carrying lots fewer scientists and lots more Marines.

That told me the captain was staying close to the truth. The Comity was looking to search an abandoned alien ship or some ruins, maybe looking to find some new technology. More likely some ruins, if the colonel wanted me to plant a locator beacon. We couldn't afford to allow the Comity any additional advantages from an alien technology. Things were bad enough already. If the technology had come from the subdemons of Iblis . . . that made the possibilities even worse.

"Bond! Over to the transport tubes." Chief Stuval didn't quite yell.

I hurried. "Yes, chief?"

"They'll be calling battle stations before long. Word is that there are Sunni bandits chasing us. We need to start loading torps into the transport tubes. For the needleboats. Get the small slider. You and Ciorio load it from bank one. Just four to the slider."

"Yes, chief." The small slider could only carry four torps. The larger one took six. The armory had transport tubes that shuttled torps to the firing ports and the bays. They were one way. Any unfired torps had to be brought back by slider and reserviced. According to what I'd learned, sometimes repeated temperature differentials affected the internal systems. As a precaution all torps that went out in needleboats and came back unused were checked out before being sent up to the needles for use again.

I had the slider in place before the loading rack in bank one when Ciorio showed up. Even with the dolly and loaders, wrestling the torps onto the slider was work.

"Too bad we couldn't go null grav," I said.

"Don't even think it," Ciorio said. "That's how the *Flewelling* got scrapped. Torps still got mass. You get it moving in null grav, and it doesn't stop until it rams into something."

"They're safed," I pointed out.

"They're *supposed* to be safed. Just like all the 503s weren't supposed to need reworking." Ciorio grunted as he fastened the safety clamps in place on the first torp. "What's the first rule for an armorer?"

"Don't trust anything you can't verify yourself." That was one of those sayings I'd been conditioned with. It didn't appear anywhere in writing, but all the armorers knew it.

"Right. You want to guess that a loose torp ramming into a bulkhead in null grav won't explode? Predetonator could anyway."

"Nope." I eased the dolly back into position under the second torp in the bay.

By nine hundred we'd gotten all the torps into the transport tubes.

"Make sure everything's secured. Everything!" The chief pointed at a stylus on the edge of the bench. "Even that, Bond."

"Yes, chief." I grabbed the stylus and slipped it into the toolkit.

Ciorio grinned from the other side of the compartment. He didn't say anything until the chief was away. "He's still got a scar on his shoulder from when he was a tech third on the *Collins*. The first left one of those loose. Just a null-grav high-speed drill, but it went right through his shoulder. Says he almost bled to death 'cause the first didn't believe a stylus could do that."

I could see that, but I wouldn't have if Ciorio hadn't pointed it out. "Lots of things you don't see until something happens."

"Especially here." He tilted his head to the side. "Chief said the Sunnis were after us. Thought the Sunnis only went after Covenanters. Why us? Got any ideas?"

"No more 'n you. Maybe we're headed into systems they're claiming."

"Can't be that. One of the nav techs was saying that no one's been where we're going."

"You got me."

"Never could figure out the business between them," Ciorio mused. "They both think there's a big Juju that created everything. Most of the Galaxy doesn't. But they fight each other when they got more in common than other systems. Go figure."

I understood. It was simple enough. The unbelievers were damned to Hell or limbo for eternity, and nothing would change that. They couldn't see, and wouldn't. The Sunnis understood that God had been, was, is, and would be— but not truly what He was. They were worth fighting because they were so close that they just might see. They might even feel the same way about us because Covenanters also believed in the Word of God. I wasn't about to explain. I only said, "The Galaxy's a strange place."

"You can say that again."

"All hands to stations. Stations! This is not a drill. All hands to stations."

"See you later!" Ciorio headed for his station. Mine was the restraint couch in the armory's aft bay. I'd been briefed on the harnesses, but my fingers still felt like thumbs.

For a standard hour, outside of twice—once when the lights flickered, and once when we had a minute or so of null grav—nothing seemed to happen.

As I sat there in harness waiting, I couldn't help but think. How had the Sunnis found out so quickly what the *Magellan* was doing? The CIS objective was to obtain the technology, but we couldn't obtain it if the *Magellan* didn't get where it was headed. From a personal point of view, destruction of the *Magellan* would be a double disaster. Not only would I get turned to energy and small chunks of matter, but the worlds of the Covenant would lose the chance to get the location of that world. At the same time, I had to question some aspects of my mission. If the technology represented the Morning Star, did we really want to see that loosed again?

"Stand down from stations. Stand down. Class one stand-down. Class one stand-down."

From up the passageway, I heard Chief Stuval. "Ciorio, you and Bond take the slider up to the bays. The boat techs will already be there. Don't get in their way, but you clean and service the launchers, then unload any torps they didn't fire. Bring them back on the sliders."

I hurried out to join Ciorio. He was sweating.

"I hate waiting. You never know what's going on."

"The boat techs will tell us," I pointed out.

"After it's all over."

He had a point, but there wasn't anything we could do about it. We had to take the aft maintenance lift, and that meant guiding the sliders a good hundred meters aft, then up—just for one deck. On most combat ships, according to my briefings, the armory was practically beside the launch bays, but that wasn't so for the *Magellan*. I'd guessed that was because she'd been designed as a colony ship first.

We got the slider through the shipside equipment locks and into the bay. A maintenance chief appeared. "About time you guys got here. There's one torp on two, and one on five."

"None on the other one?"

"Not here. After you're done here, you'll have to go over to bay four. Needle Four was a recovery job. It still has two torps on board. Only fired one. My crews aren't working on it until you've got the torps out."

"We'll take care of it, chief, after we finish here." Ciorio smiled.

I could tell he didn't mean it.

Once the chief stepped back, we eased the slider across the bay and up in front of the full tube on Needle Two.

Ciorio glanced back at the chief, then mumbled, "Shit! Friggin' recovery job. Just hope the tubes aren't bent. Have to go back down for metal benders and who knows what else."

That didn't bother me. What else was I going to do? "What about the pre-detonator?"

"We'll read that first. If it's bad, and the tubes are bent, they'll have to jetti-son the boat. If the tubes are straight, then we pull it and they put a jetpak on it and jettison the torp."

Ciorio did the readouts. "Predetonator's fine on this one." He took a deep breath. "Let's get this one out first. Least they left the tube ports open for us. Got the sticktights?"

I handed him the twin batons. He placed one on each side of the torp nose. I tightened the tension on the slider's winch.

"Begin reeling," Ciorio said.

I eased the winch into retraction. For a moment, nothing happened. Then the torp began to ease forward out of the tube.

"That's it. Keep it slow. Now, bring up the cradle . . ."

The other torp was salvageable as well. We got both torps out and stowed in the slider. Then we had to turn the slider, without scraping the needleboats or running over the maintenance carts that were everywhere, and guide it back to the shipside maintenance lock, up along the maintenance passageway, then through the shipside lock for bay four.

Needle Four had gouges down the hull, and a section of the fuselage on the aft port section was crumpled in. Someone had cut through the access hatch locks. They'd probably been jammed. The aft drive section was bent down more than ten degrees.

"Looks like the pilot ran through a comet head," Ciorio said. "At least the tubes are clear. Better take readings, though." He stood next to the port tube. "Hand me the probes."

I handed him the probes.

"This one reads all right."

Both torps came up green. We extracted them and loaded them onto the slider. Going back down to the armory took longer. The slider massed a lot more, and neither one of us wanted to slam it into a bulkhead or hatch.

24 *BARNA*

When the ship announced "General Quarters! All personnel to stations!" I was already in my studio. It was midmorning, and I'd been trying to re-create an image of the three pilots—blonde, red-haired, and dark brown—mostly from memory.

I made sure that lightbrushes and the matrix-easel were secure in one of the equipment bins. Then I fastened myself into the seat before the board and tried to get more information. All the systems would tell me was that suspected enemy vessels were on an intercept course and that I was to remain strapped into my station. The heavy seat before the board locked itself into a forward-facing position. It took me a while to discover the screen controls on the armrest. After that, I settled into shifting views on the center screen, awkwardly.

Mostly, what I saw was lots of black, with distant points of light that were stars. An indistinct flickering of amber occasionally appeared, almost like the faintest of mists that I could barely see. I thought that might be the ship's defense shields interacting with the few molecules of gas that comprised space outside planetary systems.

I'd just as soon have gone back to working on the study of the pilots, but when I started to unfasten the harness, the system warned me, "Please remain in your harness. The ship could lose gravity at any time. Please remain in your harness."

I stayed put and tried to master the other functions of the screen controls in the armrest.

After about half an hour, while switching screens, I caught sight of something, small arrows, greenish. There were five of them, and they flared yellow-amber as they moved away from the *Magellan*. I increased the magnification gain on the screen, enough to see that they were more like cylinders that flared slightly into a conical base. They had to be needleboats. That was what I'd gathered from the basic information about the ship. I'd only skimmed through it, because I'd been looking for images, rather than text. The small craft didn't look at all like needles, but I didn't know what else they could have been. I was sure that torps would have moved faster.

In moments, they were gone beyond the range of any of the screens connected to my system. I tried the other feeds to the screens, but they all came up showing just stars as points of light, with a few dark splotches here and there. Except for one, and it just showed a small disc of amber-green, and that was only with some sort of enhancement or filters. I thought that might be our escort ship, but that was a guess.

Without access to my equipment, all I could do was switch screens and watch.

After another half hour or so, the lights flickered, and for a moment, there was no gravity. My stomach wanted to turn inside out, but didn't have a chance to before gravity returned.

Right after that, a small flare of light appeared on the center screen. It wasn't much bigger than the sun of the Hamilton system, and then it was gone.

I had everything in record mode. I pulled the image back to that and tried to get an enlargement. Even at max gain, and amplification, the best I could do was a tiny image of chunks of *something* flaring outward, then disappearing into the darkness. I tried infrared, and that outlined the pieces some, but they still faded quickly. Distance and the cold of space, I guessed.

I kept watching.

After a while one of the needleboats returned, followed by another. Then another craft eased out of one of the *Magellan's* bays. It was cylindrical and looked to be more than five times the size of the needleboats, although it was hard to tell because they were at different distances, and the needleboats had docked or locked before I could really compare them. The second craft vanished into the darkness. I went back through the familiarization information on the *Magellan* and discovered that the larger boat was one of the ship's shuttles.

Another needleboat returned before the announcement came that we could stand down, and the system didn't warn me when I finally released all the harnesses.

Because I'd wondered what the last boat had been up to, even after I'd taken out the easel and lightbrushes again, I kept checking the screens. In time, well after I'd gone to the mess and eaten and come back, the shuttlecraft finally returned. Grappled to its side was a damaged needleboat, partly crumpled in places. I hoped the pilot was all right. I wondered if she had been one of those whom I was trying to portray.

Then I realized that one of the needleboats hadn't returned. At least, the screens and the recordings hadn't shown the fifth needleboat coming back.

From what I could tell, I'd just been in the center of a space battle. I had the best visual screens on the ship—or access to them—and I'd hardly seen anything.

Aeryana would never believe that. Neither would Nicole.

25 FITZHUGH

At the evening repast, if one could term it such, although I had eaten far worse institutional fare over the varied years of my existence, Melani, Tomas, and I found ourselves at a table with Dr. Sorens and Dr. Ferward. Sorens had his doctorate in structural engineering. I hadn't the faintest idea what Ferward did, but all indications were that his expertise was congruent to that of Sorens, given how readily and animatedly they were conversing before we joined them.

Alyendra had demurred from accompanying us, asserting politely that she would refrain from partaking in order not to place more strain on her system. The so-called battle had affected her, although it had scarcely seemed to have had any impact on the *Magellan*. I had strapped into my seat and watched the screen only long enough to ascertain that the representation of hostilities would display little new to me, indeed, display little at all, and would only provoke my own fruitless analysis of what might have been done. That being the case, I'd employed the time to endeavor to catch up on the seemingly endless professional journals, monographs, and articles that I had downloaded from my datablocs into my office system on the *Magellan*.

Most of what I had gone though I'd skimmed and discarded, falling as it did in one of two categories—overanalysis of the trivial or inconsequential or reverential obsequiousness in support of long-established historical truisms.

There had been an interesting article by a singer, a Carol Ann Janes, one suggesting that the creative arts, qualitatively presented in terms of exemplary and original work, foreshadowed cultural ascension and decline more closely than more traditional barometers such as technical innovation, predominance of exchange mechanisms, military puissance, or popular cultural inundation. I suspected that there might be flaws with her approach, but it had the merit of being a real-time potential direct causative correlation, rather than delayed secondary symptomatic association. The remainder of the articles had been far less intriguing, and I was more than relieved to join Tomas and Melani.

"Good evening," offered Dr. Sorens, the engineer who looked as if he would have been more at home as an elf of ancient wish-fulfillment fantasies than on a mission where he was to determine the structural properties of alien materials.

"Good evening," returned Melani.

"What did you think of the fight?" asked Ferward, a man presenting a round face suggesting jollity above an angular physique that bespoke great physical effort in maintaining optimal aerobic condition.

"I didn't follow it," Melani admitted.

"I would have been surprised if it had turned out any other way," Tomas observed.

"What was your opinion about the events?" I asked, looking at Sorens.

"Ah . . . I was actually going over some material on anomalous composites."

"You didn't watch the screens?" asked Ferward.

"I can't say that I did, Edmund. There wasn't much to see, and some of the data in my briefing materials suggested that the aliens might have mastered wide-scale production of anomalous composites."

"What does that mean?" asked Melani with a warm smile. "If you wouldn't mind explaining?"

"Anomalous metals and composites have been around for centuries. They're materials that incorporate the best features of both glass, liquids, and metals. That's oversimplifying, of course . . ."

Ferward snorted softly, as if to suggest that oversimplifying was the least of the problems in Soren's explanation, then turned to Tomas. "Why do you think that the battle couldn't have turned out any other way?"

"The Comity has better equipment, better training, and, in this case, more modern ships and weapons. D.S.S. also would not have sent us off, after investing all the credits in this expedition, without very able officers and crew."

"Then why did the Sunnis even bother to attack?"

Even as that line of inquiry intrigued me, the trends I had seen so often had already answered my question—the internal dynamics of cultural self-preservation are far stronger than any external force or threat. I pondered what Tomas might say.

He reflected for a moment. "There are many possibilities, but I would suggest the most likely is that we present a great threat to their beliefs and way of life."

"The Comity hasn't ever attacked the Sunnis first."

"Their holy book dates back over six thousand years, and one of the key lines in it says something like 'the worst of beasts in God's sight are the unbelievers, who will not believe . . . ' In their view, anyone who does not share their theocratic beliefs is one of those beasts."

"They say that, but how can they believe it?" questioned Ferward.

" 'All truth comes from the Lord,' " countered Tomas. "If science, or a secular thinker, challenges what their imams declare as their God's truth, they will follow the imam. In a technological society, being a true believer tends to create a certain schizoid behavior."

"Even if that's true, what does it have to do with this expedition?"

"What happens if we find the ruins of a great civilization that was totally inhuman?" asked Tomas. "What does that mean? Does it mean that there is a greater god than theirs? Or does it mean that their god is fickle and will abandon a great culture? Does it provide proof of a sort, perhaps, that there is no god?"

Ferward shrugged. "God is a figment of the imagination of the weak."

"That could be," I interjected, "but political and military history has been determined as much by what people believe to be the truth as what has been accurately verified as such. Facts and established principles have been ignored throughout history in favor of comforting and scientifically impossible beliefs. Recorded history is filled with cultures that have believed what we have determined is scientifically improbable, if not impossible. On ancient Earth, people were burned alive for asserting basic astronomical facts. Until three hundred years ago, it was technically a crime to teach basic brane theory on more than a hundred worlds in the Comity. It still is in the Worlds of the Covenant."

"Stupid people. There are always stupid people," Ferward retorted.

That might be, I reflected, but enough stupid people existed to support leaders and polity governments who catered to their beliefs. The idea that the existence of aliens had made the *Magellan* a military target was less than comforting, and yet I had to concur with the basic precepts that Tomas had advanced.

Ferward shook his head, more than a few times, as if to clear away an intellectually unappetizing proposition. The specialists in the so-called hard sciences have always had difficulty in comprehending, on an emotional and empathetic level, the inability of large segments of any population to embrace verified and unequivocally demonstrated aspects of the universe at variance with their personal comfort-values, all the while insisting that they were rational individuals. That phenomenon had been recognized early on by the political thinker Exton Land, who had categorized it as "the illusion of rationality." Thousands of years had passed, and human beings continued to demonstrate the validity of his proposition.

Knowing that anything I said would fall on ears unwilling to comprehend that rational discourse had little effect on true believers of all stripes, I took refuge in a strong cup of synth-tea, and turned back toward Sorens and Melani.

26 CHANG

Four hours after I docked shuttle two, I was back in the ready room. Didn't have to be, but I wanted to use the big high-res screens there to see if space looked different when the *Magellan* translated. I was betting it wouldn't, that translation mass had an effect.

Braun wasn't there. She'd just finished standby duty. Major Tepper was in the corner talking to Rigney about something. Rigney was the only pilot I'd seen with a big bushy beard. Didn't look that good on him. Be a mess, too, if he had to stay in armor for long.

Lerrys was watching the main screen. Turned around and gestured to me.

I walked over and settled into the restraint couch next to him.

"You came back here just to watch a translation on the farscreens, Jiendra? After your day?" He grinned.

"Nice boring translation ought to settle me down. What about you?" Fastened the restraint harness so I wouldn't have to later.

"I just wanted to see if it's as dark as the books say it is."

"Books? The actual bound ones?"

"They're my hobby. If you want to be accurate, I was talking about system manuals on-screen, but I think of all long written material as books."

"Don't they fall apart? Books?"

"Some do. Some don't. It depends on how often they're read and how well they're cared for. It's amazing how accurate some parts of the old science books are and how wrong others are. The older ones say that it's dark in the void. Don't see how it can be, but . . ."

Ten minutes to translation. Ten minutes to translation. Prepare for translation.

Got the announcement twice, once through the links and once through the speakers in the ready room. Military for you, redundancy in action. Checked my harness anyway.

The Gate filled the screen, a greenish white torus with a black-silver center opening almost a kay across. Frigging big Gate . . . biggest one I'd ever seen. Had to be to handle the *Magellan*. We seemed to hang short of it, while the Gate got bigger and bigger in the main wall screen.

Tepper dropped into the couch to my right. Didn't look at me as she strapped in.

Five minutes to translation. All personnel in secure stations . . .

"Can't be many other Gates that big." Wanted to get a reaction from Tepper.

"I doubt there are many left that large. It's based on the original Gates for colony ships."

"Was it a colony Gate?"

"I'd doubt it, Lieutenant, but I don't know. Some things they don't tell majors."

"D.S.S. doesn't seem to tell anyone much."

"It's called 'need to know,' and they think that makes it harder for people to find out."

Major sounded skeptical about need to know. I'd always been skeptical. Seemed like the other folks found out anyway. The only ones who got hamstrung from lack of information were the ones who needed it most. The bureaucrats insisted on the secrecy. That might have worked back before nets and microtronics. Once data could be compressed so small that masses of it fit in speck of dust, most security measures were only delaying tactics. The Comity had used all the secrecy it could. We'd still been attacked before we got to the first Gate.

Stand by for Gate translation. "Stand by for Gate translation."

Looked up at the screen again. Before we had seemed to be holding in space, short of the Gate. Now, we hurtled at the silvered blackness in the center of the Gate.

Translation was like all the others. So much of mass differentials. Everything flashed white and black simultaneously, and we went null grav. Then black turned white, and white black, and all the colors inverted into their frequency complements. White and black strobed, seemed like forever, except it wasn't, and we were back in normspace with full grav.

The screens had all blown—first impression I had. A moment later, I could see the faintest patches of white, really faint. Kept trying to find stars, real stars.

Caught Major Tepper looking at me, amused smile on her face. "Commander Morgan told you we were heading into an intergalactic void, Lieutenant. Didn't you believe him?"

"Some things . . . have to see for yourself."

"That can get dangerous, crack pilot or not."

"Two more translations?"

Tepper nodded.

"How long in normspace before the next Gate?"

"That depends on how accurate the translation was for us and for the *Alwyn*. I'm not linked to Control at the moment. So I don't know."

"You don't?"

"No. The possible errors are too large." Tepper unfastened her harness and stood. Didn't look back as she left the ready room.

"Were you trying to piss her off, Jiendra?" asked Lerrys.

"Me?"

"You." He unfastened his restraints, stretched as he stood. "This is the biggest expedition in human history. Tepper's only Morgan's number two. Morgan's probably got orders to keep everything quiet until we're close to our destination."

"No one could follow us through a Gate."

"Unless they're on board. I'm sure there are some agents in the crew or the scientists."

"You sound like a spy type yourself, looking everywhere."

"I'm not. You're not. Braun's not, and I doubt if any of the senior officers are. Beyond that, anyone can be compromised, and the stakes are higher than you seem to understand."

"So there are aliens, or there were. So what?"

"So . . . after more than five millennia of thinking we're the pinnacle of intelligent life in the Galaxy, if not in the universe, we're about to bring back proof we're not. If Morgan is right, these departed aliens may have known far more than we've discovered. What's a technology like that worth? What would the Sunnis or the Covenanters give to have that? Or to keep the Comity from getting it? What about Old Earth and the League? Or the Middle Kingdom or the Chrysanthemum Worlds? Go ahead, tell me I'm full of crap, Jiendra."

Didn't say a word. If I did, I'd regret it. Who the hell was Lerrys to lecture me? Sure, we might find tech stuff like that out where we were headed. But who said we'd understand it or could even use it?

After he left, I looked at the screen again. Mostly saw blackness. Not much in the way of individual stars. Figured what looked like nebulae and stars were distant galaxies. Few enough of those. Meant that there was dust of some sort out there. Wasn't anything anywhere near, and we weren't any more than a third of the way to Danann.

Lerrys might be right. Damned if I wanted to tell him.

27 GOODMAN/BOND

"Duty stations for Gate translation!" The announcement blared everywhere.

Chief Stuval looked at me. "To your station, Bond. You can finish the inventory after translation." He frowned. "Even on a new ship, there's always something missing. You'd think that they do it on purpose."

I laughed. It was expected. "Maybe they do."

"No. They just don't know any better. Ground-huggers never do. They don't understand ships or space or translations. They never have. You got to wonder how many ships have been lost over the years because some numbers numbnuts wanted to save a few credits."

"There are always people like that."

"You're right, but when you've made as made translations as I have . . . you have to wonder." Stuval shook his head, then gestured toward the aft bay. "Better get strapped in."

Another minute and I settled into the restraint couch in the aft bay of the armory.

"Five minutes to translation. All personnel in secure stations. All personnel . . ."

I checked the restraints again. I didn't need to. Nothing ever happened during translation except null grav and disorientation. I sat there and thought how people had different reactions to Gate translations. Yet . . . why should a translation be different for every person? Everyone on a ship went through the same process and ended up in the same place. Did the translation affect different people's brains in different ways?

I almost laughed. *Everything* impacted people in different ways. Even looking at the stars affected them differently. How could anyone look at the vast order of the universe and not accept that there was a Creator? Yet some people denied it, as if chaos could ever create order, as if, in a galaxy where there was no intelligent life except mankind, that was an accident. But were we still in our Galaxy? Or did God limit intelligence to one species in each galaxy? If He did, where had the aliens come from?

With that thought, I had to consider my mission, again. I would have liked to send a message with the locator I had yet to construct. I needed to let the colonel and CIS know that the Sunnis were also trying to obtain whatever alien technology D.S.S. might find. There were two problems with that. First, I didn't know how to modify the locator enough to send a text or verbal message. Second, the colonel had emphasized that I wasn't to start on the locator until we were actually at our destination. Over the time since I'd been aboard the *Magellan,* I'd scoped out where most of the parts I'd need would be, but I'd have to cannibalize part of a working torp for the rest of it—in a way that couldn't be detected or traced to me.

"Stand by for Gate translation. Stand by for Gate translation."

I'd made enough Gate translations in my time, but not nearly so many as a midlevel D.S.S. tech would have. I still got nervous. Going through artificial hawkings seemed to violate something about the Lord's universe. I couldn't have said what, but to me it did.

When we went through the Gate, white turned black, and black was white. It took forever, yet it was over before I could think about it. After full grav returned, my stomach was still protesting the null grav during translation. I swallowed hard and forced things back where they belonged.

I waited several moments to let my guts settle.

"Translation is complete. Dismissed from stations to normal duties . . ."

I unfastened the restraints. I had an inventory to complete, and I was looking forward to it, because it gave me a far better sense of where everything was, and what would be easily missed, and what would not.

28 CHANG

After the first Gate translation, things quieted down. Farscreens didn't show that much, except the faint and distant galaxies. We spent three days moving at high sublight to get to the second Gate. Before I'd become a pilot, I'd always wondered why Gates couldn't be reprogrammed to send ships to different places. That was before I understood the stress relationships between atrousans and gravitons. You try to use a Gate for more than one destination, and pretty soon you don't have a Gate. You put two Gates too close together, and pretty soon you don't have either one. That was what happened to some of the military Gates in the Dirty War and why Gates are spaced far apart outside inhabited systems.

After the second translation, the captain had announced we had another day and a half of sublight travel to the third Gate. Ship seemed quieter, subdued.

I was one of the last into the mess at the evening meal on threeday. I'd been in bay two inspecting shuttle one, checking things out, trying to get a better feel for it. Powered up the internal systems and ran through the checklists. Some say you can do that sort of thing with a simulator. You can't. Not the same. Feel's important.

Only table with much space and anyone I wanted to talk to held Lerrys,

Morgan, and Tepper. Soon as I sat down beside Morgan, Liam Fitzhugh and Alyendra Khorana took the last two seats. Fitzhugh sat next to me, Khorana between him and Tepper.

Rather would have had Khorana next to me. Fitzhugh was always spouting something. Not exactly loud, but firm.

I turned to Morgan. "What ever happened to all that debris? The stuff that piled up against the shields? I was thinking about our return. There was enough there to strain shields if we hit it at any high-sublight velocity."

"The captain decided to push it out of the way and leave it behind," Morgan said. "She accelerated, pulsed the shields, and changed headings twice. It's still somewhere around the second Gate, but shoved far enough away so that we won't run into it coming back."

"Debris? In space?" asked Khorana.

"The debris from the destruction of the Sunni ship . . ."

As Morgan explained, I looked toward the captain's table, where some of the physical scientists had been invited, probably to explain their specialties and what they hoped to find to the Special Deputy Minister. I recognized the faces, but couldn't put names to all of them. Ferward was there, along with Koch. He was an organic chemist.

". . . while space is big, and it's unlikely that we'd actually run back into that debris," Morgan was finishing up, "it certainly doesn't hurt to be cautious and shove it out of the return corridor to the Gate."

"Such residues wouldn't include anything explosive, would they?" asked Fitzhugh.

"There might be a torp predetonator, or something like that. There wouldn't be anything else explosive in and of itself. It we hit a lot of mass at high sublight, it could wreak havoc on the shields, and that could be as bad as a torp."

"My understanding was that shields were deployed in a curved array designed to divert such masses from actual physical impact with the vessel . . ."

"They'll divert a few tonnes," Morgan replied with a laugh. "They won't divert large metallic asteroids or other ships of significant mass. Or planets or suns."

Morgan was oversimplifying. The shields would also throw the *Magellan* out of the way of such large masses. Doing that would make a mess out of the insides of the ship, and anyone who wasn't restrained. That was why all sorts of detectors were focused ahead of the *Magellan*. Ships still got lost. I didn't want to hear any more about what I already knew. I turned to Fitzhugh. "You're a historian, aren't you?"

"After a fashion. My expertise lies in historical trends. That includes studying nodal points to determine which factors are causal and which are merely correlative, analyzing seemingly unrelated aspects of a culture's history to ascertain whether they are part of the trendlines, symptomatic, or merely noise surrounding the signal, so to speak."

"If . . . if we find something alien, do you think you'll be able to make sense of things?"

Fitzhugh paused. "That's a good question, Lieutenant Chang. I doubt that, if we do find remnants of an alien civilization, there will be cultural referents that will be meaningful, or even intelligible. In fact"—he laughed nervously—"I've pondered the rationale for my inclusion in this expedition. Not that I'd give up the opportunity willingly, you understand."

Had to admit I liked his honesty. Wished he'd give up using the largest possible words, though. "Do you think we'll find anything worthwhile?"

"To discover remnants of any intelligent life that is nonhuman would be of immense value, if only to disabuse the anthropic principle and those who have used humanity's apparent uniqueness as a rationale for theistically rationalized tyranny and ignorance."

"Surely, you don't consider the Covenanters and the Sunnis as theistically tyrannized?" That was Tepper, sardonic smile after her words.

"No, Major Tepper, perhaps my clarity was lacking. They tyrannize their own people, and would do their best to tyrannize others, rationalizing their actions on the basis of ancient theistic beliefs that state such a deity gave humanity dominance over the universe, but only so long as men, and I use that gendered term advisedly, placed that deity above all and followed the deity's commandments and those of the deity's prophets."

"I don't think you'll be on their list of the saved, Professor," suggested Morgan.

"Nor would I wish to be, not under the conditions they specify for such salvation."

Had to admit that Fitzhugh's attitude—under all the words—was more to my liking than a lot of the civilian experts I'd heard. Not that I'd ever see him outside the mess or talk to him once the expedition was over. Still . . . there was something about him. Talked like a professor, but nothing else was professor-like. He was as big as a Marine, no fat, either. He moved quickly, and his eyes flicked from point to point, like a cat's. Maybe like his mind did, too.

Didn't think anyone else saw that, either. They just heard all the big words.

29 BARNA

I wasn't about to ask the three shuttle pilots to sit for a portrait. Instead, I managed to sneak some imager shots of them in the officers' mess, and once in the ship corridors. There was plenty of time to work on that composition, because the farscreens just showed dark patches with faint hazy white globs. I could only get them magnified to barely recognizable images of galaxies. I hadn't seen much of Elysen for days, not since after the second Gate translation. She and the other astronomers and astrophysicists were already buried in some project.

I just kept working on what I could. I'd created a replica of the *Magellan* itself, based on the closescreen images I could get and upon the material in the ship's system, and I'd finished a portrait of Elysen that both she and I liked.

On fourday, just before lunch, she appeared at the door to my studio work space. "Could I persuade a hardworking artist to accompany me?"

"You could." I rose. I wished I were clever with words, but I never had been. "You've been busy."

"Very busy. It's been a great amount of work for not much of a result. Not so far, at least." She smiled. "I'll tell you about it after I get something to eat. It won't take long."

"To eat?"

"To tell you."

We walked down the passageway toward the lifts.

"How many of you are working on this?"

"Just four. Another astronomer, an astrophysicist, a physicist, and me. Cleon and I are limited in what we can add. He's the physicist and does the calculations. I comment and ask inane questions."

I couldn't imagine Elysen asking inane questions.

When we reached the mess, she pointed to a table in the corner, where an older major sat with some of the scientists. I knew their faces, but not their names. "Let's sit over there. Kaitlin Henjsen can be very interesting, even if she is a close friend of my grandniece."

Her grandniece? I didn't know what to say about that, or about her grandniece's choice of friends. "Which one is she?"

"She's the thin blonde. She's an archeological technologist."

"I didn't know such a profession existed."

"There aren't many. She was the lead on the New Cumorah project."

I'd never heard of New Cumorah.

"That was an archeological expedition to the New Zion system. A solar flare wiped out all life on the inner planets more than two hundred years ago. Recently, there was some question whether the flare was caused by New Zionist technology. The Sunnis had claimed it was the Will of Allah . . ." Elysen broke off and nodded to Henjsen. "Might we join you, Kait? This is Chendor Barna."

"Please do. I'm pleased to meet you, Chendor. Ely has told me about the portrait you did of her. It must be marvelous. She's a perfectionist."

"You're too kind." What else could I say?

"Neither Ely nor I is kind." Kaitlin offered an expression that was wry, not exactly a smile, but not disapproval. Her forehead wrinkled slightly, and her thick blonde eyebrows lifted. Unlike Elysen, while she was tall, she was fine-boned, with a small but squarish chin and gray eyes that could look as cold as rain-soaked stone when she was angry, I suspected.

"Perfection is hard on kindness." I eased into the seat across from her and on Elysen's right.

"Spoken like a true artist," added the black-haired man to Kaitlin's right. "I'm Royal Torres. Paleontology."

There was a momentary silence. I looked at Elysen. "You never finished explaining."

"It's something I've always wondered about, and since we were here . . ."

"Wherever 'here' is," murmured Torres.

". . . it seemed like a worthwhile idea. We've been making observations— the ones that we can with the relative velocity of the *Magellan*—trying to determine the gas density of the hole in the Small Wall."

"Small Wall?" My murmur was almost inadvertent.

Elysen turned to me. "I'm sorry, Chendor. The Small Wall of Galaxies is a section of the universe. Generally, the spacing is regular, far too regular for chance, except there's nothing that suggests it's anything but coincidence, but there is a hole in that spacing, and we have a chance to take observations that the earlier astronomers who studied it could not do." She smiled. "They were called the Hole-in-the-Wall gang and never had the data to reach a consensus. Since the exact center of the graviton trace line of Chronos appears to come from the hole in the Small Wall, persuading the commander that it might be relevant was not too difficult, particularly since there appear to be traces of some unusual energies involved. This could be of import, because the concentration of matter in the hole in the Wall is extraordinarily low and comes from a later date than the galaxies of the Small Wall, all of whom are true second-generation population-two galaxies."

I was still lost, but nodded.

"We're not that far, not in astronomical terms, from where Chronos and Danann started, and they represent at least a high Type II civilization . . ."

"How did you know where they started?" asked Kaitlin abruptly.

"Once we knew that Chronos and Danann were on the opposite ends of the same course," Elysen replied, "that wasn't too hard. We did have to persuade Commander Morgan to surrender some navigational information. When we explained the significance to Project Deep Find, he provided it. He wasn't totally enthusiastic, and he made us sign a secrecy agreement of sorts."

"What have you discovered?" I finally asked. "And what's a Type II civilization?"

"A Kardashev Type II civilization is one that can harness all the energy from a single star. A Type III civilization should be able to harness all the energy from a single galaxy. Not that anyone knows how that might be done. We humans are roughly a low Type II." She paused to take a sip of wine. "As for what we've discovered . . . nothing. That's what's surprising. We'd always thought that the hole in the Small Wall was just a random effect, or even a thick intergalactic dust cloud. It's not. It's truly a hole, and the samplings and observations we've taken over the last day seem to support that."

"A hole? A hole in the universe?" That seemed unlikely, but I was only an artist. I depicted what was there, usually, not what wasn't.

"In a way. It's as if something had been removed once, somehow. Over the eons, gases have drifted in, pushed and pulled by various forces, but the area that we think is where the two bodies started out is closer to a pure vacuum than anywhere else we've found in the universe. That's a preliminary observation, of course. We'll need more and better data to confirm that."

"What does that mean?"

"It's unprecedented." Elysen shrugged and smiled. It was an expression that even the ancient Leonardo would have called enigmatic. "If . . . if the finding holds . . . who knows?"

"You don't use terms like 'unprecedented' lightly, Ely," Kaitlin pointed out.

"It's anomalous, just like Chronos. Two connected anomalies generally mean that either the data or the observations are wrong, or that our understanding of that aspect of the universe is about to change. I don't know which it might be yet. There's no point in speculating."

"Do you think that Danann will help?"

Elysen shrugged again.

I looked to Kaitlin. "Do you think you'll find anything of interest on Danann?"

"Even the preliminary data suggests there is a great deal of interest on Danann. Whether we can make any sense out of it . . . that's another question."

"You may be able to accomplish more than any of us scientists." Elysen looked at me.

"Me?" As I spoke, I could see a tightness in Kaitlin Henjsen's face. She didn't like the idea that an artist might discover more than an archeologist.

"Images spark ideas," replied Elysen. "That could be because most artists work more directly from the subconscious. My only suggestion would be that you don't be secretive with your work. Let people see it, even before it's finished."

I couldn't stop the wince. I hated to display unfinished work.

"Chendor," Elysen went on, "you don't have to show it publicly. Just let a few of the scientists working in that area see it."

I *might* be able to do that.

30 CHANG

Sevenday night was when we went through the third Gate. I didn't have duty, and it was late. Knew we had another day or more after translation before we got near Danann. Didn't watch. Just strapped into my bunk. Barely woke up for the moment of null grav, then went back to sleep.

Oneday, I spent another couple of hours in the shuttle, going through systems checks, running sims, until Morgan chased me out. He told me some of the backups needed time, too. Braun and Lerrys would have told me. Besides, I'd checked with them.

Went back to the ready room at fifteen hundred for the pilots' briefing. Braun and Lerrys were already there. Morgan wasn't in the ready room, but Tepper was. So were the surviving needleboat pilots, all but Shaimen. She was still in sick bay, but likely to get out before long.

Tepper had the farscreens focused on Danann. Could barely see it. Not much more than a dark orb, even with full enhancement.

"We won't be in orbit until tomorrow around ten hundred. The *Alwyn* is already running sweeps. There's no sign of any life or energy concentrations except for the expedition. Even so, we'll be maintaining full defensive surveillance the entire time the expedition is here."

Full defsurv in the middle of an intergalactic void? Couldn't fault it, but had to wonder whether we had to worry more about alien defenses billions of years old than Sunni or Covenanter attacks. How would anyone track us through three Gates?

They couldn't. Didn't mean they didn't know our location. In a universe where nanosnoops were common and anyone could be adapted to be anyone else, nothing was secret for long.

"Can you tell us, Major," began Rynd slowly, "what happened to the ships that vanished from the first expedition?"

"No. I'd like to. I'd like to know myself. So would everyone else. One instant, the *Norfolk* was in orbit and on station. She'd fired a flash torp to get a ground reading and spectra. The next moment she was gone. There were no traces of standard energy release, no weapons tracks or disruptions . . ."

Sounded like the *Norfolk* had been translated. "There aren't any Gates around Danann?"

"No, Lieutenant Chang. That was Commander Danegel's first thought."

Tepper hadn't really answered the question behind the question. Should have phrased it better, but didn't want to try again.

Rynd looked to Lindskold, then to Rigney. All three looked at Tepper. Beurck didn't look at anyone.

"When something snatched a D.S.S. frigate, you want to know why we're back here?" asked Tepper "Isn't that in itself a good enough reason?"

That made sense. D.S.S. would love to have some sort of weapon that removed ships without a trace, and without evidence. Then, so would the Sunnis and Covenanters. The godlovers could use it to claim all sorts of things as the will of their god.

"It's risky, but as Commander Morgan pointed out, we don't have that much time before no one will be able to research what may exist on Danann. If we don't look now, we don't get a good look at all. The *Alwyn*'s security sweeps haven't revealed anything unexpected." Tepper looked at me, then at Braun. "We'll be using the shuttles to set up an orbital commnet to cover the whole planet. Outside of tasks like that, the next few days will be orbital surveillance only."

Had to wonder how much good that would do. I hadn't forgotten how big the complex was that lay under the ice on that dark orb ahead of us.

31 GOODMAN/BOND

I'd just reported to the armory after morning quarters. I'd thought I'd round up a few connector blocs before the chief arrived. The aft bay was my work space, and over the last few days, I had begun to assemble some of the smaller items necessary for the AG signaler. Those were the components that looked harmless enough, and wouldn't be missed, except in a complete inventory, and we'd just completed one of those. Even if they found them in my work bins, no one would give it a second thought.

At breakfast, Klyseen had told me we were getting close to orbit. She'd know. She was one of the nav techs. I'd looked at the farscreens in the tech lounge after breakfast but couldn't tell that much. The renegade planet—they were calling it Danann, after some heathen god—looked featureless and gray to me. It could have fit the Prophet's definition of Gehenna, all cold and gray and filled with the souls of the damned.

I'd slipped a pair of the connector blocs into my bin and was laying out my gear for an inspection of the last torp that had been brought back by the needle-boats. We'd needed to replace most of the nav sections of the pair from the damaged boat. There hadn't been a mark on the two torps, and the accel monitors hadn't shown an overstress, but we couldn't get anything in the green. Ciorio couldn't tell me why, and neither could Chief Stuval.

I'd just gotten out the diagnostic kit when Ciorio came puffing into the bay. "Been looking for you."

"I've been here."

"You're always here, except when you're not. Anyway, we got to get ready for orbit," Ciorio announced. "We'll be there by ten-thirty, Major Sewiki says. Chief wants us to transfer four surveillance torps topside soon as we can get the slider ready."

"Did the chief or the major say anything about what we're orbiting?"

Ciorio snorted. "He doesn't know any more 'n we do. We don't even see the surveillance packs. Comm techs add them topside before launch."

Why was Ciorio telling me that? I knew, and so would any armorer tech second. Had I said something to indicate I knew less than I was supposed to? "What else is new? They've always been like that. They trust us to take out the warhead, but not see a frigging datapak."

"You got it."

"You really think there are alien ruins down there?"

"Got to be something, Bond. Got to be. Comity and D.S.S. space marshals wouldn't spend all those credits if there wasn't something."

"But what? The place is billions of years old."

"Beats me. Anyway, we got to get the surveillance torps up to the comm techs. Chief 'll burn both of us if we don't get moving."

As I maneuvered the slider toward the end bays, I wondered just how much Colonel Truesdale really knew. C.I.S. must have some idea where Danann was. The Galaxy was too big to scan everywhere for the signal from the locator I needed to get assembled. Still, I'd have to be careful . . . very careful. Ciorio and the chief kept close tabs on everything in the armory.

 **CHANG**

Soon as we got to orbit, Special Deputy Minister Allerde announced it on ship-wide screens, something about our real work just beginning. After the Sunni attack, I hoped the real work was a lot more boring.

The *Magellan* and the *Alwyn* orbited Danann twoday, threeday, and fourday. Sent out surveillance torps, imaged the planet with every kind of technology the Comity had. Lerrys, Braun, and I studied all the information about Danann. On twoday and threeday, we used the shuttles to place surveillance satellites and comm relays in equidistant orbital points. Easy job—lots easier than what I'd been doing on McClendon.

After that came sims in the shuttles. Also went over emergency procedures for planetside liftoffs and descents. Hadn't done that many in a while. Not many pilots did anymore, with most of the travel to orbit by elevator.

Ten-thirty on fiveday morning, I was running through the prelaunch check-lists for real.

Navigator Control, this is Porter Tigress. Standing by at prelaunch.

Porter Tigress, Control, wait one.

Sat in my armor, except for the helmet, and waited. Aft of me were five ground support techs, five scientists. Aft of them in the cargo hold was a tractor and a bunch of support equipment, including an interim power supply. Mass load was seventy percent of T-norm, the most I'd want to drop with onto Danann.

Porter Tigress, this is Navigator Control, stand by for null grav bay two.

Control, standing by.

Null grav gave my guts the usual momentary jolt. Boards were green.

Porter Tigress, Control, bay doors opening, atmosphere barrier in place.

Control, Porter Tigress, understand bay doors opening. Looked at the bay doors and the blackness beyond. Could sense where everything was through the links. You get used to the feeling of seeing nothing with your eyes, and yet they show you the images fed through the links.

Porter Tigress, Navigator Control, bay doors open, cleared to launch.

Control, Porter Tigress, uncradling.

Took only a moment to release the cradle blocks and pulse the steering jets—slower and more careful with the mass in the shuttle.

Porter Tigress, you are cleared for departure and descent to landing zone alpha.

Control, understand cleared for departure and descent. Eased farther away from the still-open bay door. Screens showed the *Alwyn* in a geostationary orbit halfway around Danann.

Planet hadn't had an atmosphere in eons. Not what anyone would call one. Still, there was a greater concentration of gas around the planet than in deep space, not enough for anything close to atmospheric lift. Not enough to stop me-teorites from impacting the surface. Enough to fry shields and hull if I dropped the shuttle in too fast and at too great an angle of descent.

Took it easy. Concentrated mass of the tractor and equipment aft meant I didn't want any abrupt changes in velocity or direction. Laws of motion can tear large holes in fast-moving craft from inside.

Navigator Control, Porter Tigress, beginning entry this time.

Stet, Tigress . . . good luck. Thought that felt like Morgan.

Thanks, Control.

Upper part of the entry was smooth. Dark, and that meant instruments and light-enhancers. No bumps . . . nothing. Had a straight-in to the beacon. Braun had guided it in with shuttle two earlier. Hadn't actually touched down.

Shuttle was at fifteen kays AGL. Dropped a good half kay below the opti-mum, drove me upward into the harness. How could we drop that much with no atmosphere? Did a quick systems scan. No power losses, and no drains on the system. No atmosphere, either. But . . . the shuttle had acted like it had lost power, even if the systems were functioning normally. Think about that later. I added more power and decreased the rate of descent.

Porter Tigress, interrogative status.

Control . . . status is green . . . some apparent turbulence, cause unknown. Have modified power curve.

Interrogative feasibility of safe landing.

Idiot question, even from Morgan. Nothing had changed the probabilities. Not yet. We all knew there were things we didn't know about Danann. Faint heart never conquered the unknown. *Navigator Control, Porter Tigress, feasibility remains unchanged. Proceeding with approach to landing zone alpha.*

Tigress, proceed with caution. Request abort and immediate return if additional turbulence encountered.

Have to see about that. Wild turbulence and I'd agree. A bump or two, no. *Control, will consider return if significant turbulence encountered.*

Stet. Good luck, Tigress.

That was as much of a concession as I'd get from Morgan. Concentrated on the last part of the approach. Dark as shit. No sun, no stars. Used low-intensity wide-angle light beams and enhancement to get visuals and match the instruments as I brought the shuttle across the flat expanse of ice toward the landing zone and the towers beyond. Beacon was set in circular open space with a three-kay diameter. Flat enough that it might have once been a lake.

Checked the course line and descent toward the beacon. Slowed and added more power.

Navigator Control, Porter Tigress, approaching landing zone alpha this time.

Tigress, understand approaching zone.

Slowed the shuttle. Through the screens, could detect towers, blue-silver-metallic. They rose out of the dark gray ice. Never seen ice that color. Some of that might have been enhancement coloration. Wasn't water ice, but frozen atmosphere and a few billion years of accreted material. Roughly twenty-five to thirty meters deep. Had no idea what the atmosphere had been, not exactly. Some sort of nitrogen-oxygen mix, according to the samples and the analysis, with oxygen almost twenty-five percent.

Checked the towers' height. I had the shuttle level with their tops when the altimeter hit a hundred meters AGL.

Set-down was gentle and full-power. That was to pressure the ice and make sure that it wouldn't collapse under the shuttle's mass. Ground scan showed solid before I eased off power.

Steam rose around us. Not really steam, but unfrozen gases. After a minute or so, concealed gases pattered back down on the hull, where some turned back into gas. Hull probably wouldn't cool to ambient while we were down. Made a note to mention the "steam" gas to Braun and Lerrys.

Shuttle sat on the gray icy stuff, just short of the beacon the Braun and the remote had landed on threeday. Checked the shuttle systems again.

Navigator Control, Porter Tigress landed at zone alpha. Situation green this time.

Stet, Tigress. Cleared to unload and proceed at your discretion.

Nice of Morgan to allow me discretion. How could he tell from where he was?

Hit the local shuttle links. "Tech leader, science chief. We're down. You're cleared to disembark and unload according to plan."

The plan was that each group would leave one member aboard the shuttle to coordinate unloading for the techs and data transmission for the scientists. Lead scientist was the number two chemist—Willis Synor. Tech crew chief was Suryvan Patel.

Patel came back first. "Lieutenant, we're letting the science crew take their initial scan and measurements before we brace the ramp and unload the tractor and support equipment."

"Stet. Keep me posted." I felt heavy sitting at the board. I was. Instruments confirmed that Danann had surface grav of one-point-one-nine Tellurian. Outside temps weren't that much above absolute zero, somewhere just above 35 K, enough to have most atmospheric gases, the commoner ones anyway, frozen solid.

In between running systems checks, I used the farscreens to study the towers. Just blue-silver towers, shimmering with light reflected from the low-intensity lights beaming from the shuttle. Lights were necessary. With no heat to speak of and no suns or stars nearby, even enhancers didn't work—not without some radiation from somewhere.

One of the first items of cargo on shuttle two was a fusactor tractor. Braun would be bringing that down after I got back to the *Magellan* and debriefed her. Morgan and the captain were cautious that way. Suited me fine. Captain had laid down the law—only one shuttle below orbit at a time. The *Alwyn* had a standard shuttle for a battle cruiser, the kind that could take twenty passengers comfortably and fifty packed to the gills in an emergency. Both the *Magellan* and the *Alwyn* also each had one auxiliary flitter that could land planetside and lift off with four passengers, but they'd take a long time to move things with all the scientists and equipment.

We had the first small section of the portable quarters for the planetside teams. My second drop would have more. They could have them. I'd rather be aboard the *Magellan*.

Ran another set of checks, then focused one of the screen imagers on the towers forward and to the right of the shuttle, trying to get a magnified image. That was one of my tasks, gathering images of all sorts, so long as it didn't interfere. There was an artist on board *Magellan,* name of Barna. I'd seen him. Looked at us pilots strangely, more than once. Never had said anything, and I hadn't been about to ask. He'd be planetside once the science teams got set, but he and the nonimmediate priority team members needed what images I could get.

Towers didn't seem all that tall, less than a hundred meters above the ice, and wider than those I'd seen in places like Hamilton or Fiorenza. No battlements, merlons, crenellations—just smooth spires ending in a rounded dome. Took me several minutes to realize two other things. Nothing had stuck to the towers, and there was no external damage. None.

Shivered at that thought, and it wasn't because of the cold outside the shuttle.

"Lieutenant, science crew is clear. We're going to move some of the gear before we take the tractor down the ramp." Chief Patel's voice came in clear.

Reminded me how much I'd missed good equipment. Comm at McClendon had been scratchy, off-freq; and that had been when it worked. "Stet. What's it like out there?"

"Vacuum with heavy grav." Patel's tone was wry.

"Take care." Things fell faster and harder in twenty percent stronger gravity. Just hoped that all the specs for the gear had taken that into account. "What's a good estimate for off-loading time?"

"Hard to tell, sir. Judge another two stans, no more than three once we get the portables up for the team."

"Thanks."

Accessed the comm again. *Navigator Control, this is Porter Tigress. Off-loading proceeding. Estimate three stans to liftoff.*

Tigress, understand three stans to liftoff. Please keep Control informed.

Control, stet.

No way I wouldn't let Control and ops know. While I waited for Patel to finish unloading and for the crew to set up the first units of the portable base for the science team, with their largely self-contained atmospheric pressure and recycling systems, I went back to directing the imagers to pick up as many unique views as I could. Had to use low-intensity lasers to get even outlines in the darkness. The towers and the city—if it had been that—rose out of the eons-old gray ice. Almost looked as though it had been fresh-built, then abandoned. Also looked alien, not like I would have expected. The proportions were all wrong, but not any way I could have described. Color was off the same way. Could have been an effect of the light-enhancers, or maybe time had changed the color, but I didn't think so.

Kept thinking about the power loss on the descent. With an atmosphere, power loss on descent wasn't as critical. Without one, like now, power loss on ascent or descent was a problem. Began to run diagnostics on the power system between my efforts at catching images.

After half a stan, I'd run every test I could think of—that I could do planetside. Results confirmed momentary power loss, so momentary that it almost hadn't been there. But it had.

Problem was that shuttle one couldn't be inspected, not on Danann. Too many microtronic and nanotech components. So how did I get back with a lift profile that provided enough power before something blew?

Ran a profile of standard lift pattern, then identified the most vulnerable section, assuming a one-grav baseline. Danann wasn't, but most techs wouldn't have the equipment to make that kind of mod. If I used everything, and cut back on the internal grav, I could get us to midorbital velocity well before standard. That *might* do it.

Sat back in the couch . . . thinking. Did I want to try?

What was the alternative?

Shuttle couldn't be repaired planetside, not if what I thought had been gimmicked had been. Taking it apart to discover that would leave it grounded—permanently. Whole mission would be compromised—and if the captain had to deal with one shuttle lost to sabotage, how could they risk the other one to carry the heavy loads? If I got shuttle one back, claiming guts and dumb luck, Morgan might suspect I knew more, but he wouldn't be able to prove it.

Whole thing pissed me off. Chance to find out about the only aliens—or alien ruins—we'd ever found, and someone was trying to stop the whole expedition. Didn't know whether it was politics over who got the technology or politics over religion. Didn't much care. Just knew they weren't going to blow the expedition by disabling or destroying any shuttle I was piloting.

If someone had rigged the shuttle for power failure, they'd want it where the shuttle couldn't recover or be recovered. I went back and recalculated an ascent profile. *Ought* to work. I shook my head. It would work just fine if nothing went wrong—and Morgan would call me a torch jockey then. I'd still ask for an inspection. Tell him I'd worried about the turbulence that wasn't.

I didn't do as good a job on getting the rest of the images for the science types still on the *Magellan,* but they'd have enough to study.

Wasn't that long—or didn't seem that long—before Patel's voice came over the shuttle voicelink. "Sir, everything's off-loaded and clear. Be another fifteen before we're buttoned up."

"Thanks, chief." After a moment, I added, "Chief . . . coming down was a little rough in places. We'll be using a higher-powered ascent because of the higher grav here. I won't be able to hold the internal grav at one. So make sure you're all secured."

"Thanks for the heads-up, sir."

I began the prelaunch checklist—longer and different for a lift out of a gravity well.

"We're clear and secured, sir."

"Stand by for liftoff."

Finally, before I powered up, I made a last check of the area around shuttle one. The science team had used the tractor to tow all the equipment and the portaquarters practically to the edge of where the towers were—a good kay away. Local west, I figured. Their portaspots were the only real light on Danann.

Navigator Control, this is Porter Tigress, commencing ascent and return this time.

Porter Tigress, Control, cleared to orbit and return.

"Chief . . . crew ready?"

"Ready, sir."

"Commencing liftoff." Took a slow deep breath, then took the internal gravs off-line. Every erg of power went to the drives. Shuttle exploded off the ice. No air, so no backblast for the team below. They were well clear anyway. Felt like one of the alien towers was pressing down on my chest. Kept pressing . . . Pressing.

Five kays AGL, ten . . . twenty . . .

Kept watching through the pressure.

. . . Fifty . . . hundred . . .

Just a little more . . . a little more.

Half the mass-weight vanished.

Amber flashed across the boards. Left converter had gone off-line. Not blown, just off-line, with no way to get it back. Dropped the power to the max for one converter.

Porter Tigress, Porter Tigress, interrogative status. Interrogative status. Morgan again, an edge to his words even through the links.

Control, wait one. Kept my voice level. Didn't know what the frig my status was. Quick check showed we had enough power left in the right converter and enough mass left in the steering jets to adjust course to make the *Magellan.* I'd done it well enough that we were almost direct on, anyway. *Control, Porter Tigress, status is amber, on course for return as planned.* Slower and later, but we'd make it.

Tigress, Control confirms return course. Morgan sounded worried and pissed.

Whole inside of my armor was damp—stress sweat—by the time I had shuttle one cradled in bay two and the outer locks were closed.

"Clear to disembark, chief."

"Yes, sir . . . could you tell me what happened?"

"We lost power. We'll have to check out why."

"Yes, sir . . ."

I unstrapped slowly. Sweat had puddled in my boots. Helmet in hand, I dropped out of the pilot's hatch.

Morgan was waiting outside in the bay. Didn't even wait for me to say a word. "What happened? Why did you overboost? You could have blown the whole shuttle, the whole expedition."

"I didn't overboost, Commander. My lift was within all safety parameters, sir. I certainly couldn't help it if the left converter dropped off-line."

"Dropped off-line? With your accel profile, are you sure you didn't—?"

"I didn't. It went. Have someone check the supercon lines to the converters. Someone who's never done the maintenance on shuttle one. If you find what I think you'll find, have him check shuttle two before you clear Braun to drop."

He frowned, the anger gone. "Why do you think that?"

"Shuttle's new. Built for this mission. Been everywhere except planetside. Couldn't prove it, but the converter cut out just above transition point. A couple of minutes earlier, and we wouldn't have made it back to orbit. Might have had a long-shot chance at making it back to the landing zone, but maybe not."

"I'm not following you, Lieutenant."

"Seen this sort of stunt once before. Grav cutout switch. They're not designed for one-point-two gees. We have to have greater initial accel . . ."

Could see the sudden understanding. "A tech . . . of course. Could be even deep-compulsion." He shook his head. "I'm crazy, buying into that until we know."

"I had to stretch shuttle one to its limits to do that pickup of Needle Four. If the converter had been the problem, a system glitch, it should have shown up then."

"We'll have to inspect and see."

"I'm going to write up the flight report, then get a shower."

"Stay in the ready room for a bit, Lieutenant."

"Yes, sir." Didn't see any point in arguing. So I sat down at one of the maintenance consoles at one side of the ready room and began to write up the report.

Didn't finish the report before Morgan was back in.

"You were damned lucky, Lieutenant. Or more than that." He was scowling.

"Damned good, Commander. If I hadn't recognized what was happening, the shuttle and everything in it would have been a pile of metal and composite somewhere down below us."

"You *knew* something was wrong. I had ops go back over your ascent track. You practically blew every propulsion system in the shuttle before you lost the converter."

"That's not true, sir. I stayed within parameters." Barely—but I had. I couldn't have used the photon-thrusters at all. No point in mentioning that. "I got to thinking about the power loss on the way down. Thought it was turbulence, but it might not have been." I shrugged. "The way the systems are engineered, I figured that a fast ascent would be safer. If I'd been wrong, it wouldn't hurt. Just wanted a safety margin, sir."

Commander's eyes narrowed into a squint. He opened his mouth, then snapped it shut. "Chang . . . your background says that you don't trust authority, and you don't share information . . . I don't like that."

Shouldn't have drafted me if he'd known that and didn't like it. Wasn't about to tell him. "Sir. I couldn't have explained something I started to feel on liftoff. As soon as I got back, I told you what I thought. Besides, even if I'd figured it out planetside, what could we have done? Left the shuttle down there as part of the ruins? And maybe lost shuttle two as well?"

He looked at me.

I looked right back at him.

"We'll talk about this more, later, Lieutenant. There are a few matters more pressing." Then he was gone.

More pressing than attempted sabotage? Or was he talking about dealing with my so-called attitude?

The shakes didn't hit me until I was halfway back to my stateroom. Hot shower helped.

I still wondered why anyone would go to such lengths. There was a good chance that the towers didn't hold anything humans could understand, let alone use. Yet the expedition had been attacked, and we had one case of sabotage, and Morgan was worried about more than the shuttle.

After I got warmed up and cleaned up, I almost didn't hit the mess, but I was starved. Sneaked in just before the captain and the Special Deputy Minister did, and sat with the recovery and archeological types—Kaitlin Henjsen's team, plus the silver-haired astronomer, Dr. Taube. She had to be really old. Mostly just ate and listened.

". . . first indications are that there aren't any obvious ways in . . ."

". . . definite measure of high tech . . ."

"What if it's not a city, just a technological system tied to Chronos? Then what?"

"Then, we do what we can," Henjsen said, "and help the technical and technological types figure out exactly what kind of machinery and equipment it is and why it was put there . . ."

Sounded like a straightforward type. I kept listening.

Morgan cornered me after dinner, right outside the mess. "We need to talk. Privately." He was still angry. Could tell it from the stiffness of his posture. "My office."

He turned, and I followed to the ramps. His office was up in the control sections of deck fifty. It wasn't any bigger than the one he'd had on Deep Find Station. Had hatches, not doors.

He closed the hatch. Didn't sit down and didn't suggest I should. "I told you I wouldn't stand for this kind of shit, Chang. We don't have room for hot-shit individualism."

Didn't feel like playing games. So I let him have it. "Morgan, I put my life on the line, and Patel's. That shuttle doesn't get back, and you don't have much of an expedition. Didn't see you risking your life. I didn't give Patel a choice, and I'm sorry about that. Anyone else but me, maybe Braun, in that shuttle, and all you got is junk, either sitting on that frozen-assed lake, or as wreckage strewn all across Danann. You're pissed because I didn't give you a choice. You ever think that I saved your frigging ass and your blessed career? Either way, you come out better. You really want to explain to His Highness the Special Deputy Minister why you grounded a shuttle that looks fine? Or ordered one up that went to energy and quarks?"

His lips tightened. But he didn't blow. Had to give him credit for that. Been in his skintights, and I would have reamed me halfway to the void and back. Showed why he was a commander, and I'd never be anything like that.

"Lieutenant . . ." He took a deep breath, then another one. Then he shook his head. "You are a piece of work. I tried a sim. Crashed every time, and I *knew* what was going to happen."

"That's why I'm a pilot, and you're a commander."

"I don't need more smart-ass shit."

"I'm sorry." That stopped him. He didn't expect that. "I didn't mean it that way. Meant that you plan. For organization and running things, planning is better. Piloting is as much instinct as planning. I told you it was feel. I've got a better feel for piloting than you do. I'd also make a mess of what you do."

"Have you told anyone?"

"No, sir. I hadn't planned on it, and I don't intend to." Would have been stupid, too. Letting anyone know that I'd known there had been sabotage and that I'd lifted off would make the crews nervous. The way it was, word would get around that there had been a problem and that I'd handled it. That was all anyone needed to know. "Did you find out how it happened?"

"Junior mech. He's in the brig. Not that we'll find out anything from him. The moment he realized he'd been caught, nanite routines kicked in. Most of his adult memories are gone."

Shit! That meant either a big multilateral or one of the major intelligence services—CW, Middle Kingdom, or the League.

"Exactly." Morgan could see I'd understood. "This stays between us."

I nodded. It had to be, mostly. "The captain might know. She's sharp."

"You actually admit someone else might be?"

"There are people smarter than I am. They just can't do what I do." I stopped, then added, "Sir."

"Chang . . . you are an interstellar—make that an intergalactic—pain in the ass. It's too bad you're such a damned good pilot." He almost smiled, but it wouldn't have been a good smile. "Lerrys will take the drop tomorrow. You need the time off."

Didn't protest that. "So long as I've got the one on sevenday."

"You're on the schedule."

We just looked at each other. Both understood how it stood. He was a better officer and commander. I was a better pilot. Wasn't a lot more to say.

Still felt shaky when I headed back to my stateroom. Hoped sleep would help.

33 CHANG

I might not have been flying for the next day or so, but I wanted to know what sort of inspections had been done on the shuttles. Also needed to smooth things over with Morgan. No sense in having him pissed for the whole mission. Could be more than a year.

Knew he ate early. I hated getting up so long before quarters. Did anyway on sixday. Struggled into skintights and vest and shorts. Got to the mess before he did. Lagged to one side, looking for him.

He saw me, looked away.

"Commander . . ."

"Yes, Lieutenant." His voice might not have been as cold as the ice on Danann. Close, though.

"If I could speak to you for a moment?"

He stepped to the side of the corridor. "You've got your moment."

"Sir . . . I wasn't subverting your authority yesterday. I was trying to do what I thought best to keep you from being put in a difficult situation. I'm not D.S.S. Never will be. You know that, but I wouldn't have . . . presumed to question your authority . . ." What else could I say?

"Lieutenant . . ." He actually sighed. "Is this an apology?"

"If it needs to be, sir."

For a moment, he looked at me. Hard. "Let's have breakfast. I'll fill you in on what the mechs found out. You need to eat. You look like shit."

"Yes, sir."

He shook his head again. "Pilots." The word was spoken low enough that he could have denied it.

"Yes, sir. They're almost as bad as . . ."

"As what, Lieutenant?" There was a trace of humor in his words.

"Bureaucrats . . . politicians . . . maybe ship captains."

"Sometimes, pilots are worse." He gestured to one of the tables where no one was sitting. "Pilots as a species are actually indispensable. Politicians and bureaucrats only think they are." Morgan sat down.

I decided against asking if he'd had troubles with Allerde. He'd told me.

A steward arrived with coffee. I was more than ready for it. Six hundred ten was far too early for me to be functioning—except on duty, and I'd always hated the early shifts.

When the steward left, the commander looked at me. "You were right. We checked over both shuttles. There were cutouts on shuttle two. There was also a device of unknown capabilities attached to shuttle two's fusactor controls. We blew an armor jetpak pushing it clear of the *Magellan*. We've put the shuttles under extra surveillance, also certain other sections of the ship, and we're looking for . . . irregularities . . . in other areas."

"What about the *Alwyn*?"

"We messaged them suggesting a similar inspection. They found nothing."

Caught the dubious tone in his voice. "You're worried about that?"

"I'm worried that they didn't find anything."

"Better hidden or not yet planted?"

"I'd guess the latter." He took the coffee mug and sipped, held it below his chin, with some of the steam rising into his nostrils.

Waited for him to say something else. He didn't.

Steward delivered an omelet—looked like yellow plastrene with embedded mushrooms. Took a small bite. I'd tasted better. Eaten a lot worse, especially on the McClendon contract. Had to keep that in mind.

Morgan didn't even look. He just ate.

Decided to see if Morgan would say more. I chewed the egg stuff and finished a mug of coffee. Steward refilled it.

"We knew this would be tough," he finally mused.

"Everyone's afraid D.S.S. will get better technology from the expedition."

"That's some of it, but not as much as people would think." He swallowed more coffee, gulped rather than sipped. "Humans have been alone in the Galaxy for millennia. There's not been any trace of other intelligence. When you think about it, there's not even that much life that seems to have the possibility of evolving sentience. I'd say that's because the conditions for life evolving above the microbial level are rare. They're even rarer for intelligence evolving. It took something like three tries before it happened on Old Earth, and it was a perfect incubator."

"Makes sense." He was going somewhere.

"Does it? Or is it because some prime mover, some deity, arranged it that way—the old intelligent design theory?"

"I'd opt for chance."

"So would I. Most people won't. Most people believe there has to be a cause. Most of them believe humans are something special in the universe."

I snorted. Seen too many people who were anything but special.

"So what happens when we prove that we're not special?" he asked. "When we discover that the only other intelligence we ever have encountered vanished billions of years ago, and that they were smarter and accomplished more?"

"You think so?"

Morgan's laugh was low. "All of our high-tech equipment, and we can't even find the entrances to that city, or whatever it is. The material they used would survive anything up to a nova, and I'm not sure it wouldn't survive that unless it were in the center of the star. It's likely that these Danannians created Chronos as well. It's a mass almost exactly the same diameter as Danann, except that it's two hundred eighty times denser. We can't even get close to it—but it's semicollapsed matter, or an entire sphere composed of something incredibly transuranic. Danann isn't even the center of anything. It looks more like a colony or an outpost. Just one city, or hive, or station on a planet, and they sent it spinning off into the galactic void . . . ."

"You think they *sent* it?"

"They had to, if you consider it. There's no trauma to the planet, no apparent damage to the structures. They just sealed everything and left."

"Where did they go?"

"The scientific types are working on it. Dr. Taube says she has a theory, but she needs more information before she'll say more. Something about a possible Type III civilization."

Just sat there for a time. Held the coffee mug. Supposed I was more like most people than I'd thought. Aliens . . . smarter than we were. Lots smarter. They'd built an outpost on a planet and whipped the planet through space. The outpost was bigger than any single human city, and it had lasted unchanged for billions of years. Then they vanished. Or they went back where they'd come from.

"You see, Chang?" Morgan said softly. "What does that do to everyone who thinks we're special? Or to all the religions who believe in an anthropic creator? It's the biggest threat ever to their beliefs and their existence."

Guess I hadn't seen it quite that way. Always had thought anyone who felt people were a divine creation was deluded beyond belief. How could anyone believe that an omnipotent being would create so many frigging idiots?

"Way back in history . . . they burned the first scholars who suggested that

Old Earth's sun wasn't the center of the universe. Millions have been killed because they wouldn't accept this or that god. We've been fighting the believers for
millennia. What do you think they'll do if we present them with Danann? Do
you really think they'll accept the evidence?"

Saw where he was going, and I didn't like it at all. "Danann's out here in the
middle of nowhere."

"And in a few years no one will be able to reach it at all," Morgan pointed
out. "If the expedition doesn't return . . ."

And I'd thought he was worried about holding his rank.

Now I'd be looking at every tech cross-eyed.

"Thanks, Commander." Tried to make the words light and ironic.

"You're most welcome, Lieutenant."

Almost wished we hadn't talked. But Morgan wasn't glaring at me anymore.

34 FITZHUGH

Professors of historical trends were neither necessary nor invited to be among the first of those descending to Danann on the shuttlecraft. While I awaited my turn in the scholarly queue, so to speak, I passed the hours in scrutiny of the images and preliminary reports sent up from the world below, breaking the monotony with ever-more-strenuous workouts, if undertaken at times when few were present, especially in the high-gee section. After a week, I was finally summoned to the boat deck—or whatever it was called—and was fitted for space armor, most necessary because Danann had no atmosphere, other than what was solidified and exceedingly chill, from which protruded the metallic towers, and elsewhere low peaks of a singularly rounded and worn appearance. I was not told when I might actually be required to wear the armor.

I was no geologist, but the worn nature of the peaks suggested erosion and antiquity. Since Danann had no atmosphere, however, I doubted that any measurable erosion had occurred for eons, if not longer. Paradoxically, the precise and preserved rounded architecture of the towers and the other structures implied a less ancient origin or great powers of endurance and preservation, if not both, and that, in turn, implied a stable political system. That degree of stability could most likely only have come from either great power or a unique degree of social consensus, if not both.

None of the Danannian structures had yet been opened. According to the briefing messages posted on the expedition net, all the entrances were buried under the ice of ages, and none of the structures had discernible windows or means of entrance or egress. Cleon Lazar—one of the physicists—noted that the seeming lack of upper-level access might be deceiving because the outer walls appeared to be a material with the most adamantine features of anomalous metals and the temperature indifference of the best structural composites. Such a material could be transparent from the inside and opaque from the outside. It would also be a perfect material for interstellar vessels—if anyone could ever figure out how the Danannians had created it.

Because the towers appeared featureless to the imaging technology used to penetrate the ice and frozen atmosphere, the technical crews supporting the archeologists and scientists on site had decided to pick one tower and just melt their way down to ground level, but progress was slow because of the cold—water refroze instantly, and gases turned into atmospheric snow inside the tubing designed to vent and carry the melted material away. At the same time, no one wanted to destroy anything in the process.

To me, the towers themselves seemed . . . low. Their comparative lack of height, given the vastness of the city, if that was what it was, and their failure to soar skyward, suggested alienness to me far more than did their silvered-bluish metallic surface, a surface, the scientists had also reported, reflected light and all other forms of radiation in a nonimaging, almost inchoate waveform. No matter what was placed before the surface and how it was lighted, the surface appeared silvered blue without any images being reflected.

If the Danannians had observed the universe around them as we do, brilliant image-radiation-reflective exterior surfaces would have made perceptions outside the structures difficult under any sun, if that world had once been within a solar habitable zone. Conversely, if their perceptual senses were radically different, they would not have needed to employ such a modified-reflective material, unless, of course, the level of reflectivity happened to be irrelevant, and that would have seemed highly unlikely for a city—or a gathering of structures—that extended across an oval three hundred kays at its narrowest point.

The initial images and reports had not revealed any sort of internal mass transportation system other than the radial "boulevards" on each side of the "canals" that linked the perfectly oval "lakes." Depth imaging suggested that the "lakes" and "canals" had indeed been designed so that they would hold water. Whether they had or not remained to be determined.

Then there was the putative connection with Chronos, suggested in the briefing materials. I liked the name "Chronos" to the same degree as "Dannan," that is, not at all. Chronos meant time, and a planet was not "time." I suspected that someone had meant "Cronus," after one of the ancient old Earth gods who had predated another ancient deistic tyrant, and, thus, Cronus would have made more sense . . . but most obviously it had been named by a scientific type, because mythology was one of the few nonmilitary subjects with which space officers had a more than nodding understanding, as opposed to the scientists, all too many of whom dismissed mythology as part and parcel of irrational superstition.

"Liam?" Tomas had eased the doorway open.

I turned from the console. "Yes?"

"Have you been told when you might—"

"Have an opportunity to actually see what lies on the orb beneath us? Why would a mere professor of human historical trends, particularly one duped into believing he was on a magnificent Diplomatic Corps fellowship, think that such an opportunity might be afforded to him?" As soon as I'd spoken, I wished I hadn't. "I'm sorry, Tomas."

He laughed. "The words were well-spoken, Liam. You're as frustrated as anyone else still up here, but there's only so much space below. You'll get a chance, and before long. The gravity's twenty percent heavier, and some of the physical scientists will need a break."

"You're right. Besides, my presence would be superfluous at least until I could peruse the insides of the towers." I might not be able to learn anything from the interior, either. While the building shells had been preserved, had anything besides the structures themselves endured? For all that, I still wanted to observe and touch actual alien construction.

"They haven't even called me to fit me for space armor," Tomas said.

"I'm sorry. We will be here for a while."

"That's if the Sunnis or someone else doesn't track us," he pointed out.

"They can't use Comity Gates, and they don't know where we are. It took years for the Comity to locate Danann."

"All they have to do is find the right person to pay off with the appropriate spy technology, and they'll have the location."

"They'll still need to build Gates and get them into position."

"That's a matter of months if they want to cannibalize existing Gates. It could be less."

"You're such an optimist, Tomas. If their spy systems are good enough to find where Danann is, why don't they just wait and steal what we find out."

"Pandora's box. I doubt that the Sunnis or the Covenanters want it opened."

"Oh?" I had my own thoughts on that, but I wanted to hear what he had to say.

"All theocracies are based on limited truths—political, technological, and spiritual. The very existence of this planet widens human horizons and threatens those limits. The evolution of secular human governments is based on finding ways to increase individual freedoms while maintaining societal order. On balance, technology widens freedoms. Wider freedoms threaten the limits required by theocracies."

"Not always. The Saints have managed to integrate technology into a religiously limited society."

"They stopped being a viable society a millennium ago."

"They're still there."

"You argue well, Liam." Tomas laughed again. "You're right. But there's been a change over the centuries. They used to be able to expand their influence into other systems and cultures. Now, those who can't accept a more open culture, technology, and lifestyle retreat to the Saint worlds."

I couldn't argue that.

After Tomas left, I looked at the latest data from Danann. I hoped it wouldn't be too long before they were able to gain access to the enigmatic towers. I couldn't help but worry that the Sunnis—or someone—might appear out of the void and that I would never descend to Danann. In the meantime, all I could do was study what was being relayed to the *Magellan*.

35 GOODMAN/BOND

Once the *Magellan* was in orbit, Chief Stuval established a routine. The operations officer was sending out surveillance torps daily. When they returned, we had to retrieve them from the boat deck and cart them down to the armory. They had to be inspected, repaired as necessary, and returned for another run. Torps weren't designed to be returned, not time after time. Doing the repairs was a real chore, but it kept us busy. It also made more of the parts I needed to assemble an AG signaler available. I could remove a directional bloc and test it, fail it, and install a new one. The old one still worked. I'd certify it as junk, but slip it aside.

A week in orbit passed, and a second.

I had the signaler in sections, hidden in various parts of the aft bay. I had to, because it would have been close to the size of a torp warhead altogether. Once I managed to get three more components—and the power module—I could assemble it and get it up to the boat deck, hidden in the slider's large tool bin. Then I could stash it in one of the shuttles in the cargo compartment, marked as replacement equipment to be sent down to Danann. The timer would be triggered by any grav shift, and the signal would go out, and would keep going out. Even if someone disassembled it on the surface, there'd be no real way to tell where it had come from, not for certain—and that was if anyone even recognized what it was.

On fourday of the third week after we'd reached Danann, I was working on replacing the nose assembly on a surveillance torp. One of the recovery mechs had bashed it with something. That was what it looked liked, in any case.

Chief Stuval appeared. He watched me for a time, but he didn't say anything until I had the replacement cone in place. "You did that neat-like, Bond."

"Tried to, chief. Thank you."

"You hear about what happened to Vaio?"

"Vaio?" I couldn't place the name.

"He's a repair mech for the shuttles. He was. He's in the brig. He has been for two weeks. The Marines have kept it real quiet. He did something to one of the shuttles, tried to get it to crash on Danann. The pilot managed to bring it back, and they tracked it back to him."

"Why would he do something like that?" It didn't make sense. If you wanted to sabotage the expedition, you'd need to do something that would damage or destroy the *Magellan*. That would amount to suicide, and no one sane would try that. Destroying a shuttle wouldn't stop the Comity from obtaining any alien technology. It might slow them down, but anyone intent on getting Satan's handiwork would find a way. Thinking about that, I still wanted to know why Major Ibaio had been so insistent that the alien technology was the Morning Star. He couldn't have known what might lie on Danann. If he had, wouldn't he have known the location?

Besides, so far, according to the techs in the mess, even the scientists hadn't really discovered anything. There was only the one city or whatever it was, a big silver-blue oval in the screens. To me, it looked more like a huge anthill or a sandwasp colony.

"Could be he's spy," the chief went on. "From the Covenanters, or even the League. They slow us down and demand we share the knowledge. They show up with a fleet, and the Comity might agree."

"Do you think so?"

"Is it worth another war, Bond?" Stuval snorted. "They've been pawing through that deep freeze for almost three weeks, and they still don't know any more than when we got here. The Danannians *were* aliens. We might never find out what it means."

I wasn't sure about that. Who knew what kind of secrets were buried down there? No one was going to let the techs know.

After the chief left the aft bay, I eased the torp onto the slider cradle, then stopped. There had been a Sunni attack. Now a shuttle had been sabotaged. I'd been inserted to send a locator signal. Yet no one even knew if there was anything of real worth on Danann. Or did they?

In the end, all I could do was my duty, and pray that it would be enough— and that whatever was down there wasn't the Morning Star . . . or anything close. Anything that had lasted billions of years and had once nearly sundered Heaven wasn't something meant for the hands of men.

36 BARNA

We'd been orbiting Danann for almost two weeks before I was fitted for space armor. After that, more than a week passed before I got word that I'd actually get a chance to use it and see the ruins of the city on Danann—the only one, from what the orbital surveys had confirmed. My "tour" planetside was set for three shipdays. In the meantime, I'd done what I could. I'd studied all the images sent up from the team on the surface, but they were only images. Images lacked the solidity of either reality or of art, although the ancient photographers would have argued that. They would have been wrong. An image is not what it portrays. That is the strength of art, because it allows a good artist to capture the essence of reality. A bad artist, unhappily, is worse than a photographer or an imagist.

I hadn't tried to create anything based on the images. That would have locked me into preconceptions when I hadn't seen the underlying reality. I'd never painted a portrait—or anything else—to my satisfaction when I'd relied exclusively on captured images. Rather than try to work from images when I hadn't seen what was behind them, I was still working on a group portrait of the three pilots.

Even before sixday finally came, I couldn't work on the portrait any longer.

I paced around in my spaces, but it was still more than an hour before I had to report to the shuttle in bay two up on the boat deck. When I heard Elysen murmuring from the adjoining work space, I left the portrait I hadn't really touched for the last day. It was one that would take more work. Some just do, no matter what you can visualize in your mind. I knocked gently on her half-open door.

"You can come in, Chendor."

Elysen sat before a console. Her short fingers flicked across the board, and on the screen above her star images appeared, then changed, and changed again.

"What are you doing?"

She did not look up. "I've programmed a regression analysis here. I'm not certain what it will show, but there's something not quite the way I would have expected it. Rather it is the way I had calculated, but not dared to expect."

That was a different way of saying it. I would have said it was not quite right, but "right" implied that a particular expectation was correct. Yet, as I observed Elysen, who hadn't even looked at me, I could see a regal and detached expression, as if she were the empress of the ancient skies her programming had re-created.

"I'm finally going down to see what the Danannians created," I said.

"Good. I'll look forward to seeing your paintings."

"You're not going down?"

"What point would there be to it?" she replied. "At my age, twenty percent more gravity would be less than pleasant. It could be worse than that. My work is up here. The *Magellan* is stable in orbit. I've got a remote system tethered off the hull, and I'm getting incredible images."

To go so far beyond the Galaxy and not take at least a look at the Danannian city? "You're certain you don't want to see it?"

"Later, I might. You *need* to see it. I'd like to see it, but it's not necessary. I'm getting to make observations I never thought would be possible. They're critical, I fear."

Fear? What was she observing? I decided not to ask. She wouldn't say, anyway. "I almost feel guilty about going down there. You're a scientist. I'm an artist."

"You feel guilty about too much, Chendor. Go. The rest of the Galaxy needs to see your images. They need those more than we need the science. They may need them even more." She still didn't look up, regally engrossed in the pattern of the stars changing on the wall screen before her. "Go."

I went, and I pondered Elysen's words as I took the lift up to deck forty-eight. I'd have to walk up the ramp to the boat deck. The only equipment I carried was a small bag with skintights for three days, toiletries, and a portable imager with every function I could afford. It was the kind that would work in a vacuum. There was no way I could paint directly, not with no atmosphere and such a low temperature. I'd just have to look and study what was there, as intently as I could, and use the images I captured as a way of recalling more than what the images showed.

I was glad I'd left early because it took me an extra fifteen minutes to find the equipment room where those of us traveling down to Danann were supposed to get helped into the space armor we would be wearing. When I was finally in the armor, I walked down the passageway to the ready room, carrying both my helmet and equipment bag.

I knew the other four expedition team members waiting there, if only by face and name. Melani Kalahouri, the alien psychologist, was listening to Reynol Torres.

". . . no sign of any remains, but I insisted that I could determine something of the nature of the Danannians from the interiors and exteriors of the structures . . ."

Maejean Polius stood alone, muscular and dark-skinned, more so in space armor. She looked toward the closed lock. I'd only spoken to her briefly. She was the expedition geologist.

Another woman entered the ready room—Kaitlin Henjsen. She wore armor that had more than a few scrapes and scratches. I couldn't help saying, "You must be on your second or third descent."

"Just my second. Dr. Chais sent me back up here for two days standard grav—and some sleep. Doctors can be tyrants."

"Only for people who drive themselves beyond their bodies." The words came out matter-of-fact, but I wished I hadn't said them.

She gave a small start, and a glare that quickly became a wry smile. "You sound like a doctor, not an artist."

"I'm sorry. I have this habit . . ." I didn't finish what I might have said.

She nodded, then looked away as a chief tech appeared beside the lock to the bay.

"You'll be boarding in just a moment. You'll each take a couch in the passenger compartment. Your equipment must be stored in the padded bins behind the passenger compartment. Your helmet must be secured in the bracket beside your couch, and must remain within your reach. After touchdown, you'll be instructed when to don it." The tech gestured to the lock door. "The shuttle is ready for you to board."

I let the others go first. The couches in the shuttle were oversized, at first glance, but as I saw Kaitlin Henjsen—wearing space armor—I realized the reason. There were ten seats, in five rows separated by an aisle, each seat by itself. I settled into the back, opposite Maejean. She didn't look at me. She didn't look at anyone. Behind me, I heard the lock close.

"Please remain in your couches until we have touched down at landing zone alpha. We will be going to null grav until we're clear of the ship."

Nothing happened for several minutes. Then my stomach tried to float up into my throat, and I was glad I hadn't eaten recently. No one said anything. I could feel some motion, but without windows or ports, it was hard to tell exactly where we were headed. The descent was smooth. The shuttle didn't bounce as I had expected. The pilot set us down with hardly a thump.

"You can release your harnesses now. Before you leave the passenger compartment, please put on your helmets. I'll be checking each one of you before you enter the lock. Make sure your comm unit is turned on."

I fumbled on my helmet and checked the comm. I discovered I was first in line. That made sense because I'd entered last. I recovered my equipment bag and walked to the lock door. Everything felt heavier. I hadn't thought it would be that noticeable.

The tech checked my helmet seal. "Is your comm on, sir?"

The sound in the armor was better than I'd thought. "Yes. I can hear you."

"Good. I'll cycle the lock for all of you once I've checked everyone. We don't have nanite barriers on shuttles. After the outer lock door opens, take the ramp down and hold on the dark plastrene waiting area until everyone is out. The groundside team will have someone there to escort you to the briefing room."

I nodded. Another briefing? I stepped into the lock and waited for the others to join me. Less than five minutes later I walked out through the outer lock door and down the ramp. The only sounds I could hear were those of my own breathing. The sole lights were those from the shuttle and from our own suits, Beyond their radius was a darkness that showed no signs of ever having seen illumination.

Plastrene or something like it had been sprayed in the form of walkway to a rectangle ten meters west of the ramp. The dull gray surface of both walk and rectangle was only a shade or so darker than the ice around it. A figure in armor waited for us.

Kait Henjsen didn't bother with waiting or the briefing. Unlike the rest of us, she nodded to the waiting tech and kept walking. I didn't hear anything, but she must have used another band for her communications.

"Good day." The voice was male and professionally cheerful. "I'm Tech Nuovyl. Please follow me. If you say on the path, your feet will stay warmer longer."

Nuovyl led us into a lock in a portable building, bright blue plastrene that clashed with everything, then through the inner lock and down a narrow corridor to a room that held ten armless chairs—made out of some sort of spray composite. The color was supposed to be cherry, but it was just reddish ochre-brown, not even close to the wood.

"Please take a seat. You can remove your helmets."

I sat down. I wasn't breathing hard, but it felt good to get off my feet for a moment. I took off the helmet. The air in the room was chill and had a faint odor of oil.

A trim woman in blue skintights and the gray shorts and vest of the D.S.S. appeared. They clashed with the walls. "I'm Lieutenant Hvaro. I know all of you want to get on with your work, but we do need to brief you on several matters . . ."

I glanced around. Maejean was looking at the floor. So was Torres. I found Melani Khalahouri looking at me. We both smiled.

". . . be very careful. Twenty percent more gravity might not sound like much, but the difference is enough to make what might be a minor bruise into a severe contusion or turn a bruise into a broken bone. I can guarantee that you don't want to take a shuttle back to orbit with a broken arm or leg . . . Try not to touch the walls. Although your armor is nonconductive, it's still far warmer than anything here. The frozen stuff might look like ice, but it could easily be frozen oxygen or nitrogen. If you touch it for long, it will vaporize and fog up things, perhaps your viewplates . . .

"You'll be assigned bunks in the quarters section . . .

"No one is to travel alone. Several of you are not part of a team. We've worked out arrangements for you, and we'll tell you individually right after we finish this briefing . . ."

All of what the lieutenant said was common sense. Some of it I wouldn't have thought about. Some, I didn't see how anyone could not have figured out.

She came over to me first, after the briefing. "Ser Barna? Tech Nuovyl has been assigned to be your escort. You're cleared to go anywhere you wish, but it's recommended that you take frequent rests or stops . . ."

After listening to another round of cautions and instructions, I escaped.

Nuovyl was waiting outside the briefing room. Like many of the techs, he had shaved his head. His smile matched the cheerful voice. "Ser Barna!"

"You're cheerful."

"Yes, sir. I get to look at everything when I'm escorting you, and I don't have to carry much. Do you want me to carry your gear?"

"No. Let's dump my personals on a bunk first. I'm only carrying an imager."

The quarters for the groundside team were very spartan. Rows of bunks in two bays. Everything recycled. Already, it bore the odors of an orbit station. I was glad to get back into my helmet and follow Nuovyl out through the lock and toward the cluster of towers closest to the flat area on which the shuttle had landed. The suit light wasn't that bright, but it was adequate.

I glanced back toward the shuttle. Figures in armor were carrying containers and loading them into the shuttle's cargo bay. Under the lights, they were metallic shadows.

"Nuovyl . . . I need to circle back."

"Yes, sir."

I took several shots, all from different angles, trying to get in the figures in armor, the shuttle, and the more distant towers. With the lack of light, the towers would be shadowy at best, if they appeared on the image at all, but I could re-create them from other images I took later. It might be a composite, but the composite would be more truthful than a technically accurate image. What I was after was a fundamental contrast—the alienness of the armor and the shuttle opposed to the alienness of the towers. Once I was done, a viewer would see representations of two different civilizations, never quite sure which was alien and which was not.

Nuovyl didn't say anything.

Before long we were headed back toward the first set of towers.

Even with vision enhancers built into the armor, and the suit lights, I could only see the lower part of the tower closest to me—even when we were less than ten meters away. The images that I'd studied on the ship had been silvery blue, but before me, they appeared almost totally silver, with the barest hint of blue. The tower was far bigger than I had realized. It had to be a good two hundred meters across. It wasn't exactly circular, either, more oval I would have judged, but I really couldn't tell. My lights didn't show enough. I was going to need some higher-powered illumination to get any large-scale outside images.

"Sir . . . we have to go down the ramp through the ice there."

"In a minute." I walked off the plastrene-sprayed path and over to the side of the tower. I looked up. The tower curved outward from the base—not much, but noticeably from beneath. I took several images, not that they would show much, but the imager was more sensitive than my eyes, even with enhancers. There would be something of the tower in the final image.

Even when I put my faceplate almost against the wall, the surface appeared shimmeringly smooth, without a hint of damage. Up close, there was no hint of blueness at all, just silver. The silver showed no reflection, smooth and shiny as it looked.

I stepped back and took several more images.

"This way, sir," Nuovyl pointed down a ramp, cut through the ice at a gentle angle.

We had to walk away from the tower to take the ramp downward.

"How did they figure out where the entrances were?"

"Where they were wasn't too hard to see once they cleared away the ice and frozen air," the tech answered. "There were places that looked to be entrances. More like nowhere else they could have been. Getting them open was harder. It took more than a week. They finally figured out how and where they could cut the latches, or whatever. Had to boost one of the cutting lasers almost to burnout."

"The doors were that tightly locked?"

"No, sir. Something about the material flowing into itself, because the latches were different from the casings. One of the physicists—that was Dr. Lazar—he was amazed at the whole setup."

"Can they open the others now that they've found out how they work?"

"No, sir. Only from inside. Unless they cut through."

That seemed odd, but maybe the means for opening them from outside no longer existed.

At the base of the ramp was an opening to the tower. It was a circle with the base flattened. The high point of the center arc was only ten or fifteen centimeters above my head. I studied the door itself, which consisted of two sections. Each had been slid about three-quarters open. There was *something* about the door. I looked again. The door melded with the tower wall. It was neither farther in nor farther out than the wall itself. How had they done that?

"Sir?"

"The door. It shouldn't open. It's part of the wall." I wasn't expressing myself that well, but Nuovyl would understand.

"Yes, sir. They're like that. The material, whatever it is, deforms to do that."

"When it's this cold?"

"It's slower. It took almost half a stan to open this one just a few centimeters. That was until Dr. Lazar suggested using the laser on low power to heat it some. Then it opened real quick. Well . . . quick by comparison."

I looked at the door again. Metal doors that changed their shape to open? After a moment, I took a series of images of the door from the outside, then from the inside. The material was seamless on both sides, with no signs of joins or joints.

Inside the door was a circular room about fifteen meters across. It would have been a foyer in a human building. The silver walls were smooth, and slightly curved inward. Floors, walls, and ceilings seemed to be made of the same material as the outside of the tower. There were no protrusions, no roughness—and no furniture. There was also no dirt, except smudges created by the boots of others in space armor. The surfaces held and reflected the suit lights. That created a faint illumination from everywhere. I didn't see a single reflection of our images.

I captured more images. "Were there any furnishings, any equipment? Anything?"

"No, sir. Dr. Lazar doesn't think they had anything like that. They wouldn't need it."

Wouldn't need it? Why not? Because the walls or ceilings or floors could form anything? I moved to the nearest wall and pressed my armor-stiffened fingers against the wall. I could feel some give. It wasn't from the gauntlets I wore. I could tell that. "Are all the buildings like this?"

"So far as I know, but I've only been inside a few, sir."

Two corridors opened from the foyer, one to the right and one to the left. They looked like they paralleled the outer wall. I took the one on the left. The corridor was the same shape as the outer door, if larger in diameter and almost seven meters wide. The ceiling was low for the size of the tower, since I could reach up and touch it without stretching. There were no sharp edges. Even the corners where the walls melded into the floors or ceilings were curved arcs. Every surface was a curve or an arc.

We passed another door that had been cut and left half-open. I stepped through the opening and into a chamber. The outer wall clearly followed the curve of the tower wall, and so did the inside wall. The entire room was an arc, barely, given the size of the tower, and the end walls bowed inward slightly.

There was something about the outer wall. The faintest shift in shading, a darker silver, outlined an oval on the wall. "This was a window."

"How do you know?" asked the tech.

"It's on an outer wall. If it faced that flat area where the shuttle is, when it lifts off, we might see something."

"You think so, sir?" I could see the skepticism through the body armor.

"Well . . . not here. We're too far below the ice. Can we get up several levels? How long before the shuttle lifts off?"

"Another half stan, sir. The captain doesn't like to leave them groundside too long, but it does take a while to turn them around, with the samples and all."

"How about going up?"

"There are ramps in the center of the tower. They circle up. There are two."

I followed Nuovyl out of the chamber and along the corridor, past a number of doors that had been opened, then to the center ramps. Unlike the other chambers, there were no doors to the ramps, just open circular archways When I looked down at the silvery floor of the ramp, it appeared just a shade rougher. "You said that there were two ramps?"

"Yes, sir. They each circle."

"One was an up ramp and one a down. They probably carried the Dananni-ans each way."

"That was what Dr. Lazar said. He couldn't explain how, not in any terms I understood."

I doubted that I would have understood either.

We left the ramp through another open arch off three levels up. I hoped that there were some open doors and that I could figure out which side of the tower faced the flat area where the portable quarters and the shuttle were. Only a handful of doors had been opened on the fourth level, and none was directly op-posite the shuttle. I picked the one that might offer an angled view and stepped inside. The chamber was larger than the one on the first level, but just as empty of anything as it had been. I could make out a far larger oval, one that stretched a good six meters from end to end, taking up most of the outer wall, and cap-tured an image of it.

"Now what, sir?"

"We wait, and we look at this blank wall. You tell me what else you know about the towers, or this one."

"Sir?"

"How many towers has the team entered? Do you know?"

"I'd heard that they've only gone into five or six. It takes a lot of power to melt the ramps through the ice . . ."

Nuovyl didn't seem to know that much more about what was inside the tow-ers. He did know a great deal more about what was outside. ". . . we've found five of these circular lakes, and the towers are spaced the same around each one. Each lake has a wall around it, and the ground-imaging equipment shows they're all smooth. They don't have any decorations at all . . .

Abruptly, the oval on the wall—or a small section of it to my right—turned hazily transparent. I could see what looked to be bluish lines around the shuttle, in addition to the ground lights focused on the craft. I quickly used the imager and hoped the pictures would turn out. As the shuttle lifted, the transparency faded quickly.

"Sir—it is a window. But . . . what were those blue lines? I never saw those before."

"I don't know." I didn't. I had an idea that the window had displayed or translated some form of the AG-drive energies in a visual image, but I could have been wrong.

"How did you know?"

"I was just hoping." I'd guessed. Intelligent aliens who had intelligent doors and buildings—if they looked at anything—might have had intelligent windows. The windows were probably one-way, and they needed energy to work. There wasn't that much visual light, and almost no heat energy on Danann. Only something like a shuttle or a high-power laser would activate them. Even so, someone had to be looking when it happened.

I'd found windows. I doubted that my discovery would even make the footnotes in the scholarly papers. Someone else would have found them sooner or later, but I enjoyed the idea that I might have been among the first.

"We can head back, Nuovyl. We might as well report this to Dr. Lazar or Dr. Henjsen." I took a few images of the chamber. The only thing special about it was that I'd seen a window work there for a moment, but I wanted a personal record.

"Yes, sir."

Besides, I was getting more than a little tired, and my legs were beginning to ache, really ache.

37 *FITZHUGH*

At five minutes past eleven—or eleven hundred five in military terminology—on the morning of oneday, a mere two days before I was scheduled for my descent to Danann, the console in my work space flashed on with the image of the *Magellan*'s operations officer.

"Professor Fitzhugh, this is Commander Morgan."

For all that his image was clear, and the announcement of his identify unnecessary, I merely replied, "Yes, Commander?" I refrained from rhetorically offering assistance that he neither needed nor probably desired.

"You are currently scheduled to go planetside on threeday."

"That is what I've been informed by Major Tepper."

"I would like to suggest that we postpone your descent for another week. It's taken more time and a great deal more equipment to gain access to the towers and structures below. We'd like to retard the schedule for those members of the expedition team whose specialties deal with cultural artifacts other than the shells of the structures and with the culture itself." Morgan paused. "That's because, frankly, as you may have noted from the images and findings made available to you, we have yet to find anything besides empty buildings, and getting inside those has been more difficult than we imagined."

"I understand, Commander." I could have lodged some sort of protest, perhaps with the Special Deputy Minister, but it would have been in vain—and self-defeating over any length of time. Morgan was in charge of the exploration schedules, and he had encountered a problem, certainly not the last, I suspected, over which he had little control. Moreover, as he had intimated, it was most highly improbable that I would be likely to discern additional new insights about the Danannian history from looking more closely at the few structures to which the team had gained access. The greater the range of structures and artifacts to which I had access, the more valuable and potentially accurate my analysis and contribution would be—if I could make any real and meaningful addition at all.

Still, I did have questions and decided to ask one or two. "I have not seen any reports on any life-forms, even lesser life-forms—"

"You haven't seen any reports because there haven't been any found yet. There isn't any uncovered ground in the megaplex. Torres is attempting to get core samples outside the built-up area and from underneath the lakes."

"Nothing like cemeteries, memorial garden, statues?"

"Nothing, Professor. Believe me, everything that's been reported is routed to all of you on the project. Now . . . if you will excuse me?"

"I'm sorry. If you would let me know when my time on Danann will be?"

"We will, as soon as we know. Thank you, Professor Fitzhugh."

When the screen blanked I leaned back, cogitating upon the unmentioned possibilities raised by the commander, dismissing the least probable immediately and accepting provisionally the most likely—that, as the flow of images from Danann had suggested, unforeseen difficulties in obtaining access to the ancient structures had indeed occurred. Even so, perhaps a closer analysis of the building sizes and positions, revealed by overhead imaging, might suggest something more of the culture.

Already, the preliminary images I had scrutinized suggested that Danann was neither a colonized world nor one that had been long inhabited. The architecture was all of the same style, and the patterns of structural placement strongly indicated that the entire complex, the huge oval of structures and boulevards or canals, of open spaces or lakes, or both, had been designed as a unit, and built within a short time—short for that culture, at least. Likewise, the geographical scans of the planet itself were unusual. It had a number of the telltale features of a standard "water" world that had evolved in the habitable zone of a "G" class star—except that several had been adapted. The depressions that were filled with ice and seemed to be frozen oceans displayed a regularity of depth and gradient, as if they had been modified or engineered, and the "continents" were regular, without the fractal-like features that naturally evolving coastlines displayed. While I had not seen any more detailed reports from the geologists, I would have been more than mildly surprised if they had not come up with better-supported conclusions along the same general thrust as mine.

The ratio of structure heights to their breadth in the single "city" was also unusual, because, first, those ratios remained constant by area across the entire urbanized area, and, second, the tallest towers in one section were exactly the same height as the tallest towers in the next section. Not only that, but there were exactly the same proportions of buildings of various sizes in each area, although their arrangement within each of those areas varied to some degree, and all the buildings were arced or curved. Most of the boulevards seemed to be curved in some fashion as well, and all the lakes were ovals. The lack of organic remains— of any type—were also suggestive of a planet not inhabited for long.

By the time I had gone back over my preliminary conclusions, doubtless duplicating the analyses of others, the time for the midday meal was approaching. If I could not descend to Danann myself, it might prove of some utility to obtain information from someone who had done so, perhaps one of the pilots, since I was not aware of the return of any team members who dealt in subjects related to mine.

The mess was but two-thirds filled, and there were a number of tables with spaces. There were two shuttle pilots at the mess—Lieutenant Lerrys and Lieutenant Chang—but Lerrys was seated with a number of others, and there were no vacant seats at that table. Lieutenant Chang was seated beside Major Tepper, but the chair on her other side was vacant.

"I hope you won't mind if I join you," I offered.

"Of course not, Professor," replied Major Tepper.

Lieutenant Chang nodded, politely and distantly.

The steward served the lieutenant coffee, and returned shortly with bergamot tea for me—formulated, but better than ersatz coffee. I listened, hoping for a conversational opening, not wishing to insert myself excessively.

". . . Lerrys had shuttle one early this morning . . . brought up more ice samples . . . say there are frozen microorganisms in the ice . . . but different . . . still carbon-based . . . and something like DNA . . ." That was Alexa Neison. She was a linguist, and she was probably in the same situation as I was. It is incredibly difficult to study a language when no one has found any records of such, or even if the Danannians communicated in a fashion similar enough to us that we would even recognize such communications as language.

". . . Dr. Koch contends that any life that evolves in what we term the habitable zone will have to be carbon-based . . ."

". . . could still be totally alien to us . . ."

I finished a sip of the tea and decided to risk opening conversation with the silent lieutenant to my right. "You have made a number of descents to Danann."

"A few."

"I know it's not in the best of manners, and I would not presume to intrude, but I would greatly appreciate any insights you might have, Lieutenant, about what you've seen."

"Asking me, Professor? Pilots pilot. We're not scientists."

"You are a professional, and I am most certain you have observed things that others have not."

"You'd better answer him, Lieutenant." Tepper laughed. "Professors are known to be tenacious."

"Don't know what that could be."

"You have doubtless seen the inhabited area from above more than others."

"You can't see anything. Not with your eyes. It's dark. Have to use imaging and radar to get your descent angle to the landing zone."

"That suggests that the images reveal something . . ." I let my words slide away, wondering why she was so reluctant to talk about what she had seen down on Danann, or even what she had not.

Had she concealed a sigh? I waited, although patience has never been the greatest of my virtues. Part of the waiting time was mitigated by the arrival of the meal, served quickly by a pair of stewards, who set plates before everyone at the table—nanite-formulated fowl in white sauce with ersatz rice and equally ersatz snap beans.

I kept looking patiently at the lieutenant until she answered.

"The screens show patterns. Leastwise, they look like patterns—interlocking ovals. Can't recall seeing any straight lines. Everything's curved. Even what they call the boulevards." Lieutenant Chang looked at me. She had deep gray eyes. "What do you think that means?"

"Everything about the design of an artifact or a city conveys a meaning. Whether we discern the rationale for such a design is another question." I'd noted the prevalence of curves, but had not considered that there were no straight lines. Had I seen any? I couldn't recall.

"Professor?" asked Lieutenant Chang.

"I'm sorry. I was thinking about your observation. I had noted the predominance of curves and arcs in the layout and construction of the city, if that is indeed what it is, but I honestly had not recognized that there were no straight lines at all."

"The screens don't show any. Saved some of the images and checked later. Don't have images for the whole complex, just the sections we overfly and those adjoining. None of them have any straight lines."

"Then it is unlikely that there are any straight lines in the design and layout of the complex, because each section replicates in some fashion the components of every other section, and each section is somewhat like an interlocking oval."

"You're taking my word for that?"

I inclined my head to the lieutenant. "I have no doubt that, if you have observed something, it is indeed as you have observed it."

Major Tepper smothered a laugh. "Lieutenant Chang is known for her straightforward manner."

"I appreciate that. While I have some expertise in unraveling historical indirections, my abilities at such in personal interactions leave much to be desired."

The interplay between the two officers suggested that there was much more there than met the eye. I wasn't about to pry into it, especially not at lunch among the lieutenant's superior and others I knew little more than by name.

Because I was at a loss at how and with what I might further engage Lieutenant Chang without revealing more than I desired, I took immediate refuge in the meal before me.

"You're a historian, aren't you?" asked Alexa Neison after a time.

"I specialize in the analysis of historical trends."

"This is an isolated outpost. Is it possible that it's left from some war?"

"Anything is possible, but the design of the buildings and the openness of the plan would suggest that this was not a warlike culture—or that they were so successful that they were unchallenged. I would opt for the former, based upon our own history of warlike expansion, because we've seen no other evidence of this culture. Then, Danann may have been their greatest expansion and simply abandoned." I shrugged. "The possibilities remain numerous, far more than would be the case were this an abandoned human settlement."

"You don't think that's possible?"

"Given the designs, the sizes of doors, the lowness of the ceilings, and the extensive patterned similarities in structures, the probabilities that this is an alien, nonhuman world approach unity, in my opinion. Moreover, it shows no vestiges of the kind of warlike history that a human settlement would."

"You've suggested several times that humans are warlike. Do you think that for us war is an inevitable historical trend?"

I'd considered the question before, but I would rather have avoided replying in simplistic terms, and any other response would have been hedged by so many conditions that a nonhistorian—even some historians known as oversimplifiers—would not have considered it an answer. "I'd be reluctant to term war a trend, or to say that any trend might be inevitable."

"I've read that there has never been a time in recorded history where some nations or worlds were not actively at war."

"True enough," added Lieutenant Chang. "From what I've seen. Someone's always fighting. We're just headed on an expedition, and someone's attacked us."

Tepper glanced at the lieutenant, who apparently ignored the look, yet closed her mouth. Then the major looked to me. "What do you think causes wars, Professor? You've obviously studied the matter, academically and perhaps otherwise."

While I wished she had not offered that last phrase, I quickly offered my usual gambit line for the subject. "When peace fails is when war becomes inevitable."

"That's absurd," replied the linguist. "You could say the same thing in reverse."

"No. Try it, and you will discover that it is not a proposition whose inverse is equally true. When war fails, there is total destruction., or exhaustion, but never peace, except for the terms imposed by the winner, and that is not peace in the true sense of the word, because peace implies an equality—at least a reciprocity that offers a promise of future equality. Peace is a situation where societal conflicts are resolved through nonmilitary accommodations. When those conflicts cannot be so resolved, war becomes inevitable." I paused.

"Aren't you really offering the argument that less sophisticated cultures or societies resort to war when they cannot compete in nonmilitary terms?" Major Tepper's tone was bantering.

"That has occurred. War has also occurred when societies more advanced in technology or commercial activities have been rebuffed by cultures who do not wish to accept what they regard as values or customs or other societal aspects of dubious value. What many analysts ignore is that information and technology possess values on two separate levels—those of symbolism and those of effective application. Exceedingly or even moderately advanced technology does not always ensure a triumph by its possessor. Such victories are assured only when the effectiveness of application exceeds that of lesser technology. Great military leaders have understood both the practical and symbolic value of technology that appeared strikingly advanced. From the days when all humanity was confined to Old Earth, various military forces have undertaken preemptive strikes to preclude the development, deployment, and application of advanced technology. In some cases, the preemption was merely to prevent a polity from using the technology as a symbol of power. In other cases, the technology would have posed a terrible threat to the polity making the preemptive strike . . ."

"You think that the attack on the *Magellan* was that kind of attack?" asked Neison.

"It couldn't have been anything other than preemptive, but whether preemptive for symbolic reasons or out of fear that the Danannian technology might provide a greater edge to the Comity remains to be seen. At that point in time, we had learned nothing." We still haven't learned that much. I turned to the lieutenant again. "What do you think?"

"Even the Sunnis don't send billion-credit warships if they aren't worried." She shrugged. "You know more than I do, Professor, but it seems to me that you have to be open-minded to learn new things, or learn about different cultures. Sunnis haven't shown that much open-mindedness in a long time. Maybe never. So I'd guess they just want to keep the Comity from learning more. Might be true of the Covenanters, too."

"Inflexibility, either general or selective, is, as you have pointed out, a hallmark of societies dominated by religious ideologies," I replied. The lieutenant, for all her terseness of expression, had outlined the argument far better than most politicians could . . . or would. The Special Deputy Minister had avoided that aspect of the subject altogether, and that action was one of many that classified him as a political prop. "You doubtless have noticed some relation between beliefs and effectiveness."

The lieutenant inclined her head, as if to assess whether my observation required a response. After an interval too brief to be a pause, except for someone such as she was, in a profession requiring instant decisions, she answered. "The more simple the beliefs, the more quickly people act. Most times, simple beliefs are wrong."

"It's a simple thing to believe in good and evil, or right and wrong," protested Neison. "Is that wrong?"

"Depends on how you define good or evil," the lieutenant replied.

"How would you define it?" I asked.

"I wouldn't want to try." She gave a short laugh. "One of those things that everyone wants to be simple and easy. It isn't."

"The Danannians seemed to be very simple, from the reports," suggested Major Tepper. "No furnishings, rooms and structures of similar size, designs similar throughout . . ."

"That indicates an incredibly complex society and individuals." I wasn't certain she was serious. Once human societies developed any technology at all, they displayed a tremendous range of differences in physical attributes, from housing to clothing, from commercial structures to transportation—everything. The more a society strove to minimize—in a workable fashion—the physical gaps between the richest and poorest, the least able and the most able, the more complex that society had to become. Human societies have never successfully narrowed those gaps, and serious efforts to do so have effectively destroyed both governments and societies. That alone suggested some very fundamental differences between the long-departed aliens and us. "Or vast differences between us and them, not only in terms of physiology but in terms of basic perceptions of the universe."

"That assumes a great deal, Professor," said Neison dryly.

"It does indeed." I smiled politely. "But when you analyze beyond the superficial, just about every decision and judgment we make assumes far more than we ever acknowledge." I had already said far too much on far too little concrete information.

A faint smile crossed the lieutenant's lips. After a moment, she pushed back her chair. "If you will excuse me . . ."

"Of course." Unlike me, she was on call all the time.

After Lieutenant Chang left, Major Tepper looked at me. She said nothing, and since she had voiced nothing, I merely offered a smile and took a long sip of the formulated and too-cool bergamot tea that lacked the true essence of tea in some indefinable fashion.

38 BARNA

After three days on Danann, by the time I collapsed twoday night on my assigned bunk in the men's bay, everything ached. On threeday morning, my legs were aching even before I got up and sat on the edge of the bunk. My head throbbed, and my eyes were filled with grit. I didn't even try to look up. I might have seen the blue plastrene walls closing in on me.

"It doesn't get any better, Chendor." Rikard Sorens sat on the edge of his bunk. It was one away from mine. The one between had been empty the whole time I'd been on Danann.

"How long have you been down here?" I asked.

"Five days. This time."

"How did yesterday go for you?"

"The same as every other day. We've found three kinds of anomalous composites, and they've all got elemental characteristics that suggest they were engineered on the fermionic levels. None of us can figure out, even theoretically, how they created them. One deforms. One doesn't. The third one doesn't deform, but passes radiation selectively. That's what they used in the windows you found. There's almost no difference in appearance. They all seem to have the same Mohs number. At least, their surfaces do, but the window materials change their refractive index in a passive-response mode. The material responds to radiation, but the response is skewed somehow, as if it had been engineered to fit a different spectrum . . ."

That still didn't tell me much. "I'm an artist, Rikard. What does all that mean?"

"First off—it's all impossible. The materials can't be. Anomalous metals *can't* be that stable for millions of years, let alone billions. For the universe's sake, they're effectively liquids, but these composites don't seem to know it."

He seemed more than a little upset. "What *have* you learned?"

"We can tell that their sun was significantly dimmer than ours. Of course, that's assuming that the response to radiation at present reflects what it did when the materials were designed and installed . . ."

That meant more than he was saying, but my head hurt so much that I really couldn't figure it out.

". . . the material has a refractive index of one for each type of radiation it passes, even simultaneously. And it has a threshold. It won't pass any form of radiation energy above a certain level. We think that it's about twice what the ambient level of their sun was, but that's only a guess. The physicists and the chemists are going crazy over the internals, because there aren't any identifiable controls, at least not in the small pieces we've managed to cut away, and those are mostly latch fragments. The others . . . we've destroyed two lasers. The material itself is probably intelligent on a nanetic level. If we knew how to control it, I'd bet that we could make it go negative to any degree necessary. It's the perfect window, or the perfect lens. You might even be able to use it as a telescope . . ."

"From a window?"

"Why not?" asked Rikard. "If you can do it. How many things do we do just because we can?"

Art was one of those things.

After Rikard left, I tried not to think too hard about what he'd said—especially about the impossibility of what the Danannians had done. I did manage a quick hot shower. It helped, but not enough because the water was limited by the recycling-reformulating equipment. If we had a bigger base on Danann and more power, we could have melted more of the ice, but anything outside the walls and shields froze immediately.

My feet still ached after breakfast, when I stood in the cramped operations area and looked down at the small screen display of the megaplex. That was what they were calling the assemblage of buildings on Danann. The structures weren't a city, or a country, and there was no sign of anything artificial or fabricated under the ice anywhere except within the megaplex.

I wanted to find something special. Everyone did, and no one had found anything—except the towers, canals, and lakes—not a single artifact, not a single remnant of any multicelled creature.

I wasn't after that. What I wanted was something that conveyed what the Danannians might have been. It didn't have to be a picture, or a sculpture, or a frieze . . . but something.

In seeking that, thinking hadn't done me much good. I hadn't found anything beyond what everyone else had seen. I'd gotten some images that, because of lighting, angles, perspectives, contrasts, I *might* be able to turn into truly evocative art. An artist never knows, not for certain, until he tries. Those who say otherwise lie. The least talented lie to others, the most talented to themselves.

Those images would do what I'd been brought to do. They weren't enough for me. I kept looking at the map on the screen display. Finally, I decided on a section of one of the lower oval buildings almost a kay from the first that had been opened. Because of the time constraints facing the expedition, Commander Morgan had overruled Dr. Henjsen and the archeologists and ordered more buildings opened so that other members of the team could investigate. He had ordered that nothing be disturbed until the archeological team could investigate, but so far, no one had found anything except what had been in the first structure.

With my imager and case in hand, I headed for the locker room that held my space armor. Once there, I struggled into it. Most of the other team members had already suited up and left for their sites. I tried to ignore the odors raised by too many bodies and too much equipment in too small a space.

Nuovyl was waiting for me by the inner lock. "Where to, sir?"

"Oval thirty-nine."

"That's the new one. We'll need extra lights for that. If you'd wait a moment, sir."

I nodded, holding my helmet in one hand, the imager in the other. Nuovyl was back in less than a few minutes, wearing what looked like an ancient cartridge belt over his armor, except that it held powerpaks and lights.

He checked the seals on my helmet, and I did the same for him. Then we stepped into the lock and its already-marred blue plastrene walls and dark gray floor.

"Comm check, ser Barna."

"You're clear. Comm check, Tech Nuovyl."

"Clear here, sir."

The lock cycled, and we stepped out of the lock into an arc of harsh white light. A good two hundred meters to my left was the edge of the area where the shuttle landed. It was empty. Ahead was that part of the uneven icy surface of Danann holding the dark gray plastrene path that led to the western section of the megaplex.

We walked for a good fifteen minutes before we left the area on the frozen lake where the temporary quarters had been constructed. After that, the circles of light around building entrances vanished. Lighting was another problem I'd have in depicting Danann. Without an atmosphere, light didn't diffuse. It only illuminated what it struck, either directly or by reflection. The silvery surfaces of

the buildings should have reflected well. They didn't. So much of art was the interplay of light on surfaces, and that was minimal. I'd have to work on how to
create that starkness in a way that conveyed both the effect and the alienness,
but wasn't merely an image. Just replicating the effect of light without an atmosphere would push most things into a flat characterless representation. Accurate
as that might be, it wouldn't be art.

"Has anyone found anything new?"

"Not that I've heard, sir." After a pause, the tech added, "Professor Polius
thinks that the aliens planoformed all of Danann."

"They did something to it. The continental outlines are too regular. I
thought everyone felt that way."

"She said . . . something about the geology being more ancient than the
planet itself. I think that was what she said, sir."

I almost laughed. Danann was a planet close to ten billion years old. How
could the geology not be ancient?

We kept walking westward, along the dark gray plastrene path. The farther
we left the landing area behind, the more the darkness pressed in on us. It
didn't, really, but I felt that way. Darkness couldn't really impose itself. So it had
to be that I was getting so tired that it felt like that to me. Then we were walking
along a curved canal or boulevard that ran through an area where the towers
were taller. Maybe it wasn't my imagination, but where would the light have
come from that they were cutting off—if they were?

I played my light across the base of the nearest tower. It looked to be a paler
silver than the others. *That* had to be my imagination. The scientists had measured them, and announced that they were all identical in all exterior characteristics. I didn't see them as identical, but that was what the reports said.

As we walked, my feet felt colder and colder. The armor readouts indicated
all systems and temperatures were normal. My legs felt heavier, but that was to
be expected after three days in stronger gravity.

"There it is, sir."

The structure was one of the few that wasn't really a tower. It was more like
a flattened oval with a curved roof that rose less than a meter or two above the
ice and frozen atmosphere. It looked almost underground, with the ramp melted
down to the circular entrance below.

The main door was the same circular shape as all the others, with the flattened base. Inside, our lights showed that the foyer beyond was also like all the
other foyers, except smaller. As in every other building investigated so far, there
was nothing in the foyer. I took the left-hand hallway from the foyer. All the internal doors on the lower level had been opened, but only wide enough to let a
single person at a time step through the gap between the two halves. I peered
through the first door. The chamber was like all the others. So was the next one,
and the one after.

I couldn't find anything worth looking at more closely on the entire first
level. That had been my experience for the past two days, since I'd discovered

the windows. I had taken lots of images and seen lots of windows, now that I knew what to look for, but nothing new. Would the windows be all I found out?

I trudged up the ramp to the second level. It was also the top level. Then, in the fifth chamber I peered into, I felt something was different. I stepped all the way through the narrow gap in the door sections. Nuovyl followed me. His light swept over the chamber.

"That looks different," I blurted out.

"You think so, sir?"

I knew it was different. It took me a moment to determine what about the empty room was distinctive. Then I had it. All the other rooms in all the other structures I'd been in were oval, or arced one way or another. The chamber where we stood was oval on one end and curved on both sides, but the remaining part of the wall was ran nearly perpendicular to the curved sidewalls. I looked carefully again. There was the slightest convexity, almost as if the builder had not been able to bear the idea of a straight line.

I shook my head. How could I guess what an alien had thought billions of years ago? "The end of the room here. It's almost flat. I'd bet something's behind it. Do we have the equipment to open a door here?"

"No, sir. I can tell, maybe, if it's like the other doors."

"Go ahead."

Nuovyl stepped up to the flatter wall and scanned it with some sort of detector. After a moment, he turned to me. "There's a door here. Leastwise, there's a change in the readings right in the center, and it runs floor to ceiling."

"Can you get someone here who can open it?"

"I can see, sir. It will take a moment."

While Nuovyl contacted whoever it was, I walked up to the center of the wall. I stood right where Nuovyl had been. Other than the minimal curve in the wall, I couldn't see anything that suggested where the two sides of one of the Danannian doors might join.

"It'll be a quarter stan or more, sir."

"That's fine. I'll check out the rest of the building until they get here." I left the chamber and walked to the next door, and the one after that. I made my way around the entire upper level and checked every room. All were the same size, except for the one with the internal door and one other. At the south end of the building was a room five times the size of the others. It was empty also, and its shape didn't suggest anything hidden. I thought it might have been a meeting room, but that was a guess.

When I saw another set of lights coming up the ramp, I went back to the chamber where Nuovyl waited.

A pair of techs arrived. The second one pulled a slider with a heavy power-pak. The first tech looked at Nuovyl.

Nuovyl gestured to me.

"There's a door here, on this wall." I pointed. "There might be something behind it. We don't know."

"I suppose we can try." She stepped up to the middle and pointed a scanner. She might have nodded. If she did, her helmet concealed the gesture. "We'll see what's possible."

The second tech eased the powerpak forward. The two worked for several minutes, attaching a supercon cable.

The first tech took a cylinder from her belt and ran it across the center of the wall. It left an oily sheen. "Don't look while I'm cutting. The material gives off secondaries that standard helmet filters don't block."

I turned away and waited. No artist wants his eyes injured. Was there anything behind the door, or just more empty space?

"I'm done with cutting."

I looked back at the wall. The thinnest line was visible under the lights played on it by the two techs.

"This wasn't as bad as some of them. Now we'll give it some heat. Seems to help." The tech adjusted the cutting head of the laser and checked the cable from the powerpak. Then she aimed the laser at the wall and played it across the silvery surfaces on each side of the thin line. Nothing happened for several minutes. Then the wall *split*. I couldn't see any movement, yet a gap opened.

When it was about a meter wide, the tech flicked off the laser. "Should be good enough for now, sir. Don't want to use any more power than we have to."

The two began to disassemble the portable laser cutter.

I stepped forward and peered through the gap, then played my light across the darkness beyond. So far as I could tell, there was nothing there except walls, floor, and ceiling. Still, since I'd made an issue about how the chamber was different, I stepped through and began to study what lay beyond. I tried to be methodical as I did.

I almost missed the one difference in the chamber. The first time I saw it, I thought it was a shadow from the light. I moved forward and swept the beam across the silvered floor again. There was a faint oval depression—or indentation—a meter or so back from the internal door.

I bent over and studied the silvery floor. The indentation was somewhere between a centimeter and a centimeter and a half deep, and extended more than two meters from side to side, parallel with the door, but no more than thirty centimeters in the middle, tapering to less than fifteen before the curves of the elongated oval at each end. The depth of the indentation seemed constant throughout.

"Sir?" asked Nuovyl.

"There was something here. Or maybe there's something beneath the floor."

"Do you think . . ." Nuovyl left the sentence unfinished.

I stepped back, careful to avoid the oval indentation. "You're right. We'll just report it to Dr. Henjsen."

Before I left, I used the lights at several angles and intensities to capture as many images as I could. Images of an indentation in an alien floor—was that what I was being reduced to depicting?

I stepped back through the opening in the doorway. "We might as well explore some more outside."

"Yes, sir."

From Nuovyl's tone, I could tell he was relieved that we were leaving.

Once outside, I could only hope that I'd be able to capture some images of the megaplex that might provide inspiration and interpretation.

But then, there wasn't much else I could do.

39 CHANG

While I was sitting standby in the ready room on threeday after making a supply run to the *Alwyn*—mostly raw materials of the rare stuff for their formulators—I got to thinking about Fitzhugh. Had put it off ever since lunch on oneday. Had avoided Fitzhugh as well. Couldn't quite figure him out. Certain I'd seen him somewhere, besides in the mess, but couldn't recall where. Still couldn't see him as a professor. He was taller than average, well muscled, too. Moved like a cat, a well-behaved big cat, always on edge. He'd been the one to approach me. Men looked at me. Some women, too. Fitzhugh certainly looked at me more than once. Didn't see him look below the neck. Even Morgan had appraised me there once or twice. Also thought the professor heard every word I'd said. He was interested in what I'd had to say. I wasn't sure I could have said that about many men. Wished I knew why. Was he just after information?

Thing was, he wasn't gay, wasn't a neuter. Could have been he was just well-mannered. Hard to say, because pilots don't see that side of people too often. For all his big words, he had manners. Still wanted to know what he wanted. Wouldn't find out unless I talked to him, and I wasn't sure I wanted to. Tepper suspected something about him. That phrase about studying war academically and otherwise—meant to prod him. He'd ignored it like she'd never said it.

Lieutenant Chang, start the prelaunch on two. Jumped for a moment when Major Tepper's links hit me. She came through harder on link than Morgan did. *You'll be headed planetside with some special equipment as soon as shuttle one is inbound on the final return leg. They'll start loading as soon as they can. No more than a few minutes.*

Yes, sir. What's the problem? What equipment?

Commander Morgan's coming over to explain. Tepper broke the link.

Sounded like Lerrys and shuttle one were all right, but "special equipment" loaded in a hurry suggested trouble. Headed for the locker bay. I was deliberate in getting into armor.

Morgan arrived when I was unracking my helmet.

"What's the problem?"

He grimaced. "The lake they put the temporaries on is heating up. No one knows why, except there are heat sources registering all across the bottom. There's actually liquid underneath, and there are a few cracks in the ice. Some of the water is coming up as steam jets that freeze straight to snow and fall."

"Danann's too old for volcanic activity that close to the surface." Even I knew that.

"The science types think it's some sort of automatic mechanism. They want to study it, but they're afraid the whole base will collapse through the ice if the heating continues. You'll be landing in a new zone and taking down a second tractor and some big slider pallets. That way they can move everything before the melting gets out of hand."

How much power was there under that lake? How could it possibly be active after billions of years? Or had the science types been wrong about that, too?

Morgan went on. "You're to unload the sliders and the tractor as quickly as possible, then get shuttle two out of there." He didn't want any of the *Magellan's* equipment caught on the ground if anything happened. Couldn't say I blamed him.

"You want me to bring back some reaction mass? Or any returnees?"

He laughed. The sound wasn't quite harsh. "All the science types are excited. No one wants to leave." He looked worried, more worried than from melting lakes.

"What else is going on? Graviton traces? Atrousan tracks?"

Morgan looked hard at me. Real hard.

"Melting water doesn't bother you. We already had one attempt at sabotage and two Sunni ships attacked. All of a sudden, you're nervous. Tells me you're worried about company."

"There's a possibility." He shook his head. "We'll talk about it later. Your job is to get the tractor and sliders down there." He ran his fingers over the armor, checking it. Then he gave me a last look and hurried off.

It wasn't more than ten minutes before I was strapped into shuttle two, starting the prelaunch checklist. Ysario was crew chief this time. She was wiry and old enough to be my mother and then some. Didn't miss much, either.

"I double-braced the ramp, sir. They're backing the tractor in. Wouldn't let 'em use sliders. It took a while for them to get the message."

"Thanks, chief." That much mass on a slider, and one mistake could blow out the shuttle's hull.

"What I'm here for, sir."

I finished the prelaunch. After the tractor was secured, the empty sliders didn't take long, and Chief Ysario reported "all secure." Shuttle two carried one crewman besides the chief.

I went link. *Navigator Control, this is Sherpa Tigress.* I almost said "Porter Tigress" because I usually piloted shuttle one, rather than shuttle two.

Sherpa Tigress, Navigator Control, bay doors open, null grav in bay. You are cleared for departure and descent to landing zone beta—blue-white beacon.

Control, understand cleared for departure and descent to landing zone beta.

I eased shuttle two clear of the *Magellan*. I was more deliberate, because shuttle two was close to max mass with the tractor and the other stuff that they'd piled in.

Descent was smooth. I'd programmed the scanners to make readouts on alpha area as we neared the zone. Morgan had been right—all sorts of temperature plumes there. We made the alternative landing zone without using full power. Didn't want to use any more power than necessary. Not if water might be building up under the ice. They'd said beta area was still solid, but I had my doubts how long that would last. Like every time before, the unfrozen gases rose around the shuttle like steam, then came back down like hail on the hull.

Sherpa Tigress, interrogative status. Morgan didn't even let me finish the set-down check-off.

Navigator Control, Sherpa Tigress at zone beta. Situation green.

Stet, Tigress. Proceed soonest to unload. Report ready to liftoff.

I ran through the postlanding checklist, but left everything hot for liftoff, monitoring everything as Ysario took care of the off-load. I watched the mass indicators, ready for any instability, but the shuttle only wobbled slightly. Still . . . took a deep breath when the big tractor was off the ramp. The sliders and the extra formulator provisions took another quarter stan.

"Cargo's clear, sir," reported Ysario. "They've got the ice pallets coming up the ramp. Looks like half what we usually take."

"Commander said not to wait. We'll take what they have." The ice was dirty and sealed in plastrene. Once we got back to the *Magellan,* the mech crew would off-load it, strip the plastrene, cut it, and tube feed it to the purifier. Never hurt to keep your reaction mass tanks full.

Another fifteen minutes went by before Ysario reported. "We're secure and set to lift."

"Thanks. Starting the liftoff checklist."

Everything was in the green, and we lifted clean. Quick scans showed everything normal. Detectors registered heat from where zone alpha was—low-level, but nothing had registered before. Scary when I thought about it—equipment still operating after being frozen solid for billions of years. I was just as glad to be quartered shipboard.

Concentrated on the return, but couldn't help wondering if we'd see company before too long. Also wondered about Fitzhugh. Had the feeling there was more about him than he let on. Frigging thing was that there was more about everything than showed.

40 GOODMAN/BOND

On fourday, Chief Stuval sent me up to the shuttle bay with a slider to pick up some diagnostic equipment the shuttle mechs had borrowed.

A mech appeared from somewhere. His namestrip read KLEZEK. "You the armory tech?"

"That's right. Bond. Chief Stuval sent me up to get the diagnostics . . ."

"They're over in the insulated subbay there, past the shuttle."

Three people stood just inside the lock, wearing space armor, but not helmets. Two were shuttle pilots. The taller one's armor was stenciled LIEUTENANT CHANG. Even in armor, she had a good figure, blonde, make a good wife on looks. The other was Lieutenant Braun. Her face was like a porcelain doll, till you got close and realized she was made of endurasteel.

"Are all pilots women?" The man wore the bulkier general armor of the expedition scientists. Those suits fit only roughly and were uncomfortable. He had a temp tag—FITZHUGH.

"Not all, Professor," replied Braun. "Lieutenant Lerrys is a very good pilot."

"Not many people have the skills," added Chang. "Need spatial orientation senses, and more men have those than women. Also need the ability to integrate multiple details and coordinate them simultaneously."

"That's where most of the men fail," Braun said.

"What about combat?" asked the professor. "Don't men have an edge in ferocity?"

Both lieutenants laughed.

I smiled as I edged the slider past the three. I didn't feel like smiling at the bitches.

"The Second Arm War proved that was a canard," Braun said. "Covenanters went after the League . . . Old Earth . . . I'm sure you know that. The League's pilots were eighty percent female. The Covenanters were one hundred percent male. Do you recall what happened?"

"The League destroyed all the Covenant fleets. How much of that was skill, and how much was due to the equipment?"

I was glad the professor asked that. I kept listening as I moved the slider past the stem of the shuttle and toward the insulated subbay the mech was opening.

"None." Chang laughed. "Every bit of equipment that the Covenanters had was newer and better than the stuff the League had. Only significant difference was the pilots."

She was lying. Old Earth had far more wealth and equipment than we'd had, far more. I tried not to frown as I eased the slider toward the open area between the shuttle and the subbay.

"Surely, in all the years of history, the male hunter-killer—"

"Men are better at killing in packs, and they're frigging better as commandos and suicide hunters," Chang interrupted. "They can focus on one thing. In space combat you have to handle multiple inputs."

"Every woman knows that most men are single-minded," added Braun.

The lieutenants laughed again.

"You may have a point." The professor smiled, politely.

"You'd better go back to the ready room, Professor. I need to finish a preflight."

"I will. Thank you."

The professor moved away. He didn't look much like a professor, not to me, even in the overlarge armor. For all his manners, he looked more dangerous than the two bitches. I'd like to have gotten each one of the women alone—for a long time. Then they'd have seen what a good man could do. That wasn't the mission, though. After I'd managed to set out a signaler, I'd be more than happy to get back to the Worlds of the Covenant and real women.

I began to slow the slider, and turn it toward the subbay.

"Over here, Bond!" called the mech.

The sooner I finished the signaler the better. If only Chief Stuval didn't watch so closely. That was slowing me down, more than I'd thought. I blocked the slider in place.

"Saw you looking at the pilots, Bond."

I shook my head. "They're too hard for me." I couldn't say they were fem-bitches, even if they were.

"Too tough for most. That's why so many pair off." Klezek laughed. "Any-way . . . all the paks on the left are the stuff we borrowed from you."

I pushed the frigging pilots out of my thoughts and got to work on loading and checking the diagnostic paks.

41 FITZHUGH

I'd arrived early at the ready room for the shuttle bay and had found both Lieutenant Braun and Lieutenant Chang. In our brief conversation, I'd definitely gotten the impression that neither cared for male posturing. Since I didn't care for posturing, including my own, to which I was more prone than I liked to admit, their views didn't bother me. I had the growing feeling that Chang liked men who were direct, strong without being overbearing. I probably came across as too overbearing, but I had enjoyed conversing with her, few words as we had exchanged.

The shuttle descent to Danann wasn't in itself particularly uncomfortable, but the space armor in which I had encased myself was scarcely bearable. No sooner had I donned it than portions of my anatomy which had theretofore been perfectly quiescent decided to itch. One can certainly scratch the outside of armor, but doing so with gauntlets presents the risk of damaging both gauntlets and suit—and thus its occupant, in this case, me—while accomplishing nothing in reducing the irritation. I would rather not have had my recollections of precisely how uncomfortable ill-fitted armor was refreshed so personally.

Once we were on Danann, as the heavier gravitational force immediately made itself known, I'd wished I had been even more assiduous in my workouts, although I could not reproach myself for the past few weeks, but few academics, I consoled myself, had been more dedicated over the years. Still, while I regretted my lapses, I would not have desired to have continued in the service merely to remain in top physical condition. The body should serve the mind, not the reverse.

The crew chief announced, "You can release your harnesses and put on your helmets. I'll check each of you before you enter the lock. Make sure your comm unit is on."

By the time we finished the necessary debarkation and postdebarkation efforts, more than a standard hour had passed, because the landing area had been relocated to another of the flat frozen lakelike areas, and we had to walk almost half a kay to the temporary quarters and buildings. They had also been moved onto a wide curve in a boulevard or canal between towers. After the briefing, I had deposited my minimal gear upon a nondescript bunk and returned to the external lock to meet my escort.

There Tech Nuovyl waited, smiling blandly. "Do you have any gear, sir?"

"No, Nuovyl. I'm here to see as much as I can, preferably as much different as possible. You can start by showing me the more interesting towers nearby." My initial tour planetside was three days. Since no one had found anything except the towers and the buildings themselves, as a historian, all I could do was to look at them and try to find the meaning in their construction, placement, and external and internal arrangements. I'd read the latest report by Lizabet Marsalis, the biologist. To date, her team had found no remnants of either flora or fauna. She was hopeful that core samples from a lake bottom might have organic traces, but after billions of years, even in a planetary deep freeze, finding remnants on the microscopic scale was problematic.

"Are you looking for something in particular, sir?"

"I'd be interested in seeing what seems to be most common, then areas that differ from that baseline."

After we checked helmet seals and comm links, I followed Nuovyl out through the main lock. The more traveled ways had been covered with insulating gray plastrene. At the edges, snowlike crystals, scuffed or kicked by boots, encroached.

When I turned to view the shuttle just visible down the ancient open canal/boulevard, harsh lights glared through the airlessness from where a crew loaded plastrene crates. The combination of the lights and their armor turned the three crewmen into white-edged stark shadows.

"What are they loading? Do you know?"

"Mostly samples of the materials the aliens used to build the towers. That's what Dr. Henjsen said. Cutting even small pieces clear is a bitch. They had to beef up the lasers into something that's half laser, half particle beam, and tighten the focal cutting edge into something like a hundred nanometers. Only the door catches cut easy."

From what I remembered from the reports and my own scattered research and education in that area, Nuovyl's statement suggested that the expedition scientists were being required to apply an inordinate amount of power to take the alien composite materials apart at the molecular level. I had read somewhere, though, that anomalous materials shouldn't behave that way.

"The door catches?" That was a datum, although I couldn't yet place its importance.

"Those oval or circular doors—they split in the middle. They're held so tight by catches that you can't even see where the two halves join, but they sort of ooze apart if you heat them with a broadbeam laser after you cut the catches." Nuovyl turned toward a ramp carved into the ice, one that led to the entrance to the nearest tower.

I stopped and focused my suit light upward, letting the illumination diminish itself as the silvered surface of the tower absorbed the quanta that flowed over it. Light doesn't follow such a pattern, but that was the first impression that I gathered. The second was that, for all their apparent height against the darkness of the galactic void, the towers were . . . short . . . almost squat. So smooth and curved and without projections were they that they reminded me of the sand towers that Cheryssa had built to hold back the tide when we had vacationed so many years before at Ballytor Beach.

Why would anyone build such gracefully squat structures, particularly an alien species whose technology and engineering clearly had surpassed our own? Had they had a totally different concept of beauty? Or was their ideal of beauty tied more directly to functionality?

"Sir?" Nuovyl's question intruded upon my silent contemplation of the washed-out silver megaliths among which I stood and marveled.

"Is there anything on top of the towers?"

"No, sir. They're curved into a slight dome, and Dr. Henjsen and the scientists say that there's no access to the top surface."

Another datum. Humans had invariably built access to the top of their structures—or at least to the vast majority of them—from the time that we had begun to build anything other than hovels. Why would a culture avoid such? If the aliens had been acrophobic, they would not have built so many towers, especially with such wide windows. If they had been agoraphobic, their megaplex would not have been so open with such wide canal boulevards. With all the lakes and canals, they liked water, but their structures had not been designed to hold water, and that suggested that they were not aquatic.

Nuovyl led the way down the plastrene-covered ice ramp toward the half-open circular doorway with the flattened base.

While I had read about the deformation mechanism and viewed images, seeing so closely in person how the silvery material of the entry melded seamlessly into the casements was an emotional confirmation of the superb design and technology embodied in the structure. That it functioned, if not as well as originally, under the extreme adverse conditions of temperatures close to absolute zero and no atmosphere—after billions of years—was nothing short of breath-taking.

"Professor?"

"I wished to observe the deformation of the entry closely. Do they all deform in the same fashion?"

"Yes, sir. That's what the science types say, anyway. I haven't looked that close."

I stepped through the half-open door. The ceiling in the entry foyer rose into a low dome, presumably in shape similar to those that capped the towers, since the Danannians repeated the same shapes and patterns, just arranged in seemingly endless differing combinations. I could easily touch the highest point of the foyer ceiling. The surface gave slightly, then stiffened against more pressure, demonstrating elasticity at temperatures that would have fragmented most human-developed elastic composites. Yet the material resisted cutting except by high-power, tightly focused lasers.

I had some ideas about the Danannians—or aliens, since it was all too obvious that Danann had been an outpost or colony—but I submerged them, letting the surroundings immerse me. I could only trust in my senses and reserve the analyses for later. Observation first, with interpretation and analysis only after far more lengthy familiarization with the structures.

"Ah . . . Professor."

"I need to take my time, Nuovyl."

As I proceeded, I also hoped that Nuovyl wouldn't continue to prod me every time I stopped to observe some aspect of the structures, their design, or their architecture. Without inscriptions, written or oral histories, the only record of the aliens lay in the structures themselves, and, unless the other members of the expedition discovered more than they already had, the towers would have to speak for the Danannians—if I could but decipher what they had to tell.

42 *Barna*

The first day after I returned to the *Magellan,* I spent most of my time sleeping. That was sixday. Sevenday wasn't that much better. I'd been so tired on sixday that I hadn't realized how sore I was and how many bruises I had from the armor and my own clumsiness in higher gravity. The stiffness was worse on sevenday. I really didn't begin to get down to serious work on sorting through the images and selecting possible composition subjects until oneday.

Twoday, I started in on a simple light-matrix image—one of two towers set in a halo of illumination. The source of the light had been the light-belt Nuovyl had worn, but I wasn't showing that. I wanted to show the alienness of the setting, with the light just *ending,* except where it was held by the surface of the towers. At the base of the left-hand tower was the crudely melted ramp mat led down through the dark gray ice. I was trying to contrast the rudeness of the cut with the alien perfection of the towers, while still attempting to convey a feel of just how long the ice and frozen atmosphere had been there.

After an hour or so, I stepped back and studied the image. It was simple enough, just a narrower section of one of the canal boulevards between two towers. I had a sense of what it might have looked like. That would have to wait. I first had to depict what I had seen, not what might have been.

"It's beautiful, Chendor." Elysen stood in the studio doorway.

I thought I'd closed the door, but perhaps I had not. "It needs work."

"It's still beautiful. It's haunting."

That was the idea, but I wasn't satisfied. The silver of the towers held a shade too much blue. The darkness beyond the rounded dome of the tower on the right wasn't ominous enough. It didn't press in with the hunger that I'd felt when I'd looked at the blackness beyond the lights that Nuovyl and I had used.

"The painting doesn't do it justice." Not yet anyway. "You'd understand if you'd gone down and seen the towers."

"I'm better off not going down. Twenty percent higher gravity would be too much of a strain for any length of time."

"I wish you could have seen the towers." And I did.

"That's why you're here." She smiled, warmly. "So that everyone everywhere can see them as you saw and felt them."

"That makes it my interpretation."

"Who better to make it?"

"I'm not sure I want that kind of responsibility. What people think of the Danannians—they're not really from Danann, are they? So why do we call them that?"

"All human cultures are cultures of names. All too often we think we know something once we give it a name. That's why what you're doing is so important."

That didn't make the sudden weight on my shoulders any lighter.

"Are you going to include pictures of the pilots?" she asked.

I could tell the question wasn't casual. "You think I should."

"It's another aspect of contrast."

I understood what she hadn't said. The more effective I was at portraying the alienness of Danann, the more necessary the touches of human faces and human artifacts would be, in order to convey that Danann was real—and not just a series of representations from my imagination. Creating that balance might be harder than representing Danann accurately.

43 CHANG

Barely made it to the mess for the evening meal on threeday evening before the captain did. Had to take the first seat I could find and ended up beside Major Singh. He was the navigator. On the other side was Lieutenant Tuala, the one needleboat pilot I'd really never met, just seen infrequently in the ready room, the mess, or on the ramps or lifts.

"Are you in navigation as well?"

Tuala nodded, almost shyly. "Assistant navigator."

"Most of the time," Singh added. "Except when he's getting an adrenaline fix in one of the needles."

"I'm just a backup pilot," Tuala added. "Qualified, but I don't see much time in the cockpit, except for fams or routine runs."

Almost suggested that he might now, but realized nothing had changed. The *Magellan* had one less pilot, but one less needle.

"Better for you," Singh pointed out. "Mortality of needle pilots in combat is thirty percent."

Noted that Singh didn't wear wings. Most navigators were pilots or former pilots. "Were you ever a pilot?"

"Fifteen years was enough." He chuckled. "I could have kept the wings if I'd spent another five as a needle pilot or a command pilot, but I couldn't handle multiple links and didn't want to risk another five years when the politicians were talking about a limited border action against the Covenanters. Limited border actions are hard on needle pilots." He looked past me at Tuala. "Keep telling the young fellow that, but he likes those wings."

"The extra pay isn't bad, either," Tuala quipped.

"Youth . . ." Singh shook his head. "It's a miracle any of them survive it."

Didn't know whether to be complimented or insulted by the assumption that I wasn't "youth."

Major Singh took several sips of the coffee, then set the mug down. "I always hope, but D.S.S. coffee tastes the same in every ship."

"Better than the stuff on a lot of orbit stations," I pointed out.

"I had hoped it might be different here, but the cooks are still D.S.S."

"Where did you come from?"

"I was the engineer on the *Tours*. The exec, she came from the *Dauntless*."

Didn't know either. Wasn't surprising with so many D.S.S. ships. "The *Dauntless*?"

"She's one of the older dreadnoughts. Commander Lilekalani was the exec there. Thought she would have gotten her own command, or at least become an exec on a new dreadnought. Same's true of Captain Spier. Pulled her from command of *Courageous*."

"They probably wanted experience."

"That was my thought. Commander Morgan, he doesn't fit that, though. He was the exec on the *Bruce* years back, then went to D.S.S. headquarters, some say logistics, others say he spent time on the planning staff. I even heard rumors about intelligence. I thought he'd retired."

"Logistics or planning . . . maybe he was in on the planning of the expedition," I suggested. Intelligence made as much sense as the others. Maybe more, but I wasn't about to say so.

"So D.S.S. stuck him here to make sure everything went the way it was supposed to?" Singh looked at the coffee mug. Didn't pick it up. "That could be. He caught every detail when he was number two on the *Bruce*."

"He catches them now," Tuala said, almost under his breath.

"You expected something else?" asked Singh.

Half the table grinned. So did I.

44 FITZHUGH

The first day on Danann, Nuovyl and I went though seven towers, one of each of the general configurations used in the megaplex. In an area of over a quarter million square kays, there were only seven basic structures, although the necessarily sketchy surveys suggested that each tower differed slightly from every other one of the same type.

The second day, I dragged myself out of the bunk and stood there, stretching sore and tight muscles—not so sore as they could have been without the workouts.

"It doesn't get any easier." Dashiell Grant-Wong grinned at me from the adjoining bunk. He was an electrical engineer, but I'd never encountered one with three separate doctorates who understood every aspect of electronic flows beginning with weak and strong atomic forces.

"How long have you been down here?"

"From the beginning, with two breaks up on the ship."

"Have you discovered anything of interest?"

"It's what I haven't discovered that's interesting."

Because I was experiencing a headache, I merely looked at him.

"There's no discrete framework or infrastructure for power or energy transmission. The towers would require more energy than could be supplied by solar energy, and that's assuming that the anomalous composites provided one hundred percent efficiency of conversion. They're also atmospherically permeable under certain conditions. Those conditions suggest an atmosphere with twenty percent more oxygen than Tellurian norm."

With an effort less than supreme, but more than normal, I stretched another set of protesting muscles. "So we have towers constructed out of a material we cannot analyze or replicate powered by electricity or other energy flows we cannot trace—"

"We're getting good analyses." Grant-Wong's mouth twisted into a grimacing smile. "We just can't figure out how they created what we've analyzed. Then, it also could be that the TOE is wrong."

"TOE?"

"Theory of Everything."

How could TOE be wrong? Close to three thousand years of experimentation had validated its basic precepts and structure.

He must have understood my incredulity. "It could be that TOE is correct—and has been for billions of years. There are measurements of light and gravitons from more distant galaxies that don't quite fit. They've been dismissed as measurement errors. What if they weren't?"

I knew some science, but I was no physicist. "Then what?"

"Maybe something changed in the universe." He grinned again. "Or maybe we don't understand things as well as we think we do."

My wager, were I an aficionado of betting upon matters about which I knew little, for that was the fashion of most who gambled, would have been upon our lack of understanding of a universe about which we knew less than we thought we did.

I made my way to the facilities before getting cleaned up and dressed. Breakfast helped. After eating, I donned the armor in the locker room, later than most of the expedition members, who had already departed for various alien locales.

Nuovyl was suited and waiting for me by the main lock, holding his helmet. I scrutinized him. "Were you able to arrange the transport and opening the towers?"

"Ah . . . yes and no, sir. Commander Morgan had already insisted that sections of towers be opened all across the megaplex. There is an area where narrow ramps have been melted and doors have been opened some thirty kays to the northeast of here. It has not been investigated, except briefly by the tech crew that cut the door catches." Nuovyl glanced past me.

I turned. Kaitlin Henjsen stood there, her visage not quite so dark as the airless sky outside of the temporary base where I stood.

"Professor Fitzhugh?"

I waited for her to continue whatever peroration she was about to disgorge upon me.

"You have requested transportation to an unexplored area. Given the vast expanse of the megaplex, we will never be able to explore all sections in the limited time allotted to us. For that reason, more standard archeological practices have been modified. Still, I would request that, should you discover any artifact at all, or any internal attributes that present a new or different aspect of Danann, you do not disturb it, but leave it untouched and contact me immediately."

"I have no difficulty at all with that stipulation, Doctor, none whatsoever."

"Good. Best of luck." Her countenance lightened only slightly.

Within another quarter stan, I was seated on the front bench seat of a slider-sled that was speeding silently northeast along the curved boulevards that had been canals billions of years in the past. The towers conveyed an impression of dark canyon walls, except when the sled lights—or those I trained upon them—momentarily created abstract patterns of silver and shadow.

By the time we had covered twenty-five kays, every new section we passed through looked just like every other one, no matter how often I told myself that that each structure varied from every other tower. My anticipation was that such similarity would soon become unnervingly overwhelming.

45 CHANG

On fiveday, I was scheduled to take shuttle one planetside with the next set of scientists and pick up the returnees. Wondered if Professor Fitzhugh would be coming back up. Had no way of knowing. Made it to the ready room with ten minutes to spare before officers' call.

Morgan was already there. He motioned me over. "You won't be doing the regular shuttle run today. Lieutenant Braun will handle it after you finish another assignment. Dr. Lazar and Dr. Polius need you to take shuttle two and make slow passes over the lake where landing zone alpha was. They need to observe what's happening below the ice, and they want an overview that they can't get from the surface."

"The shuttles aren't designed for that."

Morgan shrugged. "We all know that, but Danann doesn't have an atmosphere. Their equipment is too heavy for the flitter. The shuttles are all we have that will carry the instrumentation that they want. They can't monitor the activity beneath the lake effectively, because all those anomalous composites block or distort the heat patterns and any other signals. We can get some readings from low orbit, but not all, and the ones we have been able to get aren't precise enough."

"None of us took anything into low orbit."

"I took the flitter. That's why I know its equipment won't work. You three have been busy enough."

And he hadn't? Just looked at him. Hard.

"I needed the practice."

I understood that.

"You're not to put the shuttle in any position or configuration that over-stresses the hull or drives—or you. . . ." Morgan went on, hurriedly, as if he needed to get back to operations. ". . . the receivers and receptors are compatible with all equipment they have down there, and they can tap into the shuttle's system. If they have questions, link them to Major Hondohl in Comm . . ."

By the time he finished, he'd made it clear he didn't like what the scientists wanted, but couldn't say no. His point was clear—no strain or hazard to the shuttle or its equipment.

Took my time in preflighting and running though the checklist. Told Ysario to do the same. Even so, shuttle two and I were planetside by eleven hundred. By eleven-fifteen Maejean Polius and Cleon Lazar were standing with me in the shuttle's main cargo bay. We all stood in full armor.

Lazar was a big man, huge in armor. Too big to be a physicist. He watched two techs slip equipment into the empty receptors on the bulkhead aft of the pilot's section. "Fine." He turned. "There's enough space here, but will the receivers be able to handle the signals?"

"The equipment is completely compatible," I assured him. "Let me link you to Major Hondohl in Comm. You can verify that." Wasn't about to argue on secondhand reassurance.

Lazar and Hondohl talked for less than five minutes. Polius looked annoyed in a pinch-faced way. Lazar was nodding at the end.

"Better than I'd hoped," he said, after I broke the link for him.

"Could you explain what you hope to do?" I finally asked.

"We've begun to detect various energy emissions," Lazar began, "but the angle and composition of the confinement basin effectively block any monitoring except on the lake's surface itself. The emissions seem to be intermittent, or they're moving, and we don't have enough equipment to cover the lake in order to monitor what's happening . . ."

"And the ice beneath is melting fast enough that you don't want to risk it, either?"

"That won't happen. There has to be an equilibrium reached because the surface temperature is so low and the radiating area so large that it can't melt all the way to the surface. We're more limited by the lack of enough remotes to cover the surface. By flying higher above the lake, we can obtain the data simultaneously in real time . . ."

Understood that part, but still wondered about his "equilibrium." Seemed to me that what the ancient aliens had done didn't fit a lot of expectations, scientific or otherwise.

"How high do you want the shuttle?"

"We'd like to try a thousand meters, then go higher, if we need to."

With the power of the shuttle, a thousand meters AGL was almost on the deck. "That will limit the time we have."

"Can you hover over the lake at that height?" That was Polius.

"For maybe a quarter stan before I burned out the AG drives, and we went straight down."

"Flitters can hover."

Ignored the exasperation in her voice. "Only in an atmosphere, and that's not here. There, they can use diverters. That gives lift because they're acting against atmosphere." That was a gross oversimplification, and not really correct, but I didn't care. The basic point was the same. You couldn't hover for long without burning lots of power, and the less atmosphere and the more gravs, the faster you burned it.

Lazar smiled faintly. He knew I'd oversimplified, but he wasn't saying anything.

Polius turned to him. "Cleon . . . is she . . . is that right?"

"Lieutenant Chang may be slightly conservative. I would judge that she might be able to hold position over the lake for so long as seventeen and a half minutes before all systems failed."

Polius missed the glint in his eyes. I didn't.

"How slowly can you go?" demanded the geologist.

I linked to the shuttle system for the calculations. My own estimate had been close, but I'd wanted the backup. "It's a power trade-off. At a thousand meters AGL, the shuttle's limited to roughly two hours at max power in this grav field before the heat dissipaters—"

"The temperature out there is close to absolute zero, and you can't dissipate heat?"

"Not inside the shuttle."

Clear that Polius had trouble understanding trade-offs. Greater heat dissipation meant either less endurance in deep space or even greater systems complexity. Complexity is the enemy of effectiveness and survivability in space.

"What about two thousand meters?" asked Lazar.

"You'll get another thirty to forty minutes. Either way, we'll have to return to the *Magellan* before I can set you back down on Danann."

"Power constraints?" asked Lazar.

"Exactly."

"You mean we have to go back to the ship?"

"Only for fusactor mass."

"But . . ." Lazar was frowning.

"We're getting the water from the surface, as ice, but it has to be melted and purified." Purification wasn't absolutely necessary in emergency situations, but I didn't want the shuttle sidelined for feed-line cleaning and repairs just to accommodate a pouty geologist—and there was always the possibility of power surges with impure mass. Not something I wanted to experience in dealing with a higher-grav planet without an atmosphere.

"We'll try two thousand meters, then," Lazar stated.

Polius glared. Kept her mouth shut, though. Physicist ignored her. I would have, too.

They settled into the couches mounted before the equipment boards. I went back to the controls and began the liftoff checklist.

Navigator Control, this is Sherpa Tigress, commencing mission liftoff this time.

Stet, Tigress.

Couldn't tell if Morgan was pleased, worried, indifferent.

While I circled the shuttle over the frozen surface of the lake, I used the screens to catch and record images—all through temperature differentials. Still pitch-black below. Images had to be enhanced, and enlarged. Mostly recorded, but occasionally even took a look. Saw one gout of steam shoot up through a crack in the ice—so thin that it quick-froze and fell like ice dust.

Also monitored the internal comm between Polius and Lazar.

". . . temperatures at the bottom more than four hundred Kelvins . . ."

". . . readings . . . circular pattern . . . ovals again . . ."

". . . look at that! That plume is almost a hundred meters high . . ."

I kept a close eye on the fusactor and the AG drives. The slightest excess heat trend, and we were headed to orbit and the *Magellan*.

Surface of the ice was covered with humps and small peaks. They hadn't been there two days before. Whatever was under the lake was something different. No radioactives I knew lasted billions of years without significant decay. No device humans built would create that much heat that soon, especially not after even a century of disuse. Danann had been abandoned billions of years back.

Seeing those gouts of superheated steam turning into icefalls sent chills down my back, insulated armor or not.

46 FITZHUGH

Despite the lack of artifacts and my inability even to suggest where such might be found, the three days I had spent on Danann had been more than worth the exhaustion and inconvenience. No matter what Dr. Taube and some of those who had demurred from visiting the megaplex said, seeing and walking through a city—even an alien city—imparted a feel that no amount of statistics and maps could have conveyed. Rational and considered analyses may be the coin of the realm of academia, but such analyses are worthless unless backed by intuition grounded in experience.

In the days following my return, I stepped up my exercise program and tried to find greater meaning in the positioning of the Danannian structures.

On twoday, I had spent the morning deep in analyzing ratios and arcs . . . and getting results, but not ones that contributed much to my understanding of the Danannian megaplex, save that there seemed to be a relationship between the length of each canal and the angular value of the arc formed. So engrossed had I been in calculations that doubtless would heterize nothing that I was more than slightly tardy in reaching the mess.

For whatever reason, the captain was only settling herself at her table as I hastened into the mess. While Special Deputy Minister Allerde was already seated, two chairs to the captain's left, the executive officer was not present, nor was Commander Morgan, but Major Tepper and a number of the pilots were seated at the table closest to the captain's table. Lieutenant Chang glanced in my direction, then looked away quickly. Had I offended her in some untoward fashion? I hoped not. For all her terseness, and despite her considerable pulchritude, behind both lay a mind of considerable power and depth, and I would have liked to talk with her far more.

Yet . . . how could I broach the diffidence she cultivated? One could not say, even indirectly, "I believe you have a beautiful mind, and I would appreciate the chance to know you in greater depth," without being instantly categorized as lupine in character and lecherous in intent.

There was a space at the table adjoining the one occupied by the pilots, and I eased into a seat across from Chendor Barna, the almost reclusive artist, and beside Bryanna Nomura. As the expeditions cryptographer, Bryanna's utility heretofore had been as marginal as my own. "Good evening."

"And to you, Liam." She smiled.

"I fear we represent a convention of the underutilized . . ."

"Perhaps." She took a sip of ersatz merlot. "I have been thinking. About linguistics and codes. We need them, but would the Danannians?"

I passed on imbibing the merlot, ignoring the carafe to my right and sipping plain water instead. "That's an old argument. Given our physiological evolution and limitations, language is a necessity if we wish to function above the most basic level of hunter-gatherers. Therefore, we assume that language, especially a written language, would be a necessity for all species, including ancient aliens."

"Could the megaplex have been a hive, and could the Danannians have been the ultimate social insect species? All this similarity suggests great regularity, and to me, that suggests a culture more like intelligent social insects . . ." She paused, tilting her head, her black eyes intent upon me.

"That would appear to be the initial and obvious conclusion, and one borne out by our own experience, but I would question the validity of an assumptive determination based on unconscious application of anthropic principles."

"An explanation might help, Professor."

Restraining the urge to comment upon Bryanna's lack of perspicacity and unfamiliarity with the richness and depth of language, I forced a smile. "We might do better by taking into account ser Barna's disciplines, and regard the structures and dwellings below as blank canvases or untouched light matrices."

"Their apparent emptiness does suggest something like that," Barna replied.

"The physicists have determined that the walls and floors and ceilings of the structures are composed of an anomalous composite that can extrude itself into any shape. The exact mechanics and physics of this technology have not yet been discerned, but the fact that it existed suggests a very different social structure. I would submit that decor and decoration rested upon the creative ability of the individual inhabitant—and that the shapes, even the colors, of the basic furnishings and accessories were molded by and to the will of whoever lived in each set of quarters."

Both Bryanna and Chendor nodded.

"Initial indications are that they also possessed devices—built into each unit—that resembled nanetic processors that could provide such items as clothing, food, bedding, and the like. This suggests that wealth—if you will—or power—was based on the ability of the individual to create and conceptualize, and not upon the ability—as in our societies—to manipulate the physical elements of survival in order to create a position of superiority . . ."

"Not all human societies based power on that—"

"Or those that use the illusory promise of rewards in a hereafter that has never been proved to exist by any scientific test or experimental methods ever developed over more than five millennia," I added quickly.

Two stewards appeared from the kitchen area, each in the white garb so traditional in military vessels and so impractical for all its tradition. They glided toward the captain's table. Nearing it, they turned, and in almost measured cadence, each moved toward a different end of the longer rectangular table, each carrying a basket heaped with bread. Both used both hands and arms under the pseudowicker baskets.

Bread shouldn't have been near that heavy. Ancient alarms went off, and the chair where I'd been seated went flying back as I took three steps, trying to keep my body level.

"What . . ."

The steward turning toward the head of the captain's table lowered the too-heavy bread basket slightly. My aim was off slightly, and my shoulder hit the outside of his right shoulder blade, an effort useless except to throw off the aim of the neural disruptor concealed by the basket.

Lieutenant Chang—it had to be her, the only blonde at the pilots' table—was moving before any of the others.

Thrumm! The ugly whine from the weapon of the other steward filled the mess. Someone yelled, and others screamed.

The steward I'd struck tried to bring up the disruptor—and that was a mistake. My elbow crushed his throat. He turned, still trying to bring the weapon to bear. A spray of neural damage slammed across the table where some of the pilots were sitting. Two went down—I thought, but wasn't looking for that.

I broke the arm holding the disruptor, and the heavy weapon hit the floor with a *clunk*. His face was turning red, and he kept struggling—deep-conditioning against pain. I levered him to the floor and snapped his good arm out of the socket, then slammed my bootheel where it should stop his heart.

The second steward had been staggered by a platter thrown into his face, but stepped back, his face totally immobile, and raised his weapon once more, aiming all too deliberately, not toward the captain's table, but toward the pilots. People were moving, but most all too slowly, as if they could not believe that such an occurrence might befall them.

Chang had tried to reach the surviving steward, but one of the other officers had bolted and knocked her sideways momentarily. Lerrys was behind her, but he'd been blocked as well by someone trying to escape.

The remaining suicider was bringing his disruptor to bear on Chang.

I couldn't have that. Not at all.

Everything moved so slowly. I'd forgotten that. I snatched a chair, but couldn't get a clear throw. The only tactic left was to keep the steward from taking out any more officers. Chair in hand before me, I jumped onto the table where the pilots had been sitting and took two steps—and launched myself at the remaining attacker. The chair might deflect some of the disruptor's flow.

He jerked the disruptor around—away from Chang and toward me—and another *thrumm* filled the mess, so loud . . . so very loud . . . until the darkness swallowed it.

47 CHANG

Fourteen hundred, and I was in Morgan's ops office up on the command deck. Lerrys had taken Braun's afternoon duty. Shook my head. Still couldn't believe she was gone, not the way it had happened. Morgan had a black expression. Even without the name, I could have told that his background was ancient Welsh. He didn't say anything for long minutes after I sat down. Neither did I.

"Thank you." His words were flat.

"You're welcome. I did what I could." Wished it had been more. The first steward had taken out Braun and Rynd. Second had managed to wipe out Major Tepper, Major Alynso, Beurck, and Rigney. All six had died in the mess, brains and nerves scrambled. Couldn't believe that Braun was dead. Sitting there, eating one minute, and dead moments later. You expect you might die piloting. It's dangerous, no matter what they say. Don't expect to get your nerves fried by a disruptor eating lunch. Gone . . . just like that.

Fitzhugh had hit the phony steward targeting the captain just in time. She'd escaped being hit. So had the Special Deputy Minister. Except for Braun and Rynd—who'd been caught by the blast misdirected from Fitzhugh's attack—all the damage had been done by the second steward.

If Major Singh hadn't gotten in my way, I might have been able to do more. Might have gotten killed, too. Something like that, you can never tell. "If you'd been there, you might have done better."

"This noon was the first time in days, maybe weeks, when the captain was there and I wasn't."

"Sounds like they waited until you weren't there."

"It could be. Or it could be coincidence." Morgan frowned. "Neither one aimed at the Special Deputy Minister. They never even looked at him. They should have. If they'd taken out both him and the captain . . ."

Hadn't thought about that. Should have. "Allerde couldn't be involved."

"You can't say that about anyone these days." He paused. "You're right, though."

Had to think about that for a moment. Didn't like what I came up with.

"Do you know what it means?" Morgan asked.

"Probably not."

"What do you think?"

"Took time to get the stewards, replace them or deep-condition them. Means that someone knew about the *Magellan* and Danann from the beginning. Maybe they didn't know who'd be the Comity rep on board—or if there'd even be one."

"That's my guess."

"Guess? Did you and DeLisle get anything out of him before . . ."

"No . . . he had an autonomic nerve bloc. Heart, lungs, they all stopped. In the chaos, it took too long to get him to sick bay. Revival wasn't possible." Morgan's lips tightened. "You and Professor Fitzhugh acted before anyone else. How did you know that there was something wrong?"

"I didn't, not until the professor threw himself . . . how is he?"

"He took a direct shot from the disruptor. He's in a medcrib, but he'll make it. He shouldn't." Morgan didn't sound happy.

"That bothers you? Without him attacking the first steward—"

"It could have been much worse," Morgan admitted. "The one he got was after the captain. That shot took out Braun and Rynd instead."

"The professor couldn't have known that. The man he hit only got off one blast."

"The professor crushed his windpipe, broke both arms, and triggered instant heart failure, then vaulted a table with a chair and distracted the second killer long enough for you to take him out. Does that sound like your typical professor?"

I'd figured that from the beginning. "He isn't a professor?"

"No. That's the problem. He has been for years. He's got awards and publications, even. But . . . how many professors have that kind of reaction and training?"

Could tell Morgan was pissed at not knowing more about the professor. "You think he was planted by D.S.S.?"

"Comity Diplomatic Corps, more likely. I think he's an unconscious plant."

"Conditioned? Like the two stewards, except by our side?"

Morgan shook his head. "No. Not for the expedition in particular. He already had the conditioning. They went out looking for former commandos or operatives who had the academic or professional background for the expedition. I'd bet Fitzhugh was a single termer who used the service to get his education and never looked back. Their conditioning runs deep, and trying to remove it is usually worse than leaving it. They plant social mores and morals all over it. It takes something like what happened to trigger it, and intelligence types figure that in such situations, it's justified."

Another aspect of the Comity I'd never known. Made me just as glad I could go back to being a civilian. Hoped I could, anyway. Also explained a lot about the way the professor moved. Made sense. Just hadn't thought of it that way. Stopped.

"What?"

"Nothing." Wasn't about to tell Morgan I'd realized where I'd seen Fitzhugh before—in the high-gee workout room.

"Lieutenant."

"Didn't realize it until now. I'd seen him in the workout rooms once."

"So he stayed in shape. That figures. They'd pick a compulsive."

Didn't know that I'd like to be called that. "You think there are others?"

"Some . . . but not many. He might be the only one. That combination's hard to find." Morgan shook his head. "Bastards."

Knew he meant Comity Diplomatic.

"They *knew* we'd be infiltrated."

"That's three subverted so far, isn't it?"

"So far." He sounded resigned.

For the first time, I began to worry. Really worry. "What else?"

"Pilots. We lost Ungera in that Sunnite fight, and Rynd, Rigney, Beurck, and Braun in the mess. That leaves us with four needleboats, and just Shaimen, Lindskold, and Tuala." Almost asked why the *Magellan* didn't have more needleboat pilots. Then I realized why. Most times, when a needle was lost, so was the pilot. What I'd managed to do with Shaimen was the exception. And in modern warfare, either all the officers on a capital ship survived a battle—or none did.

"I can handle a needleboat." Couldn't believe I'd said that.

Morgan smiled, faintly. "I might have to take you up on that, Lieutenant, but not until we're on the way back. While we're here, you're more valuable as a shuttle pilot, and with only you and Lerrys as first-class shuttle pilots . . ."

"What else?"

"A CW flotilla is missing. No one knows where it is. So is one from the Worlds of the Covenant."

"How did you find out that?"

"We've been running the couriers. That came from the *Bannister* when it came back yesterday." He shrugged. "They could be anywhere. They could be out to fight each other. It's a big galaxy, and they don't like each other much."

"You don't think that."

"Not anymore."

"Why them?"

"The Chrysanthemum Worlds and the Worlds of the Covenant are both pressing the Middle Kingdom, as well as each other, because they're worried about the recent tech advances in the Middle Kingdom. The CWs don't want to see the Middle Kingdom regain a tech advantage. The death-conditioning on the second steward was typical of CW neural work. That's what Major DeLisle thought."

Made a sick kind of sense. Weaken the pilot and command structure of the *Magellan* . . . "What about the *Alwyn*?"

"Two pilots died from a malfunction of the *Alwyn's* shuttle and a needle yesterday. They haven't traced how it happened. They probably won't. There's not much left of either craft. Collided, partial explosion, and the vector imparted blew them into Danann's gravity well."

"Just happened that way." I snorted. "It wasn't any coincidence."

"Neither captain thinks so, but it is a combat mission."

"Just not the kind of combat anyone expected."

"Not yet." Morgan was telling me that would come as well.

"That why you haven't told anyone?" I could see why he hadn't, but it bothered me.

"Do you think that would help anyone?" he countered. "Anyway, we'll have to handle all the replenishment runs to the *Alwyn* now."

He was trying to change the subject away from the combat angle. He was probably right, but it still nagged at me. Whatever I thought, Morgan was going to do what he was going to do. "You don't like to tell anyone anything unless you think it's absolutely necessary, do you?"

He laughed, once. "You should understand that."

Almost shot back that I wasn't the ops officer, either. Didn't. Didn't know as I wouldn't have done the same. Instead, I backed off. "Have the scientists found anything that's worth all that?"

"They've got samples of those anomalous composites. Sorens thinks that he can duplicate some of the properties on one now that he's seen how the Danannians did it. The others, he's not even certain how it's possible. Lazar says it will take years of observations and investigation to determine what's occurring under the lake. Whatever that process is, he's convinced that it's somehow linked to Danann itself and its velocity and position."

"We don't have years."

"We may not have even weeks."

"Anything else?"

"No one else has managed to figure out anything. Not yet, anyway. There's nothing else down there except the towers and the canals and lakes. Every building is empty. I've told Dr. Henjsen to step up the process of opening and scanning towers. That's whether she and her team can ever investigate them all."

His smile was sour. "She's not happy with that, either. It's highly improper archeology."

"Proper is fine when you have the time."

"She understands that. She just doesn't like it. None of us do." Morgan stood. "I need to meet with the captain. I'll have a revised schedule ready for you and Lerrys later."

"We'll split the duties until you have a chance to get to that."

Morgan gestured to the hatch. All the spaces on the command deck had airtight hatches. I went out and headed for the down ramp. He headed toward the bridge.

After I left the ops area, I went down to the thirtieth deck.

The medtech on duty there looked at me. "You're checking on Dr. Fitzhugh, Lieutenant?"

I nodded.

"His reactions are better. He'll be in the crib for at least another week, though. That's what Major DeLisle said."

"What about his mind? His nerves?"

"Hard to say, sir. Most people don't survive that kind of jolt. His brain is functioning on all levels, though."

How it was functioning was another question. No one could answer that now. Hoped he'd recover everything. Hoped . . . but you never knew. My guts twisted. If he hadn't gone for the second steward, I'd be the one in the med-crib—or dead.

I made my way back to the ready room. I wanted to check the schedule. Lerrys and I would have to cover all the shuttle drops between us. Still hard to believe that Braun was gone. Just like that. We hadn't had that much in common, but she'd been a good pilot. Wished I'd made an effort to know her better.

Kept walking up the ramp, going up in circles. Hadn't wanted to take the lift. Might have had to talk to someone, and I wasn't ready for that.

48 GOODMAN/BOND

We'd been orbiting Danann for almost two months. So far as I could tell, we were alone in whatever part of the galactic void where the *Magellan* had ended up. Rather than do make-work, I'd taken on trying to repair and replace a torp power converter I'd salvaged, for my own purposes, although the chief didn't know that, since he was happy at the idea of getting a spare converter.

After a week, I was almost ready to give up. It was like attempting to weld spider silk with a battle laser. It was one of those things that was theoretically possible, except that very few would ever be successful at it. I didn't have many options, though, because I needed a converter, and I was running out of time.

Right off, I'd found what amounted to a mech tutorial on the ship's micro-tronics—including power converters. The first message was clear enough.

This is an emergency procedure. Do not attempt unless no other alternatives are available . . .

From there it got more difficult. I didn't have any choice, though, not the way the major and the chief kept track of the active torps and the spare converters. Still, I'd managed to get the damaged converter disassembled without further damaging anything. Half the time, the problem wasn't doing something, but figuring *how*. The tutorial would say that the filament control submodule needed to be removed before working on modulator beta. It even gave detailed directions for repair of the modulator. My problem was that there were no directions—or practical schematics—for the removal of the submodule. That meant working with indirect optical enhancement to determine the method of attachment and attachment points.

It took me half a day to discover the pair of inert attachment pins on the underside, perfectly matched in color, flush with the adjoining surface, each less than half a millimeter in length. Removing them without destroying them took less than fifteen minutes each—after I'd created a special tool to do so. Making the tool took several hours.

When the chief summoned us together late on twoday afternoon, I was more than ready for a break—until he announced that two stewards had smuggled disruptors into the ship and murdered something like six officers. Most of them had been pilots. He'd gone on from there. ". . . we don't know what's down on that planet, except a lot of towers. Not yet, anyway. What we do know is this. It's important enough that our enemies would kill every one of us to get what's there. Our duty is to make sure that they don't get it, or we'll be dead and your families and children will be speaking something else—if they even survive."

That was all fine, but what if that duty turned the Morning Star or the Spear of Iblis over to those who had no concept of their power? From the Garden and the first Fall, from the Tower of Babel, from the Harrowing of Old Earth, there had always been those who placed their judgment above God's, and the results had always been devastating.

"Keep your eyes open for anything that looks strange, and let me or the officers know." Stuval looked at Ciorio, then some of the shield techs, then at me.

I looked him back and gave him a nod.

"That's all."

"Chief laid it on pretty thick there," said Ciorio, as we eased back aft.

"If you were him, wouldn't you? It's getting scary."

"Yeah . . . you expect crazy stuff from the Sunnis or the Covenanters, but D.S.S. stewards frying officers . . ." Ciorio paused. "I've known one or two that deserved it, but not here."

"You think we'll get attacked again?"

"Out here in the middle of nowhere? Doesn't seem likely." Ciorio laughed. "None of it seems likely, does it?"

I shook my head. How likely was it that the Morning Star would reappear? If it did, it wouldn't be by coincidence. Only God or Lucifer could have engineered that, and it would mean great trials—even perhaps the beginning of the end, and the coming of the Final Kingdom.

"How are you coming on that converter?"

"Slowly. They weren't designed to be repaired and rebuilt." Of course, the colonel wouldn't accept that as an excuse. In his book, I should have just stolen a converter from one of the torps in the armory. There were a few problems with that. First, the array was locked. I could get through any lock. Second, there were alarms, and some of them I had yet to figure out, not because I couldn't, but because I'd have had to take them apart to do so, and the whole area was under continual surveillance. The third problem was that it took time to disassemble the power system to get the converter out.

Now . . . I could run fake feeds when I had armory duty, and break into the array, and get the converter and put the AG signaler together by the end of the watch. The only problem was that I'd be caught with the goods in hand, with nowhere to go. And when the questioning started, my internal defenses would go to work, and, before long, I'd cease to be. That approach didn't appeal to me.

If I failed to get the signaler assembled, and the *Magellan* returned, I'd at least have a fighting chance to go to ground. The Galaxy was a big place. I'd have been a failure, but I'd be a live failure. I suppose that was one of my faults. I believed in living for a cause, not dying for it, at least not needlessly. The colonel would have found that a fault, too.

But I couldn't dwell on that. I already had recorded the monitor feeds I'd use. I'd done those weeks before on a midwatch, and I'd created hidden bypass ports to override the real visuals. Those had been easy compared to what lay ahead.

49 *BARNA*

When the stewards started firing at the captain's table, for a moment all I could do was look. I should have ducked under the table, or done something sensible— or heroic like Liam Fitzhugh. I never saw anyone move so fast. Big as he was, I'd never have picked him as a martial arts specialist. Nor Lieutenant Chang. Between the two of them, they saved some lives, maybe a lot.

I just looked, and the scenes burned into my brain. I couldn't describe them in words. I'd have to paint them, too, along with the alien towers and lights of Danann.

Strangely, after the attack, I wanted to get back to work. I knew I had to finish as much as I could, and the pieces had to be good. More than my pride—or credits—was at stake. I couldn't have made that clear to anyone, even Aeryana, even if she'd been standing at my elbow.

No one said anything except clichéd phrases, the kind I'd never mastered, and the rest of twoday passed, and so did most of threeday, with the expedition experts still on the *Magellan* in a fuguelike shock. The remaining ship's officers were even more distant, and Commander Morgan seemed to be everywhere. I didn't see Lieutenant Chang and Lieutenant Lerrys together, just one or the other. The third shuttle pilot—Braun, the small dark-haired one—she'd been one of those killed. Liam was still alive, but no one was saying whether he'd pull through or not.

I kept painting. I alternated between a tower scene on a large matrix, an oil rendering of Liam in motion just before he struck the first steward, and another mixed-media portrait of Lieutenant Braun. It was the least I could do.

"They're all good."

I almost dropped the light-wand. I turned.

"You make me see Liam Fitzhugh in a way I never saw him," said Elysen. "He's the kind of man who does what he must."

"I didn't see it, either, until he acted."

She settled into the good chair in my work space. "They picked well when they chose you, Chendor. You live what you paint. Good artists do."

"I don't know about that. I feel some of it. A little, anyway." I leaned against the side of the console. I didn't like to talk about painting. "How do you feel? About the attack in the mess yesterday, I mean?"

"I was more astonished than frightened, I think. At my age, death doesn't offer so great a threat." She laughed. "Not that I'm in the slightest ready to give up or die. It's just not a threat, but an inevitability."

"How is your work coming?"

"We're hopeful."

"Can I ask about what?"

"I don't want to say too much, because the results are preliminary, and we're still comparing baselines. That's tedious, because even the ship's systems are limited."

"Baselines?"

"We have observations from five radically different points. That means parallax and temporal adjustments, because each different observation point represents not only a different location but a different time period. That is, the light we've observed comes from a different point in time."

"You didn't answer the first question," I said. "What are you trying to find out?"

"What everyone else is seeking in their own fields—the origin of Danann and Chronos. It's a long process for all of us. Cleon Lazar and the physical scientists are convinced that the alien anomalous composites were designed to do more than they have discovered so far. Yet they have not been able to discover even the theoretical basis for the subatomic mechanisms that make them operate as they do. They've attempted all manner of tests and experiments, but as of the other day, they had little success."

"That was a polite avoidance of what you're working on," I pointed out. "Have your astronomical observations shed any light—" I avoided wincing at the inadvertent pun—"on Danann and Chronos."

"I said that it was premature—"

"Have you?"

"We don't know yet. The observations we've processed and analyzed to date suggest we have an unprecedented astrophysical occurrence. We're beginning to think that the Danannians were possibly a true Type III civilization."

"You need all those observations to say that? From what you and Commander Morgan have already said, the existence and speeds of Danann and Chronos already proved that."

"The cause of their existence might be something even more unprecedented."

"Their existence is unprecedented enough. It's clear that these aliens had technology that we can't match, and may not match for years—even with what we've found here. So they sent two planets hurtling across the universe on exactly opposite courses. If we wanted to throw enough energy at a pair of planets, couldn't we do it?"

"Possibly. It might bankrupt all of humanity. What we're pursuing is far more elegant."

"Elegant? Even higher technology? Or are we talking about the hand of God?"

Elysen laughed again, warmly, then smiled. "Let's just say that it's a bit more controversial than that."

"More controversial than the hand of God?"

"Chendor . . ." The smile vanished. "We really do need absolute certainty, or as close as we can get, before we announce even a hypothesis. I promised the others I wouldn't say anything. Please don't press me."

"It's that momentous?"

The trace of a smile appeared, and it was a sad smile, the kind that, had I captured it upon a canvas, would have made a masterpiece. "Yes."

"I'm sorry."

"So am I, if we're right. It will change everything." She stood and looked at the portrait of Lieutenant Braun. "Beautiful, and such a waste."

Then, she was gone.

After Elysen left, I realized that I really wanted to get back down to Danann. There was something else down there. It wasn't something missing, but something not found. I didn't know that I could find it, but I wanted another chance.

I supposed everyone did.

50 FITZHUGH

Blackness, and white-hot stilettos slicing into my body—those were what I sensed after the steward's weapon. Then came the needles, infinite points of pain, all with the same receptor locus—those were my first thoughts . . . when I could finally attain some semblance of cogitation muddled and inchoate as my self-awareness first was.

In time, subjective eons, the worst of the agony subsided, and I could discern that I was encased in a medcrib. When I saw a hazy figure standing above the crib, I attempted to talk, but discovered that I was immobilized, either physically or physiologically, and the figure perambulated out of my restricted range of vision.

When they finally removed the upper part of the crib, more eons having passed, a major looked down at me. "Don't try to talk yet, Dr. Fitzhugh. There were some spasms in your throat, and we restricted things there. You're going to be fine, but it will be a little while before the effect on your voice wears off. You've been in the crib almost four days, but you should be out of here in just a day or two." From his tone and insignia, he was a doctor.

What had happened in the mess? How could I ask? Was Lieutenant Chang unharmed? What about the captain?

The doctor smiled. "You're somewhat of a hero. I've let Commander Morgan know that you're awake, and he'll be down here shortly. The captain was here earlier."

I managed a slight nod. Even that sent paroxysms of beloid agony through my neck and throat.

"Shortly" was most definitely a generic and personal relevant term, because several long hours went by, their passage eased not in the slightest by the holo-drama displayed above me, entertainment, if it could be termed such, clearly se-lected for plebeian tastes, before the commander peered over the edge of the medcrib.

Commander Morgan's face bore a touch of gray, but the dark half orbs un-der his eyes suggested exhaustion more man age-induced physiological debilita-tion. "Dr. Fitzhugh, I understand that you can hear, but not speak."

I nodded, tentatively and slightly.

"Good." A sardonic smile appeared. "At least, I won't have to explain in endless detail, not until you recover your voice. The stewards killed six people, but you kept the number from being much higher and saved some lives. How many I don't know, but one was the captain's, and she is most grateful. So am I. For better or worse, the casualties were all ship's officers . . ."

How many of them had been pilots? They'd been the closest to the assas-sins, besides those at the captain's table.

". . . I am curious, however. I've never seen a history professor who moved like a commando. Were you in a service commando group at some point?"

I nodded, although I'd tried for years to minimize that aspect of my preaca-demic career. I was just as glad that I wasn't in a position where I was expected to elucidate upon the details.

"I'd imagine that you only stayed in long enough to get basic educational benefits."

That wasn't quite correct. I struggled, but managed to lift a hand that was shaking and show two fingers.

"Oh . . . you spent two tours so that the service would pay for your doctor-ate as well?"

I indicated that I had.

"So you put in forty percent of the time for a full pension, then walked away?"

I would have shrugged, but decided against it.

"Did the Comity Diplomatic Corps talk to you about your service when they offered you the fellowship?"

I shook my head again. I hadn't really been offered it. For all the generous remuneration, I'd been given the choice of accepting it or facing severe adminis-tration disapproval for the rest of what would have been a severely shortened academic career. Morgan evidently thought I'd been selected because of my commando background. That was not only possible, but, in retrospect, highly probable. Even more chilling was that someone had noted my ongoing dedication to physical fitness and to my continued practice of basic commando moves and techniques.

Morgan's questions blurred together around the same topic.

"Did anyone ask you if you had maintained your conditioning?"

"Have you ever engaged in any martial arts competitions since your release from duty?"

"Do you know of anyone at the university who was aware of your commando past or your abilities?"

"Have you ever written or published any articles or books that demonstrated a personal knowledge of commando operations or tactics?"

Finally, the commander surveyed me, taking in my inert status. "One last question. Did you apply for the fellowship you were granted?"

That was an easy headshake.

All Morgan had done since arriving in the infirmary was to question me as though I'd been somehow guilty of some obscure failure of military jurisprudence, which I was not. What made it more irritating was that I'd never really even asked to be a part of the expedition. I'd been pushed into it. Exasperation doubtless manifested itself in my eyes—and the set of my jaw.

"I'm sorry, Professor, for asking all that, but we're still trying to make sense of things."

I managed a weak snort. He wasn't trying to do that. He was trying to find out more about the composition of the scientific team and wondering if he'd been outmaneuvered by the Comity Diplomatic Corps. From his reaction—and mine—it was more than obvious that we'd both been manipulated, and that the Diplomatic Corps had been far more concerned about infiltration than they had indicated to anyone. Morgan was justifiably irritated, but he didn't have to take it out on me, especially in the state in which I found myself.

"I'm lucky that you can't talk, because I have the feeling you have more than a bit to say. Just remember, Professor, we're in this together."

I scarcely could have forgotten.

When he left, I was still fuming, if bottled and exasperated rage qualified as such, and worried about Lieutenant Chang. She had been headed straight toward the second assassin when I'd been hit, and I still didn't know if she had been one of the casualties.

The doctor reappeared. "You need to calm down, Professor Fitzhugh. I know that you must be upset about learning about the deaths—"

I shook my head and nodded, attempting to convey the idea that what he said wasn't precisely correct.

I held up my hand and mimed writing, then keyboarding.

"I'll see what I can do." His expression was one of concern, far more than Commander Morgan had expressed.

Within moments, he returned with a stylus and an impression pad. "I don't have a keyboard that I can use around the medcrib."

The tremors in my hand almost triumphed over my will, but I managed to scrawl two words: "Who died?"

The doctor warred with the major, but finally he spoke. "You're well enough to know. Not the captain, and the exec wasn't there. Mostly pilots . . ."

I tried not to wince, but waited.

"Major Tepper, Major Alynso, Lieutenant Braun, Lieutenant Rigney, Lieutenant Rynd, and Lieutenant Beurck."

I crabbed out two more words. "Other injured?"

"You're in your own company, Professor. No one else was injured, except for scrapes and bruises."

I nodded and mouthed the words, "Thank you."

"You need some rest. I'm going to step up a touch of relaxants."

More blackness and hot needles weren't anywhere near the top of my desires, conscious or unconscious, but he had already programmed the medcrib, because my eyes began to close even before I could lift a finger to express a contrary opinion on the impression pad.

51 CHANG

Morgan insisted on cutting the number of shuttle runs down to Danann and back. Also worked out something with the mech chiefs so that none of the techs ever worked alone on the shuttles. Still, days were long.

From what I overheard from the experts I carried planetside, no one had found anything new. Same kinds of buildings everywhere, all sealed, with nothing inside. No sign of any life, except maybe something on the microscopic goo level. Water still boiled under the first lake, but it reached the equilibrium that Lazar had predicted. Just got steam that froze soon as it cleared the lake ice. Glad he was right. So far, anyway.

I'd checked on the professor several times, but he was still in the medcrib. Early oneday, found a message for me on the system from Major DeLisle. Since I'd stopped to check on Professor Fitzhugh several times, he thought I'd like to know the professor could receive visitors.

Had oneday as a standby. Lerrys was duty with shuttle two. Midmorning I went down to deck thirty. Most times, I'd dealt with the medtech. This time, DeLisle was there, brown-haired, blocky, muscular. Didn't fit the image of his name.

"Lieutenant Chang, I thought you might like to see the professor. That's why you're here, isn't it?"

Ignored the question. "Has anyone stopped to see him?"

DeLisle smiled faintly. "One of the other professors. She didn't stay long. The captain was here briefly. Commander Morgan has stopped several times—and the artist. He was here earlier this morning."

Morgan wouldn't give up on the Diplomatic Corps. Didn't understand why he was pushing Fitzhugh. Unconscious agents were just that, and that was why they used them. Ser Barna seemed decent. He'd been sitting with the professor when everything went to shit. Probably came to thank Fitzhugh.

The professor didn't look bad. Not for someone who'd almost died, and should have. He was propped up in a bed, but his left side was partly encased in an extension of the medcrib.

"Professor."

"Lieutenant Chang." His voice was low and raspy. "I must apologize for the less-than-acceptable resonance of my speech, but I've suffered a certain debilitation."

Couldn't help but smile at the wryness in his tone and words. "Anyone else wouldn't have been debilitated. They'd have been dead. I wanted to thank you, tell you . . ." What could tell him that wouldn't sound patronizing?

He lifted his right hand, waved off my words. Did it in a courtly way, though. "You did the hard part, I heard. If you had not incapacitated the remaining assassin, what I did would have been immaterial and irrelevant."

"You were commando, weren't you? First elite?"

He lifted his eyebrows.

"Team leader, too, I'd bet."

"I trust that I have the sagacity never to wager anything against you, Lieutenant. You perceive far more than others are willing to credit you. You were doubtless far more effective than I, since you have not spent days unaware of what transpired around you, and you are not surrounded by medical apparatus, with every bodily and mental function fully monitored."

"I was lucky. The one you took out was faster."

"You will pardon me if I refrain from accepting your facile but flawed proposition. Your reflexes are indubitably far swifter than mine and your training and conditioning far more recent."

Laughed. "You don't like people to make a fuss over you, do you?"

"Let us say that my reluctance springs from experience in dealing with praise, both that which has been bestowed when undeserved and that which has been withheld when deserved."

"Don't like people that much, do you?"

"I am as enamored of them as any rational being might be, but experience suggests that impartiality and wisdom are seldom exhibited at the same time, and even less frequently are actions meriting commendation recognized, let alone praised." He coughed.

I could sense the pain, but he didn't even wince.

"Have they discovered anything more below?" he asked.

"Nothing that they haven't already found elsewhere."

"Have you seen anything more of note?"

Managed a smile. "I've been using the scanners. So far they don't show any straight lines in the megaplex."

"That signifies more than mere artistic inclination, but I am without the insight or specific expertise to determine what the rationale for such might have been."

"Could it be that straight lines were impractical for some reason?"

"Curves are often stronger, but with the strength of their composite materials, that wouldn't . . ." Fitzhugh paused.

Waited for him to go on.

"Cultural patterns embody, either through affirmation or rejection, past lessons or perceptual requirements. The curved lines doubtless reflect one of those, if not both." He smiled, another wry expression. "Since we know virtually nothing of their culture, their physiology, or how their anatomy enabled their perception, determining more might be somewhat difficult."

Somewhat difficult? Couldn't help grinning at the way he put it.

Abruptly, he closed his eyes for a long moment, then opened them.

"Can I do anything for you?"

"Dear Lieutenant, I would love a dark bock, the genuine brewed kind, or failing that, actual bergamot tea that has not been formulated. You have worked miracles, but I fear those are beyond even your powers." He forced a grin, clearly fighting off pain.

Saw Major DeLisle moving toward us.

"I think the doctor is about to tell me you need rest, Professor."

DeLisle nodded.

"I fear he is correct." Fitzhugh's voice was weaker. His eyes closed again.

Looked at DeLisle. Just looked.

"He'll recover completely, Lieutenant. He will."

Hoped so.

Morgan met me outside. "What did you find out?"

"You don't give up, do you?"

"Would you, after everything that's happened?"

"Wouldn't be leaning on Fitzhugh. He's in it just like us."

"Did you find out anything new?" Commander's voice was hard.

"He likes bergamot tea and chewy dark beers."

"Sometimes, Chang . . ."

"I asked if he'd been an elite commando team leader. He wouldn't tell me, not exactly, but he didn't deny it, and he would, if he hadn't been."

"A frigging elite commando who's kept himself in shape for twenty years without letting anyone know? In good enough shape that he took out a conditioned assassin without raising a sweat? We're supposed to swallow that?"

"He's a very private man, Commander."

"You believe that?"

I did. More than clear enough.

"You like him? You never use a word when a syllable will do, and he never uses a word when a paragraph will do."

What could I say? That Fitzhugh's excessive verbal elegance was as much armor as my terseness? That Fitzhugh was a professor because he was the type to do what was right and necessary, whatever the cost to himself? That he'd realized as much, that in the service too many commanders would have sent him to his death, playing on that weakness?

Could be I was guessing too much. Could be. Didn't think so.

Smiled at Morgan, politely. "I'd better get back to the ready room, sir."

Felt his eyes on my back when I walked away.

52 BARNA

Once Liam Fitzhugh could have visitors, I'd stopped by sick bay. It was the least I could do. He was happy to see me, but embarrassed and tired, and I didn't stay long.

After that, I had gotten around to thinking. I'd settled onto the stool in my work space and glanced at the racks built into the walls. I'd been working long hours. There were more than forty oil and light paintings that I'd completed, based on the images from my trip. That didn't count the portraits of the pilots. The ones that showed scenes from Danann were good, but they weren't enough. There was something missing, and I couldn't describe it. I only knew that something wasn't there.

I needed to get back down on Danann. Commander Morgan had said we'd be on the mission for a year. We'd been in orbit for two months. We'd had one attack from other warships and one attempt from within the *Magellan*. I didn't see the attacks stopping. Sooner or later, someone else would find us. If enough hostile ships appeared, the mission was going to end. If it hadn't been for Liam and Lieutenant Chang, we might already have been on our way back to Hamilton—or dead.

There was more to see on Danann, and I needed to see it.

For all that, I couldn't have explained why my presence on Danann was important. I didn't have to. When I told Commander Morgan I needed another trip down, he nodded and said, "I'll let you know."

Three days later, I was strapped back into the shuttle. All the way down, I asked myself if it had been a good idea. I wasn't a scientist like Elysen or Cleon Lazar. I wasn't an analyst like Liam. I was an artist who felt something was missing, and who had no idea what that might be or how to find it.

As soon as I could, I was studying the illuminated map of the megaplex, with the golden lines that showed the areas that had been fully mapped and explored, the green lines that indicated those that had been opened and quickly surveyed, and the red lines for the areas that had been opened, and scarcely more than looked at.

In the end, I selected a red-lined section to the "southeast."

"Nuovyl, I want to go there." I pointed.

"Ser Barna . . . that is a good stan by slider."

I said nothing.

"If we leave now, it will be very late when we return."

"Does it matter? There's no sunlight here anyway."

"As you wish, sir." He wasn't pleased, but I wasn't there to make people happy.

Less than a stan later, we were seated on a slider, gliding over the frozen surface of the canal boulevard. Behind us, the base was an island of light in a world of darkness. The lights of the slider created a tunnel into the blackness, and a washed-out spray of illumination ahead and to the side, just enough so that the lower sections of the towers showed their silvered surfaces.

As we slipped through the endless night, heading southeast, I wrapped myself in the silence within my armor. Rather than staring at the silver towers and concentrating on their enigmatic similarities, I tried more to absorb not just the towers' appearance but their feel. I wanted to experience them without classification, without judgment, without trying to fit them into the patterns of my past. I let the silvered shapes, illuminated only by the lights of our passing, blued in infinite variations, more hues than I'd realized, appear before me, slip past, and vanish behind the slider.

"Sir?" Nuovyl's voice broke through my silence as the slider slowed. "Ah . . . this is where you said you wanted to be."

"Thank you." I unstrapped myself from the plastrene seat on the slider and stretched. It was a careful stretch. I'd learned about that on the first time on Danann.

Then we began to walk, following the beams of white-silver light, down the ice ramps and through the near-circular doors. Each door had been forced open with laser cutters—careless technology. It struck me as the equivalent of using a medieval battering ram to smash through a ship's air lock, wasteful, destructive, and necessary because we had no other way to enter.

I walked down each corridor, peering into every chamber, looking for something small, even minute, but different. We walked every ramp and every corridor in five towers, before my feet and legs couldn't take any more.

In the end, I didn't find anything. Not on this excursion.

Nuovyl said nothing on the way back. I couldn't blame him. He took his leave as soon as I was inside the temporary base.

Dr. Henjsen was appeared as I left the locker room after getting out of the space armor that chafed in too many places.

"You returned rather late, ser Barna."

"Yes."

"Did you discover anything?"

I shrugged. "Not yet."

She laughed. It was a brittle sound, echoing harshly off the plastrene walls. "Everything is the same everywhere."

How true was that? I thought for a moment. "No. We see the same things everywhere. That doesn't mean that they are."

"When it's all hidden within the composites of the structures, that amounts to the same thing."

It wasn't, but I was tired and had no interest in arguing. "Perhaps."

"If you plan more late excursions, ser Barna, I would appreciate your informing me. It complicates maintenance, and that requires additional preparation."

"I trust that they will not be necessary." I wasn't promising that they wouldn't occur. I was hoping that I wouldn't need them. I could understand Kaitlin's exasperation. She'd spent most of her time planetside. Her face was drawn and grayish, and she'd lost weight. For all of the efforts everyone had made, the expedition didn't know all that much more about Danann and the aliens who had built it than we had learned in the first few days. That had been clear from what Elysen had said and from my own small efforts.

"I would hope not. The techs are strained enough as matters are."

"I understand."

"Good night, ser Barna." She turned and left me standing in the corridor.

Every muscle ached. I knew sleep wouldn't take away all the discomfort.

There had to be something—something that showed the aliens' art and being. My lips curled. Lazar was trying to find something of their physics, Fitzhugh of their history, Sorens of their materials . . . and with all of our technology and expertise none of us had discovered anything new in nearly two months.

There had to be something . . . but I was too tired to ponder it at that moment.

53 FITZHUGH

On a fiveday, three days after I was out of sick bay, finally, I received an invitation to the captain's table for the evening meal, as she had indicated when she had visited me in sick bay, not that I recalled it well. I found myself placed immediately to her right. To the captain's left was Special Deputy Minister Allerde, wearing, as he always did, an old-style shipsuit, rather than the skintights, shorts, and vest of the space service. His shipsuit was all gray, of a shade I could only have termed faded. Even his iron gray hair had more color than the shipsuit. He surveyed me with eyes that were close together, deep-set, and black.

Neither the executive officer nor Commander Morgan was present at the table. I thought I'd seen Lieutenant Chang slip into a chair at one of the outer tables, but I was essaying to keep my concentration on the captain and the minister. I was still more tired than I would have liked, and Dr. DeLisle had suggested—more than firmly—that I was not to resume any strenuous exercise until he checked me over in another three days. He'd also defined exactly what light exercises he wanted. The manner in which my muscles inadvertently contracted in unexpected and unanticipated fashions had convinced me that his advice was to be heeded.

I tendered a pleasant smile to Captain Spier. She was anything but physically impressive, far smaller and more slender than Lieutenant Chang, and with short-cut red hair without the intensity of flame, nor the depth of mahogany, yet not washed-out. But when she turned to me, the gray eyes focused with the energy of a D.S.S. laser.

"It's good to see you back on your feet, Professor." Her brief smile was as intense as her gaze, and warm, rather than cold.

"Thank you. My present position is most definitely superior to the one in which I've spent much of the last weeks."

"His wit hasn't suffered, either," murmured someone farther down the table.

The captain smiled, suffusing even more warmth, if possible. "I've always appreciated those whose acts reflect their beliefs, especially when they speak directly, as you do, Professor. I'm not terribly fond of *sotto voce* commentary, although some individuals tend to forget that unless their memory is frequently refreshed."

The captain's integral directness suggested an officer whose awareness was magnified by her intelligence, an intelligence capable of assessing threats both obvious and insidious without being constrained by paranoia. That considered, I had no desire to be one whose actions displeased her. "An ancient saying suggests that there are those who forget nothing, but learn nothing as well. I can see it would be well not to follow that misguided precept."

The hint of a frown appeared on the Special Deputy Minister's face. The expression suggested that he was more courtier than politician or trusted technical staff with a title. While I preferred not to displease Allerde, either, my mind was not so sharp as it could have been.

"Memory, of course," I added as smoothly as I could, trying not to flog myself mentally for stupidity, "is an essential tool in politics, but one subject to misuse by those less experienced than, say, Special Deputy Minister Allerde."

The captain laughed. "I see how you have survived and prospered, Professor."

"No, Captain, you see that I have survived in spite of my excessive verbiage."

Even Allerde laughed, if in a more restrained fashion.

Very little conversation—other than polite phrases and requests—occurred until the captain was initially served.

"In addition to your considerable martial arts skills, Professor Fitzhugh," Allerde said into the thickening silence, "you are reputed to be quite the scholar. With all that background—and wit—what historical perspective on Danann can you provide?"

"I have only been on the planet for a few days, Minister Allerde, although I have perused many of the reports and images that have been transmitted to the *Magellan*." How far should I go? I offered a laugh. "And, given my physical condition, it may be some time before I'm allowed to return. Still, there are some factors that appear intriguing and suggest possibilities." I cleared my throat and took a sip of the wine—Riesling, formulated and exceedingly ersatz.

"Would you share those . . . possibilities?" Allerde pressed, his voice unctuously polite.

"I would be more than happy to do so," I lied, "but I would also reiterate that they are nothing more than possibilities based on egregiously inadequate information and data."

"Isn't that always the case?" The captain's voice was simultaneously warm and dry.

"It is often so, Captain, particularly for historians, because everyone believes that since the past has already occurred, determining what occurred is merely a process of unearthing enough facts and sifting through them until the truth spontaneously emerges, pristine and inviolable, from the broken shards and crumbled buildings and incomplete writings and records. It is even more difficult in the case of the aliens below, because, with the exception of the buildings themselves, they left no traces whatsoever, not so far as experts far more capable than I have been able to discover." I paused for another sip of the wine before continuing. "The aliens were not from the planet below, but from somewhere other than our Galaxy. They were physically shorter than we are and probably broader. They may have had an aquatic evolution, but they were carbon-based air breathers, as we are. The structure and spacing of the towers suggests that Danann was a temporary outpost world of an extremely high-technology society, and I suspect that some of the towers were never occupied at all, and that the population density was extremely low. It may be that each tower was in fact the habitat of a single individual . . ." Some of what I recited came from the work of others, but it was necessary in providing some of the background for what I had decided to present.

"That sounds rather fanciful, Professor," replied Allerde. "Some of those towers are more than a hundred meters tall. You are suggesting that individuals perhaps smaller than human beings each lived in what amounted to an individual high-technology hacienda tower."

"That is indubitably true." I smiled politely.

The captain leaned forward, ever so slightly, but did not speak.

"All races, all living creatures, require nourishment and create waste products. All of more than minimal size have internal systems by which oxidation is used to create energy, and all exhale in some fashion or another. Those exhalation products do in fact circulate in the atmosphere. Likewise, there is a food chain in naturally evolved planets, and on those which have been planoformed, there are traces of the original ecology as well as the modified one. So far, our scientists have found absolutely no traces of any life-forms larger than what one might generously term microscopic, and the remnants teased from the frozen depths suggest a mechanism something like DNA—perhaps—that is carbon-based. Is that the same life-train as that of the aliens? Or was it there before they arrived and rebuilt the planet?" I shrugged.

"I had hoped for answers, Professor, not questions," Allerde said dryly.

"I'm getting there. My answers will only be conjectures, however, until there is more hard evidence. The lack of waste products, the lack of a varied and distinct ecology, and the relatively pristine state of the single megaplex suggest a number of conclusions, First, the entire planet was modified for a single, one-time project of some sort. Second, in terms of the life span of the aliens, this was a long-term project, but not a multigenerational project. Third, they knew that whatever they did would have a deleterious effect on the planet after they finished and departed. Fourth, they had a far higher ethical standard than do human beings at present—"

"Wait a moment. How can you conclude that?"

"Because," I said quietly, "there is absolutely no sign of any significant waste products nor that any higher-level life-form was left on the planet. Both our technology and our economic system would preclude us from leaving an entire planet so waste-free, and the lack of life-forms would require either not bringing such here or removing them. We could not do that for a planet and settlement of this size, even with formulator technology."

The Captain nodded slowly. "You are suggesting a civilization with a far higher level of technology and culture than we have attained. If that is so, where are they now?"

"I can't answer that, Captain. I can only make my conclusions on what I've seen. I doubt that they ever entered our Galaxy. Even after billions of years, their materials would endure."

"After billions of years on any geologically active planet, they'd be buried," suggested someone.

"That is possible. It is also most likely that some isolated traces would be still found. Nonetheless, it seems unlikely that, if they had entered our Galaxy, that a race that could move planets and create such an anomaly as Chronos would have left undiscovered traces."

"Point taken," said the captain.

"You are asserting that this . . . megalopolis . . . this megaplex . . . was built just as a base for a project of some sort. What sort of project? Why?" asked Allerde.

"Those are questions for which I have no answers, Minister Allerde. I can but conjecture that the project was indeed massive and major since it required this kind of support. I can also conjecture that the alien civilization was far more glorious than we can conceive of if Danann is their equivalent of an outpost or company town—something to be used and abandoned."

"I can see that," reflected the captain. "Your conclusions do leave one unresolved aspect, however."

"I'm certain that they leave many, Captain. They are but conjectures based on inadequate information."

"You point out that these aliens effectively cleaned up everything. Why didn't they just clean up Danann and leave no traces at all?"

"My only response would be that it was not possible, but *why* it was not possible—for that I cannot even conjecture a possibility."

"Could they have been wiped out by an even greater culture?" asked Allerde.

"That is always a possibility, but I would guess not. There are no signs of damage, and nothing that resembles a defensive structure." I smiled. "If they were wiped out so entirely, there is no physical record of it—and that would suggest a culture of even greater superiority."

"There's another question," the captain said. "According to the astronomers . . . Danann has been traveling at unheard-of speeds for billions of years. So has Chronos, if in opposite directions. Yet there is absolutely no sign of anything in space—except a void—at the point from which their journeys began."

"I would submit, Captain, that such observations merely add weight to what I have hypothecated in suggesting that Danann is the product of an exceedingly advanced technology—Type III, I believe, is the category."

"If it was so advanced, then, what happened to it—or them?" demanded Allerde.

"That is, I believe, one of the purposes of the expedition." I smiled as politely as I could. I wasn't about to enter into speculations about the hypothetical fate of vanished aliens who had left technology we could not only not duplicate, but, in many cases, not even understand. "I am but a poor historian, attempting to discern cultural patterns from the dimensions within empty buildings and from the placement of those seemingly eternal structures."

"Eternal structures—you make these vanished aliens seem almost godlike."

"As has been quoted so often in history, there is little difference between miracles ascribed to deities, magic, and sufficiently advanced technology."

The captain laughed. "On that note—or quote—I'm going to suggest that the end of this discussion await further discoveries from Danann."

Even Allerde didn't press her on that.

As I ate, slowly, I did have to speculate on Allerde's last observation. If human beings had discovered such structures on the back side of Old Earth's moon at the time of the dawn of spaceflight, most would have ascribed them to an advanced technology, but not all. If they had been discovered upon an Olympian peak in the pretech era, certainly the towers would have been credited to gods. Yet Danann was more remote to us than the ancient Mount Olympus had been to the Bronze Age civilizations of early historical Earth. What was the difference? Knowledge? Arrogance?

Science had found no proof of gods or angels, and so most who believed truly in the superiority of intellect and reason had drifted away from belief in a supreme deity who created the universe. We believed—for I was certainly among that group—that with time and sufficient knowledge human beings could eventually unlock all the secrets of the universe, from the smallest components of fermions and bosons to the vastness of the universe itself.

Yet . . . after all the reports I had read . . . I had the feeling that Danann would not yield its secrets easily, and a part of me wondered if we ever would understand what lay there, let alone be able to replicate it.

54 CHANG

By sevenday, after almost three months in orbit, I was dog-tired. Forced myself to concentrate as I brought shuttle two down toward landing zone beta. At least the lake bottom under the ice there hadn't been heating up. Could be that Henjsen's precautions had worked. No equipment anywhere on the lake. No power, no fusactors.

Energy emissions noted, EDI traces two eight seven. The alerts were from the system.

Frig! Had Morgan's predictions come true? Switched concentration to the scanners. Emissions were from a lake to the west-northwest of the landing zone. Scanners reported two sets. One looked to be something like a fusactor. The other was vaguely familiar, but I couldn't place it.

Once shuttle two was on the ground, and the locks were open, with unloading proceeding, I went to the links. *Danann Base, this is Sherpa Tigress, reporting energy emanations approximately two hundred twenty kays from you at two eight seven, local north.*

Say again, Sherpa Tigress.

Repressed a snort of exasperation and repeated my report, adding, *Interrogative any local observations in that area.*

We have your report, Sherpa Tigress. Wait one.

Someone should have known. If they didn't know . . . Didn't want to think about that.

"We're off-loaded, sir. Ready for passengers up, if we have any."

"Thanks, chief. I'll check." Shuttle two was only configured at present for two passengers. Usually there weren't any because shuttle two runs were later in the day—unless Henjsen or one of the long-timers wanted to go up and then catch shuttle one when it returned the next day—if it was on a day when a run was scheduled.

Danann Base, Sherpa Tigress, unloading complete, interrogative return cargo or passengers.

Tigress, understand three crates for return. They should be there now.

"Chief . . . they say there are three crates."

"There's a slider coming. I'll let you know when they're on board and secured."

Danann Base, slider with crates in view. Interrogative emanations.

Sherpa Tigress, Danann Base, emanations at two eight seven are from multiteam project.

Interrogative second emissions.

Wait one.

A long silence followed. Finally, another "voice" came through the links. Recognized Henjsen. *The second set is from the lake heating up. There's something there that recognizes fusactors. We haven't located or determined what it is or what the mechanism might be.*

What's the lake project? Looking for that mechanism?

Another silence.

Finally, Henjsen spoke again. *I suppose it won't matter. Cleon's sent a report. Some of your cargo has samples for analysis. We've found traces of another landing, not one of ours.*

Another landing? Had the CWs or the Middle Kingdom been here already? *Interrogative informing the operations officer.*

The laugh over the link came as rueful. *Operations knows. We haven't dated it yet, but it's anything but recent. Cleon thinks it's over a million years.*

The aliens came back?

We don't think so. We had a team looking into the towers there. Some of the doors had been battered open, a long time back. Preliminary measurements show that some of the ice on the lake there melted and refroze. We've found traces of materials in the ice, and a few scraps of metal and polymers . . . a few small items. We'll know more after the analysis of your cargo. I'd appreciate your keeping that to you and Operations until we know more.

Will do.

Someone—something—had landed on Danann in the past, maybe millions of years ago.

To do that, they'd needed technology like ours. Where had they come from? Where had they gone?

"Sir, we're loading the crates now."

"Thanks, chief."

I'd keep my mouth shut—except to Morgan—but I didn't see how news like that wouldn't spread through the *Magellan* like air pouring from a holed needle.

55 BARNA

I'd spent another three days on Danann and returned the day after Henjsen's team discovered the traces of the aliens—the second aliens. I got more images, including a few of one of the doors that the second aliens had forced and a ramp cut or melted into the ice—wider and shallower than our ramps, but not much different otherwise. I had a few more ideas to go with the images. I still hadn't found the elusive "something" that I *knew* was down there. What I had seen fueled ideas for another round of work.

One of the pieces I tried was another interpretation—of what that ancient past might have been. From Fernard and Marsalis and some of the others, I'd picked up what they had learned about Danann. So I'd shown the sky as a deep blue, because they'd said that the atmosphere had been thicker, and a sun that tended slightly to the orange. The setting was two towers above one of the canal boulevards, set just at sunrise, with the sun halfway out of the water of the canal, and nothing around. One of the tower doors was half-open, with the hint of a shadowed figure.

I stood back, looking at it and wondering if I should have made the indistinct shadow taller and not quite so dark.

"You probably can't show that one as purely representative or historical." Elysen carried a mug of tea as she slipped into my work space.

"No . . . but it might be easier to sell."

"I suppose it might. It's a touch less alien." Elysen eased herself into the good chair, slowly. "You're good enough that you don't have to be blatantly commercial, Chendor."

"Tell that to Aeryana."

"You make her sound so greedy. You couldn't love her as you do if she were."

"She's not. She is more practical than I've been." I set down the lightbrush. "She's seen what happens when an artist suddenly becomes unpopular. Her cousin lost everything, then jumped off the Palisades."

"I imagine he was trying to find a commercial niche. You don't need that. Paint your best, and success will find you." She smiled. "It already has. You both find that hard to accept, don't you?"

"Probably." I didn't want to talk about it. There wasn't anything I could do about it on the *Magellan.* "What do you think about the other aliens? The ones that landed only a million years ago."

"The visitors? That's what I prefer to call them." Sitting in my sole good chair, Elysen sipped tea from her mug, while I paced across my work space, avoiding canvases and matrices.

I paused to study her. There were deeper circles under her eyes, with hints of redness in them. She was thinner, and she'd shuffled slightly when she'd come in.

"I'm not a fowl to be studied, Chendor." Her voice was gently acerbic.

"You're not well, are you?"

"No. I wasn't well before we left. They knew that, and I knew it."

"What—"

"Extreme old age. At some point, medical science can't do any more. You can only spur regeneration so long before the system says no, or before you get carcinogenesis so rapid and widespread that no treatment is effective. In my case, it's just the former."

"But . . . why did you come?"

"Why not? My children are dead, and I have great-grandchildren older than you. I'd rather keep working." She smiled and her eyes brightened. "I've never had such an interesting project, either."

"Can you tell me yet?"

"Not quite. The cross-checks on the last observations—and on the mathematics—should be finished in the next few days."

"Is it as big as you thought?"

She shrugged, then sipped her tea once more. "If the evidence all turns out the way it's looking, it will be one of the most astounding discoveries in astronomy and astrophysics. It will also confirm the Kardashev civilization classifications. Most people will reject it. Possibly even most astronomers. It will be very controversial, to say the least."

"You're making it all very mysterious." I knew better than to ask. I'd already tried more than a few times and gotten nowhere. Elysen would tell me when she was ready, and not before.

"You don't like to let people see what you're painting until you're ready."

She looked tired, and I didn't point out that I had let her see works in progress. She and Aeryana were the only ones who had. "You never said what you thought about the visiting aliens."

"From what Cleon has sent me, I don't think the visitors' technology was as advanced as ours, but it's difficult to tell from so few scraps. One of the items left was a projectile weapon, gas-powered, from a reservoir. Of course, it wouldn't have operated on Danann unless it had a heating element."

"The only way they could get into the towers was to pound open the doors."

"Some form of massive hydraulics. They've found traces of that, too. From the metal shavings buried in the ice, Cleon thinks that they had mechanical difficulties and finally gave up."

"Why didn't they use lasers?"

"I would surmise that they either did not have them or did not have them with the ability to focus sufficient energy in a fine enough cutting edge."

"But they reached Danann."

"They did. So did we. And we could have traveled here centuries ago. I have my doubts that we could have had much success either if we had arrived right after the development of the AG drive."

"Why didn't they come back, then?"

Elysen raised her eyebrows. "There was only one flurry of expeditions to Chronos. Why didn't we go back?"

"Oh. You think it was too costly, with no hope of financial return? But surely, sometime . . ."

"How long do civilizations last, Chendor? We don't know. We look at the ruins down there, and we know that something ended . . . at least it appears that it ended anywhere that we can reach or observe. We almost didn't survive the early nuclear age on Old Earth, or the postdiasporan conflicts, or the Covenanter-Sunnite Conflagration. If they hadn't called a truce when they did, most of the known galaxy would have been dragged in. Would we have had a civilization to come here—or return to Chronos?"

"But we haven't seen a trace of the visitors' civilization. Our Galaxy is by far the closest to Danann, and it would have been even a million years ago."

"That's true. And what percentage of even our Galaxy's systems have we surveyed or visited? There are close to five thousand inhabited worlds—out of more than a hundred thousand million star systems."

I couldn't argue that.

"Intelligent life has to be rare," she said quietly "We know that. Intelligence also makes cultures unstable."

I hated to think that. "Liam Fitzhugh thinks Danannian culture was stable."

"He may well be right. Are we to the point of matching it? In terms either of stability or technical achievement?"

Elysen didn't say it, but I could sense what she implied. Would we ever reach that point? "Not yet."

She looked at the latest light-matrix painting, my representation of a past that might never have been. "I wonder . . ."

"You wonder what?"

"If great art and stable societies are irreconcilable."

"What about science?"

She smiled, so enigmatically that I wished I could have put the expression into oil then and there, but the half smile vanished before I could have even reached for an imager.

But that was art—trying to create a work that evoked a moment and a truth that had already come and gone—or one that had never been, but should have been.

56 CHANG

Didn't get to the officers' mess that much with all the shifts in the shuttle schedule. Neither did Lerrys, and usually we never got there together, except at breakfast. Morgan took some of the replenishment runs to the *Alwyn,* trying to give us a break and keep his hand in. Wasn't a bad idea.

Asked him why he didn't try the needle pilots with the shuttles. He had laughed. "They don't *feel* the mass."

I understood what he meant. Exactly.

Another fiveday came. Dragged myself to the mess for the evening meal. Saw Liam Fitzhugh coming the other way. Just looked for a moment.

He looked, gave me a sort of smile. "Might I join you for supper?"

"I could manage that. Don't ask me to be brilliant, Professor."

"I won't. I would request . . . if you wouldn't mind . . . that you refrain from calling me 'Professor.' When I hear the term from you . . ." He stopped speaking. "My verbiage is already excavating a depression from which I will not be able to extricate myself."

"Then stop digging." Tried not to make the words hard.

"Excellent advice."

We sat a good three tables away from the captain's. Didn't even ask each other. Just seemed better that way.

Professor deSilva joined us, and so did Nalakov, obnoxious math theorist. He always stared at me, like he'd never seen a fair-skinned woman with true blond hair and slanted eyes. Except he was blunt about it. Had to stop a smile when Alyendra Khorana plopped down between Fitzhugh and Nalakov. Gave me enough separation.

Fitzhugh poured me a quarter glass of the wine, exactly what I poured for myself. Impressed me. Also worried at me. Took even less for himself, passed the carafe to Alyendra.

"You don't drink much?" I asked.

"I like just a little good wine. This is barely passable, but I will taste some, at times, if merely to remind myself that there is a universe of superb vintages awaiting our return. Not that I could afford most of them. Still . . . if one looks and is careful, there are many that are delightful and fit the budget of academics."

Didn't want to talk credits. "Do you think the aliens had wines?"

"They did not practice viniculture as we know it, not down upon Danann, but perhaps their chemistry was as advanced as their materials science." He pursed his lips. "But then, they would never have discovered the joys of uncertainty, the combination of soil, of climate, and the fluctuations of solar radiation that combine to make a vintage that can be almost abysmal or truly celestial."

"Perhaps nothing in the universe was uncertain to them," suggested Professor deSilva.

A moment there, I thought he was serious.

Fitzhugh paused, then frowned. Finally spoke. "You meant that humorously, Tomas, even with great irony, but there is a possibility you are absolutely correct."

"How could that be?" asked Alyendra. "There is uncertainty everywhere, even for us and our technology. The Danannians were not gods."

"I will reply, if you will, by means of an analogy." Fitzhugh inclined his head. "Ancient humans believed the weather to be capricious, or dictated by the whim of their gods. Early technological humans discovered the mechanics of weather and achieved reasonably accurate predictions, Today, we are not perfect, but we are over ninety-eight percent accurate. Weather is the result of the interaction of multiple factors. A culture that could anticipate and predict such factors would operate with little uncertainty."

"Then they could have predicted our arrival here." Irony filled deSilva's voice. "Could they not?"

"Quite possibly. At least, they could project the type of culture that would seek out Danann."

At that, I had to wonder about the heating of the water under the ice. What sort of mechanism had the aliens set up? One that waited for visitors that might arrive millions or billions of years later? What else might be waiting down there? What might trigger it?

"If they could predict that, could they not also predict any other dangers to their civilization? And if they could predict all that, certainly they should still be around, shouldn't they?"

"We only know that they are not on Danann," Fitzhugh replied. "That does not mean that their civilization does not exist elsewhere. There are endless galaxies in the universe."

The stewards arrived and set plates before us. Something covered in white sauce. Watched Fitzhugh motion to the steward. "Tea, please."

"Yes, sir."

Fitzhugh fingered the stem of the wineglass.

"I don't suppose we'll find the answer to that soon," deSilva replied. "But, speaking of predictions, we've had one set of ships attack on the *Magellan*," deSilva said. "Do you think another outside attack is likely?" Looked at Fitzhugh as he spoke.

"It's possible." Fitzhugh smiled politely. "In an infinite universe, the possibilities are also infinite."

"Anything is *possible,* but what do you think?"

"I am not a military expert."

Someone murmured, "You could have fooled me."

Didn't recognize the whisper.

"What about the other aliens?" asked Alyendra, as if to cover the comment.

"They were not on Danann recently. The team has dated their appearance at close to a million years back, give or take some tens of thousands." Nalakov tried irony, just sounded ponderous.

"They found a gas-powered projectile weapon, with a grip, an odd grip," deSilva said. "The similarity seems . . . unusual."

Fitzhugh leaned back as the steward slipped his tea onto the table. "There are only so many possibilities for efficient use of energy."

"I can see that with the Danannians. One can look at the megaplex and see that it is truly an alien culture. But a weapon so similar in design to something we might have used, doesn't that suggest a similarity of evolution?"

"Their technological prowess approximated that of ours, I understand. Therefore, there should be a certain similarity."

"Still . . ."

Fitzhugh turned to me. "I defer to an expert. Lieutenant, space combat has been employing torps and screens for centuries. From what you have indicated, their efficiency leaves something to be desired. With the plethora of human cultures and the multiplicity of worlds, one would think that something more innovative should have arisen from the depths of human ingenuity and destructiveness, let alone among aliens. Yet it does not seem that such has occurred. Why might that be?"

Even asking a question, he sounded like a professor. Bet he knew the answer, but he knew Nalakov and deSilva wouldn't buy his words. Or he wanted me to support what he thought.

"Simple. Space is big. It's also essentially a vacuum. Means that there's no medium to conduct energy."

DeSilva looked puzzled.

"Not explaining it as well as I should. You explode a simple bomb on a planet. There's an atmosphere. The air carries a blast wave. That extends the force of the explosion. Doesn't happen in space. Lasers . . . particle beams . . . they're useless except close in. No ship can generate enough energy to hold a long beam; and then there's the delay factor. Torps are designed to maneuver to deliver concentrated energy at the focal point. So far . . . nothing else does it that well. Doesn't matter whether you're human or alien. A gas-powered projectile thrower is the same idea. Concentrates the force in the projectile."

"That answers my question about the visitors—"

"The aliens who built the structures that dominate Danann were more advanced than we are at present," Fitzhugh said smoothly. "If . . . *if* we ever manage to escape the current morass of irrationality and the need for ideological dominance, I would wager that our technology, should it become sufficiently advanced, would converge, at least functionally, upon what we see demonstrated below."

"Form follows function?"

"More like the laws of the universe," I put in.

"Well said, Lieutenant."

"What about the Danannians?" asked Alyendra.

"They, dear Professor," Fitzhugh pointed out, "operated in the same universe as do we. Therefore, they were constrained by the same laws. I would suggest that they understood them better or in greater depth."

"Or those laws have changed since then." Nalakov had an odd smile.

Fitzhugh shrugged. "You are the scientist, Doctor. Is that possible?"

"We know certain aspects of the early universe were not quite as they are now. If there are . . . properties . . . we have not yet discovered, it is always possible that they might have changed. It is unlikely, but one cannot rule it out."

"One can rule nothing out tonight, it seems," said deSilva dryly.

Fitzhugh looked at his platter. The formulated and sauced fowl still lay there. Untouched.

We looked at each other. Smiled. Briefly.

57 *Barna*

The images from my last trip planetside had helped, but I was still missing something. I couldn't even draw a rough image of what it was. Not even a mental picture.

On oneday, I went back to Commander Morgan.

He looked up at me with red-rimmed eyes. "You want to go back down." Those were his words before I could take a seat.

"Yes." I didn't bother to sit. Morgan didn't dither about decisions.

"Why?"

"Because my work isn't done."

"There's a place on the cargo shuttle this afternoon. I'll let Dr. Henjsen know you're coming down. She won't be happy. Nothing I can say will make it easier. You understand that?"

"I do, Commander."

He nodded. "You'd better go make sure there's a set of armor that comes close to fitting."

That was all there was to it. Morgan was absolutely correct. There was one passenger seat on the shuttle, and I was in it. The cargo space was empty. When we landed, I saw why. Crates and sliders were stacked up on the dark gray ice in the blackness waiting to be loaded. Lights glared on the shuttle. Droplets of refrozen atmosphere skittered across the cargo ramp I walked down.

There wasn't even a tech waiting. So I made my way to the temporary base. I just followed my lamp and the gray plastrene pathway. After checking in, and asking for Nuovyl, I went back to the illuminated map. There were more golden lines, showing where more exploration had been done, but not that many more, and a few more green lines, and a few less red lines.

None of them felt right.

I kept studying the map in the silence.

Nuovyl appeared. He was wearing armor, carrying his helmet, like me. His face was drawn, his left cheek smeared with dark grease. He coughed several times. He didn't say anything.

"We'll be leaving in a bit. I'll need a slider and a cutter that will open doors."

"Sir?"

I didn't answer. I'd found something. There was one part of the megaplex that looked different. I couldn't explain why. Superficially it looked like all the other interlocking ovals holding towers and canals. It wasn't.

"Nuovyl, I want to go there." I pointed.

"Ser Barna . . . that is almost two stans by slider at full speed. It is late in the day. You know how Professor Henjsen feels about that."

"That's where I need to go. I'll need the equipment necessary to open any doors." I'd said that before, but it hadn't registered.

"It's late, sir." Nuovyl repeated.

"It's very late, and we don't have much time." I could feel that. I'd felt it the moment I'd seen Commander Morgan that morning, and all the crates headed up to the *Magellan* reinforced my sense that we were running out of time.

"You'll have to clear that with Dr. Henjsen."

"Then, let's take care of that."

I followed him to the small cubicle off the main lock.

Henjsen looked worse than Nuovyl or Morgan. She was skin stretched over bones, eyes beyond red with purpled half circles under them. Her hands shook, and her left eye twitched.

"Whatever you want, Barna, I can't do it. You can walk where you want, but no equipment. We can't spare any equipment. We don't have much time to find clues to the technology . . ."

"And you certainly can't spare it for a mere artist?"

She did not meet my eyes.

"You haven't had any success. I discovered the windows, and one hidden room. Has anyone else done that?"

"I just can't spare the equipment."

"Then we should talk to Commander Morgan."

"I'm in charge here."

"Commander Morgan thought enough of my ability to send me down now. Do you want to cross him?"

"You . . . you think . . ."

I just looked at her. "You've had three months, Kaitlin. I found more in six days than most of your teams found in all that time."

Her eyes finally dropped. "Morgan'll still have to approve. One day."

"The rest of today, and tomorrow," I countered.

She touched a small console. Shortly, Commander Morgan's image appeared.

"Yes, Doctor?"

"Ser Barna—the artist—has requested a slider and two techs for some explorations. He wants them today and tomorrow. I can't meet your schedule and spare them."

Morgan looked up from the small screen at Henjsen. "You've had control of all the sliders for three months, Doctor. I think you can spare one slider and the necessary techs for the rest of today and tomorrow for ser Barna. I'm sure you can find a way to meet the schedule without two techs and one slider for such a short period. I think that an extra day on such matters as paleontology and geology will be marginal at best. I could be wrong as to which area is of marginal use. I leave that to you." His smile was wan, almost ghastly. "I do know that ser Barna's artistic renderings may be as necessary as all the scientific findings, particularly for later funding."

Henjsen stiffened. "As you wish, Commander."

"As the captain commands, Doctor." Morgan's voice was tired—and cold.

Once the screen cleared, Henjsen looked at me. "Today and tomorrow."

"Yes, Doctor. I understand." I doubted Kaitlin Henjsen would ever hold a kind thought about me again, but I had been given, effectively, twelve to fifteen standard working hours. It wouldn't be enough, but a century wouldn't have been enough for anyone, not with the size of the megaplex.

Nuovyl was waiting outside. "Sir?"

"We're cleared. You can check with the doctor if you want."

"Have Zerobya handle the cutting laser," Henjsen said from behind me. "Whatever ser Barna wants with you two and one slider until tomorrow night."

If I could have captured her voice in oils, even abstractly, it would have made a glacier—or the surface of Danann—seem warm.

"Yes, sir."

Nuovyl said little at all until we were on the slider with the other tech.

"Ready, sir?"

"I'm ready. There's a duplicate map in the system." I'd made certain it had been downloaded and linked, to ensure we got exactly where I wanted.

"Ah, yes, sir. I see."

Nuovyl eased the slider away from the welter of lights behind us where some of the tech crew was completing the loading of the shuttle.

Along the way, I'd only caught one fragment of his conversation with Zerobya. She was a squarish woman who muscled the cutting equipment with ease. Nuovyl must have triggered the wrong channel because his words cut off abruptly.

"He may be an artist, but he's got enough clout that the ops officer overruled Henjsen. She'd just as soon have us all freeze—"

I could guess what he'd been about to say. He probably did say it to Zerobya.

By the time we were halfway to the area I'd picked out, the alienness of silver-blue towers appearing in the light and vanishing in blackness beside and behind the slider had dulled into routine. Another three-quarters of a stan passed before Nuovyl eased the slider to a halt in front of a tower. In the lights from the slider, blackness looming behind it, the tower looked no different from hundreds of others.

"Think this is it, sir."

I looked past Nuovyl to check the map again. Expanded on the slider's small screen, it was obvious. The tower before us was larger, if just slightly. It was also subtly set in the center of those surrounding it. Because of the interlocking arcs, that could have been said of a number of the towers, but the arcs were slightly more pronounced around the tower I had discovered, if only by a few degrees of curvature.

Lifting the imager I had brought, I followed Nuovyl from the slider toward the tower.

"We're lucky, sir. Looks like someone melted the ramp down to the door. Didn't open it, though."

"We haven't been out here, I don't think," Zerobya offered from where she was working to off-load her equipment onto a handslider.

"But there's a ramp down."

I looked at the ramp. Although the edges were crisp, it felt old, and the gradient wasn't as steep as those I'd been down before—except once. Not so old as the towers, but we hadn't melted it. "We'll worry about that later." I eased down the ramp, stepping carefully, but the ice under the armor's boots didn't feel any different from any other of the ice surfaces.

The door to the tower was unmarked. I didn't see any debris anywhere near. If the visiting aliens had melted the ramp, they hadn't done much more. At least, I couldn't see any sign of that.

"The door needs to be cut and warmed, Zerobya," Nuovyl called back. He turned to me. "When are you going to report about the ramp?"

"When we find what I'm looking for—or if we don't." I gestured toward the sides of the ramp and the ice underfoot. "I don't see any signs that anyone left anything."

"Yes, sir." Nuovyl's voice was even and polite. That meant he disagreed, but that could have been because, if I reported the ramp, we were through for the day, and he could head back, rather than working late. Then, too, I was undoubtedly breaking yet another archeological rule.

"You two will need to back off to the top of the ramp," Zerobya said "There's not enough room for me to get the equipment past you."

I edged back up to the top of the ice ramp. There, Nuovyl and I waited at the top of the ramp—and we waited. From time to time, I looked down, but I couldn't see that much.

Nuovyl didn't say anything, and I had nothing to add.

"It's open. But it was a real bitch," Zerobya finally called.

I tried not to hurry back down the ramp.

Zerobya was replacing a laser cutting head and didn't look up immediately. "The latch placement was different here, and there were double catches, instead of single ones." She straightened and turned more directly to me. "Do you want me to open the inside doors, like usual?"

"If you would. If I see something, I may call on you."

"Yes, sir."

Once Zerobya was through the door with her equipment, we followed into the foyer. It might have been my imagination, but the oval foyer seemed slightly larger than those in the other towers I'd surveyed. The first level was similar to all the other first levels I'd looked through. Similar, but not identical. I had the sense that there were fewer chambers—even though the tower was larger and each chamber seemed no larger than those elsewhere. But there were no hidden alcoves.

Around each door was a scattering of ice or atmospheric droplets from the heat created when Zerobya had cut and warmed the doors to let them deform themselves open. Some of the droplet patterns were most intricate. I only took a few images, though.

Still, I inspected each chamber, well enough to ensure that nothing obvious was concealed and that there were no hidden alcoves. There were neither.

With our lights cutting through the darkness and creating a silvery light from the largely nonreflecting silvery walls, we made our way to the ramp and headed up to the second level. I was convinced the ramps had once actually propelled the Danannians up and down the towers, but I hadn't seen reports about any possible mechanisms.

When we emerged on the second level into the upper-level foyer, I turned toward the left branch of the corridor. I had taken only a few steps out of the foyer when I realized I had seen no doors. Also, the corridor swung to the left. According to the pattern in all the other towers, the corridor should have curved to parallel the outer wall. Instead, it turned outward.

"This is different. We might have something here."

"Walls look just the same to me, sir," Nuovyl replied.

I played the light across the walls and floor. They were no different from any other interior surfaces, except for the lack of evenly spaced doors into chambers. I kept walking. Unlike all the other corridors, this one widened as it continued, then opened into a second foyer. I stopped and used the light to search the foyer. Directly across from me was another entrance, a duplicate of the corridor down which we had walked. To my right was a curved wall, one that roughly paralleled the outside of the tower. It was the only time I'd seen an interior wall of any size on an interior chamber that was convex. In the middle of that wall was one of the flattened circular doors. To me, it looked slightly larger.

"Nuovyl . . . we'll need to open that."

"I've already called Zerobya. She went the other way out of the ramp foyer. Said there were more doors that way. She'll be right here."

I walked toward the door in the convex wall. It was larger than all the interior doors, even a trace wider than the outer building doors. My light showed no separation between the halves of the door.

"Here's Zerobya, sir."

The light from the other corridor strengthened. Behind it came the other tech, pulling her equipment slider. Once she entered the foyer, she stopped as well. "This is different. Haven't seen one of these with three entrances before."

"Can you open that door at the side?"

"Hasn't been one I haven't been able to open yet, sir."

Like the main door, the foyer door took longer. It could have been that I was impatient. I didn't think so.

Finally, the door halves separated, but they came to a halt when they were less than a meter apart.

"This one'll take more power to get wider, sir."

"I can see that." Still, the opening was enough to enter whatever lay beyond. I stepped through into a dark cavernlike chamber. I almost stumbled, because the floor sloped down from the entrance. "Careful. It slants down."

"Yes, sir."

I swept the beam from my light across the chamber from left to right. I could sense immediately that the hall was far larger than any interior space I'd seen. Then, as the beam crossed the middle of the dark chamber, light cascaded everywhere, flaring like a fountain up into the domed ceiling that was at least ten meters overhead.

"What the frig . . ." Nuovyl's exclamation reverberated through my helmet.

I finished the light sweep of the hall. It looked to be almost forty meters in diameter, and more circular than oval. Then I trained the light on whatever it was in the center of the space. Once more light flared upward, in a spray that illuminated the entire space. The intensity was so great that the helmet filters kicked in, and my eyes had to adjust again.

What stood on a low circular dais in the exact middle of a perfectly circular hall was . . . I didn't know what to call it. It had two bases—if they could be called that—each silvery gray. There were seemingly perfect and identical spheres. From each sphere, something crystalline swept up in an arc, and the two sweeps joined about three meters from the base. Each of the crystalline arms or arcs was about thirty centimeters across, until they joined. They looked cylindrical in cross section. From where they joined, they extended another meter and a half straight up—then just ended. But when I put the light on either arc, the light filled the arc and *flowed* upward. But it didn't stop when the crystal did. Instead it focused into an intense single point of light that was both brilliant and black—simultaneously. That tiny light point illuminated the entire hall.

"Frig . . ." muttered Nuovyl, again.

"What's . . ." Zerobya peered through the partly open door. "Oh! What is it?"

I didn't have the faintest idea. "I don't know."

I kept the light on the point where the two arcs joined and tried to study what I saw. After a moment I could see that a black line ran between the two spheres—but it was dark light, not whatever crystalline material made up the arcs.

After a moment, I spoke again. "Nuovyl?"

"Ah . . . yes, sir?"

"Put your light where mine is. I want to walk down and take a closer look."

"You think that's wise, sir?"

"Probably not." I paused. "Zerobya?"

"Sir?"

"Will you contact Danann Base and get a message to Dr. Henjsen that we've found something unique. Give them our location and say that I'll be in touch momentarily."

"Yes, sir. I'll have to move back outside. Signals don't travel from in here."

"That's fine. When you're done, come back and let me know."

"Yes, sir. I'll be going now."

It might have been my imagination, but I thought I sensed relief as she left.

The light intensity more than doubled when Nuovyl's light struck the sculpture. I had the feeling it was a device of some sort, far more man a sculpture. Yet the curves and the lines were so precise, so artistic, and the crystal and gray were so intense, and the light somehow so serene, brilliant as it was, that I couldn't help but think of it as art.

I lowered my light and slipped it into the clasp on the armor's equipment belt. The illumination dropped to the previous level, but it was more than enough. I unslung the imager. "Just keep the light on it. I need to take as many images as I can."

"Yes, sir."

I moved down the sloping floor, gingerly, shooting images as I moved. I'd already decided not to step onto the dais. I didn't need to, and I had a healthy respect for anything that worked as well as the Danannian stuff after billions of years.

Once I got within a meter of the dais, perhaps three from the edge of the sculpture device, I checked out the black line between the two spheres. So far as I could see, it was just dark light, not carried by anything crystalline.

"Nuovyl . . . play the light on me for a moment, not on the sculpture."

"On you, sir?"

"That's right."

"Yes, sir."

The dimness and the darkness immediately filled the room. Enough of Nuovyl's light reflected off my armor that I could see there was nothing connecting the two gray spheres directly. I could see the spheres, the crystal arcs, and where they joined, but nothing more.

I took some more images.

"Now . . . put it back on the sculpture."

"Yes, sir."

Once more, the hall was filled with light from that point source. It was definitely a point source, in the pure geometrical sense. I kept moving around the base of the dais, taking images from all possible angles and elevations. Who knew when I'd ever get as much time with the sculpture again?

Finally, responsibility caught up with me. "I need to report to Dr. Henjsen."

"Yes, sir."

"We'll go out and see how Zerobya is doing."

"You think we can leave this . . . ?" Nuovyl's voice reflected the mixed emotions of duty and relief.

"It's done quite nicely for the last few billion years."

Nuovyl didn't say anything until we were walking down the ramp to the first level.

"Do you have any idea what it is, sir? Why would they leave it here? They didn't leave anything else. If it's important . . . I mean, there aren't even any directions to it."

I almost shook my head. "We don't know that. There aren't any directions as we'd recognize them. I'd guess it's important, but that's only a guess. I'd also judge that there was a reason it was left, but we haven't had much luck in figuring out most of what's here. So whether we'll do any better with it . . . who knows?"

"Sir!" Zerobya voice was so loud it rattled my head inside the helmet. "Dr. Henjsen requested that you contact her ASAP."

"Can you put me through on the slider's comm?"

"You're on."

"Danann Base—"

"What took you so long to report personally, Barna? What do you have? More windows? Or transparent doors?"

I let the silence hang there.

"Barna. It's damned late."

"We have a significant piece of artwork, or a technical model of something I couldn't begin to understand. It transmits and intensifies light in a way I've never seen, but it's also very artistic. It might even qualify as a great work of art, but I don't think that's its purpose. It measures roughly three meters from side to side, a meter deep, and about four and half meters high. That's the physical structure. It projects light another meter above that. I'd guess it weighs at least a good five hundred kilos, maybe even double that, but that's a guess—"

"You've found an artifact that significant, and you didn't report immediately—"

"I haven't touched it, Doctor. It's been here for billions of years. It's sitting on a perfectly circular dais in a perfectly circular room. It's the first place I've seen that's perfectly circular. There's nothing at all around the . . . whatever it is. I judge that the hall that holds it is the closest thing to an auditorium that the Danannian aliens had."

"What do you mean by intensifying light?"

"If we shine a light on the crystalline part, light flows up to the top, then concentrates to a tiny point almost a meter above the crystal. That point puts out enough light to illuminate the entire hall, and it's forty meters across and more than ten high."

"Don't touch anything. Don't touch anything at all. Cleon and I will be there as soon as we can be."

"I haven't." I didn't mention that I'd taken a number of images and would keep taking them from as many angles as possible.

"Stay where you can be reached."

"Either the techs or I will be here at the slider."

Henjsen was silent for a moment. She was probably thinking about whether to demand that I stay away. Finally, she replied. "I can't stress enough that you shouldn't touch it or anything around it."

"I haven't. I've stayed off the dais where it is."

"Good. We'll be there as soon as we can."

That gave me more than a good stan to go back and look at it and take some more images. I probably ought to have taken some of the hall as well, because I'd have to paint the sculpture in its original setting.

Could it even be moved? What if it were an integral part of the entire tower?

If that were the case, I'd better get all the images I could.

Then, if it could be moved, Henjsen and Lazar would find a way. With the scarcity of real artifacts, they'd blow a fusactor to get enough power to cut it from the dais. Even if it could be moved, *someone* would want an impression of how it looked in its original setting.

"We need to head back in to get some more images."

"Yes, sir." Resignation and apprehension filled Nuovyl's voice.

I could have been mistaken, but I didn't think the Danannians would create something so artistic that could last billions of years just to have it explode the first time some alien looked at it. After all, in their minds, we would have been the aliens.

58 BARNA

We didn't get back to base until late on oneday. Actually, it was very early in the morning on twoday. I tried to sleep in. I didn't sleep well. Despite my exhaustion, dreams of light fountains and strange voices that I could not understand or recall filled my sleep. When those subsided, I got all of half a stan past the normal call time before Fernard's loud voice woke me.

"Expedition director or not, I'm not her errand boy!"

I rolled over and sat up.

"Well, you got the job done, Edmund." That was Sorens. "You also woke up everyone else who worked late."

Fernard had bushy brown hair and a wild reddish brown beard. He looked at me. "After you've eaten, Dr. Henjsen would like to see you, ser Barna."

"Thank you."

"I'd rather not be in your boots, ser Barna," added the chemist. "Most acids I've know are less corrosive than Dr. Henjsen these days." He offered a sympathetic smile and vanished.

Rikard Sorens studied me. "You know the only thing worse than not finding something?"

"What?" I wasn't ready for questions or riddles. My whole body ached.

"Being a nonarcheologist who finds it." He grinned. "Do you have any idea what it might be?"

I grinned back—raggedly. "You saw it. You're the scientist. What do you think?"

"I have no idea, except that the clear crystalline arms are another material that's unique. It also amplifies light in a way I've never seen. I don't think that's its purpose, though."

I didn't either.

Sorens rose. "I have to meet with the techs."

"Good luck."

"The same to you." He turned and headed toward the facilities.

As I stood on sore feet, my recollection of Fernard's words didn't improve my sense of well-being. I also worried about the artifact. While I had scores of images of it, such representations weren't the device. Still, I was certain that Kaitlin Henjsen had it under guard.

I did wash up, dress, eat, and make my way to the small cubicle where I'd met with Kaitlin before. She was sitting behind a square console.

"You took your time."

"I was tired."

"So are we all."

There wasn't much to say to that. I didn't.

"I'd like to know how you knew that artifact was there." Her eyes accused me.

"I told you last night. I didn't know. I only knew that there had to be something, somewhere in the city. The pattern of the boulevards—"

"There is a difference, but it's minute. Almost as soon as we established the base, I had Nalakov analyze all the arcs and towers, every one in the entire megaplex. They all differ somewhat."

"These looked different." They had, and that was all that I could say. I wasn't about to suggest to her that what was a minute difference to us might not have been so to the ancient aliens.

"While you were sleeping, I had him reanalyze them. How did you know?"

"Artists deal in patterns, Kaitlin. I wouldn't know the mathematical terms. I only saw that the pattern looked somewhat different. What did he find?"

"The tower is the center of a locus of some sort. You could have mentioned that."

"I didn't know that. I only knew it was different."

"Then there's another thing. We didn't catch it until this morning. None of our techs melted that ramp." She was presenting another not-so-veiled accusation.

"They didn't? Then . . . you think the visiting aliens did?"

"I've already talked to Nuovyl and Zerobya, Barna. You knew that, and you entered the tower without so much as telling anyone here."

"Tech Zerobya said that she hadn't been there, and she didn't know anyone who had been, but there was nothing about the doors to suggest anyone had tried to break in, the way there was where the visiting aliens had been."

"There are a few traces. You might have destroyed any others."

"We only walked down the ramp. I'm sorry if that caused a problem."

"You shouldn't have entered that hall once you saw what was there."

I'd had enough. "My dear Dr. Henjsen, I didn't see what was there until after I entered the hall. I did not touch the artifact. I did not step on the dais or touch it or anything around it. I found it when none of your people could. I know you're tired and overstrained, but I'm also tired, and I'm particularly tired of your accusations and your blaming. I haven't damaged anything, and, frankly, I think I've contributed a great deal. All you seem interested in is finding fault with what I've done. That's not an admirable trait, and I would have expected better from you." I paused for the briefest of moments. "If you don't have anything else . . ."

Surprisingly, while she had stiffened at my words, she nodded slowly. "I am tired, and you are right, given the circumstances of the expedition. But I don't have to like what amounts to smash-and-grab archeology." She paused. "You'll need to get ready to leave. I don't know whether it will be this afternoon or tomorrow."

"Leave?" I was getting even angrier. "Because I found—"

"No." Her voice was chill, but resigned. "It has nothing to do with that. Commander Morgan has conveyed the captain's orders that we are *all* to reembark upon the *Magellan*. We'll leave the basic base and power systems in the hope that we can return. There will be no more expeditions by anyone away from the main base. I trust that you understand this is not my doing."

"I do. Did Commander Morgan give you any idea why we need to abandon Danann?"

"He did not. He just said that it was necessary and to prepare." Another pause followed. "I believe we've said all we have to say, ser Barna."

We probably had.

I nodded. "I'll be ready."

After I left her cubicle, I was still seething. Were all archeologists like that? Thinking that they owned all the artifacts of the past? That intuition or feeling—or vision—had no place in discovering what might have been? Or was it just that she'd been asked to coordinate too much with too few people over too short a time?

With so much unexplored on Danann and with so many unanswered questions, the captain's orders to abandon the megaplex suggested that attack or danger was imminent. My feeling was an attack.

59 GOODMAN/BOND

Bit by bit, I had rebuilt the torp power converter. Along the way, I'd gathered everything else I needed for the AG signaler—or knew exactly where it was and how to get to it quickly. I had to set everything up so that I could assemble it all during one of the night watches assigned to me. Then, late on oneday, I finally "scrapped" the dummy torp power converter. Standing in the aft bay of the armory, I unclamped the false converter. "All right, you miserable hunk of junk! You win!" I picked it up and headed forward.

"Sorry you couldn't make it work," Ciorio said. "Friggin' fine-ass work you've been doing, Bond. Shoulda maybe been a mech. Might have gone further in ratings."

"Didn't test well enough for that. You've got to be a friggin' engineer to be a mech." I dumped the dummy into the bin that held unusable components. If the fusactors were short of mass, it would become energy. If not, some tech back at base might discover it was faked, but I doubted it. It would just get fed into industrial reformulators.

"I thought you almost had it there."

"I *almost* did," I replied. "I thought I could."

"Almost doesn't count much, even with good torps," Chief Stuval added. "All you can hope is maybe you learned something that'll be useful later. Repairs like that aren't so easy."

"No. But it was more complicated than it had to be." I'd seen several ways it could have been simplified and made more reliable. "It could have been built simpler, a lot simpler."

"Simpler is better. That's if simpler does the job you want. It usually doesn't," the chief replied. "Now . . . we need to get to work on redoing the torp array. We need a complete check-off and inspection on each torp. That'll take every minute you've got for the next few days."

I didn't need to be reminded about that. Now I had everything I needed for the signaler, if hidden around my bay in the armory—except for the power section. What I didn't have was the time alone to assemble it, or the knowledge of which torp I could pull the power supply from. The torp check-offs would mean that both the chief and Ciorio would always be around—and probably Major Sewiki as well, or Lieutenant Swallow. I didn't ever see much of the lieutenant. While I was scheduled for the evening armory duty on threeday, the chief usually dropped in on the evening watches. A midwatch would have been much better, but the way the schedule fell I didn't have one of those until sevenday.

I was running out of time. That is, I was running out of time if I wanted to complete the mission and walk—or run—away from it with my body and mind intact.

"You all right, Bond?" asked Ciorio.

"I'm fine. I'll just be glad when this tour is over." That was true enough.

"It's been easy for a combat tour. Only one attack."

"So far," I pointed out. "They don't give combat pay without a reason, and one attack isn't usually a reason."

"You worry too much."

I had more than enough to worry about. Somehow, some way, I had to get the signaler assembled and stashed on one of the shuttles. I had to get that done soon, and I might just have to take the kind of chances I didn't like taking. I couldn't afford to get caught, but if I didn't get the job done, I'd either be dead— or I'd be on the run from both the Comity and C.I.S. I didn't want Colonel Truesdale's crusaders after me, either. Just as important, I didn't want the Spear of Iblis or the Morning Star in the hands of the Comity. What the Godless would do with such a weapon wasn't something I ever wanted to think about, and Danann looked to represent a temptation worthy of Iblis. If I failed, none of the alternatives were good, either for me or the Worlds of the Covenant.

"Bond?"

"I guess I do, sometimes." I gestured toward the aft bay, where both the torps we needed to inspect were and where I'd hidden my signaler components. "Could be I've had too much time to think." I offered a twisted smile.

"Thinking—that'll get you!" Ciorio laughed loudly.

So did I, even if I didn't feel like laughing. I could feel time squeezing in on me like a vise. I needed time alone in the armory, and that didn't happen except when I had the midwatch, and I usually got those on the enddays. I didn't like waiting that long, but agents who hurried usually hastened their own discovery or death. I wasn't aiming for that, although I doubted that Colonel Truesdale would have cared, not so long as the signaler was in place and worked.

I liked the idea of reaching the Paradise of Heaven, but I was in no hurry to get there, either.

60 BARNA

In the end, I rode the passenger shuttle back up to the *Magellan* late on twoday. If Kaitlin Henjsen could have found a way to get me off Danann sooner, she would have. I was thankful I'd had the foresight to take all the images of the artifact that I had, because I never got near it again. All the physical scientists were out there—all the ones that were on Danann. I hadn't heard if they'd discovered anything. In the little more than half a day since they had converged upon my discovery, I hadn't thought I would.

The shuttle was packed, both with passengers and with cargo. I was tired. So was everyone else, and they were all experts in fields deemed uncritical to investigating the artifact.

Exhaustion didn't stop Aleya Neison from asking questions. She was in the couch closest to mine.

"How did you know it was where it was?"

"How big is it?"

"Were there any markings that might have been inscriptions or a language?"

"What do you think it really is?"

"Is it possible there are others like it . . ."

I answered them all, as well as I could, but most of my answers frustrated her, I knew, because, except for how I found the artifact and how big it was, and the fact that I certainly hadn't seen anything that might have been inscriptions, I couldn't say anything except, "I don't know," or similar phrases.

After the shuttle docked in the big boat bay, I turned in the armor to the techs. I was glad to get out of it. Then I headed back to my minuscule stateroom. Tired as I'd been, I wasn't sleepy, and it was still well before the evening meal. I showered and dressed in clean skintights, vest, and shorts—practical for shipboard living.

I took the imager to my work space and transferred all the images I'd shot in the last day on Danann. Most were of the artifact, or the hall, with just a handful or so of the tower.

Because I had to talk to someone, I sent several of the best images of the artifact to Elysen's system. Then I slipped down the passageway to her work-space door. I knocked gently.

"Yes?"

"It's Chendor. I just got back. I found something that you might be interested in."

"You can come in. I'm not at my best, but that won't make any difference."

She wasn't. She was sitting behind her console, wearing a pale blue old-style shipsuit. The color should have looked good on her, with her silver hair. It didn't. On the wall screen was another parade of star regressions. I didn't try to follow them.

"You're back rather soon," she said. "Didn't you just go down yesterday?"

"I did. I found an artifact. Kaitlin Henjsen wasn't too happy with me. I neglected to tell her that the visiting aliens had marked out that tower, too. They never entered it, though."

"Kaitlin can be, shall we say, rigorous . . . in her defense of the professional approach . . ."

"And you aren't?" I still had no idea what her grand discovery might be.

"I don't recall throwing you onto a shuttle for a disagreement." Elysen smiled, faintly. Her expression did not remove the fatigue from her face. There was a hint of grayness to her complexion as well—just a slight touch.

"They're moving everyone off Danann. She just made certain I was among the first."

"It's already coming to that?" Her voice softened. "I was afraid something along those lines might occur."

"Along what lines?" I had no idea what she meant.

"Tell me about the artifact."

"I sent you the best images. You can call them up."

"I didn't notice." Her fingers touched the board, and the stars vanished from the wall screen. An image of the artifact filled it. The image was good, but it was flat. "How big is that? I don't get a sense of size."

"Four and a half meters from the bottom of the spheres to the top of the crystal, another meter to the light point. There are three other images on your system."

She called up the others, looking at each in turn, then returning to the first before speaking. "Amazing . . . truly amazing . . ."

"It's the only artifact down there," I said.

"You did better than you know, Chendor."

"You know what it is, don't you?"

"I might. Cleon and I will have to consult on this, but it sheds some light—as you put it earlier"—that enigmatic smile crossed her face again, almost erasing the worst of the age and the fatigue—"on what we've been doing. That is, if my theories are correct."

"You're not going to tell me yet?"

"Tomorrow. The day after at the latest."

She wasn't going to say, and I'd never been the kind to browbeat people into telling me anything. "A little while ago, you said something about the removal of the team, of it 'coming to that already.' What did you mean?"

"Oh, that. I was talking about Pandora's box, or a version of it, or maybe the ancient myth of the tree of knowledge of good and evil."

"You think Danann has something like that?"

"It *is* something like that, and the rest of the human Galaxy either wants the box or the fruit of that tree for themselves, or they don't want anyone to have it."

"No one understands most of what's down there," I pointed out.

"The rest of the Galaxy doesn't know that. Even if they did know, they wouldn't want to risk the chance that we might be able to find out."

"They think it's a technology treasure hunt."

"Isn't it?" she asked archly.

I knew what she meant. "It's more than that." What exactly, I couldn't say, except that the artifact was a key. I had an idea from Elysen's reaction that it confirmed the Danannians had indeed been a Type III civilization, if not more. I should have seen earlier, but I hadn't been thinking along those lines.

"Tell me about the towers, if you would."

"They're all the same, or almost the same, both inside and out—except for the one that held the artifact."

"And they're all made of those various anomalous composites that Cleon and the others think can extrude themselves into almost any shape and function? The outsides as well?" Another enigmatic smile crossed her lips.

I opened my mouth, then shut it. I should have seen that as well. We're all so used to seeing things as they are and not as they could be. Even I had fallen into that trap. When you see towers, kays and kays of ancient towers, that look identical, the question is why they look identical. That wasn't the right question.

"They had to be an incredibly artistic culture as well," I said slowly. "Every tower was a blank canvas. Probably every single one represented the artistic abilities and views of its owner, its inhabitant." Because, if the insides changed to meet the needs of the ancient Danannians, so could the outsides. There wasn't any art because, in a way, *everything* was art that changed to match the designs and desires of those who lived there. Yet it was all functional. I paused. Was it art? In the way I understood art?

I looked to Elysen. "How did you know?"

"I didn't, not much before you. When I saw the images of the artifact, a model, but one created lovingly and artistically, there had to be a reason why there was no other visible art."

I understood that as well. Sometimes you can get too close. I'd had to look at a map to find the tower, because there were too many towers everywhere. "Would you like to go to dinner with me?"

"I'm tired, Chendor, and I'm not all that hungry, not these days."

"You need to eat."

"I'm eating enough, Dr. DeLisle says. I don't have that much of a metabolism left."

I didn't want to drag her up to the mess, but I didn't like leaving her alone."

"You're kind, Chendor. I did have a small dinner earlier, and I need to rest. I'll be fine . . . as fine as possible, anyway, and you need to eat."

I wasn't so certain about any of that.

"Chendor." The words were strong and firm. "I *will* be fine. Go and leave an old lady in peace. You can tell me more tomorrow when we're both rested."

"Yes, Dr. Taube." I softened the formal words with a grin.

"Go, you young imp."

Only Elysen could have called me that and meant it. I went, worrying, but obeying. I had my doubts about resting in her work spaces. Was what she needed to finish that important?

61 CHANG

In the days after I'd had dinner at the mess with the professor, the shuttle schedule had gotten more and more cramped. Morgan didn't take any more replenishment runs. Only said that the needle pilots had to stay ready, and he couldn't direct them if he were somewhere with a shuttle. That told me that he expected visitors of the unfriendly human kind.

Twoday came. I took shuttle one down to Danann, came back heavy on both passengers and cargo. Wondered if that meant Morgan had detected visitors, or that the *Owens* had brought information about them. But I didn't see Morgan, and didn't want to chase him down to ask.

Threeday, Lerrys had the duty. Screen plot showed he was headed back to the *Magellan*. He'd reported full load, close to max—both passengers and cargo. I was stretched out on one of the chairs in the ready room. Didn't have to be there, but I'd already done my workout. Besides, most times, it was quiet on the launch deck.

Fitzhugh peered in, then stepped inside. Looked around, saw me, smiled. "I haven't seen you in the mess."

"Schedule's been a bitch."

"I suppose I shouldn't be here, but I marched up as if I were headed to be transported or fitted for armor, and no one even looked." He grinned. "Such an approach is advantageous in that it usually works. That is, if you've been cleared before and are in the system."

"You know more about things than you let on." I gestured to the seat across from me.

He slipped into it. Gracefully. Had forgotten how he moved.

"I know a modicum about some things. All military organizations operate on essentially identical principles, requiring discipline above individual initiative, command accountability above responsibility, structural regularity above functionality . . ." He shrugged. "Unfortunately, I talk to excess, and my speech is filled not only with detailed relevancy, but with irrelevant and equally detailed digressions."

"You're more comfortable with principles, facts, and abstract concepts."

"And you, Lieutenant, are more comfortable with action and silence."

"Silence is better, sometimes," I pointed out.

"It is. I enjoy it, paradoxical as that may seem from someone as verbose as I appear."

Appear? If he enjoyed silence, then why did he speak at such length? Almost shook my head. Because it was a way of keeping people in a crowd at a distance? "You need time to yourself."

"Most people do. They just don't recognize it. They're afraid of the silence."

"You're afraid of the silence in a crowd."

He shrugged. "It's impolite to be standoffish."

"Ex-commando conditioning?" Frig! Spoke before I thought. "I'm sorry. I shouldn't have—"

"You are the first to have made that connection, at least, the first to have had the courage to verbalize it." His lips twisted. "It's easier to work within the conditioning parameters."

"You're . . . you're really a shy and private person, but all that . . . stuff . . . so you fill the space so that people won't pry . . . so that they'll keep everything on an intellectual level?"

"You're most perceptive, Lieutenant—"

"Far too blunt."

"But honest. You are honest, and that has laid a toll upon you, Lieutenant—"

"My name is Jiendra. Appreciate it if you'd use it." Couldn't believe I'd blurted that out.

"Only if you will return the favor and call me Liam."

"Done." Silence—the awkward kind. "Why did you come up here?"

"Can you think of a more appropriate locale in which to find you?" Fitzhugh—Liam—hard to make that change in my mind—flushed slightly.

"Don't know as I'm worth finding."

"I've enjoyed your company and found your absence created a void I had not realized existed."

Most would have told me they missed me. Would have been saying they missed my body. His indirection was true . . . touching. "I would have liked to be in the mess more. The schedule makes it hard."

"You're always combating fatigue."

"Happens when you're short of pilots." Felt like we were dancing, trying to get where we both wanted and not knowing how.

"Chang!" Morgan hurried in. First time I'd seen him move that fast—or breathe hard. Looked at Fitzhugh. "If you'll excuse us, Professor . . ."

"I understand. I'll leave you to your duties, Commander." Fitzhugh stood, turned to me. "Until later, Lieutenant."

"Until later." I made sure I smiled. Knew Morgan would catch that, as well as Liam, but I didn't care.

Morgan didn't say anything until Liam was out of the ready room. "You seem to have made an impression upon the professor. Or is it the other way around?"

Ignored the question. None of Morgan's business. "What's so urgent? Do we have company?"

"Not yet. The *Alwyn*'s detected some activity at the end of detection limits, but that could be interference from the singularities. They're closer than we had calculated."

"Or it could be a CW or Middle Kingdom fleet?"

"Or the Covenanters or my aunt Wauneta. That's not the only problem. Henjsen has an artifact She thinks it should come up here. So does the captain. I've got the crew stripping shuttle two."

"The artifact is the *only* problem?"

"No. We can't take a chance with the people, either. We've been pulling the team off Danann, quietly, but the artifact is something special. I've never heard Henjsen so excited."

"How did she find it?"

"She didn't. The artist—Barna—he found it through some sort of artistic sense or analysis. Henjsen blasted me when I insisted she give him a slider on oneday. She's forgotten that. When I told her she needed to evacuate, she insisted we bring up this artifact. I don't think she wanted to tell me about it. Not yet."

"How big is it?"

"It's not the cubage; it's the mass. It's almost five thousand kilos. Henjsen says it only ought to mass five hundred, from its size. It doesn't."

"What the frig is it?"

"Barna found it. Henjsen claims he says it's not art, but a technological device that's artistic in form. The scientists haven't begun to figure it out, but it was in a place that suggests it was important. Whatever it is, they can't do more than they have down there. They think it's inert."

"*Think?*" We'd had steam explode out of frozen lakes near absolute zero, energy emissions that remained unexplained, and Morgan wanted a massive unknown alien artifact in the shuttle—or the *Magellan?*

"Neither the captain nor I feel we have that much time left here."

"So we have to bring something back?"

"As much as we can. Lerrys has shuttle one full—science types and cargo."

"Those AG traces aren't your aunt Wauneta." Looked him square.

"We're not sure, but probably not, not from the dispatches the *Owens* brought. If we wait until we are certain . . ."

"Everyone on Danann's frigged."

"There's a good chance of it if we don't get them off."

Frig! Frig! Frig! Knew it had been a bastard mission from the beginning. "How soon will shuttle two be ready?"

"Another stan."

"I'd better get started on preflighting."

"Good. I've got a few more . . . difficulties to handle."

He left without another word.

Bothered me. A lot. Morgan was brusque, but not that short. Meant other trouble that I knew nothing about. I headed for the pilots' locker area to get into my armor.

62 FITZHUGH

Much as I comprehended the urgency manifested by Commander Morgan, and much as I understood its necessity, assuming that it represented a military requirement, I still resented his summary dismissal, particularly when it had seemed lively that I might have been able to engage in a less formal conversation with Jiendra. Behind her own abnegation of verbosity, seemingly the obverse of my excessive semieloquence, I was convinced that there lay a personage of considerable depth, understanding, and wit. Yet for us to navigate through two sets of shoals, erected to protect each of us from the cruel uncertainty of the interpersonal interrelations so erroneously bearing the appellation of human nature, required time and patience, and the vicissitudes of our respective situations mitigated against the leisurely approach so necessary for us both.

More directly put, regardless of Morgan's intent or situational urgency, irrational as the feeling was, I would have liked to have handled him as roughly as I had the saboteur steward. In that state of repressed anger, a return to my work space and any form of reasoned analysis would be less than productive.

Since Dr. DeLisle had suggested occasional returns for brief monitoring of my physiology, I made my way down to the *Magellan*'s sick bay by the ramps and not the lifts, trusting that the major would indeed be there. If he were not, I would have at least gotten some additional exercise, although I had begun to frequent the workout rooms once more.

As I slipped into sick bay, through the main hatchway, I heard voices. One was that of Commander Morgan. I immediately moved to one side of the passageway and dropped to the floor beside one of the slightly protruding supply bins, as if to check my shipboots, although the effect was to render me far less visible.

". . . got a problem, and that makes it yours." Morgan's voice was low, but intense. "I need some special medical support."

"What do you need?"

"We've got an agent on board. Another one, and he's from a system that deep-conditions their people. I can stun him, but I need you to flush out whatever nanites and conditioners are in him."

"Commander . . . we've got some of the latest med equipment here, but no D.S.S. ship is equipped to handle that."

"You don't think I know that? I'm asking you to come up with something that will give us half a chance to talk to this agent before his memories and personalities are flushed."

"I *might* be able to do that on Hamilton. Here . . ." DeLisle's voice trailed off. "I was pushing it to put Professor Fitzhugh back together."

"You did. Now I need this, and I need it soon."

"I told you, Commander . . ."

"Our lives—your life—just might depend on it." Morgan's voice was hard. "We've got what looks to be a flotilla gathering just at the limits of detection range."

That was not information particularly reassuring, nor something I wanted to hear, however much it did not especially astonish me.

". . . do what you can to prepare. I'll let you know when we're bringing him down."

". . . not get your hopes too high, Commander . . ."

"Don't set yours too low, Major. I'll inform you."

I stood up just before Morgan turned, like an ursinoid moving toward prey. His visage stiffened upon perceiving me.

"Whatever you heard, Professor, keep it to yourself."

"I heard very little, Commander, except your telling Dr. DeLisle to prepare. Are we facing another attack in the imminent future?"

"That's possible. I'd appreciate your keeping that to yourself as well." Behind the words was a coldness verging on a threat.

"While I doubt that anyone would find that knowledge of great surprise, I will comply with your wishes."

"My commands, Professor."

"Those as well, Commander." I met his eyes, and my orbs were as chill as his, and more adamantine. "Even though you are in no position to enforce them personally."

He paused, just for a moment, then inclined his head and surged past me like a wave spent on an unseen reef.

Morgan had admitted the possibility of an another attack, and that admission was indicative that he wanted to conceal the matter of yet another agent aboard the *Magellan*. While I would have considered an approaching flotilla as a far greater threat than a single agent, it was manifestly apparent that Morgan did not, and his use of authority and personal presence on Major DeLisle reinforced the criticality involved with such an agent. I would have like to have been clairaudient to have ascertained what about that individual constituted a threat of such magnitude.

Major DeLisle looked up, his cognitive functions focused elsewhere.

"Commander Morgan left in quite a hurry," I offered, pleasantly.

"He has difficulties."

"He often does, I suspect. His position is one where all the responsibility for execution rests upon him, but he has less-than-optimal input into making the decisions that must be implemented."

"Something like that," murmured DeLisle. He forced a professional expression approximating a smile. "How are you doing?"

"Better than I might have anticipated those days when I was in the medcrib, but you had requested that I stop by in a week or so." I shrugged.

"We'll give you a quick diagnostic." His eyes drifted toward the passageway behind me, his concerns still with the departed commander. "Are you following the exercise program?"

"Mostly. I've stepped up some of the workouts slightly." More than slightly, but I had a far better idea of what my system could handle and required than did the doctor.

"You don't look like a man who nearly died less than a month ago, but you shouldn't overdo it."

"Why don't we see what the diagnostics indicate?" As we moved toward the diagnostic bay, I was considering when and how I might work another encounter with Jiendra without seeming either calculatedly coy or overtly predatory. She wanted to be valued, but neither pursued overtly nor ignored, and that balance was more than a little difficult for a man whose personality was as inhibitedly aggressive as was mine.

But then, I had been far from facile in managing and maintaining all facets of close interpersonal relations, even with the girls when they had been children—or later. Yet there was something indefinable about Jiendra Chang that intimated that not all dreams were only for the young.

63 CHANG

I had to wait half a stan longer before shuttle two was ready to preflight. Tech Chief Patel was already going over the cargo bay when I stepped aft through the hatch from the forward section.

He looked up, shook his head. "They stripped out everything, even the emergency pods. What sort of mass load are we talking, sir?"

Frig! Morgan hadn't told me how much they were stripping. "At least five thousand kilos, the commander said."

"Has to be more, sir. We can carry 10 MT against T-grav."

"That would be a little over six, with the safety factors, from Danann."

"They stripped out a good MT of gear."

One artifact massed close to 7 MT? Didn't like that at all. "Ours not to reason why . . ." Didn't voice the rest of the words. Showed that military stupidity had been around longer than I wanted to dwell on.

"Yes, sir."

"We don't have to like it, chief, but the commander said that what we're bringing up is critical." Could see the question in Patel's eyes, and added, "How and why he wouldn't tell me except that it's the only artifact they found down there. We need to recover it before more trouble arrives." Offered a cynical smile. "Besides having no life-support backup, how do things look?"

"Everything else is sound, sir."

"Thanks." I finished the walk-around, then strapped in, and started through the first part of the checklist. Brought the fusactor online and went link.

Navigator Control, Sherpa Tigress, powered up this time. Interrogative anticipated mass load for return.

Tigress, estimated mass load at 5.5 MT. Could tell Morgan was on the link.

Thirty percent safety factor? *Interrogative estimated?*

Cargo mass varies over a twenty percent range. May be equipment measurement error, or the properties of the object.

Shit! *Request priority of cargo.*

Star double plus, Tigress.

If I were still civilian . . . that would rate triple pay.

No response to that.

Finished the prelaunch prep and checklist.

"Ready, aft, chief?"

"Yes, sir."

Navigator Control, this is Sherpa Tigress, ready for departure.

Tigress, Navigator Control, bay is clear, doors open, null grav in bay, nanite barrier in place. You are cleared for departure and descent to landing zone beta. Request immediate return upon load-in.

Null grav hit even before Morgan's link finished.

Control, understand cleared for departure and descent to landing zone beta. Will comply with return as immediate as possible.

Touched the steering jets and eased shuttle two clear of the *Magellan*.

Descent to Danann was easy, maybe too easy. We set down on the empty lake. Screens and energy tracks indicated that it was heating up under the ice as well. Not so far along as zone alpha had been, though.

Danann Base, this is Sherpa Tigress. Standing by for cargo load-in. Interrogative energy sources under zone beta.

Sherpa Tigress, ETA of cargo sliders less than ten. Energy sources same as zone alpha. . . .

That meant that they still didn't know what caused them, only that they showed the same patterns.

. . . Traces registered at detection levels late yesterday. Ice and surface will remain usable within all safety parameters for at least another week. Have informed Navigator Control, and will keep all shuttles posted.

Danann Base, thank you. Another thing Morgan had known and hadn't bothered to tell me. His secretiveness was getting to me. Mission was enough of a bastard without that. Who were we going to tell? Decided to put it aside until later.

Liam Fitzhugh was reserved, but didn't use information like a weapon. I frowned. More like a tool. Most men did. But Liam shared information. Maybe the difference was that for Liam, it *was* a tool, and he thought everyone needed the tools. Put that thought aside, too. Began a systems check.

"Have the sliders in sight, sir. Request permission to open the outer hatch and depressurize cargo bay."

"Granted." Checked to see that my helmet was racked in easy reach. Shouldn't need it, but you never knew.

Sherpa Tigress, Danann Base, interrogative cargo sliders. Even over links, the base controller sounded nervous.

Base, sliders approaching this time. Preparing to begin in-load.

Stet, Tigress.

Went back and checked the emissions from below the lake's frozen surface. They seemed lower, but I didn't have comparative records. With almost another 6 MT—or more—being loaded into the shuttle, had to hope the science types and Morgan had it right.

"Be a while, Lieutenant," Patel reported. "They've got to brace everything before they load. Sliders can't negate all the mass."

"Sliders? How many does it take?"

"They've got two and an insider."

"Can you see what the cargo is?"

"No, sir. They've got it wrapped and crated in plastrene. Crate looks to be three meters by five by four . . . something like that. It's barely going to fit through the cargo hatch. I hope they remembered to set outside tie rings on that plastrene and link-braced the inside."

"Me, too, chief. Ask them about the internal bracings."

"Yes, sir."

I could feel the vibrations through the hull—and the sensors—as they loaded the artifact. I didn't hear anything from Patel for almost half a stan.

"It's link-braced inside, sir."

"But what?" Patel wasn't telling me everything.

"Whatever it's made of is stronger than anything they have down here."

Frig! Swallowed to let the anger subside. "So if we make any violent changes in altitude or heading, they won't swear everything will hold?"

"Not with that mass, sir."

"Then our liftoff and ascent will be very smooth."

"Yes, sir."

"Let me know when everything's sealed up." Patel would anyway, but I had to say something.

I replotted the power curve for the liftoff and checked the systems again. Found I was sweating. Almost never sweated. Armor and control area weren't that hot.

"Everything's tight and green, sir. Strapped in and ready."

"Commencing liftoff checklist."

Danann Base, Sherpa Tigress. Loaded and preparing for liftoff. Didn't have to let them know, but wanted to get a reaction.

Stet, Tigress.

Some reaction.

Finished the checkoff and brought full power up in the fusactor, then eased in the drives, following the curve. Hoping nothing went wrong. Frigging little margin for error.

Navigator Control, Sherpa Tigress, lifting this time.

Stet, Tigress. Report near approach to Navigator.

Stet, Control.

Kept the shuttle on the power curve all the way out. Once I was above low orbit, I began cutting back on the drives. Began decel far earlier than I had been, but with so much mass effectively unsecured, I didn't want it crashing through me if the gravs hiccuped, or we lost power.

Sherpa Tigress, this is Control. Interrogative early deceleration.

Clear that Morgan had been watching the screens from the time of the shuttle's liftoff from Danann.

Control, Tigress. Mass balance requires . . . How the frig could I say it? . . . *phased decel in order to avoid structural damage to shuttle. Interrogative Navigator difficulty.*

That's a negative, Tigress.

Morgan was lying, but he wouldn't tell me why over an open link.

Checked the farscreens. Even the shuttle's screens showed energy distortions, but too far out for me to get details. *Any* energy levels meant we had company, and it wouldn't be friendly. Still wasn't about to hurry my approach. It'd be stans, if not a day, before the "company" got close enough for action. Still . . .

Control, interrogative immediate turnaround for personnel recovery.

That's affirmative. Crew standing by for service and reinstallation of basic couches.

Another aspect of a bastard mission. High price for getting my masters' certs back—especially since they'd been stolen. Shouldn't lose a cert for uncovering graft. I snorted. The word "shouldn't" didn't have much applicability when male pride and egos were involved.

Checked the closure with the *Magellan*, eased in a touch more decel. Only wanted minimal closure near the ship. I frowned. Screens showed the main bay doors closed.

Tigress, stabilize position outside boat bay. Stand by for scan.

Stabilizing now. Frigging great. Had me lift whatever the frig the artifact was. Didn't even know if it would blow. After I'd stuck my neck and Patel's out—again—then . . . *then* Morgan decided on a remote scan. Another aspect of a bastard mission.

Detectors protested as the beams played across the shuttle.

"Sir . . . the artifact is glowing. I can see it through the plastrene."

"We're being scanned, chief. The glow ought to fade . . ." Don't know why I said that. No reason for the artifact to glow, or for the glow to fade.

Detectors went null.

"Is it still glowing?"

"No, sir."

Really wanted not to tell Morgan, but there were others on the *Magellan.*

Navigator Control, Sherpa Tigress, reporting artifact illuminated in response to scan. Scan completed, illumination ended.

Stet, Tigress. Object intensifies all forms of radiation. You're cleared to main bay.

Another reason to throttle Morgan. He could have told me that.

"Beginning recovery, chief."

The bay doors were open now. Took my time about easing the shuttle into the cradle. Made sure everything was perfect.

Control, Tigress. Cradled and shutting down this time. Will stand by for personnel recovery.

That's affirmative, Tigress.

Morgan was worried. So was I.

64 GOODMAN/BOND

Late on threeday, I was cleaning up my work area. I was just about to head off to the mess. I'd have four stans off before I came back on the evening watch for the armory.

"Bond!" called Chief Stuval. "Ciorio!"

"Yes, chief." We hurried forward.

"I want you two to give the sliders a full inspection and check-out. They need to be ready. Then check the transport tubes, and get the sliders ready. There's a good chance we'll be needing them before long," ordered the chief.

"Needing 'em?"

I was glad Ciorio asked.

"Ops has ordered a class-three alert."

"Have the Sunnis come back?" I couldn't believe that, but it was a safe question to find out more.

"No one's saying topside, and they haven't announced class one," the chief replied.

"Then what are they going to send out the needles for? There's nothing here except that planet."

"They don't tell us why, Bond. They tell us what to do and when."

"They never tell us much of anything."

"It's called 'need to know,' Bond, and you've been around long enough to understand that." Stuval sounded angry.

"I know, chief. But it's different here. We're in the middle of nowhere."

"Gliess says that they're running the shuttles down to Danann and back up, shipping up the science types," Ciorio said. "Fast as they can."

"That doesn't sound good," I admitted. If they were bringing everyone back from planetside, the *Magellan* wasn't likely to be remaining near Danann long. That meant, somehow, I had to get the AG signaler assembled and into one of the shuttles on my evening watch. Or somewhere on one of the needles. I didn't see how it mattered, so long as it sent out the signal clear of the *Magellan*. How I'd manage either was another question, but I'd have to find a way.

"It's not good at all," Chief Stuval said slowly. "Bond . . . go on and get something to eat. Better be back here a good stan before your watch. That way, both you and Ciorio can square everything away."

"I'm on my way, chief."

I thought the chief watched my back as I headed out through the armory's main hatch. I didn't look to check. That would have made him suspicious. If I couldn't get time alone, I might have to incapacitate the chief somehow. Give him a bump on the head and claim he fell.

That'd be weak, but I was stuck on the *Magellan* in the middle of a galactic void, with problems with anything I did—or didn't do. I took the ramps up to the mess deck.

Alveres caught me in the mess line.

"You hear what's happening, Bond?"

I shrugged.

"You guys in the armory always know."

"I thought shield mechs knew." I managed a grin.

"Nah . . . we just have to repair things afterward."

"We're on class-three alert."

"Oh, we all know that. Why? You know that?"

"No one's told me anything, except they're bringing back scientists from Danann."

"That's very not good."

"What's the scuttlebutt down forward?"

"They ran a scan on the big cargo shuttle just came in. Something they found down below. Major was muttering that he'd never seen anything like it. Strange backscatter, almost like the thing amplified radiation or light."

Amplified light? The Morning Star? How had Colonel Truesdale known? Or had he just been talking figuratively, suspecting what *might* be found? Did it matter? I *had* to get the AG signaler assembled and in operation. I just hoped I hadn't waited too long. But . . . only three months into a yearlong deployment? "Anyone know what it is?"

"Who knows? They don't tell us. That's for certain." Alveres shook his head, then started for a table with another mech.

I joined them.

"Bond doesn't know any more than we do."

"We're checking torps again," I said. "I can't figure if the chief wants to keep us busy, or the major's been told something's up."

"Got to be something coming," volunteered Hastens. He was a screen tuner. "All the officers are tight. Don't show it outside, but you can tell. They wouldn't get tight just for a frigate or some corvettes."

I nodded and ate. The evening meal was another attempt at turkey—closer to the taste of a real fowl than the reformulated chicken, but still not all that good. I'd had worse, but not often, and not for weeks on end. The potatoes were fine, and the sugarcake pudding took away the aftertastes.

After that, I went to the rec hall on the twenty-fourth deck and lost twenty credits on bones. I was trying to pass the time. With what I had to do, I knew I couldn't rest. Everything I needed was in the armory.

I arrived an hour early for my watch—just like the chief had ordered.

"You're always on time, Bond." Those were Ciorio's first words. He was sitting behind the duty console. "Thought I'd wait for you to get started on the sliders. Didn't want you to have nothing to do but watch the console and stand by."

"You're even lazier than I am."

"You? Lazy?" He laughed. "I'll bet you were studying for the tech first exams."

"Not a chance. Lost twenty creds at bones."

"First time all deployment, I'd bet."

"Third or fourth." I lied. It was the second time.

"I've already run checks on all the torp transport tubes," Ciorio said. "Chief came by and signed off on that. All we have left is the maintenance checks on the sliders."

"I'll do the up-front maintenance on sliders one and two, then. You can do number three. Later, I might run them down the passageways a bit just to make sure."

"Chief wouldn't like that. He always wants the armory sealed during off-stans."

"Then I won't." That was a lie. I'd have to use a slider. The signaler assembly would be too big to carry far without a slider.

Ciorio didn't leave for almost an hour, but we did finish everything the chief had ordered.

Once he was gone, I retreated to the aft bay. First thing I did was run the feed into the monitoring scanners. One run showed the aft bay empty—the way it should have been—and the other showed me around the duty area. That part of the mission had gone as planned. I'd just recorded that one night when I hadn't been doing much. Anyone watching the feeds wouldn't see anything out of the ordinary.

After that, I had to hurry. It took less than ten minutes to gather all the components from their various hiding places. Some were in plain sight, such as in the stocks of replacement components. Others were harder. It took some effort to pry the false bottom off the toolkit assigned to me.

Forty minutes passed, and I had everything together—except for the power-pak from a torp. But the chief always came by halfway through the watch. So I stowed everything and put the almost complete signaler under my workbench, behind the toolkit. It barely fit. It was bigger than I'd thought it would be, almost a meter square.

Then I hurried back to the watch console at the front of the armory, and dropped my phony monitor feed off-line.

Sure enough, less than ten minutes later, Chief Stuval appeared, opening the hatch that was sealed during off-hours. Only he and the officers had the codes.

"How's it going, Bond?" He looked at me intently.

"Ciorio left about a stan back. We finished everything you asked. I can show you the sliders, and the check-offs." I rose from behind the console.

"That's all right. If you say it's done, it's done."

"Have you heard any more, chief? About what's going on?"

"Not a thing." He looked around, then walked into the main bay of the armory, directly behind the console.

"Alveres—he's one of the shield mechs—he said that they brought up something strange from Danann. They even scanned it, and it had funny radiation."

"Don't believe all you hear."

"I usually don't, but he's a screen mech. That's not something he'd make up."

"No one's told me. Has the major been by?"

"No, chief. The only ones here have been you and Ciorio."

He frowned. "That's right. She said that she was meeting with the ops officer about now." He gave me a smile. "When she relieves you, tell Ansaio that she should run a last check on the transport tubes around zero three-thirty."

"I can do that."

The chief surveyed the front bay, then nodded. "I'll see you in the morning."

After he left, the hatch sealed behind him, I saw that he had left a stylus on the corner of the console. I slipped it into a drawer. It looked like I wouldn't have to worry about the major, not if I hurried, anyway.

Getting a torp from the last cradle in the array single-handed was a bitch. I managed, and in another fifteen minutes I had the power section open. Ten more minutes and the powerpak was on my bench. I forced myself to reseal the power section of the torp and slide it back into position. Then I sealed the array.

With the powerpak on the bench I had one last task. The power lead connectors were different sizes, but that wasn't a problem because they attached to a transformer to step up the power. It would burn out the signaler sooner, but that kind of boost was necessary. That's what I'd learned along the way. I dipped the connectors in the conducting solution, then replaced it as well.

Only then did I pull out the signaler assembly. It had more mass than I'd recalled. Without the small slider, I couldn't have handled it. I checked all the circuits one last time, then I lifted the powerpak to slide it into place.

Click, click . . .

Boots on the deck. Who'd opened the hatch without the alarm sounding? I didn't have a weapon anywhere close. I hadn't planned on that complication, not on a sealed warship. Any sort of energy weapon would have registered on the ship's system, and any other sort would have been useless.

"Bond?" The voice was Chief Stuval's.

"I was checking something back here in the bay." I turned, moving forward from the bay. If I got away from the bench, he might not look back there. It was about the best I could hope for.

Thrum!

Stunner! I tried—

Hot blackness . . . Everywhere.

"Give him another shot . . ."

Thrumm . . .

65 CHANG

Lieutenant Chang, to the ready room!

With the jolt from the link, I bolted upright in the bunk. Almost slammed my head on the bulkhead. Frig! Hadn't gotten back to the *Magellan* until late on threeday. Universe-dragging late—and now Morgan was blind-linking, and that meant urgent.

Checked the time. Zero five hundred. Took care of a few quick necessities, scrambled into skintights and vest, splashed water on my face, brushed back my hair, and headed out. Did take the lift up to the launch deck.

Morgan was waiting in the ready room. Bad as I felt, he looked worse. "There's a flotilla out there. It's Covenanter, or I miss my guess."

"Do they really want to take on the Comity?"

"If we don't get back," Morgan pointed out, "how will anyone know? We don't have a fast courier at the moment. The *Owens* left early this morning with the information about the artifact and the initial data, and the *Bannister* hasn't re-turned yet. I need you to take shuttle two down to landing zone beta. You'll pick up one of the fusactors, and transfer it and some equipment to an unmarked landing zone. The coordinates are in the nav system. Call it up as gamma. Lerrys already made a transfer to delta zone with shuttle one. You'll have two techs. Once you unload at gamma, you'll hop back to beta and pick up the last of the planetside techs and scientists. Lerrys is about to lift now."

"We're leaving fusactors?" Didn't make sense to me.

"We need to keep the Covenanters busy once they get here. They need to think we have at least three sites active down there, and that we've got defenses. Each of the three fusactors we're leaving will power a shield once we're clear."

"Diversionary tactic?"

"What else can we do if we're outnumbered?"

"We could run?"

"They could move in at any time. We don't have everyone clear yet. Henjsen had some of the scientists out in the field."

Morgan was lying about some of that. Didn't want to call him. "We could still run, just head out angular . . ."

"No, we can't," he said. "Dust density's too low for the photon nets to gather enough mass. We've got limits, even with full tanks. We also don't know what else is there."

"You think some other systems in the human Galaxy sent ships?"

"I wouldn't bet against it. We caught another saboteur last night. Probably a Covenanter."

Raised my eyebrows. "Suicider?"

"We don't know. We stunned him before he could react. He had something that could have taken out the entire ship. He'd almost finished building it on board. That really would have made it easy for them. Doc DeLisle has him under sedation. Later, if DeLisle is successful, we might find out more." Morgan took a deep breath. "You need to get going. There's a mug of coffee by the maintenance console."

"Thanks." Coffee would help, even the weak reformulated stuff from the mess.

"Oh . . . watch Henjsen. She wanted another run. She said she had more samples that were critical. I told her no. She still pressed. She'll press you to overload. Don't."

"Appreciate the heads-up."

He was gone almost before I could finish the words.

Went to the maintenance console and checked out shuttle two's status. We were still running without the emergency support packs, stripped for max cargo load, except we had twelve troop seats. Not even real couches.

Ysario met me at the shuttle. She was tech chief on the run. Like everyone else, dark circles under her eyes. "Another heavy load, sir?"

"A three-fer. Down to beta zone, out to gamma, then a full load to orbit."

"Gamma, sir?"

"A new zone where we're dropping a fusactor. We have to pick it up at beta first. How do things look?"

"Beat-up." Ysario laughed. "All those crates. Good thing the *Magellan*'s got lots of hold space. Patel said he was here until zero two hundred getting the big cargo sliders out of the bay."

Nodded and continued with the preflight walk-around. When I finished, I headed forward. Racked my armor helmet, then slipped into the couch and began the systems checks. They came up green, and I started the prelaunch checklist.

After I finished, I linked. *Control, Sherpa Tigress, ready to uncradle and launch. Tigress, null grav in bay, locks opening this time.*

Stet, Control. My stomach lurched more than usual with the loss of grav. Too frigging early and too little sleep. Also wasn't as young as I used to be.

Once we were clear of the *Magellan,* I scanned the farscreens and detectors, but only got noise at max range. Slightly reassuring. Covenanters shouldn't be anywhere close before the time we finished. Did note that the *Alwyn* had moved well out from Danann.

Descent was smooth. No glitches. I did catch a point source of energy out to the "east." Also, picked up the faint energy emanations, the kind that had come up under alpha and beta, except they seemed to be coming from all the frozen lakes. Didn't like that at all, but past experience said it took a while for them to get really hot.

Danann Base, this is Sherpa Tigress, touchdown. I managed to set the shuttle without a hitch. Harder than you'd think without atmosphere. No wind, but no ground cushion either.

Sherpa Tigress, this is Danann Base, your in-load is standing by.

"We're unsealing. Then we'll brace the ramps, Lieutenant," Ysario announced.

"Let me know when you start loading." Put everything on standby and eased out of the couch and stood. Debated watching the load-in and decided against it. I'd have to don the helmet and lock out. Besides, Ysario knew more than I ever would.

Stood for several minutes, then settled back before the controls until Ysario reported.

"Cargo's in, and we're sealed aft, sir."

Danann Base, Navigator Control, Sherpa Tigress lifting this time for zone gamma.

Stet, Tigress. Report touchdown. That was Morgan. Didn't get any acknowledgment from Danann Base.

Control, will report.

Gamma zone was barely a hop in the shuttle. Just an empty ice lake. Right before setdown, picked up some of the diffuse Danannian energy emissions. Could be a good thing we were getting off Danann before long. Made another smooth touchdown.

Navigator Control, Sherpa Tigress, touchdown at zone gamma. Will report liftoff.

Took almost a stan to unload the fusactor and set up whatever equipment was necessary for the shields and diversion that Morgan had planned.

Finally, Ysario let me know. "Load's clear, and the automatics are set. We're sealed."

"Thanks, chief." I began the liftoff checklist for the return to beta zone.

Liftoff and return to Danann Base were smooth and quick. Touchdown was no problem, but the energy levels below the surface were the highest I'd seen. Wanted to get clear as soon as we could. Checked the monitors. Couldn't believe how much shit was lined up on sliders for us.

"Chief . . . you see what's out there? We can't take all that."

"No, sir. I'll run a mass check as we load. Stop short of point-seven."

"Sounds good."

I watched the monitors as the sliders edged closer to the shuttle.

"We're beginning load-in, sir. We'll be at max, with cargo and eleven passengers."

"Keep track of that mass." Didn't need to tell Ysario, but Morgan had warned me.

Ten minutes passed, then half a stan. I could feel the vibrations as crates were stowed.

"Lieutenant, Dr. Henjsen wants to know if we can take another hundred kilos in samples. One more crate."

"You've got the load parameters, chief. What are we running?"

"We're at point-six-nine."

Frig! With all the last-minute cargo crates and the ten remaining techs and Henjsen, we were running heavier than we had with the damned artifact. Still . . . we weren't likely to get back to Danann. "If it's *only* a hundred kilos . . . we'll still be in the green." Even two hundred would have been all right, but I didn't trust Henjsen.

"She says it's just a hundred. That's the mass calc on the crate."

"That'll be all we can take." I didn't like to cut it that close. Not at all.

I ran another systems check, then started the checklist for liftoff.

Just before I finished, Ysario clicked on. "Everything's stowed, sir. We're tight."

"Stand by for liftoff, then." Finished the checklist.

Navigator Control, this is Sherpa Tigress, lifting this time.

Stet, Tigress. Report when clear of megaplex.

Shuttle came up slow and heavy. Knew it would be that way, but still felt sluggish. Checked the drives. Could see them running up, but they didn't stop. Went right into the amber, telltales flashing.

Frig! Flattened the climb angle, but the drives were still amber. Frigging Henjsen had overloaded us! Should have done a full mass check instead of taking manifested weights.

On top of that, shuttle wanted to slew. Something aft was unbalanced.

Whole shuttle shuddered and shifted. Managed to compensate and keep the shuttle level. Decided to let Ysario handle it without asking. She'd have her hands full.

Maybe five minutes passed. The imbalance had been righted . . . somehow.

"Cargo problem, sir," Ysario reported. She was panting. "Got it under control. That last crate. Must have massed three hundred kilos. Hidden sliders, never shut down. Broke the tiedowns. We've got it now."

"Thanks, chief."

Navigator Control, Sherpa Tigress, reporting cargo shift, possible mass undercalculation by planetside personnel. Matters under control. Best always to cover your ass when some idiot screws you, except figuratively and literally, it's usually too late.

Confirm, Sherpa Tigress, matters under control.

That's affirm, Control. We were through the worst part of the liftout, and I'd managed to get the drives back in the green, just barely. Whole drive system would need checking, maybe retuning.

Went back to routine scans. Systems showed three energy sources below— strong. Had to be the new shields. Morgan had probably triggered them from the *Magellan*. The baseline Danannian emissions were also higher.

Barely got out of suborbit when Morgan linked again. *Sherpa Tigress, Control, interrogative status.*

Control, Sherpa Tigress, estimate status amber. Anticipate return and cradle green. I could get the shuttle back into the boat bay without a problem. I could even take it for short hops outside a gravity well. I wouldn't have wanted to take it anywhere else.

Thanks for the clarification, Tigress.

Made a slow and careful approach to the *Magellan*. Along the way, saw that the *Alwyn* had moved farther deepspace from Danann, but the shuttle detectors still registered noise in the distance, no clear indications of what might be there.

Did take a deep breath when the shuttle was safe in the cradle and ship grav took hold.

"Don't let them off-load yet, Ysario. Have Dr. Henjsen stay there. I need to talk to her. I'll be right there." Before I left, I put my comm on record and patched it through to ops.

"Better you than me, sir."

Henjsen stood at the top of the ramp in her armor, helmet off. "Why are you holding off-loading? Some of the samples are temperature sensitive." She actually looked put out.

I could have cared less at that moment. "Doctor, you overloaded us. And that last crate was on hidden sliders, so Ysario wouldn't know the full mass load. It had to have been close to three hundred kilos. That was more than two hundred above what you manifested. And the other crates were low-massed."

Henjsen looked at me directly. "I know. We needed those samples. I told Commander Morgan the samples were vital. Besides, there's always a bit to work with on safety margins."

"We went amber on liftoff, Doctor. If you'd cheated by another hundred kilos we'd still be on Danann. Might have been in lots of pieces. Don't ever pull a stunt like that again."

"I won't ever have that chance again, Lieutenant." The bitch smiled.

I lost it. Came up with an open palm. Boosted armor and all. She and her armor flew out the hatch and hit the deck hard.

"Ysario! Help Dr. Henjsen. She seems to have tripped."

Turned and went back to the controls. Was still seething. Had to finish the shutdown checklist and write up the maintenance report for the amber line. Took almost a quarter stan.

Commander Lilekalani—the exec—was waiting in the ready room with Henjsen.

Henjsen was out of her armor. The archeologist had a bruise along the edge of her jaw and several welts on her cheek.

"Dr. Henjsen has charged that you assaulted her, Lieutenant." Exec's voice was level, cold.

I didn't give a crap. "Commander, Dr. Henjsen tripped coming out of the shuttle. But, if there are any charges to be filed, I'll be filing them. Dr. Henjsen lied about the mass of an additional cargo crate, by the amount of almost two hundred kilos. She also deliberately labeled a number of crates with incorrect mass calculations. We were close to max load anyway. The drives went to amber on liftoff. You can check the maintenance and drive logs. You can also check with the crew chief. Dr. Henjsen's lying—or deliberate inaccuracy—almost cost you a shuttle—and the lives of everyone aboard. Obviously, I'm furious with the doctor, but I can't help it if she tripped over her own armor. If . . . if she wishes to pursue this, then I'll be happy to file endangerment charges."

"Are you certain of that, Lieutenant?"

"Dr. Henjsen admitted that to me just before she tripped. I took the precaution of recording her statement and also patching it through to ops."

Lilekalani's eyes hardened, but they were on Henjsen. "Endangering a Comity vessel is a serious charge, Doctor. I'm certain that the lieutenant would not be willing even to mention it if there were not adequate evidence to support the charge. Are you certain you wish—"

"Forget it." Henjsen glared at me, then at the exec. "You D.S.S. types are all the same. You cover for each other."

We just looked at her. Like she was a Covenanter wife, brainless, barefoot, and pregnant.

She turned and left.

"Nasty piece of work, that one," observed the exec. "You could still file those charges."

"I could. I don't see the point, not unless she starts making trouble."

The exec shook her head. "You handled that like regular D.S.S., Lieutenant."

"People remember pain, sir. They forget legalities. No one ever wins with legalities. She'll remember that she tripped."

"I'm certain of that. You've logged the maintenance?"

"I did that before I left the bay, sir. Also told the mechs to check the grav system."

"Good." Lilekalani lowered her gravelly voice. "Don't worry about the doctor. The captain will make sure that the Deputy Special Minister understands."

"Yes, sir. Thank you, sir." Hadn't thought about the politico aboard. Should have. Probably still would have knocked Henjsen ass over spaceboots. Would have preferred to have thrown her though the nanite barrier with the lock open—without her helmet.

66 FITZHUGH

My first impulse after leaving sick bay on threeday had been to find Jiendra, but I quashed that with a modicum of common sense, such a quaint appellation for such a rare quality. The commander had summoned her, then hastened to Dr. DeLisle. That suggested that she had been dispatched on piloting duties.

I had attempted to determine what those duties entailed by checking the available options on my wall screen in my work space. That was infeasible, because all options had been blocked except for the sole view of the unchanging vista of Danann, slightly light-enhanced, but still a dark gray mass against the near blackness of the galactic void, filled with hazy ovoids, discs, spirals, and points of light that were distant galaxies, barely visible even with optic enhancement.

I could not locate her at any time on threeday. Nor could I ascertain the existence of any reference on the accessible sections of the ship system to potential enemies or any intention or indication to move the ship. At supper and breakfast on fourday, in the mess, there were scientists I had not seen in days, if not weeks. While the subject of a number of conversational interactions was the sudden required return to the ship and while all those who conversed did so in great detail and volume about the evacuation requirement, solid information was not forthcoming.

To me, that suggested a high probability that our situation was less than sanguine. Yet my own options for determining the verity of any of the varied surmises were nonexistent. I was but an abaculus in an enormous politicomilitary mosaic.

In the end, I sat before the console and attempted both rational thought and analysis. What was it about Danann that had create such a maelstrom?

We had studied the remnants of an ancient culture, one that appeared both culturally and scientifically advanced. The expedition had been attacked by warships before we had even left the environs of Hamilton system, and there had been at least one and possibly two attempts at sabotage of which I was aware, and now a presumably hostile flotilla was approaching. Was the political and power balance between the various human governments that delicate?

To me, the irrationality was stupendous. Despite all the secretiveness associated with the mission, most of the major systems had learned of the expedition. If they could do that, then why didn't they just wait and steal whatever the Comity learned? Space was big enough and technology application sufficiently capital-intensive that the Comity could not conceivably develop and implement whatever it learned before it could be stolen or copied. Equally important, the lessons of history strongly suggested that while highly advanced technology might provide a significant edge in armed conflict, it was not terribly useful in subduing large unfriendly populations. I was certain that the Comity understood that proposition. That suggested that at least some of the polities involved feared not subjection, but obliteration—or wished to do the obliterating themselves. That was also not rational, because, again, with the vastness of space, the energy and financial costs of undertaking such would bankrupt most systems, assuming that they could even master the alien technology.

Yet . . . rationality did not seem to be a significant concern of all those involved.

Why?

The only possible motivating factor had to be fear—fear that the alien technology was so superior, and so potentially deadly, that every polity wished it for itself or to deny it to all.

Was the Danannian technology that deadly? Had it been so destructive that Danann was all that was left?

I shook my head. That I found a difficult proposition to reconcile with what I had seen and studied. Yet . . . the questions remained. What had happened to the species that had constructed Danann and presumably Chronos?

My other question was far less universal. Where Was Jiendra?

67 *BARNA*

I was awake early on fourday. It was one of those times when mental visions of what I should paint and had not yet put on canvas or matrix flashed through my mind. I did a quick sketch of aliens—the visiting aliens, not the Danannians—attempting to batter through a tower door. The sketch was sheer fantasy, of course. We had even less idea of what they looked like than we did of the Danannians, but space armor can conceal much, and there ought to be at least a speculative sketch of the other species to seek out and explore Danann, even if it had been a million years earlier.

Then I finished the last touches of the work showing Liam Fitzhugh taking on the subverted stewards. His eyes were the hardest, because they were that hazel color that changes from light brown to green depending on the setting.

I waited until midmorning on Fourday before approaching Elysen's work-space door. It was just slightly ajar. I could hear voices.

". . . How did you get the images?"

"Chendor, of course. He thought I should see them."

"He has better instincts than Kaitlin will credit him with. He found it, you know? She had trouble with that."

"Kaitlin should know better. I *will* have a talk with her."

When she talked in that tone, Elysen was no longer the kindly, tea-drinking, elder astronomer. I decided to knock. "Elysen?"

"Come in, Chendor."

I closed the door behind me. I didn't want any more eavesdropping. Lazar was standing. Elysen was in her chair. If possible, she looked more tired and frail than the night before. I tried to keep a pleasant smile on my face.

I'd seen Lazar on occasion, even sat at the same table at the mess. Up close he was bigger than I realized, with fine black hair that was cut short and clung to his skull, but he wasn't quite as big as Liam Fitzgerald. Nor as dangerous. Lazar had pale white skin and gray eyes. His name fit him.

"I believe you know Cleon," Elysen said.

I nodded slightly. "He's been working with you, and the artifact confirms—or supports—whatever you two have theorized."

"Supports. I have doubts that we will ever be able to prove the theory," Lazar replied, "accurate as I believe it to be."

"Why not?"

Elysen smiled, faintly. The grayness in her face held hints of blue. Her eyes were intent as she looked to the physicist.

"The universe has changed, and while we can determine that it has changed, that change is so basic that, although we may be able to theorize what conditions were like six to ten billion years ago, we may never have the technology to replicate those conditions, and thus prove that they in fact existed."

That didn't sound as insurmountable as Lazar made it out to be. "The Theory of Everything hasn't ever been proven conclusively, has it?"

"No. It has never been disproven, and it seems to explain the universe . . . as we know it. What we've discovered may require revisions."

"Then what's the problem? Theories do get revised."

Lazar looked almost embarrassed. He didn't say anything.

"It's clear to me," I pointed out. "The Danannians were more advanced than we are. They built towers out of materials we can barely understand and can't yet duplicate. The buildings responded to their wishes or commands both inside and out. They built an enormous advanced city for one project or purpose. They sculpted an entire planet for the sake of that city."

"Just tell him, Cleon, or I will."

"The were Type III plus. They created another universe and moved a whole galaxy—albeit a smaller one—into it." Lazar rushed through the words, spitting them out, one after the other. Then he looked at me. His expression was almost defiant.

"You think no one is going to believe you?"

"No one will want to," Elysen said quietly. "The amount of energy required, even under the conditions ten billion years ago, is staggering. It's beyond comprehension or rational quantification."

"There's so much we can't determine. How they created or harnessed it, how they managed to focus it . . ."

"It sounds impossible," I said. "You don't think so. Why?"

Elysen chuckled. "First, there's a missing galaxy. All our observations support that. At one time, there was a galaxy where there is now an empty expanse in space. Second, even the underlying dark matter and the associated atrousans are missing. That has created some gravitational effects in the region that have puzzled astronomers for a good millennium, if not longer. Third, there are observations that suggest certain variations in the value of the speed of light, but those observations only occur in light traversing that region. Fourth—"

". . . the building materials on Danann do not function as they were designed, even when we replicate what appear to have been the ambient conditions," Lazar continued.

"But after billions of year . . . ?"

"No. They're exceedingly stable, down to the subquark level. What we know says that you cannot have a stable anomalous metal or composite. The material can be deformed, but not destroyed, at least not by any method we can devise."

"But . . . you cut open the doors . . ."

Lazar shook his head. "We were *allowed* to cut open the doors. The metal that comprised the latches is significantly different. Or I should say that a strip of it is. All our samples of the actual composites are from sections such as that. There were certain areas of buildings where it occurred. They were obviously designed in order to give themselves access in case whatever controlling system there was failed—just as we would. All our samples are sections we were *allowed* to remove."

"What about the visiting aliens? They battered—"

"They deformed the composite enough that several of the treated access latches broke. We heated two of those doors, and they re-formed as if they had been untouched."

"You've reported this."

"Oh, no one will question about the composite. We have samples." Lazar's smile was crooked. "The trouble will come when people discover that they cannot really analyze or duplicate the materials."

"You said . . ."

"We can describe it." He shrugged again. "It doesn't analyze. That's a problem. Scientists believe that there is always a solution, that there must be a way to solve the problem, that we have the intelligence and insight to resolve all problems and aspects of the universe." He paused. "What if we don't? Or what if the universe has changed in some subtle, but fundamental fashion, so that we can understand what they did, but we can never duplicate it?"

"How could that be?"

Elysen smiled. "The universal density of dark energy and matter. The universe has been continually expanding since the primal brane flex. We've always assumed that expansion meant greater and greater space between discrete clumps of matter and energy. That is, each atom, each lepton, each quark, each fermion, retained the same energy and size. From what we can tell, this has in fact occurred, at least after the first massive inflation. From that example, we have generalized that the same has been true of dark matter and energy, since we have never been able to capture or analyze either, only to observe, and replicate some of the effects."

"Think of dark energy as a fabric being stretched," Lazar added. "When the universe was young it was like fine silk, a fabric underneath everything. As the universe expanded, the space between the threads also expanded, until now it is more like a net with huge open spaces between the strands or threads. But it *is* energy. I can only theorize, but the Danannians, I believe, used that far-more-concentrated energy, perhaps even powered their entire culture by it."

I just stood there. I understood the words and what they meant. I could also sense that there was far more beyond that. "There's more."

"That concentration of energy doesn't exist any longer. You might call it an early manifestation of entropy."

"So they created a whole new universe to be able to use the dark energy there?"

"I don't think they had any choice," Lazar replied. "I certainly can't prove it, but I think they had to create a new universe, make their own brane flex, or whatever, because they needed the dark energy to survive."

"By the way, Chendor," Elysen added. "It's only dark energy to us because we don't perceive it."

"So much for the anthropic principles," Lazar said dryly.

"Is that what the artifact is all about? It's a model or a representation of what they did?"

"It seems to be. It also holds some secrets of its own."

"The light amplification?"

"It amplifies all energy trained on it, and we can't detect any energy sources within it, or any energy flows."

"Perpetual energy?"

"I'm guessing that it draws on the remaining and dispersed dark energy or matter in the universe. It has to draw on *something*." He frowned. "That's why I've recommended to the captain and Commander Morgan that we leave the area as soon as possible."

Lazar finally lost me on that. "Why?"

The physicist shrugged helplessly. "We have discovered all manner of energy emanations, coming from all across the megaplex. Others are coming from beneath the oceans. From what we can determine, except for two, near our base and landing sites, they began at approximately the time that the *Magellan* and the *Alwyn* first detected the approach of other ships."

"Someone followed us, then."

"No," replied Elysen. "Following a ship is highly improbable. Not with our technology. Calculating where we might be would be far easier."

"Why should we leave?"

"Danann has some sort of response capabilities . . . something. What would happen if a torp or a particle beam struck the artifact?"

"You don't think it would be destroyed?"

"I not only don't think that, but I believe all that energy would be amplified."

It took me a moment, but I understood. "You think there's something like that in other places?"

"I don't know, but after all I've seen, and all I don't understand, I'm not exactly willing to bet on there not being anything there."

"So we just leave?"

"We have enough material to study, and we have the artifact."

"When you get to my age, Chendor," Elysen said, "you understand that there are times when you can be too greedy."

"Why haven't we left yet, then?"

"I would assume that is because the shuttles are still bringing up the last of the science and tech crews."

"Kaitlin is trying to squeeze in every last moment," Lazar said. "Not that it will matter in the slightest."

"We have enough material and observations that, if we can't figure things out from that, we never will?" I asked.

"I don't believe I said that," Lazar replied.

"You might as well have, Cleon." Elysen smiled.

"So . . . now what?" I finally asked.

"You paint. We try to understand. The captain tries to get everyone safely away."

I didn't think it would be anywhere near that simple, even if I didn't have a better answer.

68 CHANG

After the exec left the ready room, I tried not to think about what an asshole Henjsen was. Corrected myself—selfish asshole. Took a couple of deep breaths. It didn't help. I'd spent pretty much all day threeday and fourday trying to get the frigging artifact back, then the last of the science team and samples, and the greedy bitch had almost gotten us wiped out. Then . . . I should have listened more closely to Morgan and had Ysario mass-check every piece of cargo. Every last one had to have been somewhat over-mass.

What frigging good did it do to get another thousand kilos of samples if they didn't get back to the ship? Or if the experts who could explain them didn't? Or had Henjsen figured the mass to the last kilo and pressed right to the limit? She could have found that out. Either way, I didn't like her tactics and attitude.

I was tired, and just wanted to get something to eat—by myself—and fall into my bunk. Except I was too angry to do either. Just stood there for another few minutes, mentally cursing Henjsen.

Morgan walked into the ready room while I was still seething. Looked like he been frozen in deep space, then quick-thawed—red eyes over purple-black, half circles, lines etched across a pallid forehead.

"I heard Henjsen had an accident." His voice was hoarse.

"Wish it had been fatal."

"That wouldn't have been good. Her father is the senior council rep from Agder. He chairs the D.S.S. oversight committee."

"Shit."

"It's all right. So long as she's not permanently hurt, he won't smash orbits, not when the endangerment charge is possible. Write it up and hold it." His laugh sounded ghoulish. "I wouldn't count on a career in the D.S.S.—not that you ever had."

Ready room was silent.

"When do you expect to launch the needles?" I finally asked.

"Who said anything about launching needles?" he countered.

"The way you look. Or do you plan to wait for your 'company' to arrive and cut us off?"

"They already have. Right now, they're sitting between us and the Gate, and it's not just a ship or two. It's a flotilla. They look like Covenanters—two battle cruisers, two frigates, and a corvette."

"Why aren't they just sitting off the Gate?"

"They might be doing that also," Morgan said tiredly. "It's too far to determine."

"What do you and the captain have in mind?"

"Wait until someone commits. There's no source of fusactor mass anywhere near, except Danann. We got supplies for a year. They don't. The longer they wait, the easier for us to evade them."

I hated waiting. Would have hated getting potted by a Covenanter cruiser worse, though. "You think they're trying to spook us?"

"I'd guess so." He frowned. "If we stay here long, Henjsen will start pressuring the captain to allow some teams back on Danann."

"How far out are the Covenanters?"

"Six stans."

"Just enough so that we can't afford to put even small teams back down."

"That's right."

"How long do you think they'll wait?"

"A few hours, a few days, a week, who knows?"

"Why don't we cut and run?"

"You? Suggesting that?"

"Not an idiot, sir."

"The longer we wait, and make them come to us, the less fusactor mass they have, and the better chance we have for evading them."

Made sense to me. "You need me for anything now?" I asked.

"No. You'll know if I do."

"Why'd you come here, then?"

He grinned. "To tell you how glad I was that Henjsen tripped coming out of the shuttle lock." After the slightest pause, he added. "Get some rest. You'll need it."

"Yes, sir."

Like always, when he was pressed, he turned and left. Not another word.

Henjsen—her father a frigging, muckety-muck Comity planetary rep. It figured. Everything about the mission was bastardized.

Started for the mess galley. Didn't want to wait to go to the mess. My stomach was empty, my head light, and I wanted sleep.

Wasn't sure I was going to sleep all that well. Wondered if I should use the comm system to find Liam. At least, I could talk to him. But I wasn't ready for that.

69 FITZHUGH

By midmorning on fiveday, I'd still not seen any sign of Jiendra. The mess was full, and Tomas and Lizabet Marsalis had confirmed at breakfast that all the science team had been lifted off Danann.

I'd been in my work space, looking at the wall screen, still showing just the image of Danann, trying to concentrate on a better analysis—if one extraordinarily speculative—when the screen blanked, and the captain's image replaced that of Danann. For a moment, Captain Spier said nothing, as if waiting for confirmation that she had preempted all the outlets of the ship's public comm system. As she began her address, her voice was resonantly confident.

"The *Magellan* has been making preparations to leave Danann, and we had hoped to do so today. We have detected a flotilla of potentially hostile vessels stationed between us and our first Gate. For tactical reasons, we will not be leaving Danann immediately, but our departure could occur at any time, or it could be several days. Because of this uncertainty, I wanted to inform all ship's personnel and all expedition personnel of the situation. We have well over a year's supplies, while it is highly unlikely that the forces opposing us have any such level of resources. We intend to wait until resource and tactical considerations favor our departure and return to Hamilton system. You will, of course, be informed as matters develop."

That was the extent of her communication. Nonetheless, I was pleased that she had made the announcement, rather than Special Deputy Minister Allerde, and that she had not included some morological phrase about us having little about which to worry. With a hostile flotilla standing off somewhere in the atrous galactic void, there was ample cause for discerning worry.

There was also the possibility that Jiendra was on some sort of standby.

I attempted to return my concentration to the unfinished analysis on the console before me, but my concentration flagged, if indeed I had even truly begun to focus, and returned to thoughts of her. While I detested even the insinuation that I might be wolflike in pursuit, there was no alternative course of action. I accessed the ship's directory and finally located Jiendra, except that she was listed as "Chang, J. M., LT."

I initiated comm access, but the screen remained blank, and an insipid male voice intoned, "Please leave a message."

"This is Liam Fitzhugh. I had hoped we could continue our conversation at some point. Thank you."

My message was stilted, but what else could I have said without being either suggestive or misleading. The veracity of the content of my communication was absolute. I did wish to talk to her, and to continue from that ambiguous position where we had last been before being interrupted by Commander Morgan.

My action in accessing her comm link, ineffectual as it might have been, allowed me to return to the analysis.

Based on the amount of resources manifested in the construction and operation of the megaplex, it was more than obvious that the beings who had constructed it operated in a culture of relative abundance. The lack of differentiation in structure sizes suggested that either their nature was either not personally and relatively competitive, or that such competitiveness, had it existed, was expressed in a fashion other than size of structures, unlike human cultures, where virtually every structure ever constructed revealed aspects of a competitive nature. Yet such massive construction also intimated that they had been anything but passive in their outlook.

Another stan passed.

At a single sharp rap on my door, I looked up abruptly. "Come in. It's unlocked."

Jiendra stepped into my cramped domain, attired in the skintights and uniform vest and shorts of a pilot. "You left a message."

I stood quickly. "That I did. You didn't have to come." My smile doubtless indicated a contradiction to my words.

"Messages are . . . too impersonal." She closed the door behind her, deftly, yet without a discernible sound, but took only a single step toward me.

I gestured toward the single other chair, straight-backed, but not too uncomfortable, if a less-than-pleasing shade of plastrene green. "You could avail your-self of a chair."

With a laugh that contained a hint of both melody and amusement, she seated herself, but her eyes never strayed from me. I reseated myself, turning the console chair toward her.

"You were working on something."

"A speculative analysis of the culture that produced the Danannian megaplex."

"Have you seen the artifact?"

"Artifact? They found one?" My words sounded less than articulate, far less, and I disliked sounding inarticulate, let alone ill informed.

"Just one. Massive. Couldn't tell you what it looked like, all crated up in plastrene. Morgan said that Barna—the artist—found it."

"There has been nothing about it on the system, and I would have thought . . ."

"Henjsen. She's trying to keep it quiet, I'd guess."

The way she stated the technical archeologist's name revealed a distinct lack of affection. "You're not fond of Kaitlin Henjsen?"

"You wouldn't care for her, either. Not if she'd overloaded your shuttle and strained your drives. Few more kilos, and she could have crashed us." Jiendra stopped. "Shouldn't have said that. Had to tell someone."

"She sounds like a person who is pleasant enough upon the surface and far less than that under any sort of pressure or when she wishes things to follow her desires."

"That's charitable."

Given Jiendra's clear and understandable dislike of Kaitlin Henjsen, I perceived that avoiding reference to Henjsen would be the wisest course. "I'd wager that Chendor Barna could enlighten me about the artifact."

"Probably could. Bet he doesn't care much for Henjsen, either."

"Did you ascertain much about it, other than its mass."

"It intensifies any form or energy that strikes it. Morgan had it scanned, and the tech chief said the whole crate glowed."

"That might be one of the reasons why the captain—"

"No. All tactical. No fusactor mass near here, except on Danann. We can wait. They can't."

"Will you do any piloting . . . in combat?"

"If they need to use the needles. Morgan's short a pilot—after the mess attack."

"You?"

"I'm the best qualified."

"Let us trust that such will not be required. I suspect that both the captain and Commander Morgan have an excellent grasp of applied tactics."

"Suspect you do, too." She paused, but only briefly, before asking, "Why didn't you stay in the commandos?"

Her inquiry roiled the depths of memory, depths I had not desired to disturb. "There were multiple reasons, and rationales . . ."

Her nod confirmed the question. "You must have been good."

"Good enough that they requested I remain," I conceded.

"You didn't."

"No. Remaining would have subjected me to too much of a temptation."

"Afraid that you might like the power and the violence too much?"

"The power. Disciplined use of force is actually antithetical to violence, but creates an illusion of and a need for control."

"An illusion? Wasn't any illusion to that steward you put down."

I couldn't help but smile. "You're more than correct, but I was referring to the user of disciplined force. The more successful the application of force, the more those who have the ability to employ it are willing to authorize its future use. Force cannot create anything; it can only prohibit or inhibit other actions. It is an extremely useful tool, but because its results are so easily measurable it is overapplied, and in time that creates an overreliance upon its use . . ." I halted myself before I launched into a full discussion. "You'll have me lecturing, and that's something I have tendency to overdo all too often."

"Lectures are a wall of words, Liam. Were you married or contracted once?"

"Yes." It was for the best that I not launch into yet another extended explanation. "It . . . worked for a while. What about you?"

"Never tried anything extended. Never found anyone I trusted that much."

"You don't trust men?"

"Trust some about some things. Trust others about others. Never found one to trust about what matters."

I found myself nodding about her last words. She hadn't expected to find someone to trust about everything, just about what mattered. Would that I had thought that clearly years earlier. "Well-chosen words, Jiendra."

"Thought about them. Years, I think."

"Whether to think and blind one's self to what one feels, or to act and blind one's self to what one thinks . . ."

"Either way, it's a wall." She looked directly at me. "I'm tired of walls. Aren't you?" Her eyes were gray, but a gray so dark it was close to black.

As the ancient poet once asked, in a line I had never forgotten, if there would be "time for a hundred indecisions" or revisions. But there was no time, not this time. My throat was dry, and I couldn't stop looking into her eyes. Time extended across the billions of years Danann had waited, and I was stretched tightly across those years.

She waited, dark gray eyes willing to accept what I said, yet clearly taking the most dangerous step first, wanting me to know that, but, like me, being unwilling to say it directly.

"Yes. I'm very tired of walls." Protection in the extreme is also confinement, and that I had also known, but never known anyone worth the risk of leaving that protection.

Her mouth curled ever so slightly at the corners. "Hard admission for you."

I shook my head. "Far harder for you, and braver. For that, I will always owe you." I stood.

So did she.

We stepped toward each other.

At that first moment, we only held hands. It was more than enough.

70 CHANG

I wasn't thinking all that straight when I left Liam.

Strangest lovemaking. Just stood there and held hands. Like we both knew stepping out from behind walls was more intimate than sharing bodies. We didn't even talk that much. I didn't want to. He was afraid the words would build another wall.

His eyes were hazel, the kind that switched from gold-flecked brown to green.

Finally, I squeezed his hands and leaned forward. Just brushed his cheek with my lips. Had to. "Thank you." Didn't say more. Let go of his hands and stepped back.

"No more walls, Jiendra?"

"No. Not between us." Wasn't quite true. We both knew not everything was down, but that was what had to be. "I'd . . . better go."

"For now."

"For now," I agreed. Slipped out of his work space. Felt both drained and exhilarated, and scared shitless. Morgan had told me to get some rest, and now I'd gone and screwed that up, too.

Hadn't wanted to press it with Liam, but didn't want company. Also didn't want to be alone, rest or no rest. Found my feet taking me up the ramps to the launch deck.

Lerrys was the only one in the ready room. Made sense. The needle pilots had auxiliary duties on the *Magellan*. We didn't.

"Are you all right?" he asked.

Appreciated his concern. "Yes. Could be getting to be more right."

He nodded slowly. "Pardon me if I intrude too much. Fitzhugh?"

No point in denying it. Not to Lerrys. I nodded.

"He might actually be good enough for you."

"Is that condescension . . . ?"

Lerrys grinned. "From me?" He shook his head. "I meant it. He talks to everyone else. He listens to you." Another grin. "Most of the time, I hear." He paused. "He's not *that* much older. You wouldn't have to worry about taking care of him."

"You didn't worry about that with Ilendra." Braun had told me that. Almost winced when I thought about her.

"When I'm not piloting, I need someone to take care of me. Ilendra does. I admit it. You could use someone taking care of you now and again."

Knowing that hadn't been the problem. Finding the someone had been. Was Liam the one? Thought so, but . . . wanting it to be so has always been women's greatest self-deception and weakness. Maybe for men, too, but they bull through. We bleed. Inside. Hate that.

Lerrys didn't say more. Probably figured he'd said too much.

"You hear anything about the Covenanters?" I finally asked.

"They're not moving."

"Anyone else?"

"Morgan said he didn't expect anyone else out this far. The others can't spare the ships and don't have the science to track where Danann is."

"He expects trouble on the return."

"He didn't *say* that."

I snorted. "Lots he doesn't say."

"Like you." Lerrys laughed.

Decided to go suit up and run sims in one of the needles. Might let my subconscious sort some things out.

71 FITZHUGH

After Jiendra left, I just stood there.

A line came to mind, something about how the quilled rodents of Old Earth had made love—most carefully. That was us. Were we so prickly, so armored against unwanted intrusion?

My laugh was somewhere between self-acknowledgment and outright rue.

Then I looked down at the analysis, less than half-completed, on the console. Would it matter what I determined? Not to anyone besides myself, because the amount of speculation involved was so great that it would not withstand the criticism of any scholar determined to dismantle it. While my logic was as sound as my expertise and intelligence could make it, the assumptions were all open to question. But then, so were most of those on which we based our actions and our lives. Those were just not questioned.

More to the point, why else was I present on board the *Magellan*, and what else would I do while Jiendra was possibly risking her life as a pilot? What else besides analyze?

Such reasoning was impeccable—and manifestly incorrect, since I just sat and stared at the console. After a time, I leaned back and began to search for Chendor Barna's commcode.

He answered, leaning forward. "Chendor Barna." When he glimpsed my visage in the screen, he tilted his head. "Liam . . . I hadn't expected . . ."

"Might you have a moment to discuss something with me if I stopped by your studio?"

"I could do that."

His work space was one deck down, and I took the ramp, passing several techs—a shield mech, a screen mech, and a quartermaster. All three moved quickly and barely glanced at me.

When I reached Chendor's space, I rapped.

"Liam? You can come in."

As I entered, he turned away from a canvas that he had just covered and set a palette on a small table beside the covered easel.

The walls were filled with canvases. I had to stop, just halt and limit my scrutiny to one at a time, or the intensity of those images would have overwhelmed me. Everyone on the expedition was reputed to be one of the foremost in his or her field, and I had not considered the impact of encountering the work of such an artist. The painting that caught my eyes first was not one of the haunting scenes of Danann, but a composition of three pilots—Jiendra, Lieutenant Braun, and Lieutenant Lerrys. To me, Jiendra stood out, but objectively, they all did, and yet, in a fashion that I could not have described, Chendor had captured each one, both as an individual and as a part of a unity. Braun embodied strength beneath apparent doll-like delicacy; Jiendra the wiry resilience of an unbreakable cable beneath breathtaking beauty; Lerrys an adaptability and competence with sensitivity.

Beyond that, farther to the right, was a portrait of Braun. Without inquiring, I knew that Chendor had painted it as a memorial. Beyond that was one that must have been Chendor's imagination of how I had dealt with the false steward. While artistically impeccable, it conveyed a heroism that was far beyond anything I had ever felt or attempted.

Rather than dwell on that, I turned my concentration to the scenes of Danann. Had I not seen them, I would not have believed it possible to have captured so much diversity when the towers had all seemed so visually alike. Several stood out, but the one that caught my attention was not one of the towers as they were, but one clearly as Chendor had visualized it as it must have been, billions of years in the past. There were no figures, and no direct sunlight, yet it was definitely a morning scene, and one where I could feel that one of the aliens was just about to appear beside the stillness of the canal.

Finally, I turned back to him.

"You didn't do one of Lieutenant Chang, did you, by any chance?"

"No. Just the portrait of the three."

"I understand that you found an artifact down on Danann. Could I ask you to tell me about it?" My eyes drifted to a canvas—covered—the only one so masked. "Is that—"

"It is, but it's so unfinished . . ." His words drifted off. "I can show you some images. I'd appreciate it if you would keep the information to yourself for now."

"I can do that." I certainly could honor such a commitment.

When the first image appeared on the wall screen, I found myself staring, drawn into the curves and the artistry of the object. From its balance and proportions, it could have been almost any size, although, from the background of the tower chamber in which the image had been captured, it was unlikely to have been exceedingly small. I had to wonder about the intensely bright point of light captured in midair above it. "The proportions are so balanced that its size could vary . . ."

"From the base to the top of the artifact is almost four and a half meters. It's about three meters wide."

"The image doesn't capture its mass and magnitude . . . its grace minimizes its stature . . ."

"That's right," Barna said.

"What about that point of light?"

"It captures and intensifies light."

"Do you have any idea of the artifact's purpose or employment on Danann?"

"It's a model of some sort, according to several of the scientists. They have an idea, but they're still working on the mathematics behind it." Barna did not look at me in replying, and it was more than obvious that discussing its usage discomfited him.

"I take it that you've been requested not to comment."

He nodded. "There could be considerable controversy."

"I won't press." I studied the image for a time. "Those spheres . . . could they be Danann and Chronos? A representation of those bodies, that is?"

Barna did not reply immediately, but the tightening of his brow and lips—almost an incipient frown—intimated that my suggestion was accurate.

"If it is a model," I continued, "the clear or crystal sections imply some sort of flow or force that joins, and the dark line between the bases suggests a link."

"That's one possibility." The words were almost grudged forth.

"I had considered that because the briefing materials had suggested the initial link between the two bodies. There is certainly some linkage, but I imagine that the nature of that link is something that the scientists have yet to determine."

"They're working on it."

"It is magnificent. You're certainly to be congratulated on finding it."

The trace of an ironic smile played at the corners of his lips. His eyes dropped to the console, and the fleeting smile vanished.

"Not that Kaitlin Henjsen was totally pleased, I would judge." That was a calculated approximation to the unknown truth.

Chendor laughed. "She was appalled that a mere artist could find it."

"That merits double congratulations." I hesitated. "If I did not display it to anyone else, would it be possible to have a copy of the image to study—for my own work on Danannian culture?"

"I don't see why not. The scientists are studying the artifact. You should certainly be able to use an image."

"Thank you." I gestured toward the covered canvas. "When it is done . . . might I see it?"

"When it's done, Liam, you'll be among the first to see it."

"Thank you."

"That's assuming that we don't run into difficulty with the ships out there in the void. Do you know who they might be?"

"I have no idea. I would judge from the political situation that it is unlikely that they are League ships or ships from the Middle Kingdom—or certainly not from the Comity. Other than that . . ." I could only shrug.

There was little enough either of us could add to that, and a silence swelled into the studio. Chendor glanced to the console, again, as if he expected a message or an in-comm.

"If you'd transmit that image . . ." I offered.

"I'll do that now."

"Thank you. The best of fortune with the work in progress."

He smiled faintly.

With another nod, I took my leave. As I progressed up the ramp back to my own space, I did wonder why he seemed quieter than usual, almost sad and preoccupied, but I had not wished to be excessively inquisitive—and I worried about Jiendra.

72 BARNA

Once Liam Fitzhugh had left, I uncovered the canvas again. I'd been trying to capture the depth, the *aliveness* of the artifact. The Danannian artifact was far more than a model or an object. Anyone with any sensitivity at all who looked at it knew that. The problem was that none of the images I had made of it conveyed anything close to that energy.

I supposed that I shouldn't have told Liam about it, but he was the type who'd keep his word, and he'd put his life on the line for everyone in the mess. Perhaps for everyone on the entire ship. How could I have said no to him when every physical scientist on the expedition knew about and probably had studied the artifact personally?

He was also interested in Lieutenant Chang. The way his eyes had lingered on her image and his question about a portrait of her showed that. At first glance, no one would have thought that they matched, but they did. Behind the big words and the professorial demeanor, Liam was a big cat, and he'd turned his predatory nature into academic excellence, I suspected. I wouldn't have wanted to cross him professionally. Like most cats, he was a loner. Unlike most, he needed a soul mate. Jiendra was much the same, if I couldn't have described her quite as conveniently.

Neither liked to reveal what lay within. Whether they could with each other, and whether Jiendra was even interested in Liam, beyond conversation and a similarity in outlook, I couldn't tell.

I paused. Together they would also make a good composition, and one that was important in its own way. They had saved lives, in more ways than one, between the two of them. I smiled, and took out a sketch pad.

As I laid the lines on the pad, I realized that I hadn't heard from Elysen in more than a day, and that had been unusual. After I roughed out the sketch, rather than return to the canvas of the artifact, I left the studio—what else could I call it, with all the canvases and matrices stacked everywhere?—and walked to her work-space door. It was closed.

I rapped on the door, firmly. There was no response.

"Elysen?"

That wasn't like her.

When I got back to the studio, I immediately tried the ship's comm.

Elysen's image appeared. It was one that she must have recorded soon after boarding the *Magellan*. The silver hair was still alive, and her eyes danced. "I'm sorry not to be available, but please leave a message . . ."

"Elysen, this is Chendor. I hadn't seen you in a while. I was just calling to see how you were. I'll check back later."

I told myself that she well might be off making observations, or inspecting the artifact with Cleon Lazar. At that moment, I realized that I didn't even know where the artifact was. I'd found it, and I hadn't even been told where they had put it.

I shook my head and removed the cloth covering the painting. Then I stood back and studied it.

I wasn't getting anywhere with that version. Something was missing. I took the canvas off the easel and set it aside, turned to the wall so that I couldn't look at it, even casually. If I started again, first painting part of the silvered blue background of the chamber where I had found it, could I better capture the feel of the artifact?

I decided on using a taller canvas, but one that was proportionally narrower. That might help in conveying the upward sweep of the crystalline sections. Then, it might just make it worse.

I tried to keep my concentration on the canvas as I prepared it. I still worried about Elysen.

73 CHANG

Lieutenant Chang! To the ready room.

Didn't have that far to go since I was already there, dozing in one of the couches. After a sim run, I'd finally drifted off. Slept through the midday meal. That figured, the way things were going.

Looked up and across at Lerrys. "You get a link?"

He nodded.

"Anything on the screens?"

"Nothing different."

We waited until the others arrived. I listened. Didn't feel like saying much.

". . . Convenanters . . . what I heard . . ."

". . . could be anyone . . ."

". . . wouldn't be Middle Kingdom or the League."

Tuala was the last one to arrive. He smiled shyly at me and took the seat next to Lerrys.

"You don't know that, Lindskold . . ."

"Know what?" Morgan half grinned as he stepped into the ready room, closing the hatch behind him. Grin didn't help. He still looked like gray shit.

"Nothing, sir," replied Shaimen.

Morgan looked across the ready room. Took in the pilots there, all five of us, one by one, starting with Lindskold and ending with Lerrys.

I waited. No one else said anything.

"We have more than one flotilla out there. We think the first ships are Covenanter for a number of reasons I won't go into here. They're beginning to close. We've received word from the *Bannister*. She just arrived. She managed to evade them, but reported another and larger flotilla has made a Gate translation and is also en route to Danann. The courier has offered us enough information that we can plot an exit course that gives us a good chance of evading both flotillas. This seems the best option, since we're outnumbered by even the smaller flotilla. Our course will be closer to the smaller flotilla. We will attempt to use it as a screen of sorts."

Two frigging flotillas heading for Danann? Why? From what I'd overheard, it'd take years for the scientists to develop anything worthwhile, even from the damned artifact I'd carted up.

"Do we have any idea of their objectives or intentions, sir?" asked Tuala.

"Their objective is either Danann or us, Lieutenant. There's nothing else out here."

"Ah . . . yes, sir. I had wondered if we knew whether they were actually hostile."

"If we wait to discover that, our options are likely to be significantly reduced, possibly to extinction." Morgan's tone was dry, irritated. "If we depart, and they're not hostile, they'll let us go. If they are . . . that's where you all come in. Lieutenant Chang will take Needle Four, and Lieutenant Lerrys will be primary pickup, if it's necessary . . ."

Morgan didn't sound happy. I couldn't say I was either. Not frigging, likely.

". . . We won't launch needles until it's clear that you're needed. By then, we should be well clear of Danann. With luck, you'll all remain on board the ship. We'll be breaking orbit in about one stan. It will be at least three stans before you're needed. It could be five or six. I'd suggest an afternoon nap. It could be a long night. Once you're summoned to flight quarters, you'll stand by here. You'll go to armor when we're stan or so from contact. Any other *relevant* questions?"

Clear Morgan didn't want any questions. I didn't ask. No one else did, either.

Didn't really want to leave the ready room.

Tuala and Lerrys stayed, too. The others left. I wasn't sleepy. So I went over to one of the briefing consoles. Wasn't anything new there. Accessed the farscreen plot. Plot showed six ships incoming. From the signatures, I made out two battle cruisers, one heavy and one light, two frigates, a corvette, and a scout, trailing. Bet that the scout had been there all along, just had been masked by the emanations of the heavier ships. Plot also showed four signaler satellites, or something like them, each in a geostationary orbit, each a quarter orbit from the next.

I glanced up from the console. "Tuala? We've left some signalers out there, it looks like. You're nav. Know anything about them?"

"Not much. Commander Morgan took shuttle one yesterday and placed them himself. He said all the other pilots needed the rest. He hoped that the Covenanters might leave them, since they're just nav beacons. According to him, there was no reason not to leave them now. He said the whole Galaxy must know where Danann is by now."

"Anything else?"

"No."

Didn't believe that. Morgan wouldn't have wasted nav beacons, not without a reason. Had he gimmicked them somehow?

Kept watching the energy signature plots. Less than a quarter stan passed before the beacons flared into the energy signatures of a frigate, a courier, a light cruiser, and something like the *Alwyn*. Morgan had probably waited until just before the Covenanters were within detection discrimination range. Harder to pick out clear signals around a planet, even a cold one like Danann.

Even so, somehow, didn't think that the Covenanters would let us off. Someone was still going to come after what looked to be two cruisers and a courier. Might slow them down, or split their forces, though.

Nothing was going to happen for stans, anyway.

I went and took a shower and cadged a meal from the mess. So did Lerrys. We sat at one of the tables that wasn't yet set up for the next meal. Reformulated chicken with brown sauce. The brown was better than the white.

"Why would the Covenanters risk it?" Lerrys asked.

"They haven't risked anything yet." Kept eating.

"They will, even with another flotilla out there."

"Maybe it's theirs, too. Or someone who's thrown in with them."

"No one can use what's down on Danann. Not for years, if ever," Lerrys said.

"They don't know that."

"You think they're that desperate?"

"Don't know what to think. I know that there are two flotillas out there, or one big one, and that doesn't look good for us. Don't think they'd send that many ships out here if they weren't after more than two D.S.S. ships and a courier or two."

"How would they know?"

"Just like we know. Intelligence. Can't keep anything a secret in a high-tech world. You can only move faster and be smarter. Looks like we weren't."

"You're so optimistic, Jiendra."

"Realistic."

At that moment, the wall screen in the mess switched from the view of Danann to one of the captain. She looked alert, rested—unlike Morgan.

"This is the captain. We will be breaking orbit in a few minutes. For the next three stans or so you all may continue normal operations. After that, I may sound General Quarters at any time. That is all."

The screen returned to a view of Danann.

Neither Lerrys nor I said much more. We separated, and I tried to get some sleep. Dozed some, but kept thinking about Liam . . . wondering. Why now? Was he that different? Or was it me?

It was almost a relief to go back to the ready room. Got there after eighteen hundred. Missed another meal in the mess, but stopped and cadged some stuff from the cooks. Was I missing meals because I wasn't ready to face Liam so soon again?

Frig! Didn't need all the complications.

Lerrys, Lindskold, Shaimen, and Tuala were already waiting in the ready room. They looked about as pleased as I felt.

Morgan was nowhere around. Had mostly expected that, not when he had no second after Tepper's death.

I went back to the briefing console. Nothing new there on our launch or ops. When I checked the farscreen plot, I could see the vector arrows showing direction and velocity of the *Magellan* and *Alwyn* relative to Danann. The *Bannister* was running between the two capital ships. Then I frowned. The captain was using shield energy to damp our emanations. Both the *Alwyn* and the *Magellan* were radiating like frigates. Deception might have been worth the waste of power.

Before long, Morgan walked into the ready room.

"You're all dismissed to your quarters. Get some sleep. Or rest. One way or another, you won't see any action until late this evening. It could be tomorrow."

I left. Wasn't sure I could sleep.

 CHANG

Lieutenant Chang! To the ready room!

Frig! Checked the time. Zero four-seventeen. I'd struggled to get sleep, finally dropped off at sometime after zero one hundred. Hated early morning.

Washed quickly, scrambled into vest and shorts, shipboots, and hurried up to the ready room. Lerrys was there. He looked like a frigging recruiting poster. Bet I looked like warmed and flattened shit. Tuala straggled in after me. Then the others followed.

No Morgan.

I heaved myself out of the chair and went to one of the briefing consoles. Lindskold was already at another. Nothing new. Checked the farscreen.

All six Covenanter ships were making for us, but I could see we were pulling away. Captain had dropped the power shields and funneled all power into the drives. Didn't want to think what the gravs would have been without internal gravity control. We had the angle, and the power.

Looked like we might get clear—of those six. Could see some distortions ahead of us, but the plot I had didn't discriminate. Hoped we could clear the others, but there wasn't much I could do at the moment.

I went back to one of the chairs. Must have drifted off. Woke up with a jolt when Lerrys touched my shoulder. Least I got a nap. Checked the time—zero five-forty-one—another stan.

"We cleared the first bunch," he said.

He didn't look happy.

"And?"

"There's another flotilla—five fast frigates between us and the Gate." He gestured toward the wall screen.

Morgan appeared there.

Everyone in the ready room sat up.

"Those of you following the plot have noticed that we've been able to outrun the first attackers. Unfortunately, the second flotilla was not a flotilla, but a full Covenanter battle fleet. While the majority of those ships have moved to engage the CW flotilla . . ."

CW flotilla? Morgan had said the flotilla was Covenanter. What had happened?

"Five of their new class of fast frigates have moved to intercept us. In about one stan, we will be launching all needles. Please check the briefing consoles. After you're briefed, all needle pilots will don armor and stand by for launch."

I checked the middle console.

Tactics in space depend entirely on the relative motion of the ships. In-system combat has slower velocities. That's for lots of reasons, but mostly because really high speed in a system increases fatalities—even without combat. Out-system combat is rare. Generally, you can escape in one direction or another—except in a case like ours, where the Covenanters knew where we had to get. That was the Gate.

We had high absolute and relative velocity compared to them. Morgan and the captain were counting on that. The frigates would attempt to use that speed against us. If they could overload our shields—at our velocity even something like a grapefruit or a chunk of ice, any kind of debris, would be catastrophic if we impacted it. If our shields went, a single torp would reduce a vessel the size of the *Magellan* to dust and insignificant chunks of metal and organic glop.

The needles would accelerate ahead of the *Alwyn* and the *Magellan,* building on their absolute velocity. We'd attempt to use the kinetic energy of our speed to boost the power of the torps. The objective was to create a hole in the linked shields and torp barriers thrown up by the frigates. The frigates would accelerate and attempt to concentrate their torps and the torps of their needles on one point on the shields of the D.S.S. capital ships.

The primary task of the four needles from the *Magellan* and the five from the *Alwyn* was to eliminate the opposing Covenanter needles in order to reduce the pressure on the shields of the two ships. The secondary task was to fire any remaining torps at the Covenanter frigates. Simple strategy, but frigging tough execution.

Looked up from the briefing console. None of the other pilots looked at me, except Lerrys. He just gave me a thumbs-up. Liar! Close to a frigging suicide mission. Idiot that I was, I'd volunteered.

Took my time getting into the armor. So did Lindskold. Tuala and Shaimen were out in the boat bay long before we were.

"Covenanter fleet? What do you think?" Lindskold asked as we walked toward the needles. "Why would they send a fleet?"

Wondered that myself. "Maybe they think we found more than we did." Laughed. "Like their Morning Star or Spear of Iblis."

"They'd fight for holy objects. We know that. But for devices of an ancient demon? One that probably never existed?"

"They believe it did," I pointed out.

"So we're fighting because they want to keep us from obtaining non-existent mythical devices used by a nonexistent mythical demon?"

"Sounds about right."

"Maybe, but how would they even know that was a possibility? Even the Covenanters would have to have some information that would lead to that conclusion." She shook her head and turned to her needle.

Good question. It'd have to wait.

Needle Four was the last one in the bay.

Patel was standing by it. "It's a good needle, Lieutenant."

"Glad to know it. Thank you." The preflight walk-around was quick enough, and I made it into the cockpit before the link message.

Ten minutes to null grav in the needleboat bay. Ten minutes to null grav.

Donned the armor's helmet. Pilot's armor was different. Wider field of vision and internal heads-up displays. Hadn't needed that with the shuttle, but it was necessary with a needle. I settled into the couch. Made sure the comm connections and the habitability connection at the hip were both secure. Needles didn't have ship habitability. It all came through the armor. Then I tightened the harnesses and ran through the checklist—shorter than the shuttle's. Needle was pretty much drives, shields, and torps. Internal grav control was rough at best. Three torps, two preloaded in a launch tube, third one had to be shuttled after one was fired. Frigging poor design. I'd thought that before, not that it changed things.

Navigator Control, this is Needle Tigress, standing by for launch.

Wait one, Tigress. Estimate ten plus to launch.

Stet.

Wasn't that long before null gee hit the bay, and my guts lurched. Still hated that initial feeling. Swallowed and waited. Watched as the bay doors opened.

Needle One—Lindskold—was first out. Then Shaimen and Tuala. I was last. Wasn't sure I liked that, either.

Once I was clear of the *Magellan*, I formed up on the left of the other three needles. Lindskold had us oriented in a wedge outboard on the starboard from the ship. Farscreen showed the *Alwyn* directly ahead of us—far enough that I had no visual. Yet, at the speeds we were traveling we were covering the distance between the two ships in microseconds or less.

Screens showed the five Covenanter frigates ahead in an inverted wedge—formation designed to concentrate max power on the *Alwyn*. Our own courier—the *Bannister*—was tucked up tight behind the *Magellan*. Made sense, but I'd have bet the junior major commanding her hated it.

The *Alwyn* had more needles than we did—eight—and they formed a tight wedge ahead of the big cruiser, close together, but not close enough for their shields to overlap.

Readouts showed less than two minutes to closure. No visuals. Relative speeds so quick, it'd all be by displays.

Navigator Needles, two zero starboard. Now!

Immediately brought the needle onto the new heading. *Magellan* followed.

Just before the *Alwyn* reached torp range, the battle cruiser turned toward the rightmost frigate of the five screaming toward us. Because of the course change, we were already directly behind the *Alwyn*.

The frigates reacted, turning their inverted wedge to envelop us. Torp tracks flared from all the frigates—then from the Covenanter needles.

After an instant, torps flashed from the *Alwyn* and its needles, all concentrated on the one frigate.

The Covenanter's shields went amber, bright red, and dropped. A wave of energy replaced the ship.

The next Covenanter turned in and toward the *Alwyn,* a straight suicide run.

Before the D.S.S. ship could evade, the shields of the two ships touched—just as another salvo of torps targeted the battle cruiser. The *Alwyn*'s shields flickered amber, but the second Covenanter converted itself to debris and energy.

Perhaps a third of the Covenanter needles had vanished, but so had more than half of the *Alwyn*'s needleboats.

The remaining Covenanter needles launched torps—their last, if I'd been counting right—and all were headed for the *Alwyn*. The three other frigates followed with another salvo.

The *Alwyn* concentrated its next salvo on the closest Covenanter frigate.

A surge of energy blanked my farscreens. Safety cutouts had desensitized my receptors for a moment. Only a moment, but when blast passed, screens showed that the *Alwyn* and the frigate were both gone. Two of the Alwyn's needles remained.

Navigator needles, on my mark, fire on starboard frigate. On my mark, fire at starboard frigate. Mark!

At the mark, I released both torps, then shuttled the remaining torp into the port tube.

Eight needle torps slashed through the darkness toward the Covenanter frigate, preceded by five from the *Magellan* and followed by another ten.

The frigate went to energy and dust.

The remaining Covenanter frigate turned toward the *Magellan,* not quite head-on-head. Both shields and drives were flicking in and out of the amber. Covenanter was overloading everything to get enough velocity to hit the *Magellan.* Another frigging god-squad suicider!

Scanned the farscreens. Five enemy needles were leading the frigate. All of them headed straight for the *Magellan.* All of them suicide runs. Shields piled in front.

Navigator needles, concentrate on the incoming needleboats, one on one. Tigress, take the one most starboard . . . Morgan ordered each needle directly.

Just as he finished, one of the *Alwyn*'s needles fired a torp that backsided one of the Covenanter needles.

I went head-to-head with the other needle. Wasn't about to suicide, but Covenanter wouldn't know that. He wouldn't suicide against me. He wanted the *Magellan.*

He'd slewed his shield strengths forward, and I only had one torp left. Ideally, if I dropped, flipped, and fired a torp into his stern as he passed, the torp would hit the weakest section of his shields. Problem was that I couldn't risk a tail shot from beneath. Torp could angle back and impact the *Magellan*'s shields. I'd have to drop, then overcorrect, faster than he could react, and aim for his midsection.

Only had seconds by the time I fired.

Torp went where I wanted. His shields went amber and vanished—but only his shields. He still had a torp, and the needleboat was a weapon itself.

I was out of torps. If I'd counted right, so was he—except for the one he wanted to lay on the *Magellan* at the same time the last frigate salvoed it.

Idiot didn't even hesitate. Just kept driving for the *Magellan*'s midshield nexus. My detectors said the *Magellan*'s shields were taking a beating from the other needles and the frigate. Not obvious yet, but close as I was, I caught the quick flickers of orange from both the *Magellan* and the Covenanter.

Covenanter needle had a torp, but no shields. I had shields, but no torps.

Checked the screens. We'd lost two needles, but so had the Covenanters. Frigate would impact the *Magellan*'s shields in less than a minute. I pressed the needle's drives past max, and aimed at his aft section—or where it would be.

He tried to evade, but my shields clipped him, crumpled the foresection of his needle.

His torp blew. Energy flared all around me. Didn't know if the torp went in the tube or he'd launched it at the last moment.

Amber telltales appeared everywhere across my displays.

Shields had gone. Fusactor was dying.

Farscreen showed the *Magellan* had taken out the last frigate, but half the shields were amber.

Turned the needle on an intercept course for the *Magellan.*

Navigator Control, Needle Tigress, on return course this time.

Tigress, interrogative status. Interrogative status.

Status is amber/red. All systems amber or worse. Amber systems deteriorating this time.

Stet. Report visual.

Checked the screens again. Plot showed I was on closure. Showed two Magellan needles left and two from the *Alwyn*—besides me. Took a deep breath. Shouldn't have.

Yellow waves appeared on the farscreen. Came from "behind"—the direction of Danann. Yellow! Never'd seen yellow on a screen. Had to mean more power than I'd want to have hit me, especially in a needle.

Damned yellow waves had to be moving at multiples of light, the way they flashed across the screen toward me. That *couldn't* be happening.

The needle bucked—only term for it—and the farscreen flared, then went black. Flat dead. Frig!

Drives were dying, and I was in the middle of nowhere in total blackness. Even the backup power storage was gone. Every detector in the needle was dead. Had suit habitability . . . and not much else.

Tried transmitting. Emergency burst. *Control, Needle Tigress, all systems red. All systems red. No nav, no drives, habitability marginal.*

Kept listening. No link response.

Looked through the visual port. All I saw was darkness.

Hoped Lerrys could find me. Hoped Morgan or the captain hadn't changed course. I'd been on intercept. If they'd changed heading, without energy radiation from the needle not even Lerrys would be able to find me.

Swallowed. How did I know if the *Magellan* hadn't been blinded by the yellow energy waves? What had they been? Some remnant of Danannian technology? Why now? Why couldn't it have waited five minutes?

Stared at the board before me. Dead.

Didn't know whether to laugh or cry. I'd survived a battle that had killed all but five of something like thirty needle pilots—and I was going to freeze or suffocate in deep space.

Thought about Liam. Wished I'd done more than hold his hands. Hadn't thought things would end this way.

Swallowed. They hadn't ended yet . . . Wouldn't end.

My last course changes *would* get me close enough to the *Magellan*. They would.

Lerrys *would* be able to grapple and bring me in. Maybe I could get close enough for a jetpak.

Checked the time. Only five minutes.

Decided on another burst transmission. Hoped it went out. No way to tell. Hoped they could use it to find me. Hoped the *Magellan* was still there to find me.

Navigator Control, Needle Tigress, all systems red. All systems red. No nav, no drives, habitability marginal. Awaiting pickup.

Didn't hear any response, but didn't expect any, not with all other receptors fried.

Could hear my breathing in the suit. Raspy, fast.

Forced myself to take slower breaths. Watched the visual port. Still could only see darkness.

Another five minutes passed. It felt like thirty. All I could see was darkness, inside the cockpit and out.

Thoughts went back to Liam. Wondered how he'd feel if things didn't work out. Pushed those thoughts away. Things would work out.

After seven minutes more, thought I saw a darker oval on the right, where the *Magellan* should have appeared, but the oval began to get smaller.

I tried another burst transmission. *Navigator Control, Needle Tigress, all systems down. No nav, no drives, habitability marginal. Awaiting pickup this time.*

In the silence, the only sound continued to be my breath. Peered at the dark oval. Without power, there wasn't a thing I could do . . . just watch myself drift away from the *Magellan*.

The oval diminished more.

Another five minutes went by that seemed like a stan.

Was there a flash of light?

I squinted. Was I seeing what I wanted?

Another three minutes passed, then two more.

The armor beeped. Meant that I had less than a stan left. Such irony. Survive a fire fight, and freeze or suffocate after almost passing beside the *Magellan*. Perfect example of how close doesn't count.

Couldn't believe the way time passed. The whole fight hadn't taken much more than five minutes, if that. I'd been drifting without power for five times that.

Another flash of light glinted on the fuselage beyond the visual port.

Rrraspp . . . thunk!

Bolted upright in the armor. Had to be grapples. Couldn't help smiling as I felt the needle being moved.

Once we got back, I just might embarrass Lerrys and give him a hug in public. As for Liam . . .

DETERMINING

 **FITZHUGH**

"All personnel to General Quarters . . . all personnel to General Quarters. This is not a drill."

At something like six-thirty in the morning, the announcement definitely did not declare a drill, as it shattered through a collage of troubled dreams, phantasms that mixed Jiendra with the artifact whose image I had studied at all too great a length on fiveday.

For General Quarters, I could, as I understood the parameters of action, remain in my stateroom or go to my work space, in either case ensuring that I did not hamper those who had more urgent duties relating to combat and safety.

I decided upon and embarked upon a swift shower, doubtless violating the letter of the General Quarters decree, but not the spirit, since I was remaining well out of the way of those engaged in defending the *Magellan*. My decision to undertake that ablution was predicated upon the observation that detection of intruders and antagonists in space was likely to occur well before any physical proximity was attained. My quickness in completing it was based upon the possibility that I might be mistaken.

Nonetheless, by six-forty-one, I found myself dressed, generally in a state of consciousness, standing in the middle of a closet-sized stateroom. With little to do in that locale, save to undertake reading of the least-intriguing sections of the professional material I had downloaded to accompany me, I made my way, if cautiously, up the ramps—deserted by the time of my peregrination—to my work space, and my analyses of Danann and the artifact, an eternity artifact, of sorts, I had decided.

I did strap myself into the chair before the console, the one anchored to the deck, with a safety harness, before calling up the sections of the analysis I'd been working on. I began to reread what I had set forth, trying not to skim through my words.

While not all sections or towers of the megaplex had been thoroughly investigated, more than fifteen percent of the towers had been opened and viewed in a cursory fashion, according to the reports filed on the system by Kaitlin Henjsen. Less than five percent had been inspected in any detail. Even so, given the gridding and the sampling used, the fact that only a single artifact of any size whatsoever had been discovered suggested most strongly that it had been left deliberately.

My tentative conclusion along those lines was bolstered by the expedition's theoretical mathematician. Misha Nalakov had entered an analysis of the patterns of tower placement, and his analysis, which employed abstruse mathematics the accuracy of which I could not verify from my own expertise, concluded that the tower in which Chendor had discovered the artifact did in fact occupy the sole unique position within the entire megaplex. To my mind, that suggested the placement was neither coincidental nor meant to be easy to discern.

In turn, that intimated that the megaplex—perhaps all of Danann itself—had been constructed from its inception for multiple purposes meant to be accomplished over an infinitely long period of time. From that, and from the anomalous materials used in construction, few of which we could even analyze accurately, and none of which we knew how to duplicate, even theoretically, one could also conclude that the builders had not only possessed great technological talents, but equivalent skills in cultural self-patterning, social organization, and prognostication of the development and exploration patterns of other intelligences.

For a culture less advanced than ours, those capabilities might well have been considered godlike . . .

At that thought, I stopped. Was it remotely possible that the Sunnis or the Covenanters entertained such an idea? No. Any creation by humans—or even by other intelligences—by definition could not be divine. But how would they regard something so far advanced?

If mankind—and the leaders of those theocracies all thought of human beings primarily as men—were indeed the creation of a deity, would that deity allow a greater creation to usurp mankind? Theologically speaking, as well as politically, that was not conceivable, and that would suggest that, since there was but one God, with no others above, before, or beside Him, any such technology had to be, by definition, the creation of some incarnation of the devil, or Satan, or Iblis. The fact that its possessors and creators had vanished, doubtless extirpated by the One Deity billions of years earlier, would be proof enough that the artifact discovered by Chendor—the Eternity Artifact—was a creation of the evil one, the Hammer of Lucifer, the Morning Star, or the Spear of Iblis. That might be bolstered by the fact that the other aliens had vanished as well. Any monotheistic theologian could sermonize that even the attempt to obtain the knowledge of Lucifer had resulted in their demise, and that the same could indeed befall humanity.

By extension, that suggested why the Sunnis had attacked the *Magellan*. Since I had not discovered what polity's fleet currently threatened us, I could not complete that section of the analysis, but, in general terms, the Comity faced opponents of both secular and theocratic origins. Those of a secular nature would most likely be interested in obtaining the technology for an advantage, and in destroying us only if it could not be detected and reported and could allow them to obtain such technology.

At that point, the entire ship lurched, and my mass was restrained from impacting the overhead by the harness straps with which I had secured myself, even while doubting their efficacy.

The first disruption was followed by three more, each of decreasing severity.

After a period of silence, in which I pondered remaining strapped into my chair, I accessed the general information net, but found nothing that had not been there previously. The wall screen options were nonexistent, the single image available showing only the darkness of a galactic void, a blackness sprinkled with the distant faintness of other galaxies.

I attempted to concentrate upon the analysis, but the conflict between curiosity and apprehension effectively annihilated my capacity for concentration.

After another few minutes, the wall screen displayed the image of Captain Spier. She did not speak immediately.

"This is the captain. We have engaged a hostile force. All the hostiles who attacked have been destroyed. The engagement was not without casualties. The *Alwyn* destroyed three enemy frigates and more than ten needleboats, but was lost in that effort. We have suffered a few casualties, but we are on course for the first of the Gates required to return us to Hamilton system. At this time, it appears that there are no further obstacles to reaching that Gate . . . You may return to normal operations at this time . . ."

Return to normal operations?

Suffered a few casualties? Battle cruisers, even former colony ships rebuilt with cruiser drives and armament, were not designed or operated to suffer minimal casualties. Such casualties were either nonexistent or maximal. Why . . . who . . . ?

A cold feeling slithered along my spinal cord. Pilots . . . needleboat pilots, and Jiendra was a pilot.

I unfastened the harness straps, but saved what little I had added to my analysis before putting the console on standby.

Then I hurried toward the ramps, the one leading up to the boat deck. As before, I found the ramps effectively deserted, save for one junior tech who did not even glance at me as he headed inship.

The ready room was empty, the gray chairs equally vacant, under lighting bright and cheerless. I had half expected Commander Morgan, but had rationalized that he well might have remained on the bridge with the captain. I stepped inside the hatch and to one side.

Then a single pilot appeared, not from the boat locks, but from the lockers where they racked their armor. Her hair was damp and plastered to her skull, so short that it was not even helmetlike. Her eyes narrowed as she surveyed me and my obvious lack of official uniformed status. I didn't recognize her, and that indicated that she was not from the *Magellan*. I could only surmise the obvious.

"You're from the *Alwyn*, I take it."

Before she could answer, Lieutenant Lindskold appeared, as disheveled as the unidentified pilot. Her eyes flicked to me, but her frown was succeeded by a nod. "Professor Fitzhugh. You shouldn't really be up here, but . . ." She glanced toward the hatch through which I'd entered. "I'd suggest you take one of the corner chairs."

"Do you know . . . ?" I hesitated to finish the question.

"Ops thinks they have her needle. Lerrys is trying a pickup. She reported that she'd lost all systems after the last Covenanter went to energy." Lindskold turned to the other pilot. "We might as well wait here until Shaimen and your . . ."

"Eyler."

"Until they're clear of the bay," Lindskold finished.

"Why's he here?" murmured the other pilot.

"Interested in Chang. He's a professor . . . former commando . . . took out one of the assassins . . . probably saved a bunch of us . . . Ops boss might kick him out . . . not me."

Had the situation been otherwise, I might have been tempted to smile at her last utterance. I settled into one of the chairs well out of the way . . . waiting, ensconced in apprehension.

Before long, two more pilots appeared in the ready room, both women. I recognized Shaimen, although I'd only talked to her in passing in the mess. The other had to be the one mentioned by the other Alwyn pilot—Eyler.

"We're all supposed to check with sick bay," Lindskold announced. "Told the major we'd wait until Lerrys and Chang were back." She turned to the two pilots from the *Alwyn*. "You can go . . . if you'd like."

"We'll wait," Eyler stated flatly.

With no warning, Lindskold turned. "Professor? Ops reports that the recovery shuttle has secured Needle Four." Her visage remained sober. "That's positive, but without power, there's no way to tell . . ."

"The habitability situation," I noted.

She nodded.

Still, as I recalled Lindskold had said, Jiendra had reported in when she had lost all systems, and that had meant she had been alive then. Space armor, if unbreached, as I had learned all too well in a past I had thought long divorced from my present, provided between two and three hours of survival, even in deep space at close to absolute zero.

I could but trust that her armor was intact—trust and wait.

The moments oozed past me, and all those in the ready room, more slowly than water dripping from the ancient timepieces once employed to measure such passage of elapsed time. My forefingers rubbed the tips of my thumbs.

Shaimen paced back and forth, looking toward Lindskold, ignoring me, which may well have been for the best, while her eyes alighted but infrequently upon the two pilots from the *Alwyn.*

"She's all right!" Lindskold announced. "They had to manually open the needle. Everything was fried, and then some, but she's on her way to unsuit."

Shaimen smiled. "Wouldn't have been right . . ."

I agreed, even if I had no idea why the younger lieutenant had voiced the words.

Even so, it was another ten minutes before Jiendra walked out into the ready room, her eyes going to Lindskold and Shaimen first, standing, awaiting her. "Glad to see you two . . . wish . . . wish I were seeing more . . ."

Lerrys appeared behind Jiendra, his face slightly flushed, his demeanor almost embarrassed.

I rose, slowly, not wishing to intrude, knowing that the majority of the needle pilots had not been so fortunate as those before me, and yet wishing to convey, by my presence, my concerns for one particular pilot.

At that precise instant, Commander Morgan entered through the main hatch, his iron gray hair more than slightly disheveled, and his eyes reddened and set in darkness, suggesting long stans under high stress. "Welcome back, Lieutenants. All of you did well. All of you."

Not one of them offered a direct reply.

Lindskold and Jiendra nodded. Shaimen looked down. Lerrys looked at me, and provided the slightest of nods, clearly approval at my presence.

Jiendra looked straight at Morgan. "What were those waves of yellow energy? They burned out all my systems."

"The Danannian defenses." Morgan smiled. "They took out all the remaining Covenanters and the CW ships that had been chasing us. If we'd been much closer, they would have taken us as well."

Jiendra stiffened. "You'd thought there might be something like that. That was what destroyed the *Norfolk,* wasn't it. That was why you modified the satellite beacons and left the fusactor sites you left on Danann, wasn't it?"

The commander did not deign to reply, but I could see that Jiendra had been right, although I had but a general concept of Morgan's strategy, based on what her question had revealed.

As the silence extended itself, Morgan finally spoke. "It was worth the gamble." Abruptly, he saw me, apparently for the first time. That, or he wished to use me as way to avoid saying more. "Professor, the ready room is off-limits to civilians."

"Commander . . . I believe you have a point there, but do you really wish to press it?" I observed him as if he were a Covenanter crusader, lower than the underside of a sand snake and uglier than a fire roach. While I didn't care for either Covenanters, sand snakes, or fire roaches, I wasn't sure I cared much for an officer who had apparently lured two fleets to their destruction by ancient technology and probably denied all of humankind the possibility of more in-depth investigation and inquiry.

He met my eyes, but I wasn't about to give in, not at the moment, and not until I'd had a chance to assure myself that Jiendra was indeed as strong as she appeared and that she understood the significance she had brought to my existence.

I could sense her eyes taking me in for the first time, but I continued to observe Morgan.

"I'll leave you as Lieutenant Chang's responsibility then." The commander inclined his head to Jiendra. "If you would act as the professor's escort, Lieutenant, as necessary. You do need a check at sick bay. All of you."

"I can manage that, Commander." Jiendra smiled politely. "I think he has more than proven his loyalty and trustworthiness."

"After sick bay," Morgan continued, pointedly ignoring me, "you're relieved of all duties until morning quarters tomorrow."

Jiendra eased up to me, and smiled. "Will you escort me?"

"That might be in the optimal interest of all." I did not bother to mask my relief and elation.

". . . most polite she's been to anyone . . ." came a murmur. I thought it might have been from Lindskold.

I offered my arm to Jiendra, and she accepted it.

76 BARNA

In between the General Quarters and the escape and fight with the Covenanter ships, and afterward, I kept working on the differing paintings of the artifact. From each angle, each image, it conveyed a different sense of what it was. I didn't even try light matrices. Those didn't seem right. While I thought I managed, especially in one of the larger oils, to combine several of those different "identities" into one painting, even that work didn't catch everything.

I also spent some time on the study of the professor and the pilot, and that kept me fresh for the work on the renderings of the artifact.

I also worried about Elysen. I'd stopped by her work space often, but she wasn't there. I'd even slipped down to sick bay, but the medtech on duty there insisted she wasn't there, and promised to let Major DeLisle know I'd inquired.

I hesitated to try to find her stateroom, or to go there, but the comm gave me the same response every time, and she hadn't returned any of my messages.

For perhaps the eighth time in less than half a stan, I stood back from the canvas and studied the work. I had the silvered blue of the hall in which I'd found it correct, and I was happy with the crystal flaring sections, but the silver-grayish bases didn't convey what I wanted.

"Ser Barna?"

I turned from the easel. A major stood in my work space/studio doorway. He looked familiar.

"I'm Doctor DeLisle."

"Yes?" Was it about Elysen? "Is it about Dr. Taube? What can you tell me?"

"She asked to see you, and, well, it's not something I wanted to handle over the comm."

"Is she . . . she said there was nothing anyone could do." I didn't know what else to say.

"I'm afraid there isn't." The doctor smiled, sadly. "Not that I can do. Not that anyone could have done anywhere. Remedial actuation of telomerase only works for so long, even under the best of conditions. She was fortunate that she's one of those for whom it works at all. It doesn't for most people."

Fortunate? I wondered. Watching your children and grandchildren die before you? Even partial immortality—or extreme old age, active or not—had a price. My eyes strayed back to the canvas. Had that been a problem for the Danannians? Would we ever know?

"Where is she?"

"I'll take you."

"Just a moment. I want to bring something."

DeLisle waited while I gathered up the best of the portraits of her. Then we took the lift down to the quarters deck.

On the lift, a solid-faced lieutenant I didn't know looked at DeLisle, me, the portrait, and back at me. He almost shook his head. I could tell.

"She's dying." I wanted to shake him.

He started to retort something, then caught himself. "Your friend?"

"In a grandmotherly way. She's an astronomer."

We got off, leaving the lieutenant. He had other things to worry about, I surmised.

"He doesn't understand," DeLisle said quietly. "He's young, and if he survives combat, he still believes he'll live forever and never grow old."

Did I feel that way? Or somewhere in between—not young, but ageless? Didn't we all?

DeLisle stopped at a doorway. "I can't stay. There's a monitor, and if there's any problem . . . when . . ."

"Can you do anything?"

"No. Nothing more than relieve the pain and discomfort. We've done that."

"Do what you need to. I'll stay with her."

"I can send a tech if you have to leave."

"I'll stay with her."

DeLisle eased the door open and motioned for me to enter.

Elysen lay stretched on the gray plastrene bunk in her quarters, plain white sheets tucked neatly across her chest, white counterpane folded across a gray D.S.S.-issue blanket, her upper torso and head propped up with two white pillows. Somehow, she should have been in a solid wood bed with fine linens, and an antique china tea set beside her. Then, perhaps not. She had wanted to keep working. The only sign of any medical equipment was a wide wristband, with a narrow strip that led to a miniature console on the low table beside the bunk.

Her head turned. "Chendor?" Her eyes went beyond me. "I told you not to tell anyone."

"Medical discretion, Dr. Taube." DeLisle smiled, almost boyishly.

"If you were not a D.S.S, doctor, I'd report you." Her voice was thin, wheezy, and slightly rasping.

"But I am." He inclined his head. "I'll be back later." The door closed behind him.

Elysen snorted, but the sound was a soft wheeze.

"I thought you might like to see the final version." I stepped forward and turned the canvas so that the light fell on it.

"You . . . do have a great gift, Chendor . . . shouldn't have wasted it on me."

"It wasn't wasted. You made a great discovery, and there ought to be a real portrait of you."

"Looking too old to have done anything."

I wasn't about to get into that. "You're not in pain?"

"No. There's no pain, except feeling the universe close in around me. It's hard to think for long at a time, and soon, I won't be able to at all."

"You'll be fine," I lied. "You're just tired."

"I'm more . . . than tired . . . but there's nothing to be done."

I propped the portrait against the bulkhead where she could see it, then settled onto the stool beside the bunk.

Her eyes closed, and I just sat there for a time.

She coughed and opened her eyes. "You asked what we had discovered, Chendor. It's very simple. The Danannian aliens used their technology to move their entire galaxy—a small one, as galaxies go—into a new universe that they created."

Was Elysen getting delusional? She'd already told me that.

"I am not losing it." Her voice became gently acerbic. "I am not imagining things. That was what your device or model was all about. It was a representation of what they did . . . or, at the time it was made, a representation of what they were trying . . . Cleon doesn't think that part of their science will work now . . . don't understand the physics . . . something about the understructure of the universe . . . when dark energy and matter . . . atrousans and gravitons . . . once the density of the universe drops below a certain value . . . there's an attenuation effect . . ." Her voice dropped off.

"You told me some of that. You and Cleon made it very clear. Just rest."

"I suppose . . . I did. It's hard to remember . . . I can recall when everything was so clear . . ."

I reached out and patted her shoulder. "We all have times like that."

"Don't humor me, Chendor."

"I'm not. I've forgotten and told Aeryana and Nicole things I've said twice before. They look at me as if I were crazy."

"Artists can . . . repeat themselves . . . Scientists . . . should not." Her eyes closed once more. "Very . . . unprofessional . . ."

She seemed to doze, or sleep, and a half smile crossed her lips. I could see that she once had to have been a stunningly beautiful woman.

After a time, a good half stan, if not longer, she bolted up halfway, and her eyes darted to the portrait. "Who's . . . that old woman?" She sank back onto the pillows. Her eyes remained on the canvas, searching to identify who the woman was.

"Someone I know. She's a good person." What else could I say?

"Oh . . ." Her eyes cleared. "I feel . . . so stupid . . . Please go . . . Chendor."

I patted the back of her hand. "Would you like anything?"

"You're . . . humoring . . . me."

"A little. We all need humoring sometimes. Can I get you something to drink?"

"No . . . there's nothing . . . I need."

I thought she'd drifted off again, but her fingers, those fingers that had been so active, grasped my wrist. "Chendor . . . please go . . . now."

"No. I'm staying. You don't have to talk, and I won't." I leaned forward and took her hand. It was cool, not cold.

"Give the rest of the tea . . . Liam Fitzhugh . . . He'll appreciate it . . . especially . . . bergamot. He . . . has . . . high standards."

"I will," I promised.

After a time, she closed her eyes once more.

Before long, her hand was cold. I still sat there for a long time, until after the medtech came.

77 CHANG

Much as I wanted to, some ways, Liam and I didn't make love . . . not beyond holding each other. Didn't want sex out of relief, just because I'd survived. He just held me for a long time. Held him, too.

We both knew we wanted more. Still not sure how to get there. Could be we were both afraid that sex would be a disappointment.

We slept some, but D.S.S. bunks are too frigging narrow.

When we got up, I did have to explain to Liam what Morgan had done. Whatever the Danannians had left behind distinguished between hostile and nonhostile by use of weapons. Bet that when the *Norfolk* had fired a torp at the surface, that triggered the defenses. Morgan had made sure that the Covenanters would fire weapons. Don't think even he'd realized the extent of the defenses. Wasn't sure anyone would have.

We'd lost the *Alwyn*. Covenanters had lost a fleet, something like fifteen ships, and the CWs had lost a flotilla of five ships. Bet the Comity and D.S.S. would be happy with that. Wondered if anyone really cared about the technology or the artifact.

Anyway, Liam and I washed up—separately—and went to the evening meal in the mess. We sat with Lerrys and Lindskold. Chendor Barna joined us. He looked worse than I'd felt when I'd gotten out of the needle.

Liam saw it too, asked, "Chendor . . . is there anything we might help with?"

"No . . ."

"Anything at all?" I added.

He gave a sad smile. "Elysen . . . Dr. Taube . . . she died this afternoon."

"Died? How did that happen?" asked Lindskold. "Not because of the ship . . . ?"

"No. She was old . . . too old for anything to hold her together, but she'd wanted to come on the expedition. She was working on something. It was a big discovery. I imagine Dr. Lazar will announce it before too long." He paused, then looked at Liam. "Oh . . . she brought tea, an enormous amount. She said to give it to you."

"To me? I cannot imagine why . . ."

"She had her reasons. She always did."

"I'm sorry, Chendor," I added. He needed consoling, not questions. "She seemed . . . special."

"I think we would have been friends for a long time. It's hard to lose friends. There aren't that many."

Reached out under the table and took Liam's hand. He squeezed back, and smiled at me.

"No, there aren't," Lindskold agreed. "We've all lost someone today."

Swallowed as I thought of Tuala. He'd gone out, enthusiastic. Hadn't come back. The *Magellan* had lost five needle pilots and Braun. That didn't count the *Alwyn*. Still wasn't certain what we'd gotten from it. One artifact and a bunch of samples, and probably lots of images.

"A battle in the middle of nowhere." Lindskold looked to Liam. "Are we all that desperate?"

Desperate? Wouldn't have called going out and picking fights desperate, not the way the Sunnis, the CWs, and the Covenanters had. Stupid, maybe greedy. But desperate?

"That is a definite and distinct possibility," Liam began, clearing his throat in his professorial manner.

Almost broke into a grin, but wanted to hear what he had to say.

"There have been no new or significant substantive advances in technology or the underlying sciences in close to a millennium, even longer than that so far as the basics of understanding the universe might be considered. For the fundamentalist cultures, those of the theistic believers, particularly those such as the Sunnis and the Covenanters, this scientific *status quo* has been not only acceptable, but desirable, insomuch as it has reinforced both established religious doctrine, theocratic practices, and the subconscious belief that the scope of knowledge available to and understandable by human beings is limited and finite . . ."

I had to admit I hadn't thought of that.

". . . and that greater knowledge is the providence of the deity, whoever and whatever that deity might be. Even the *possibility* that greater knowledge is potentially available disrupts cultural, political, and social norms—as it has in the past throughout history. The theistic cultures must either obtain or stifle such knowledge. If they obtain it, then it was vouchsafed to them by the deity, and if it is suppressed, it is as though it had never existed, and life and culture will continue as before. For the nontheistic cultures, knowledge is the basis of power, and the 'rightness' of their cultures is proven by success and survival, which is, in turn, determined by comparative advantage over other cultures, and that advantage is, of course, provided by the first and most successful application of new knowledge. Thus, the culture that can obtain and apply such knowledge first attains an advantage over all others. The Comity was and remains in a position to do so, and since it is already first among equals, so to speak, additional advanced knowledge and technology would place the leaders of other polities in a position of extreme desperation, as suggested by Lieutenant Lindskold." Liam nodded to her, took a sip of water.

"Then, things will get worse, not better," I pointed out.

"Most probably."

"You're so cheerful, Liam," Chendor said.

"I am sorry, especially at the moment, but I do fear that great instability awaits us."

Things were depressing enough, without that.

"Did you get any good paintings from Danann?" Lerrys asked Chendor.

"Good? Only time will tell that. I do have quite a number . . ." He looked almost embarrassed to speak about his paintings.

"Tell us, if you would," I pressed.

"I just painted what I saw. I had to enhance the light, of course . . ."

All of us were happier letting Chendor talk about painting. Even Liam.

 GOODMAN/BOND

Once the blackness hit me, I hadn't thought, or felt anything.

Fuzzy gray—that was the only way to describe it—replaced the blackness. It swirled over and around me for ages.

I woke up in a medcrib. It wasn't a CIS crib, either, and I was restrained. I was surprised that I was awake and could still think. I felt feverish and weak.

"He's coming around." I didn't recognize the voice.

"Good afternoon, Tech Bond, or Goodman, or whatever your real name is." The man who spoke wore a commander's uniform. His hair was iron gray, and his eyes were bloodshot. He didn't sound happy.

The other figure, barely visible behind his shoulder, was a major.

"When is it?" I figured that was a safe question. Better to ask questions than have them ask the ones that would trigger the nanites in my system. It was a fool's game, because I was playing for time I didn't have. Sooner or later they would get to the questions, and I'd be dead in all the ways that counted. But I had to try.

"Not quite a week after we caught you."

"What happened?"

The commander laughed. I didn't like the sound of it. "By the way, I'm Commander Morgan."

I should have recognized him. Why hadn't I?

"You're damned lucky that Chief Stuval was so careful. At least, I think you're fortunate," Morgan said. "You don't fit the profile of a suicider."

Suicider?

"That device you were assembling was a very small—but very powerful—AG capped-drive vortex bomb."

I had no idea what he was talking about. I'd been building an AG signaler. Hadn't I? That was what I'd been trained to do.

"I'm sure that your controller didn't tell you that. If there had even been the slightest grav shift after you connected the power source, there wouldn't have been more than a few coupled molecules within several thousand kays—and that would have included you. You should have wondered why you were placed in an armory, and why it was so easy to get the equipment you need . . ."

What could I say? If I revealed what my assignment had theoretically been, I was dead, and if the commander asked any leading questions along those lines, I was dead.

"Oh . . . those SAD nanites they dumped in your system are gone—at least most of them. That's why you've been under so long. Major DeLisle figured that most of them had to be in the brain and bloodstream, and he's been flushing your system for days. You're feverish because formulated blood isn't a perfect match, and we don't have the equipment for that. We do have enough to read whether you're telling the truth and understand a great deal of what you won't say." He laughed again, harshly. "And you've probably lost sections of your memory, and you'll lose a bit more, but not enough that you won't remain you. I wouldn't want you to get the benefit of a quick death or a personality death through nanite amnesia. After what you planned, you don't deserve quick oblivion."

I had a feeling that, bad as matters had been, they were about to get worse, and I couldn't even move.

"What was the device you were building? Or what were you told it was?"

There wasn't much point in answering. If Morgan was lying, I was dead. If he was telling the truth, I was also dead—just a little later. Still . . . "Where are we? What was the thing the scientists brought back up from Danann?" Better to ask questions than to answer them, one way or another.

"We're on our way back to Hamilton system, and neither the captain nor I is very happy that we ran into a Covenanter fleet or that you were planted to blow us into cosmic dust. If I were a sadist and didn't have to account for equipment, I'd put you in a needle with all your little pieces and let you either suffocate or assemble your device and turn yourself into dust and energy."

"But what happened?"

"We stunned you before you could put the pieces together. Both the Covenanter fleet and the CW flotilla are scattered debris, and Danann is probably off-limits to human exploration for a millennium or so."

I had to keep the interview away from more questions. I had to. "You said I was putting together some sort of bomb. That wasn't my assignment at all." I had to risk one sentence. "I was supposed to build a signaler."

Morgan's gray face froze. "That may have been what they told you, whatever your real name is, but the device you almost assembled was effectively an old-style vortex torp warhead. They were abandoned centuries ago because they were so unstable."

A coldness settled over me. I'd been set up. Because I was pragmatic, because I was practical, I didn't fit the suicider profile—and the colonel had been counting on that. What else could I say?

"You know what really tripped you up, Goodman, or whatever your name is?"

I didn't say anything. There wasn't any point in saying anything. If I did, the nanetics would turn my memory to mush. Or they might. Even if they didn't, the Comity would execute me if I admitted anything.

Morgan shook his head, looked down at me. "You tried to be an armorer. You were too damned good. According to Chief Stuval, when you came aboard, you were a typical borderline tech second. You learned more in two months than most techs learn in three tours. When he found out you fixed that power converter . . ."

I'd hidden it. How had Stuval known?

"You don't think a chief knows every hiding place in his spaces? He checked it out and put it back. That was when he let me know."

One way or another, I was dead.

"You'll be under restraint for a few more days yet, until we decide. I wouldn't want you to escape seeing what happened as a result of your actions—and those of Colonel Truesdale."

I tried not to swallow. The commander had known of Truesdale, and his connections?

"You're going to have to pay, especially for this assignment," Morgan added, "since I doubt we know of all the others for which you won't pay."

He turned to the major standing behind him. "Put him back under."

As the grayness rose around me, so did the questions. Why had I been set up? What had really happened? What had the artifact been? Had there ever been a Morning Star or Spear of Iblis . . . ?

79 FITZHUGH

We'd made two successful Gate translations of the three necessary to return us to Hamilton system, and the wall screen in my work space now showed stars—those scattered at the edge of the Galaxy, but individual stars discernible to the unaided eye—and not just distant clouds of light or points of light that represented entire galaxies.

More than a day at high-sublight travel remained before we reached the final Gate on our return. With attacks by three different polities in slightly less than four objective months, I retained certain doubts that the remainder of our return would be as uneventful as intimated by either the captain or by Commander Morgan, although we had encountered no additional obstacles after the first two return translations.

Jiendra and I had eaten together when she had not been occupied with the various duties that devolved upon junior officers, particularly when casualties had abbreviated the duty rolls, and those few stans we had spent together had been the most enjoyable in years, so much so that, for that reason alone, I was not anticipating with relief the conclusion of the expedition and mission. After what I had heard from Command Morgan and from what Jiendra had appended in private, accurate postulation of any return to Danann within the temporal limbi of current human civilizations appeared improbable, and that was the most generous assessment foremost in my personal analyses of the situation.

I'd also been considering Chendor's artifact, and the limited information surrounding it. My foremost thesis was that it was a model, perhaps even one designed to replicate on a smaller scale, a massive stellar engineering project. The two silver-gray spheres had to represent Chronos and Danann—

The rap on the door to my work space was firm, but not percussively excessive. It couldn't have been Jiendra, since she was on duty as a junior operations officer, another result of the attrition of the officers of the *Magellan*.

"Yes?"

"It's Chendor, Liam."

Rising posthaste from the console, I opened the door. "Please come in."

The artist carried two plastrene boxes, each a third of a meter long, half that in width, and a good twenty centimeters in depth. Once inside he raised them slightly, conveying an invitation. "These are for you . . . the tea from Elysen."

"For me? Chendor . . . there must be some misapprehension. While I respected her and held her in esteem—" far more esteem than many of the other scientific team experts whom I had come to know, and with whose acquaintance my respect had diminished on close to a logarithmic scale in proportion to the time spent with them, every fleeting contact with Dr. Taube had reinforced my respect—"I scarcely knew her." Chendor had mentioned the tea, but I had not appreciated the quantity involved, but should have. Chendor did not offer idle remarks.

"She felt that you would appreciate the tea, Liam." He pressed the containers on me.

As I took them and set them beside the console, I noted that he also carried an imager. Such a device would have been vital on Danann, but on board ship?

"She said the bergamot tea would more than meet your high standards." Chendor went on.

High standards? When had I ever said a word about tea since embarking upon the *Magellan*? Regrettably, I had discoursed upon wine, and upon the fact that formulated wine was close to unimbibable, but never had a word about tea escaped my lips. "She must have been most observant, in addition to her other qualities."

"She was very observant. I wish I'd met her earlier." He shrugged. "Without Project Deep Find, I wouldn't have known her at all."

His observation was more than slightly true, and the same applied to me and Jiendra as well.

"What had she discovered, Chendor? It is indubitably linked to your artifact, is it not?"

He smiled. "Before we get into that, I have a request."

"A request?"

"I'd like to capture a few images of you, if you would. Part of my charge is to document the entire expedition."

"I'm certain that you can do better than my image," I demurred. "But . . . as you wish."

"If you would just walk around for a few minutes, and let me take images as you move and talk."

"What had Dr. Taube discovered, Chendor?"

He took several images before replying. "I promised I wouldn't tell anyone until it was announced."

"If I tell you what it is, and promise not to convey the information to others, will you confirm that?"

"I couldn't say, Liam."

"From what I can ascertain, Chronos and Danann have been separating for in excess of ten billion years, perhaps as little as six, depending on whose report I read. The two gray spheres of your artifact represent them, while the black is the tie that binds them or the track along which they were propelled by the builders of Danann. Those builders only created or modified Danann as part of their greater project, and the artifact suggests that they used the two as some sort of graviton/atrousan fulcrum by which they moved their entire cluster somewhere else, most probably into another universe . . ."

"Who have you been talking to?" Behind the imager, Chendor's face bore traces of both amusement and apprehension.

"No one, except Lieutenant Chang. She provided some details about the radiation intensification."

"I would ask you, Liam . . . I'll even beg you not to mention this. Elysen was so concerned that nothing be said until Cleon Lazar completed the mathematical proofs. She was afraid, I think, that people would dismiss the theory if everything didn't get presented properly."

Had it not been Chendor, I would have laughed. Virtually all the scientists at the University of Gregory had displayed traits in that vein. They ridiculed, in fashions both kind and unkind, historical or sociopolitical theses, while being perfectly willing to speculate about all too many matters of which they were effectively ignorant, but became incensed if someone speculated about their own theses prematurely, even while the aspects of what they investigated were, if not obvious, certainly not exactly unknown.

"I will not say anything, except to Jiendra, for the moment. She is not exactly effusive. I take it that you are confirming, at least in a general sense, what the artifact represents?"

"As I understand it." Chendor paused. "Please . . ."

I wanted to tell Chendor that it would make little difference what I said. I was not a hard physical scientist, and anything I suggested would be disregarded as beneath consideration by those who were, but he would regard any such statement as an excuse for me to speak. "Please don't worry about it. I'm not about to try to take credit for what they have found, and I certainly would not wish my words to cause you distress. I will say that Cleon Lazar had best finish his work fairly quickly, though, or someone else may well be able to calculate the supporting evidence and take credit it for the discovery first. Just because he and Dr. Taube were the experts in the field here on the *Magellan* doesn't mean that someone else couldn't try for the credit. If you're concerned about that, you could tell Lazar that you've heard that someone has already mentioned the possibility."

"He wouldn't think you were that credible," Chendor pointed out, proving that I'd underestimated his judgment. "Not in a scientific sense." He clipped the imager to his belt.

"You don't say that it's me. You tell Lazar that I mentioned hearing someone talking about it, and that I couldn't say who it was." I laughed. "I can certainly hear myself talk, and I can't tell anyone, you know, because I promised you I wouldn't."

"I could do that"

"I might try to talk to Lazar myself, but I won't mention your name. It's known that he worked with Dr. Taube."

"Do you think he'll say anything?"

"I won't know until I try. If I try."

Chendor frowned, momentarily. "You won't say—"

"I wouldn't even consider that a remote possibility, but if I intimate that I deduced his and Dr. Taube's theory, as a nonscientist . . ."

"It might work." After a moment, he spoke. "I did want to make sure you got the tea. And get a few more images."

"A few more?"

"I captured several off the ship's systems. When you disabled the assassins."

My wince was involuntary. I should have realized that such would have existed. All sections—or all public spaces—of Comity and D.S.S. ships were monitored.

"Don't worry." He started to turn.

"I'll thank you for the tea, since I can't thank Dr. Taube. I will enjoy it. That I can promise you."

He smiled before he closed the door.

What was he painting that needed me? I refrained from shaking my head, a useless gesture in private, particularly as I contemplated a strategy to gain access to Cleon Lazar and to obtain more details about his and Dr. Taube's theory.

80 FITZHUGH

Several hours of cogitation and calculation followed Chendor's visit, and in the middle of threeday afternoon, I attempted to reach Cleon Lazar through the comm system. He did not deign even to respond, nor to return my message requesting a few moments of his time. From what I had seen and heard of him, that lack of courtesy toward a non–physical scientist was what I had anticipated.

Determining Cleon Lazar's location required a certain amount of drudgery, including exerting percussive announcements on a few wrong doors, but by midmorning on fourday, I stood looking at him, through little more than a slip between the edge of his plastrene door and its equally gray plastrene casement.

"Dr. Fitzhugh . . . this is the physical science area, not the social studies section."

"That is a fact of which we are both fully cognizant, Cleon, and in this particular instance, irrelevant. I presume you did receive my message."

"I thought it was more like a threat."

"I don't make threats, Cleon, but I do chase down information, and if I can determine what you have in the artifact on the few clues I have, so will any competent physical scientist." I managed a facsimile of a pleasant smile. "I think it would be best if you offered me some hospitality."

"I'd rather not." He started to close the door.

His efforts were ineffectual, and after several moments, he reeled back, and I closed the door behind me.

He moved toward the console. "If you do not depart immediately, I will summon ship's security."

"You do, and Commander Morgan will require you to divulge far more than I want, and he will not be precisely pleased to be required to deal with such a matter at a critical time. Because of my particular skills, I can ensure that he will have to focus on this issue, and when he discovers why, and what you have withheld, he will be exceedingly less than pleased."

He paused. Some of his fine black hair had fallen across his low forehead, almost touching his dark brows. His gray eyes were bright, and his skin far too white, if not quite that of an albino.

"Dr. Lazar . . . you appear not to be terribly understanding of the situation your discovery has precipitated, a situation which will most certainly deteriorate. Either that, or you prefer a time of galacticwide warfare." Lazar might well laugh at my presumptuousness, for if my own sociopolitical calculations were correct, that period of warfare had already been proclaimed with the arrival of the CW and Covenanter ships off Danann.

"What are you talking about?"

"Your discovery shatters some very basic social truths, and it is upon those truths that a plurality, if not the majority, of human polities have been constructed and operated." I managed a smile, one far less amicable than the first I had offered.

"Are you always so . . . direct?"

"No. Usually those I deal with tend to be less isolated from the social and political aspects of the universe that surrounds them, and thus more inclined to at least listen before reacting."

"I believe in only what is observable, provable, and verifiable, and, ideally, what is scientifically replicable."

"Then we agree in principle. I'd like to tell you what I *think* you've found, and I'd like you to correct any basic misconceptions I may have."

"For what purpose?"

"For my own research and publications. If you choose to announce what you and Dr. Taube discovered within the near future, I will be more than pleased to refrain from publication until your announcement."

"And if I do not, then you will publish . . . anyway?"

"You may have overlooked the fact that everyone on the team was given great incentive to publish their results once we returned. Not when every fact and mathematical proof was laser-edge perfect."

Cleon actually sighed. "Do you beat up your students this way?"

"If necessary."

"It will come out. You're correct about that. I had hoped for a bit more time to refine the mathematics and the proofs while the rest of the expedition was exploring Danann." He paced toward the blank wall screen, then turned back, halting. "As you have deduced, and as I told Barna, the artifact is a physical representation of what the culture that created Danann did in creating an entire new universe . . ."

I listened, attempting to correlate everything he said to what I had attempted to set forth logically.

After he finished, including providing responses, doubtless oversimplified, to my inquiries, his eyes narrowed as he asked, "What does this have to do with history and its trends?"

"Everything," I replied. "Just about everything." I inclined my head, in courtesy, and added, "Thank you. I look forward to seeing your initial announcement."

Then I left. I had more work to do than I'd thought, especially based on Lazar's initial response to my concerns and his apparent inability to grasp the magnitude of the artifact's impacts—technological, scientific, and particularly, cultural.

81 CHANG

At fourteen-seventeen on fourday, I sat at the ops junior duty officer's console. Tiny space in the corner of main operations. Gray plastrene bulkheads, decks, and overheads, no wonder Morgan looked gray all the time.

Just a junior command pilot under instruction . . . that was all, but I had passive access to all the screens and systems. Could access anything, but couldn't do anything unless the command pilot—that was the captain at the moment—shifted the conn to me. Wasn't about to happen. Still, getting to know a ship as big as the *Magellan* felt good. Could also put it on my cert record.

Time to translation, one stan. The link announcement was restricted to those in control.

Morgan appeared, almost at my shoulder. "You're off duty now."

I frowned. My watch didn't end for two-plus stans. "I do something wrong?"

"No. I'm shifting you back to the needleboats. I'm having all needle pilots on standby for immediate launch once we clear the Hamilton Gate inbound."

I could see that. Didn't like it, but could see it. "Trouble waiting for us?"

"That's likely."

He was lying. He *knew,* probably from the *Owens*—courier had rejoined the *Magellan* less than ten stans earlier.

"You're not surprised?"

"With three attacks already, and a bunch of attempts at sabotage? I'd be surprised if trouble weren't waiting. How bad?"

"We don't know. D.S.S. intelligence had indications of possible recon and hidden Gate translations in a number of Comity systems."

"We could wait, couldn't we?" Doubted that either Morgan or the captain would have bought that, but wanted a reaction.

"For how long? And how safely, without escorts? Two fleets found us at Danann. Also, if Hamilton system comes under attack, the *Magellan* might be critical."

"You think someone will attack Hamilton?" Managed not to raise my voice. That was definitely an act of war, the kind of war everyone had been trying to avoid for centuries.

"The Covenanters and the Alliance believe we have the Morning Star or the Spear of Iblis, or whatever the true believers call the mythical weapons of Lucifer."

"We don't have anything like that . . . do we?" While Liam had told me about the artifact and what Dr. Taube believed, Morgan wasn't going to get that from me.

"No."

Didn't like the touch of equivocation behind his denial. "But the artifact . . . it's the key?"

"The scientists can't prove what it is. They don't know how the Danannians built it, or how they even created the materials it's made from, and it's anyone's guess when we will, or if we will."

"So . . . tell the Covenanters that," I suggested.

He laughed. "Let's see. What do we say? 'We have a device that we can't analyze because it's so advanced, and we don't know what it's good for or how to use it. But it's not the advanced weapon you think it is.' Even if we offered to share the data, which I doubt that anyone in the Comity would approve, the Covenanters don't want that information loose. They think it tore their Heaven in two and loosed evil on mankind." He paused. "Enough. You need to get to the ready room and suit up. All you pilots will be in your needles when we translate."

That told me we had more trouble than he was admitting. "Who do I turn the watch over to?"

"You don't. There's no one left."

Junior ops watches were for instruction, not necessary, strictly. I got up. "The watch is yours, sir." Wanted that on the record. Even logged it.

He didn't say anything, just moved back to the ops boss's console without a word.

I'd thought Morgan had a softer inside. Beginning to think I'd been mistaken. Or it was buried so deep no one would ever find it. Not even him.

Was that my problem, too? Didn't want to think about that. Not yet.

Took my time getting to the ready room. Even made a stop at the mess and got something to eat from the cooks. Had to keep moving, because getting into armor took some time. It was still almost thirty minutes to translation when I entered the launch bay. Lindskold, Shaimen, and the two pilots from the *Alwyn* were already in their needles.

Ysario looked at me as I stopped short of Needle Four and studied it, then said, "All the internal systems have been replaced, sir."

Managed a grin. "Hope so. It's pretty dark out there without screens and shields."

"Yes, sir." She didn't smile, but her eyes crinkled at the corners. She was worried, too.

After the walk-around, and the physical inspection, I settled into the cockpit of the needle. Ran the checklist all the way to launch, then backed off to standby.

Five minutes until translation. All personnel should be secured. All personnel should be secured. All unnecessary gear should be on standby. Once in armor, we got the announcements by link alone.

Checked once more—all the needle systems were on standby, with the fusactor cold.

Could only sit in the darkness and wait for the captain to guide the *Magellan* into the Gate and translation.

Stand by for Gate translation. Stand by for Gate translation.

Translation was like always—flashed white and black simultaneously, and we went null grav. Then black turned white, and white black. Colors inverted. The white and black strobing stretched out endlessly, then stopped with no real time having passed, as black returned to black. We were back in normspace—hopefully on the edge of Hamilton system.

Full grav returned, but only for a moment.

Stand by for null grav in the launch bay. Null grav in the launch bay. All needles, prepare to launch. Report when ready. Report when ready.

My stomach lurched up within me. The double cycle from full grav to null to full to null hadn't helped. After a quick swallow, I began running through the checklist to get the needle ready to launch.

Launch doors open this time.

Morgan had the bays open and the nanite barrier in place before I finished the checklist. Not by much, though.

Navigator Control, Needle Tigress, ready to launch.

Tigress, stand by. You are number three to launch. Number one departing cradle this time.

Standing by.

Lindskold was first, then Shaimen, then me, then Eyler and the other *Alwyn* pilot.

Needle Tigress, clear to uncradle and launch.

Stet. Uncradling this time.

Used the steering jets to ease the needle out, then formed up on Lindskold. When the last two joined, we had a loose wedge ahead of the *Magellan*.

Accessed the farscreens. What came through were points of energy all over the outer reaches of Hamilton system. The majority were D.S.S., according to the identifiers, but there were still close to fifty hostile vessels—including eight dreadnoughts—in three battle groups. One enemy group was down to a pair of cruisers. One cruiser's shields flared red, and raw energy replaced it, then faded.

Navigator needles, vector three one zero relative, plus two zero.

A pair of frigates—configured like Covenanters—lay along the vector. They were accelerating, closing on the *Magellan*. Leading them were three needles.

Needle Tigress, stet.

Let Lindskold take the lead, closed up slightly, but not enough that there was any chance for our shields to touch or interlock.

The Covenanter needles accelerated toward us, moving into a tight wedge with overlapping shields. Sure sign that they were trying for the *Magellan*.

Navigator needles, concentrate on the right needle. Hold fire until minimum plus twenty. Report fire.

Kept formation on Lindskold, holding as Morgan had ordered.

Less than thirty emkay . . . twenty . . . Still no torps from the Covenanters. None from the *Magellan*. Screens showed the *Owens* and the *Bannister* tucked up tight aft of the *Magellan*. They'd have bolted for Hamilton Base or some such. Except they were probably safer following the *Magellan*. Didn't have the shields to deal with all the attacking ships around Hamilton system.

Closure at ten emkay . . . five . . . we were screaming toward each other. Could smell sweat inside the armor.

Navigator needles. That was Lindskold. Could "feel" the difference. *Stand by to fire on my mark.*

Two emkay . . . one . . .

Mark . . . fire two . . . mark . . .

Ten torps converged on the starboardmost Covenanter needle.

My farscreens blanked, then came back online after the energy wave swept past. All three enemy needles had vanished. Just dust, dispersing energy, and heat that would vanish into the chill and darkness in minutes.

Navigator needles, regroup and prepare for attack on lead frigate.

Regroup? Realized we were missing one needle. Shaimen. Hadn't even seen her go. Backlash on her shields, probably. Frigging bitch of a way to go.

Shuttled the remaining torp to the port tube. Always preferred the port.

Navigator needles, prepare to fire on frigate, link. Morgan this time. Wanted perfect synch of all torps.

The four torps from the needles and the ten from the *Magellan* slammed into the lead frigate's shields. They barely flickered amber before going to red and shredding. Just a pair of torps from the *Magellan* finished that Covenanter.

Farscreen showed a wad of stuff flying out toward us. Past me before I could do anything. Shields flickered into the amber, and the needle shuddered.

Checked the farscreens. Frig! One of the *Alwyn* needles was gone. Didn't know which, whether it was Eyler or the other pilot—Sennis, that was her name.

Navigator needles, stand clear. Form on couriers as possible.

With no torps left, Morgan didn't want us caught between the last frigate and the *Magellan*. I didn't want to be caught there, either.

Swung in a loop, small one, just enough to let the *Magellan* pass. Didn't want to get caught without enough power to recover. I'd been there. Didn't want to do it again—ever.

Could see the *Magellan* shifting shields forward. Covenanter had done the same.

Just before their shields touched, Covenanter released torps.

Had to gape . . . Magellan's shields *contracted*. Morgan or the captain released double torp salvo, then expanded the shields forward. Never had seen that done.

Covenanter never had a chance. Got fried by his own torps, shield flex, and the *Magellan*'s torps. Could have been that the *Magellan*'s mass alone, backed by the shields, might have been enough. Wouldn't ever know, though.

Morgan didn't take chances. Didn't think the captain did, either, but didn't know her as well.

Navigator needles, cleared to return and recover.

Control, Needle Tigress, returning this time.

Stet, Tigress.

Checked the farscreens again. No one left close to us. Screens still registered dissipating energy. All that was left of five needles and two frigates. Had trouble swallowing. My mouth was dry.

Followed Lindskold back to the *Magellan* for recovery. Cold sweat coated the inside of my skintights. *Alwyn* pilot trailed me.

Checked the farscreens a last time before I dropped shields. Around Hamilton system, most of the hostiles had vanished—one way or another.

Still couldn't believe that whoever it was—couldn't have just been the Covenanters—had dared to attack Hamilton system itself. More unbelievable was that the Comity had been able to fight them off. D.S.S. must have pulled in every ship from hundreds of systems, if not all thousand. But how would they have known?

Navigator Control, Needle Tigress, standing by for recovery.

Stet, Tigress.

How could Comity D.S.S. have dared to concentrate so many ships, leaving systems defenseless? Bet Morgan knew. Bet he had a lot to answer for. Didn't know as I wanted to confront him on it.

82 FITZHUGH

This time, after the battle, I'd waited outside the ready room, discreetly removed so that I could observe Commander Morgan's appearance. As fortune, chance, or fate would have it, the commander did not deign to appear, and I finally made my way into the ready room.

Jiendra looked up from where she slumped in one of the chairs, exhausted. "You didn't have to come."

Lieutenant Lindskold smiled, then looked away before Jiendra could perceive her colleague's amusement.

"You need nourishment, and separation from this locale would not be amiss," I observed, "preferably before Commander Morgan appears."

"He won't be here. He's got bigger problems." She stood. "Could use a bite to eat."

"Bigger problems?"

"Need to eat. We can talk then."

Within a handful of minutes, Jiendra and I sat at the corner table in the mess, where she cut some form of formulated beef, drowned in a tan liquid masquerading as a sauce, with quick, exact strokes of a knife, then ate them with equally swift and precise bites.

"What is the probability that you'll have to fight another battle?"

She swallowed, then sipped some lager that actually resembled closely the brewed product in both appearance and taste. "Doesn't look likely. Not anytime soon. There must have been over a hundred Covenanter ships in Hamilton system. Saw more than fifty, and that was when things were winding down. Three, four times that many D.S.S. ships. We came in, looked like, on the tail end of a big-assed battle. Could have been bigger than anything since the Conflagration. Can't say as I understand what brought it on, or why now."

"You find it unsettling that the Covenanters and Sunnis and the CWs would sacrifice so many ships?"

"Stupid, first of all," she pointed out, taking another quick sip of lager. "The CWs . . . I understand them. They wanted the Danannians' technology. They didn't attack Hamilton system, either. Just sent ships to Danann. Not that many, really. The Covenanters and Sunnis didn't want anyone to have it. Understand that as well. But sacrificing so many ships? Makes no sense."

"It does if you consider that, for them, the technology is something God never meant human beings to have. Because it came from another species, it had to have come from Iblis or Satan."

"Still stupid."

"It's not precisely a question of intelligence, but of beliefs. We all have beliefs. Certain sets of beliefs enhance intelligence while others restrict the scope of its application. True believers, theocratic or otherwise, are those whose beliefs limit their applied intelligence. Throughout history, they've always been so. This . . . conflagration merely proves that little has changed. The Covenanters are monists in a multiplex universe."

"You think it's all over?" Jiendra's vocal intonation, despite the inquiry, professed skepticism.

"You comprehend, all too well, my dear lady . . ." I shouldn't have said that. I hurried on, trying to explain. ". . . that it has scarcely commenced. The Danannians, for lack of a better term, applied their technology to create a brane flex in a higher or different dimension, or another side of reality, or whatever, and they had enough power to push through at least a globular cluster. Cleon Lazar has suggested the possibility that they may have taken an entire galaxy. How or what they did doesn't matter, except for one thing. Can you conceive of what that might be?"

"Liam . . ." She laughed. "You sound like a professor."

"Professor or not," I continued, essaying not to lecture, or not too much, "they created an entire new universe. For true believers, that's something that only a deity can do. That leaves the true believers with a number of difficulties . . ."

"Aliens as powerful as gods, for one."

"Or as powerful as they believe God to be, or as powerful as the mythical

Satan, and a universe or a series of universes that can go on forever, for another, and where humans aren't the most favored or the most powerful species, for another, and that's particularly hard for those believers who insist humans are made in the image of God and foremost among his creatures."

Jiendra laughed, and I just took in her face.

For a moment, neither of us spoke.

"Do you think the scientists will ever figure out what's behind all that stuff?" she finally asked, pushing aside an empty plate.

"Cleon Lazar has figured out some of it already, but it won't be very useful as it is . . ."

"Why not?"

"The universe has changed since then. Oh . . . not in the grandest sense, but the comparative strength of atrousans and gravitons was stronger then. They've estimated that the surface gravity on Danann might have been close to one-point-five Tellurian. Cleon tried to explain the physics of it, and I still don't understand. It has something to do with what you might call frequencies of brane flexion. Because everything is related to everything else, the relationships remain constant. One of the keys has been around for a long time, in astrophysics, where the age of the universe doesn't work out quite right if the speed of light has been a constant since the prime flex. The higher gravity might be one rationale for why all the towers were shorter than anyone thought. And why the scientists thought everything was overengineered. It wasn't."

"Did they have Gates?"

"It's not likely. According to Cleon, Gates wouldn't work in the earlier times of the universe. Atrousan density was too high."

"But . . . why did they leave?"

"That's a guess. One of Cleon's colleagues, and I'd calculate that it was most likely Koch or Chais, although Cleon refused to identify whoever it might be, theorizes that they were faced with the prospect of mental and physiological degradation because their biology was vastly different. They may even have a nervous system that was based on something similar to an AG drive. As the universe expanded, atrousan density decreased. So did everything else. It was a hotter, brighter universe . . . brighter in more ways than one."

"They wouldn't be able to think as fast?"

"I'd judge that they anticipated that possibility. Cleon won't commit on that. He asserts that he is a physicist, not a neurologist. Most of the physical scientists have concluded that what we've found doesn't work, or rather, that it functions only to a small percentage of its original design and capabilities. Not only are those functions impaired, but they will always be impaired and will continue to deteriorate as the universe continues to expand." I couldn't help laughing.

Jiendra tilted her head. "Doesn't sound funny to me."

"Don't you see? Neither the rationalists nor the true believers will be happy. The scientists want to believe that, if they can just find the proper rational key, they can make anything work. If the preliminary work is correct, no one can ever make the Danannian technological devices operate as they once did. We might be able to create a universe where they did work again, but, personally, I'm not so certain that we'd work there."

"What are we, then? The dregs of the universe?"

"I'd prefer to suggest that we're the mature vintage of the universe, the later and better wine . . ."

She did laugh at that.

83 CHANG

Finished eating and looked at Liam. Wanted some answers. He'd supplied some, but there were others, ones he didn't know.

"You have that look, lady . . ." he said.

"Lady . . . I'm no lady. I'm a pilot, and I'm frigging pissed. We go off on an archeological expedition. We get attacked. We face assassins and sabotage, and when we come back through the Gate outside Hamilton system, we're in the middle of the biggest single-system battle in human history. It's no frigging coincidence."

"That's a rather charitably captious abnegation of—"

"Why don't you just say you're pissed, too?"

He grinned. "Your expressions are more colorful."

"We need to see Morgan."

"Will he see *us?*"

"If you come, how can he say no? You're not under his command, and you can bust his butt into little fragments so small even a nanetic biologist couldn't reassemble him. He also knows you just might."

Liam stood. "We need to stop by my work space first, for some insurance."

His insurance took more than half a stan. Finally, he stepped away from the console. "That should do it."

"That to make sure everyone knows?"

"Some probably do. I just want to make sure everyone does." Liam closed his door. Didn't lock it.

We walked up the ramps.

Couple of officers looked round-eyed when we got to the ops level. Didn't stop us, though. Morgan was in his spaces.

"Ah . . . I see I'm surrounded." Morgan looked up from the console. His smile was hard.

Liam gestured for me to step inside, and then he closed the hatch.

"The captain will know you've closed the hatch, and she'll be monitoring everything."

"That's fine." My words were harsh.

"We have been pondering matters, Commander," Liam began, "and cogitation, while often difficult, also can have unexpected negative impacts."

"Get to the point, Professor. I don't need lectures or verbiage."

Liam *moved*. In instants, he had Morgan on the deck. "I don't need condescending crap, Morgan. I'm polite because I was taught to be. You have a lot of explaining to do. Especially for all the blood on your hands. And don't think that you can get out of it—not unless you want to silence or murder every member of the expedition."

In a way, I was glad Liam had acted. I might have just busted Morgan's balls and neck—in that order.

Morgan looked up tiredly as Liam released him. "Some sort of timed release?"

"It's a bit more sophisticated that that. It's a burst transmission, like a virus, that will appear in every terminal in the system, shortly. It will also appear if the system is turned off, if power is lost, and if any attempt is made to remove or tamper with it."

"How did you learn that, Professor?"

"My subspecialty was communications disruptions, Commander. I've kept abreast, mainly out of curiosity."

"Out of thousands of former commandos, we would get you."

"No. I didn't have anything to do with it, but it's transparently obvious that I was placed here as a check on you, as well."

I wondered how many checks on how many people the Comity really had. Got the feeling that there were plots within plots, stuff that I'd never know. Wasn't certain I wanted to, either.

"Diplomatic Corps, no doubt." Morgan cleared his throat. "Might I get up?"

"Why don't you just sit on the deck?" I said. "Until we get some answers."

"What do you want to know?"

"Let's start right here," I said. "How did you know that the battle here in Hamilton system was going to happen?"

"I didn't."

Just looked at him. My eyes were colder than his. Angrier, too.

"Just out of curiosity, *Commander*," asked Liam, "what were you at D.S.S. Headquarters, Deputy Chief of Intelligence? That has to be a matter of record, and I imagine that, if anyone published such a coincidence as your also returning as operations officer of the *Magellan* . . ."

"It would all be hypothetical, Professor, very hypothetical. Besides, I'm well past the time for full retirement, and I certainly haven't done a single thing against any law or regulation."

"Deputy Chief of Intelligence?" Liam pressed.

"Assistant Deputy Chief."

"Now . . . about how you knew there would be a battle here in Hamilton system?"

"As I said, it could only be hypothetical—"

"Then, perhaps you had best offer your *hypothetical* answer." Never heard Liam's voice that calm or cold. Deadly.

Morgan looked from Liam to me.

"I'll take hypothetical." For starters.

Morgan rose to his feet. Liam let him.

Morgan smiled. Uneasy smile. "Let us start with Danann itself. Just assume that a D.S.S. ship fired a flash torp at the surface of Danann. Not anyplace near the megaplex, but just a flat icy patch over one of those frozen oceans. Not out of hostility, but to get some spectral readings because the ship was leery about landing its single flitter. Let us also assume that within moments the ship vanished, and there was a massive surge of energy on the AG level, enough to rock its companion vessel, despite the other ship's having stood off several thousand emkay . . . Let us assume that, far later, another ship approached and successfully landed a flitter. What conclusion would you draw?"

"Danann protects itself." Frig! "You set up everything so that the Covenanters would fire on those fusactors, and the frigging planet wiped out the whole flotilla—and what was left of the CWs, too."

"We don't know that. Not for certain."

"How long did it take to set it all up?" I asked.

"I haven't the faintest idea what you're talking about, Lieutenant. Nor will anyone else, if you happened to be so unwise as to discuss it publicly."

"You still haven't answered why the Covenanters attacked Hamilton."

"There was another agent on board—a Covenanter agent. We caught him just before he was about to complete a device that would have destroyed the *Magellan*. That was another reason why the *Owens* was dispatched," Morgan said. "The captain felt it was urgent to report a Covenanter saboteur who was planted to disable or destroy the *Magellan* just at the time the Covenanter fleet arrived. We didn't know about the CW flotilla, of course."

Just nodded. Morgan had a pat explanation. Only problem was that saboteurs wouldn't reveal where they were from, or much of anything. So Morgan had known before and had been watching. Otherwise, he wouldn't have been able to move so fast.

"What happened to the saboteur?" Liam's words didn't sound like a question.

"He had nanetic fail-safes in his system. Major DeLisle couldn't keep him alive."

Knew both statements were true. They also weren't related. Morgan had taken care of the saboteur . . . or ordered DeLisle to let him die. Couldn't say I felt much sympathy.

"The battle here in Hamilton system," I prompted.

"No single system—not really, and especially not without advance notice—can be effectively defended, not without massive superiority in numbers," Morgan went on. "When they didn't get the signal from their agent, and when the *Magellan* appeared leaving Danann, they figured he'd been discovered, and that meant we had the Danannian technology. For them, the only way to stop us from using it was to try to destroy our installations on Danann, and the *Magellan,* and attack Hamilton and create enough destruction and disruption that it would be generations before anyone could recover or find the Danannian technology . . ."

Sounded good if you didn't think. Didn't make total sense, if you did. Just nodded. Waited to see what else Morgan had to say.

"Very good defense in depth, Commander." Liam's voice dripped sarcasm. "And just how did every D.S.S. fleet in the Comity happen to be waiting off Hamilton?"

Morgan lifted his hands in a shrug. "I can't explain that. Good luck?"

"Let *me* offer a hypothesis," Liam said. "Let us just suppose that the Comity wanted to exploit the fact that the Worlds of the Covenant had this . . . fixation on the Morning Star or the Spear of Iblis. Let us further suppose that the Covenanters received unimpeachable intelligence about just how advanced the Danannian technology was, including its potential to destroy warships at a distance and how it just might be something like the Morning Star. Further assume that they received scattered information about how to find Danann, and that most Comity fleets would be elsewhere than in Hamilton system . . . and let us further suppose that the Middle Kingdom, which was doubtless more than a little irritated about the assassination of First Advocate Tyang Ku Wong, just happened to discover that all Covenanter fleets might conceivably be engaged in occupying Danann and attacking Hamilton system . . . I would judge that the Middle Kingdom is effectively laying waste to the Zion system and New Jerusalem, if it hasn't already done so."

Morgan looked at Liam. Tiredly. "That's all hypothesis."

"Absolutely." Liam smiled. Thought his early expressions had been cold. I was wrong. "But that doesn't invalidate its basic truth." He paused, then went on quietly. "I'm not a spy, and I'm not an agent. I wasn't certain, but it would make perfect sense. The Worlds of the Covenant have been expanding. They have a high birth rate, and they don't operate with any kind of logic that meshes with the more rationalistic polities. The Middle Kingdom has suffered most, but isn't powerful enough to risk the Comity's enmity . . . but an alliance of convenience would not only remove the Covenanter threat, perhaps permanently, but neutralize the Chrysanthemum Worlds. I wouldn't be surprised if someone even suggested that a CW flotilla might be able to slip in and discover that technology after the *Magellan* left. They really didn't pursue us that hard." Liam paused. "Then, too, you even considered the most important motivation of the Covenanters and the Sunnis."

Morgan smiled, amused. Said nothing.

"If an alien species could create a universe, does that make them gods? If the Comity obtains that technology, that ability, what does that do to the myth of the divine creator, the source? What does that do to the power structure of the Covenanter worlds? The theocracies didn't want the technology. They wanted it buried. If the Comity obtains it and masters the Danannian technology, the Worlds of the Covenant become even more irrelevant—politically, theologically, and in terms of sheer power. Even if the Covenanters did manage to acquire the technology, either from Danann or by stealing it, what the technology represents would destroy their culture. Five thousand years of history has shown that."

"Can anyone master it?" I asked.

"Not for a long time, if ever," Liam said. "Dr. Taube, Lazar, Hector Regens— they're convinced that some of it may never work because the expansion of the universe somehow changed the understructure of the universe itself." Looked at Morgan. "You suspected that, didn't you?"

"Let us just say that I'm a skeptic."

"We can't go back to Danann? Can anyone?" Thought I knew, but had to ask.

"After those fireworks, I don't think either the captain or the D.S.S. would wish to risk it. I don't." Morgan's voice remained tired.

"Very effective, Commander. You managed to employ a technology we'll never master to destroy the one rival to the Comity long before it could become a significant threat, while creating an effective alliance with the Middle Kingdom and weakening the strongest other system along their borders. Do they get to keep and 'pacify' the Covenanter worlds?"

"You've been wasted as a historian, Professor."

"I think not." Liam smiled. "I've enjoyed life more—although not as much as I intend." He turned to the blank wall screen. "Captain . . . since we don't intend more violence, might we depart with your assurance of, shall we say, neutrality?"

"What do you intend to do with your burst transmission, Professor?" The captain's voice came from the screen.

"Oh . . . that. I imagine I'll leave it on standby in various locales, possibly for the rest of my natural life."

"I doubt that will be necessary." Her image filled the screen. Beside her was the most honorable Special Deputy Minister Allerde. "We have already recorded a number of speculations from others on the team. Professor deSilva has extrapolated most of what you suggested, and Professor Khorana also has had some enlightening speculations. Ser Barna knows most of this, and his absence would be noted. Besides, as a most practical matter, it is now in the Comity's interest for the rest of the Galaxy to understand exactly how far we will go against blind— and it is truly blind—faith."

"And I'll be allowed to publish a monograph or book that outlines this?"

"But, of course," Allerde replied. Sounded genuine. "So long as you can document whatever you publish in the scholarly accepted fashion."

Liam laughed. "Very clever."

Morgan looked unhappy. "What about security?"

"I am sorry, Commander," Allerde added. "It was decided that the most obvious aspects of the strategy would be made public. Since initial communications have revealed no significant damage to civilian targets in Hamilton system, there is little advantage to further secrecy, and great disadvantage. As you have experienced, it appears that secrecy is not possible concerning the . . . artifact and what it represents." He smiled politely. " I am most certain you will enjoy your well-earned retirement."

Almost felt sorry for Morgan as Liam opened the hatch, and we left.

Was still pissed, though. Could see the Comity point of view. Didn't like it. At the cost of maybe fifty ships, a few thousand D.S.S. personnel, they'd ensured Comity primacy for centuries.

Problem for me was simple. Those personnel were people. People like Braun, and Shaimen. Saved Shaimen once so she could get killed in Morgan's trap of the Covenanters. Braun got whacked by assassins trying to get Morgan's bait. To Morgan and his kind, all of us were rats in a maze. Didn't like being a rat.

Liam hadn't either, and Morgan was probably more than a little pissed that Liam had turned out to be a very tough cat . . . a tiger.

I smiled at that thought.

84 BARNA

I took a last look at the canvas before I covered it. I'd done a good job. I adjusted the drape and thought about Aeryana and Nicole, and how good it would be to go home . . . and about Elysen. At the time I hadn't realized it, but when I spent that last stan with her, holding her hand . . . that was when I was ready to return home. That was when I realized how it all fit together.

I understood now why I had not destroyed the portraits of Aeryana, and why I never would, or could. Why it would be wrong. I'd even make friends with Peter Atreos. Not grudgingly, either. He could commission my work or not. It didn't matter. Enough people would.

The Danannians had developed incredible technology and great knowledge. I don't think they'd had great art. Great art happens when the artist goes beyond mere skill and sets a part of his soul in a permanent form—a painting, a sculpture, a building, a poem, a song—for all to see or hear and defies those who follow to surpass it. The mutability of the megaplex was great technology. It wasn't art. The artifact was art, of a sort, but I questioned the artistic heritage, even the soul, of a culture with that level of technology that only left one recognizable piece of art.

I glanced at the door to the studio, waiting. I'd be leaving the *Magellan* in the next few days, with most of the paintings, but I'd always remember what I'd learned and what it meant.

I didn't have to wait long.

Liam arrived first, stepping inside the work space. He was so unostentatiously graceful. He glanced to the covered canvas.

I shook my head. "I've asked some others to come. I hope you don't mind waiting."

"No. That's fine, Chendor." He looked around the studio, taking in the renditions of the artifact and the towers of Danann, and the paintings I'd done of the shuttle on the ice in the darkness, stark-outlined by the Danann ground-base lights. His eyes drifted back to the covered canvas again. "Is that—"

"It is. But artists like audiences. It won't be long."

He laughed. "I understand. So do professors."

Lieutenant Chang was only a few moments later.

"I'm sorry, ser Barna. Commander Morgan had a few words. He won't offer more than a few these days. Not to me." She glanced toward Liam. Her expression held both warmth and puzzlement. That was fine with me. "I thought you wanted my opinion on some art dealing with piloting."

"With pilots, as well," I said. "I'd like to be mysterious. Would you both close your eyes?" I could tell that Liam had a glimmering of what might happen.

I slipped the drape off the frame. "Now . . . you can look."

The lieutenant took the slightest breath.

Liam just stood there, staring at the canvas.

I'd put him in black skintights, with a dark green vest and shorts. I didn't know that he had such, but they suited the painting, especially contrasted with the blue skintights and dark gray vest worn by Lieutenant Chang. I'd set them together, just outside the shuttle, in the boat bay. Most likely they would have been in armor there, but not necessarily. Besides, this painting was for a different purpose. They'd just turned, as if addressed, or surprised. Both of them were *alive,* and they were in love. I was pleased with it, but not surprised. I'd learned a lot on Danann. I just hadn't realized it until afterward.

The lieutenant looked at me.

After a moment, so did Liam. "Is it that obvious?"

"Not to everyone, but to an artist."

"Why . . . what?"

"You two deserve it." I couldn't help but grin. "There is one problem, though."

They exchanged glances.

"There is only one portrait," I pointed out. "One original."

"Liam will take it, for now."

"For now?" His voice was bantering, but there was an awkwardness behind it.

"Until I get released from the D.S.S. That's what Morgan was telling me . . ." She looked at him, but didn't say another word.

"What degree of certainty do you possess—"

"Liam . . . keep it simple." Her words were firm but soft. She finally smiled. "Can you deal with a history professor?"

"If you can deal with a pilot."

I left them among the canvases and in front of their portrait.